THE WARTIME MATCHMAKERS

LAUREN SMITH

Lauren
SMITH
TIMELESS ROMANCE

ISBN: 978-1-956227-81-9 (ebook)

ISBN:978-1-956227-82-6 (print)

PREFACE

This story is inspired by true events and people. I have relied heavily on firsthand accounts from the people who witnessed or experienced the events. As you read, you may think some things must certainly be fictional, and you will be surprised at the parts that are based in fact. At the end of this book, I have written a brief historical note where I explain my research and break down the truth versus fiction of this story. I've also included a detailed bibliography of the books I read while researching this story. *Please note that while this is a story set in Britain, I have used American spellings.*

I have changed the names of almost all the characters from their real names, and I have used names that are personal to me and names that I have lovingly used with permission from the families of my wonderful readers. These readers' family members served or lived during the 1930s and 1940s and experienced the war. It was an honor to use these names, and where possible, I have given these men and women happy endings because we all deserve a little more light and joy in our lives.

This is a story about war, about a changing landscape of human experience, and it is about love. This emotion is so often disregarded, especially when it comes to romance, yet it is the force that motivates humans to the greatest acts of courage and compassion. The best stories, the best myths, the best legends, all involve love in its many forms. It is my hope that someday the two real matchmakers, Heather Jenner and Mary Oliver, become legendary for their actions during such a dark time. By bringing people together while the world tore itself apart, they were unsung heroes. Now, dear reader, turn the page to finally hear their song.

PROLOGUE

B ut if we fail, then the whole world, including the United States, including all that we have known and cared for, will sink into the abyss of a new Dark Age made more sinister, and perhaps more protracted, by the lights of perverted science. Let us therefore brace ourselves to our duties, and so bear ourselves that, if the British Empire and its Commonwealth last for a thousand years, men will still say, "This was their finest hour."

—*Winston Churchill*
House of Commons
June 18, 1940

LONDON
September 7, 1940

. . .

I<small>T</small> <small>WAS</small> <small>THE</small> <small>SILENCE</small> <small>BETWEEN</small> <small>AIR-RAID</small> <small>DRILLS</small> <small>THAT</small> frightened Elizabeth Mowbray the most. The deathly hush this particular afternoon had transformed London from a bustling city to an eerie stillness that made Elizabeth pause and strain her ears to listen to the world outside the tiny grocer's shop on King Street.

"Everything all right?" a middle-aged woman in a dull maroon frock asked as she packed the handful of goods into Elizabeth's cloth bag.

"What? Oh, yes. I'm so sorry," Elizabeth murmured as she glanced through the tiny crack between the blackout curtains draped in front of the grocer's store window. The funereal cloth was in some small way better than black-painted glass or boards —at least the curtains could be drawn back during the day to let sunlight in, when one remembered. This shop, like many others, left their curtains closed over the windows, despite it being the middle of the day and no need to black out the light of the shop's interior.

Elizabeth handed over a few ration coupons to the grocer before she collected the bag and turned to leave. A few people had stopped on the pavement outside, their eyes turned toward the Thames. One man removed his black trilby hat and squinted at the sky. His face drained of color before he smashed his hat back on his head and turned to run.

Time slowed around Elizabeth as she saw more and more people stop on the street and turn to face the sky. Silence had settled over the city, like fog upon the ground in a graveyard, coiling like phantom vipers around the craggy tombstones.

A dozen black flecks appeared over the Thames on the horizon. Air-raid sirens suddenly split through the bustling crowds of King Street.

German planes.

Her mind wanted to convince her that they were just a flock of birds rather than the impending doom her heart warned was coming.

As one, the crowds around her turned away from the Thames. The hum of distant bombers was drowned out by the sirens. The screaming sirens dug into her skull, leaving her with a fierce ache as Elizabeth tried to flee with those around her. Clutching her small bag of precious food, she was swept away by the crowds and flattened against a wall in an alley not far from the grocer's shop. The hard stone bit into her back as dozens of men and women pushed past her. Her cry of pain went unheard.

Shelter . . . must find a shelter.

Like the rest of England, she'd grown used to the sounds of sirens and empty skies in the previous months. There were the repeated nights and even some days spent cramped and cold in the Anderson shelters both in London and in the back garden of Cunningham House, the rambling old manor house that she spent her time at when not in London.

Those nights in the curved metal shelter were intolerable; it smelled of decayed earth, and she had to tuck her dressing gown up around her night slippers to avoid the rainwater that filled the bottom of the shelter. Now she might pay with her life for not respecting the endless drills. Even the government had relaxed its insistence on carrying a gas mask wherever one went. She'd left hers back at her office on Bond Street. She was trapped, terrified, *frozen* as the crowds threatened to crush anyone who didn't move quickly.

The planes were already here, the roar of the engines now

overpowering the sirens. Something inside Elizabeth jolted her back into motion. She forced herself away from the alley wall just as a man in a blue Royal Air Force uniform passed by. Her shoe caught upon a rock, and she cried out, stumbling. She braced for the impact, but it never came.

"I've got you!" A strong arm banded around her waist, catching her and pulling her upright. She briefly saw a striking masculine face with blond hair and bright blue eyes beneath the RAF cap.

"Nathan, take a right!" he bellowed at another man in an RAF uniform just ahead of them who was moving briskly through the crowd despite using a cane. Elizabeth had no choice but to be swept along at the pilot's side as they exited the alley and moved toward a darkened doorway of a shop.

"Get inside!" The pilot pushed her through the doorway. Crowded racks of clothing filled the small space, and the scent of musty cloth made her nose wrinkle with an impending sneeze. A stout shopkeeper with gray hair held the door of his shop open, frantically waving to everyone on the street.

"Stay there!" the pilot told Elizabeth before he dashed back outside, catching hold of a young woman carrying a small child in her arms and hauling her inside. "This way—there's a shelter."

The shopkeeper closed the shop door behind them just as the first bombs struck the river in the distance.

The one called Nathan with dark brown hair and light brown eyes leaned heavily against the nearest clothing rack, his cane braced before him. "They've hit the docks, Philip!" Behind him, the shopkeeper fumbled to open the metal door that led to the bomb shelter. At least a dozen or so people crowded together in the shop, their breath coming hard, with eyes wide and fearful as they waited for the door to open.

"Christ, they have, haven't they?" Philip's face turned toward the windows of the clothing store, which had been boarded up. No one could see outside. They could only hear the thunder of explosions. Each impact vibrated through the floor hard enough to rattle Elizabeth's bones.

"Madam, this way," Nathan said to the young mother, who was clutching her child to her breast, her eyes tearful. The door to the shelter creaked open. "I'll follow you down," Nathan assured her, ambling on his cane as he went down the steps after her and disappeared into the dark along with the others who had crowded behind them to get to safety.

"How big is your shelter?" Philip asked the shopkeeper.

The man adjusted his spectacles. "Fifteen people . . . it's more of a basement, really."

"It's stocked with torches and potable water?" Philip pressed as the roof above them rumbled ominously.

"Y-yes."

"Good. You go on down. I'll seal us in." Philip nudged Elizabeth and the shopkeeper down into the basement and closed the door behind him, sealing them all inside. Its heavy, metallic clang made Elizabeth halt halfway down the stairs in a sudden panic at being enclosed in such a tiny dark space. She gripped the rough-hewn wood railing so hard her knuckles were white as bone in the low light. Below her, torches moved as the occupants of the shelter swung them about, their beams bouncing off the walls at odd angles. Lanterns hung from hooks on the ceiling, illuminating the pilot's face as he came down the steps to meet her.

"Go on and have a seat somewhere. We're bound to be here awhile." He offered her a smile, but she didn't miss the strain in his eyes. Her throat tightened as another wave of fear swept through her. They were trapped in this tiny room, dozens of feet below the ground. If a bomb struck, they'd be crushed to death . . . starved of air . . .

"Breathe deep, darling," the pilot whispered to her. "Focus on the air moving in your lungs and nothing else."

Elizabeth closed her eyes and did so, filling her lungs with air. The fear subsided a little, and she opened her eyes again to stare at the man who'd taken charge of the moment. The man who'd saved her. Lines of worry were carved across his striking face as he tilted his cap back on his head.

She turned away from him to check on the other occupants of the shelter. Twelve huddled figures had taken refuge with them, some settled on a few creaky folding chairs set against the walls. The young mother held her toddler in her arms, tears streaming in rivulets down her cheeks until they shone in the dim light. Her child was quiet, his eyes wide and solemn as he gazed up at Elizabeth and the pilot as they descended the last few steps.

"Should we have left the door open?" the shopkeeper asked the pilot, gravitating toward him as the natural leader of their small group.

"We couldn't—those bombs that hit the docks will burn hot and long. The flames will draw other bombers in like beacons. If you can feel the bombing"—he paused and put a hand on the stone wall of the basement—"then you're too close. Better to close the door and wait."

"The RAF will take care of them," one man said, his tone confident, but no one else said anything for a long moment afterward.

Would they take care of the German bombers? Elizabeth hadn't let herself think of the oncoming war, not wanting to accept the reality, yet here it was.

"I should be up there with them," Philip muttered to himself, grief in his eyes as he looked at the people in the room.

The man called Nathan hobbled over to the pilot, one fist gripping the head of his cane tightly. "You mustn't torture yourself. You were on leave. You couldn't have known they'd come. You've saved London enough times already. Today it's someone else's turn."

"Will is out there at the bloody front—he doesn't come home for leave. And here I am, stuck below," Philip said as he started to pace. "I have no control down here. We're just . . . *helpless.*" He halted on the word, seeming to realize too late that he shouldn't have said it.

"We aren't helpless. You know your men will fight like the devil today. You need to survive today to fly tomorrow," Nathan reminded him in a soothing voice. "Getting yourself killed won't help Will. We both know that he's a St. Laurent, with that temper of his, the Nazis will be running in the other direction with their tails tucked between their legs."

Philip calmed a little and met his friend's eyes. "They should have made you the group captain instead of a flight instructor after your injury, Nathan."

Nathan chuckled. "Perhaps."

Another explosion, this one closer, rattled the trio of lanterns that hung from hooks on the ceiling, and dust rained down on the occupants of the basement. The mother held her child close. Philip stopped pacing and seemed to notice Elizabeth staring at him.

"Would you please sit? You look ready to fall down." He urged her toward the wall, and she crumpled to her knees on the floor near the mother and child. She hadn't realized until that moment that her legs had been shaking violently, barely holding her up.

Everyone was silent for a long moment, listening to the sounds above.

"Mama, I'm hungry," the tiny toddler whispered against his mother's neck. The young woman opened her eyes, her tearful gaze meeting Elizabeth's.

"I know you are, sweetie," the mother soothed. "I know. We shall eat later, all right?" She ran a hand over the child's dark curls. The boy's lip quivered, but he didn't cry.

Such a brave little thing.

The world above them could very well be ablaze. That realization made Elizabeth sick, but she buried her nausea beneath a practicality that she always managed to summon when she needed it most. Her fist still gripped the cloth shopping bag. Suddenly she remembered that the bag held *food*.

"Would your little boy like some savory biscuits? I have some cheese and canned meat. It isn't much, but if he's hungry . . ." Elizabeth opened the bag and dug around in the contents.

"We couldn't . . . ," the mother began.

"Of course you can." Elizabeth's fingertips brushed over the tin of savory biscuits and a bit of cheese as she pulled them out and handed them to the mother.

"Look, Henry, some biscuits." The woman smiled gratefully at Elizabeth before offering the food to her son. The little boy began to take hesitant bites before letting out a tiny sigh, his shoulders dropping as he relaxed. Elizabeth knew how he felt. The ache of an empty belly was something no one liked to endure. Ever since the rationing began, there had been quite a few nights when she had gone hungry, and the grumbling had formed that awful pit in her stomach, sometimes keeping her up until dawn.

The sounds of the bombing continued above them. Perhaps it was her imagination, but each impact seemed to get closer. No one spoke again, each of them sitting in their own agonized silence, holding their collective breath. No one was prepared. All of the drills, carrying gas masks about in leather cases, the disruption of lovely gardens with Anderson shelters, and sirens going off at odd hours—nothing had prepared her for this moment, waiting in a dark, musty basement as the world above was bathed in fire.

The man with the cane walked over to sit beside her. He used the wall to carefully lower himself down, as though he was still unused to not having full use of his leg. She wondered what had happened to him. He seemed healthy, despite his injury, and he was handsome to look at, and it was clear from the cut of his suit that he was quite well muscled. He was a fitting match to the pilot, who leaned against the opposite wall, scowling, with his arms crossed over his chest.

"You don't mind if I sit, do you?" Nathan asked.

Elizabeth shook her head and gestured for him to join her. "No, please sit. I'm Elizabeth Mowbray."

"Nathan Sheridan." He held out a hand, and she shook it. "And that is my friend, Philip Lennox." He nodded at the pilot who had saved her when she had fallen. "Philip, come and sit down. And stop that dreadful scowling." Nathan's tone was teasing, as though he was used to keeping Philip's spirits up.

Philip let out a sigh and removed his cap, exposing a fall of pale-blond hair. He shook the dust off his cap with a grimace. Then he sat down on Elizabeth's other side, where there was a little more room. He gripped his cap in his hands, his gaze focused on the opposite wall.

"Philip, this is Elizabeth Mowbray." Nathan was cordial and polite, acting as though they were all meeting for afternoon tea on the lawn of an ancestral estate, not in a grimy basement during a bombing raid. It was comforting and distracting in a vital way. Elizabeth clung to the normalcy of the moment.

Philip's gaze met hers, his brilliant blue eyes glowing in the dim lantern light. "Miss Mowbray."

"Mr. Lennox," Elizabeth replied. *Lord, those eyes* . . . He would be an excellent match for so many of her clients. How many letters had she received from clients wanting to marry a man with melting violet eyes? Of course, no one had violet eyes, but women wrote to them asking for them, nonetheless. Philip's striking blue eyes were certainly the *melting* kind. And just like that, she was focused on work, and the distant rumble of bombs faded into the background somewhat.

"Are you unattached, Mr. Lennox?"

The pilot's lips twitched. "Pardon? How do you mean?"

Nathan's deep chuckle filled the room. "He's quite unattached, much to his parents' eternal dismay."

"As are you, Nathan," Philip shot back with a snort of laughter. "Why the interest in my marital state, Miss Mowbray?" Philip asked.

Elizabeth felt the familiar flush of heat in her cheeks. She had been in her particular line of business for a year, but she still had a flash of embarrassment when having to explain it.

"I . . . er . . . run the Marriage Bureau. I'm not sure if you've heard of it. You both would make wonderful clients . . . if you wish to register with us, that is. I could see you matched with wonderful young ladies."

"The Marriage Bureau," Philip murmured. "Wasn't that the matchmaking service that Russell mentioned when he . . . ?"

"Yes, it is." Nathan rested his cane on his lap as he looked at Elizabeth. "We have a friend who was a client."

"Oh?" Elizabeth settled her bag on her lap more firmly as she got comfortable. "One of our happy clients, I hope?" They didn't have too many unhappy clients, which, given that the enterprise of matchmaking involved connections of the heart, was rather amazing, especially during wartime. But she and her friend and business partner, Henrietta, worked hard to properly align people in their introductions.

"A little too happy. The bloody fool wants everyone to go to you, even us determined bachelors," Philip replied dryly.

Nathan laughed. "Speak for yourself, Philip. Miss Mowbray, I would be most interested in your services. But how on earth did you come into such a profession in the first place? Usually it's a meddlesome mother or great-aunt who takes on such tasks."

An explosion shook the basement, and Elizabeth flinched, her breath halting in her throat. More dust drifted down, catching in the light before showering on everyone's heads. She lost focus on the conversation as she tried to steady her panicked breath. Philip put a hand on her arm; his gentle firmness encouraged her to draw in a few deep breaths. She buried her trembling hands in her skirts and remembered Nathan's question. He wanted to know how she'd ended up as one of London's first official matchmakers.

"You wish to know how we started it?"

"I certainly do. Spin us a tale, Miss Mowbray." Philip added with a soft, charming grin, "Something to chase away the sound of those bombs. We could all do with a good story." He spoke earnestly as he glanced about and nodded to the other occupants of the room.

Elizabeth realized that everyone in the basement was watching her with interest. The light moved back and forth across dusty, weary faces as the lanterns swayed.

This was why she'd opened the Marriage Bureau in London's darkest hour. There was no greater light to fight the darkness of war than love, and the Marriage Bureau's sole focus was to help people find the right person. Love was hope, and Philip was right—they needed hope now more than ever in this dim little room. If her story could help them forget about the bombs falling above them, then she was happy to tell it.

"It began about two years ago. I had traveled to India to visit my beloved uncle George in the remote hills of Assam, and I found myself on the brink of scandal . . ."

PART I

CHAPTER 1

ssam, India
September 1938

THERE WAS AN UNDENIABLE MAGIC TO INDIA. THE WARMTH OF
the sun settled into the stones, and for long hours after sunset,
Elizabeth could lay her palms on the white stone terrace railings
and absorb the sunlight into herself. But the magic was so much
more than light and heat. The earth *breathed*. The green plants
shimmered with dew, and the golden langur monkeys in the trees
called out to each other, reminding Elizabeth that she was a
guest in this world, that the soil and the water in the river
belonged to old gods, and she was only here to glimpse their
world briefly before returning to the earthy fens of
Cambridgeshire.

She could see why her uncle George had fallen in love with

this place as a young man. The sky above her head turned from blue and gold to red and purple as the sun fell beyond the horizon, and the vast Himalayas loomed like craggy monoliths in the fading light.

The smell of foxtail orchids hung heavy in the air as the rare white flowers spotted with pink draped down from hanging pots above her, the thick green tendrils full of dozens of blooms. Elizabeth reached out to touch those nearest her, a faint smile curving her lips at the delicate velvet petals. The Assamese women often adorned their dark, lustrous hair with the blooms when they danced the Bihu at the onset of spring.

She closed her eyes, picturing the swirl of colored silks and gold bangle bracelets.

"You should be inside, Lizzie." Her uncle's deep voice pulled her from her musings.

She dropped her hands from the blooms. Her mother's older brother was fifty-two and still rather dashing, with his dark silvery mustache and features slightly weathered by so many years beneath the Indian sun. He gazed at her with such affection that Elizabeth's chest tightened. He was more of a father to her than her own back in Cambridgeshire.

"Am I missing the dancing already?" She looped her arm through her uncle's as he joined her at the terrace. Ahead of them, the endless rows of tea plants, thick and green, covered the rich soil of the rolling hills below. It was a testament to her uncle's hard work and his relations with the locals that the plantation prospered.

"Not yet, but Mr. Britt was looking for you."

Elizabeth's heart kicked into a faster beat at the mention of her fiancé. "Was he?"

She'd only been here four months and was already engaged to

be married. Her parents had sent her to visit Uncle George for her twenty-third birthday in hopes that she would finally be married off, like many of the other young women sent to India. The "fishing fleet" of young women, as society called them, were the girls who had found no matches at home. Some were considered *troublesome* girls who simply wouldn't settle down and behave respectably. And what better way to be rid of them than by packing them up and shipping them to the farthest corner of the British Empire, where their only hope of a future lay in marriage?

It was a fate that society girls and farm girls like herself all faced. A woman simply had to be married to be useful, no matter what her situation. Elizabeth had no problem with marriage herself; she only didn't want to be *bored* with life.

Elizabeth would have hated the idea of being shipped away somewhere as a punishment, but coming here had made it an adventure and a way to escape from the dull tedium of an English farm. When she'd first arrived, her uncle had led her through a series of glittering balls and lavish parties, something she hadn't ever experienced before. He'd lived a much more adventurous life than his sister, Elizabeth's mother, had chosen.

It was one of the reasons Elizabeth adored Uncle George so much. His life was exotic and exciting compared to the quiet farm life she was used to. In the midst of all the parties in Assam, Elizabeth had stumbled, quite literally, into Algernon Britt's arms. Tall, dark-haired, and a wonderful dancer, he had quickly swept her off her feet.

He helped manage another plantation not too far from Uncle George's, and Elizabeth could think of no better place to be. It would be exciting to live here, and she would have a life full of passion and fulfillment. She had immediately accepted Algernon's proposal and sent word back to her family in England of the engagement.

"You had better go find your man, my dear," her uncle teased and kissed her on the cheek before returning to the party.

Through the gold-and-red gauze curtains draping the arched entryways, she could see the men and women drinking and talking. Strains of classical music carried upon the breeze, momentarily masking the sound of laughter and the clink of crystal glasses. She moved down the long terrace that bordered the ballroom and paused as she saw Algernon standing close to one of the entrances opening on the terrace. He was ringed by male companions who were enjoying a drink.

Elizabeth, hidden by the evening shadows, took a moment to observe Algernon, her heart swelling with quiet joy. He was the tallest man in the circle, his handsome face accented by his well-tailored light-gray suit. His natural air of command was apparent now as he fielded questions.

"Tell us, Algy, what's it like to have a girl on the hook?" one man asked. "You have the prettiest little creature for your fiancée. That impish face and flashing eyes—she'd captivate any man."

Elizabeth blushed, the compliment making her smile. She wasn't beautiful enough to model, she was only five foot three, and her curves were a little fuller than the slender beauties painted across advertisements. But her hair was a lovely shade of auburn, and she was told her blue eyes sparkled with mischief. She loved to be busy and was always up to something interesting if she could manage it. She hoped that her love of excitement was what had drawn Algernon to her.

"I do have the prettiest fiancée," Algernon agreed, and

sipped his drink. "I think she'll turn out well, once we're married. She needs a firm hand, though, that one."

At this, the other men laughed, and the sound sent a shiver of dread through her.

"Don't they all?" another of his fellows jested.

Algernon snorted. "Some women are perfectly meek. Others need that necessary meekness to be reinforced. My Beth is one of those. Someday soon, she'll have figured out that I am her lord and master. Once she knows her place, she'll be the perfect little shadow to enhance my reputation here."

The other men chortled in agreement.

A sharp, metallic taste filled Elizabeth's mouth as she sank deeper into the shadows. The draping blooms of foxtail orchids teased her skin as she closed her eyes and tried to breathe through the sudden rush of panic. Algernon's words pierced her chest with dread.

I am her lord and master . . . she'll be the perfect little shadow . . .

Elizabeth didn't want to be a shadow. She didn't want to serve a tyrannical husband. Part of her wanted to excuse him for what he had said. Didn't men often boast in front of their friends? Still, her instincts warned her that jokes came from a kernel of truth. Did Algernon truly see her as some silly little willful creature to be jerked into line like a well-trained spaniel? Elizabeth suspected that these were often the kind of men who kicked those same obedient dogs.

Elizabeth opened her eyes, fire flooding her veins. A man who loved his wife would never try to obliterate her personality or passion for life. That *wasn't* love. After watching her parents live in a frigid marriage full of stony silences, boorish dinners, and separate beds, she'd vowed not to marry until she was loved. Everyone deserved that, didn't they?

Even her uncle had made a practical, society-approved match that had ended in a painful divorce. Simply because two people were well suited on paper didn't mean they made a real match. While she'd been here in India, she'd managed to pair up several of her new friends with good men who matched them in all the ways that mattered. She'd foolishly believed she'd done the same for herself, but she hadn't. She'd been blinded to Algernon's nature because she hadn't put him through his paces and tested him the way she had the young men who were interested in her friends.

She moved away from Algernon and his companions, careful to stay out of sight as she weighed her options. A set of stairs led from the terrace down to the garden. She paused by a large lily pad–covered pond with a fountain, trying to pull herself together. She wanted to scream, she wanted to . . . she just wanted to be free of him and the marriage she'd foolishly agreed to.

Water bubbled up from the stone sculpture in the center, pouring down in smooth sheets of twilight-hued water. She reached out and traced the white blooms of a flower on top of one of the lily pads. If only she could stay here forever with Uncle George and not have to face Algernon or the expectant crowds who'd planned to attend the lavish wedding. Breaking things off could hurt Uncle George, and that was the very last thing Elizabeth wanted.

The wedding was only a week away, and they'd already received a dozen gifts, which now sat in her room. She supposed some women would succumb to the pressure and marry a man they knew was a bad choice. But she wasn't like that—much to her mother and father's everlasting dismay.

The wedding was most certainly off, but if she stayed here,

she would be a burden to Uncle George, not to mention the scandal it would cause. Everyone here knew Algernon. He was adored and loved here—*she* wasn't. Breaking off their engagement would be seen as a strike against her character.

She squared her shoulders. There was nothing to do but return to England to face the wrath of her parents. She would have to tell her uncle tonight and Algernon tomorrow.

"Ah, there you are." Algernon's deep voice froze her in place. She masked her dismay with a pleasant smile and faced her fiancé. He stood in the center of the garden path, arms crossed over his chest.

"You've missed too much of the ball. Everyone is wondering why my bride-to-be isn't by my side." There was just a hint of disapproval in his tone. Heavens, he was good at masking his commanding personality.

Elizabeth had had every intention of maintaining her cordiality toward him—until he said that. Something dark and angry flared to life inside her.

"By your side? Or *behind you* as your shadow?" Her words were forceful, but her voice was not raised. She was not one to shriek when furious.

A momentary expression of surprise flitted across Algernon's eyes. "A wife's place is to support her husband."

"And you are to be my lord and master?" she asked, wondering if he would try to deny his own words.

He didn't. His brows lowered and his voice deepened even further, now tinged with anger. "Yes, and it's time we discussed your behavior, Beth."

She winced at the nickname. When they first met, he'd called her Beth, not Lizzie, even though she'd told him she much preferred Lizzie, the childhood nickname her uncle had given her. It was further proof that he didn't care about her, only what her presence could provide him.

"I've been lenient with you, and it's clearly not the right approach. A wife's duty—"

"I'm not marrying you, Algernon. The wedding is off." She raised her chin, hoping the defiant move would give her more confidence to face him.

"Like bloody hell it is. You'd have me look the fool?" Algernon started toward her, and a wave of fear sent her stumbling back a step. He was over six feet tall; if he wished her harm, there was little she could do to stop him.

"Lizzie?" Uncle George's voice came down from the top of the stairs, gold light bathing his figure from behind. Elizabeth rushed toward him, flying up the steps so quickly that her crème satin pumps nearly fell off her feet.

Her uncle caught her arm when she tried to skirt around him to get away from Algernon. "Wait. What's the matter?"

"It's nothing, Uncle George," she lied. "I'm feeling rather unwell, is all. I thought perhaps I would turn in early." She shot a glance back at Algernon, who glowered at her in the shadows by the fountain.

What a fool she had been thinking *he* was her dream. The man was a brute, a controlling tyrant who would have broken her spirit to suit his antiquated expectations. If she hadn't heard him speaking to his friends, she might have ended up making the most terrible mistake of her life.

"Very well, go on to bed. Have Aabha prepare you some tea." George gave her arm a gentle squeeze before letting go.

Elizabeth slipped past him and rushed down the hall into the private wing of the plantation house where her bedchamber was. The rest of the plantation home was blessedly quiet; only the cries of distant langurs and koel birds intruded upon the silence.

"*Jiji?*" a lyrical voice asked as Elizabeth reached the door to her bedroom. A beautiful woman in her early forties with hair so dark it shimmered purple like a raven's wing in the light stood at the end of the hall.

"Aabha," Elizabeth greeted in relief. There was only one woman in the house who called her *jiji*.

Aabha was her uncle's housekeeper, a local Assamese woman who'd lived on the plantation nearly as long as her uncle had. She moved silently in red silk slippers, and her sari, a blend of brilliant gold and blue, glowed against her olive skin. She came to Elizabeth and clutched her hands.

"What has happened, *jiji?*"

Elizabeth hugged the woman who had become her friend and confidant these past several months. "It's awful. Algernon and I . . . it's over."

"Come and sit." Aabha pulled her by the hand into Elizabeth's bedchamber. Her eyes were warm and rich. "Now, what is this about? What has happened between you and your handsome man?"

She caught sight of herself in the tall gilt mirror in one corner, her lovely green satin evening gown with freshly cut white lilies pinned to her shoulder. She'd felt so glamorous only hours ago. Now she felt like a schoolgirl playing dress-up.

"I thought I knew who he was, but I was wrong. I'm a fool." Elizabeth hated to admit to her failings, but she knew Aabha wouldn't judge her.

"It is hard to know someone in so short a time." Her rich, lilting voice was like a lullaby to Elizabeth. She always smelled of jasmine and orange flowers, and as she curled an arm around

Elizabeth's shoulder, Elizabeth felt the pain of her impending departure from Assam all the more deeply. This was what she was leaving behind, the only family she had aside from her brother, Alan, and Uncle George that felt *real*. The magic of this place would fade from her life the moment she boarded a ship for England.

"I've ended my engagement with Algernon. That means I must leave."

The older woman didn't say anything, but held Elizabeth close for a long time. All about the bedroom, baskets of blooming jasmine filled the air with their heady fragrance, and the songs of the koel birds made tonight even more of a melancholy dream. One that Elizabeth would cling to in the coming days.

"When will you go?" Aabha asked.

"I shall purchase a ticket for the ship that leaves tomorrow." Her gaze fell to the stack of presents, all wrapped in shimmering ivory paper. They were wedding presents from the men Algernon had been speaking with tonight. The men who had laughed and agreed that she was only fit to be a man's shadow.

"What are you thinking, *jiji?*" Aabha asked, her tone wary.

"I'm thinking I should use those *thoughtful* gifts to help buy a ticket home." She didn't want a single present from those men, and it seemed only fitting to take the money from gifts that represented her shackled imprisonment to break herself free.

"But your uncle would pay—"

"He would, but I would rather him keep his money and have him buy you a new sari from the market, or perhaps a scarf."

Aabha's laughter tugged a smile from Elizabeth. "*Sahib* always does, even when I tell him not to."

"Will you take care of him for me?" Elizabeth grasped

Aabha's hands with earnestness. "I so want to stay here, but I *can't*."

Aabha cupped her face. "I will never leave him, I promise you."

"Thank you." For many years now, her uncle had shared a life with this woman in what ways he could. They were matched in temperament and enjoyed each other's company far better than the wife society had deemed acceptable for him. Elizabeth held no judgment against her uncle for loving this woman. In fact, she wished the world would allow for more people to be together, no matter where they came from or who they were. Aabha was the best choice for a companion of Uncle George's heart. But because others would condemn him, it must forever be a secret.

"Could you do something for me, Aabha? I must pack, but I need these presents sold for ticket money. Could you ask one of the servants to run to the market and see it done this evening?"

"Leave it to me," Aabha promised with a conspiratorial smile. "It is better not to keep such things for a marriage that will not happen."

"Thank you." Elizabeth hugged her again, and then the housekeeper collected the presents and left Elizabeth alone.

She collapsed onto the velvet cushioned seat at the vanity table her uncle had bought for her and removed her pearl drop earrings and delicate gold bracelets. These were the wedding gifts that mattered, the earrings from her uncle and the bracelets from Aabha. They were the only items she would cherish, wedding or not.

Then she faced herself in the mirror. The person looking back at her wasn't a worldly woman of twenty-three. She looked like a tired young schoolgirl. Elizabeth covered her face with her hands, but no tears came. No, she was too weary for that now.

Carrying an exhaustion that she wished she could banish, she packed her trunk. Long after the guests had gone, she went to speak to her uncle.

Uncle George was in his study, puffing on a cigar. The smoke coiled in tendrils up into the air as he leaned back in his chair. A lamp on a large desk illuminated a newspaper, which currently held his attention. He stroked his chin thoughtfully and turned a page. Behind him, the floor-to-ceiling bookshelves were packed with a hundred books on dozens of subjects.

Elizabeth paused in the doorway and had a moment to take in the sight of her uncle surrounded in warm light, cigar smoke clouds blossoming above his head. Something inside her cried out a warning that she might never see this again. Perhaps it was the troubling talk of Europe facing a conflict from a restless Germany again. The memories and the pain of the Great War were felt even here in India. Her uncle was one of many men who had fought on the once-golden fields of France and still bore the scars from crawling through trenches lined with barbed wire.

Something whispered in the back of her mind that *change* was coming and that this brief period of joy here with the people she loved would never be recaptured.

With a rustle of paper, her uncle set his pipe on an ashtray and glanced up to see her. He pushed his chair back and stood.

"Lizzie, I thought you would be in bed."

"I'm sorry for disturbing you, Uncle George, but I must speak with you."

"Well, come in, my dear, come in." He nodded to the leather armchair situated near his desk, but Elizabeth couldn't sit. If she settled in that worn brown leather chair, she would never have the courage to do what she must.

"What's the matter? Have you and Britt had a lovers' quarrel?" Her uncle was teasing, but he had no idea how close he was to the truth.

"The wedding is off." She folded her hands together in front of her to hide their sudden shaking.

"Oh?" That single syllable held a note of questioning and concern, but no anger or judgment. She was relieved he wasn't angry. She had known he wouldn't be.

Her parents, on the other hand . . .

"What happened?" George came to her, gently lifting her chin when she tried to look down at her feet in mortification.

"He isn't the man I thought he was . . . It became clear tonight that he and I would be dreadfully unhappy. I was so very blind about him . . . such a fool."

George's shrewd gaze left her certain that he understood. "Better to know it now than to find out later. And you're not a fool. You've done well matching your other friends, but you simply rushed your own decision. I'd rather you take your time than marry a man who would be a danger to your happiness."

"Algernon was so very upset tonight, and I shudder to think how things would be if I stayed, and . . ."

"You must return to England," he finished, shoulders dropping slightly.

Elizabeth bit her lip and nodded. "I would give anything to stay, but you know how it will be. He is an adored man here, and I'll be shunned for crying off."

George sighed. "Even here in the East, we cannot escape the reach of cultured society and its expectations, can we?"

"It seems not. Although part of me would rather brave the mess here than return and face Mama and Papa."

"That's understandable. I love your mother, but she can be

harsh at times. Marrying your father only hardened her further." He paused. "When will you leave?"

"Tomorrow."

He nodded, accepting the news gravely. "I shall buy your ticket."

Elizabeth shook her head. "No, no, I'll pay for it."

"If you're sure . . ."

Elizabeth forced a smile. "I am. I have a little money that I should really like to use for the passage back."

"And what will you do when you get home? I can't imagine you will idle your days away in Cambridge on the farm."

She pictured days mucking out a stall or throwing out feed for a brood of messy white-feathered hens. "Neither can I. I honestly don't know what I'll do."

"You know, my dear, I've had a thought . . . What if, when you get back to England, you do something about all these lonely lads here in India? There are plenty of decent chaps—the ones not friendly with Britt, of course." His eyes twinkled with the mischief that she had inherited from his side of the family.

"Do what with them?"

"Make matches, my dear. You have a good sense of people, even though you are still learning about yourself. Why not put that skill to use? You coupled Miss Palmer with Mr. Elliott last week, and by all accounts, they are blissfully happy. Think of the scores of marriage-minded women in London, each longing to escape their own farms and parents to find marital bliss. Those girls are like gold dust here, and the young men who visit England for just a few months never have the chance to meet any eligible ladies. Think of all the good you could do. Make the matches that will last, the matches that will bring happiness. Be a bridge that unites people in love."

"A matchmaker . . ." Elizabeth turned the thought around in her mind. "But wouldn't people expect some eccentric old woman with white hair and spectacles rather than me? I could scarcely trust my own judgment after Algernon—"

"Forget Algernon and forget yourself. You know *others*, my dear. That's all you need." He gave her a warm hug. "Think it over and be off to bed. I'll escort you to the ship tomorrow morning."

Elizabeth walked slowly through the halls back to her room, pondering the idea. Did England need a matchmaker? Could she even build a profession from such a thing? She lay awake long into the night, and as she finally drifted into jasmine-scented dreams, she imagined what it could mean to be a bridge that united people.

CHAPTER 2

E *ngland*
February 1939

"SOMETHING IS WRONG WITH THE GIRL." ETHEL MOWBRAY clanged a teapot hard on the wooden kitchen table. "She's not behaving the way she should, John. She's stubborn, obstinate, a silly romantic who refuses to get married when she *knows* that's what she ought to do."

"I agree," John Mowbray muttered. "We must do something. Letting her live here with us at her age, it's nonsense. I have no intention of supporting an old maid. We need her off our hands."

Elizabeth hid at the top of the stairs of the old farmhouse, just barely able to see her parents at the table, speaking. She listened to her parents discuss her future with such barely concealed disgust that her heart clenched in pain. She had expected this when she'd come home from India, but she hadn't imagined they could be so cruel as to see her as *useless*. She worked hard on the farm, just like everyone else. Why didn't that matter to them? Other daughters from the local farms didn't have parents like hers. They were the fortunate ones.

The thought that a woman's only function was to be married off so as to relieve her parents was simply idiotic. In Elizabeth's view, marriage should be about mutual desire and lifelong companionship. Uncle George had said that life was a journey best shared with another whom one liked immensely. To hear her parents speak, she was, by her unavoidable nature as a woman, a burden to be passed on to someone else.

She wasn't the only girl to face the fate of an unmarried woman living at home. Plenty of women who worked in shops, as secretaries, or even those assisting with the home were trapped in a cycle of endless days where they had no true enjoyment of life.

But what could a woman do to stay self-sufficient and still feel a sense of satisfaction? Most jobs barely paid enough for a woman to buy her food and still live with her family. Being able to have a job was one thing, but if she really wanted to get out of this farmhouse and fully support herself, she needed a business. She had to figure out a product or a service that could be offered that a lot of people would need on a consistent basis. It needed to be something that could offer her a steady stream of clients or customers, and in return, a steady stream of livable income.

Elizabeth bit her lip, thinking over what she was good at, which wasn't much. She had no special skills that people would pay for, and she couldn't create things. She would give anything to have a talent for something useful.

"She has a month," her father said. "Then she must leave. I

don't want to face any more people in town and have to explain that she's still here."

A month . . .

Elizabeth moved back from the stairs, not wanting to hear another word.

"Lizzie." She turned at the sound of her brother's questioning voice, which was soft enough to go unheard by their parents.

It was close to midnight, and Alan stood in the doorway to his bedroom, wearing his pajamas. His dark hair was mussed from sleep. He had grown up so much while she'd been away in India. The long-limbed, awkward boy was gone, and in his place was a young man of seventeen, one who would be entering university early to study advanced radio and elementary German. He'd always been so clever at school, and Cambridge had taken notice, thanks to her father's connections to several professors there.

The world had changed as she'd sailed away from the shores of India. England was bracing for another war . . . so soon after the Great War had ended with such devastating consequences. She'd been a tiny child when the Great War ended, but her parents and the others their age still remembered. Men still carried the scars, and families still carried the burden of losing brothers, fathers, and husbands. England couldn't go through that horror again.

"I didn't mean to wake you, Alan. Go back to bed." She started to walk past, but he stopped her.

Now over six foot, he towered above her. The boy she had protected with all her heart against the world was now a man, one upon the precipice of entering the conflict that Elizabeth dreaded was drawing nearer. It was like she was in a darkened wood and she sensed a shadowy presence coming ever closer, like a wolf trailing her as she struggled to find her way home. The fear of what loomed ahead, that it could take Alan from her . . . Elizabeth's chest knotted with pain and fear, but she dared not let him see it.

"You know I'm too old for you to order me about." Alan smiled and opened his door wider, gesturing for her to come inside. She did, and he sat on his bed while she paced to the window. She hoped he didn't want to talk about their parents.

"It isn't true, you know," he said.

She winced. So he had heard them talking.

"They just don't understand you," Alan added, his tone soft. "You're different. You have dreams that should carry you beyond this place."

Something about her little brother's gentleness in that moment chipped away at her carefully built defenses. He was the only one who ever saw her at her most vulnerable. The rest of the world saw her as a bubbly little creature with a bright smile and a cheerful disposition.

"I'm not sure even *I* understand me." The words came out in a whisper. "I'm no use to anyone. I have no head for arithmetic, no skill with my hands to be a seamstress or a milliner. I can't be trusted to stay focused on shopkeeping if I became a clerk."

"What would you do if you could do anything? Anything at all in the world?" Alan asked.

She faced him, wrapping her fingers in the collar of her dressing gown. "I . . ."

"Don't think with your head—answer with your heart."

"When did you become so wise, little brother?" she teased, but her eyes began to fill with tears.

"Lizzie . . ."

"Very well." She closed her eyes and envisioned herself back in India, putting away the memories of Algernon, burying those deep enough that only other memories remained. Those of dozens of faces at the social events in Assam she had attended. So many of those faces had one thing in common. *Loneliness.*

"I want to bring people together. I want to fight loneliness. Uncle George had this mad idea that I should be a matchmaker."

"Then that is what you must do."

She laughed at the thought of simply declaring she would be a matchmaker. "Just like that?" It wasn't that simple. It couldn't be.

Uncle George's words came back to her. *Be the bridge that unites people in love.*

If she started arranging matches, she would offer a path to freedom for those women, a path that led to a man who matched her, who valued her for herself and didn't see her as a burden. But how could she even begin this endeavor? Where did she start? Would people even pay for such a service?

"Papa's sister, Isabelle, is in London. You should write to her, go and stay with her. I'm sure she'll let you. She knows *everyone.* If anyone can help you, she can."

It wasn't a bad idea. Isabelle had escaped farm life to make something of herself as a model and then a fashion designer in London. No one who saw her now would ever have guessed that she'd grown up in a tiny village just outside Cambridge. She was full of gaiety, and her life never had a dull moment.

"And I shall leave you here with *them?*" Elizabeth jerked her head toward the door.

"You can and you will. Besides, I leave for school soon, and they won't be able to stop me doing what I wish, not with my schooling being fully funded by scholarships. Besides, Papa is proud of me and wants me to leave the farm."

Alan's gaze moved to the stack of books on his small writing desk in the corner. On top of the stack, a pamphlet about the Royal Navy stood out in stark colors against the old, battered books.

"Oh, Alan . . . Are you sure you should enlist?" Elizabeth wanted to keep him a child, keep him safe from the world, but that would be no different than what her parents wanted for her. A life that was built around safety. *Safety* so often could be boring. Lives were meant to be lived.

"I'll be fine, Lizzie." Alan stood and grasped her hands, squeezing them. "If I volunteer sooner, there's a chance I'll be an officer."

"But you're only seventeen . . ."

"Eighteen in four months," he reminded her. "Not even you, with all your stubbornness, can stop me from joining up."

"You should get to bed," she said. All the other things she had wanted to say seemed too much, too powerful, and threatened to choke her with emotion as they stayed trapped upon her tongue.

Alan chuckled. "You too. Tomorrow is another day to conquer."

It was a long while before Elizabeth could fall asleep. She stayed up and penned a letter to her aunt for tomorrow's post. She couldn't stay here on the farm, couldn't let the past control her future. There was only one way to go now, and that way was forward.

MARCH 1939

Living with Aunt Isabelle was easy, so easy that often Elizabeth would pause and wonder if she'd fallen asleep and was dreaming. Isabelle was a fashion designer who worked under Norman Hartnell. And as a beautiful single woman in her midthirties, she had an ever-whirling social schedule. Thankfully, she seemed to have no qualms about taking a farmer's daughter to her lavish West End parties, as she was tonight.

"Tonight, simply everyone will be there." Isabelle swiped an eyeliner pencil over her lids as she studied herself in her vanity mirror. She always knew how to put on makeup to make her blue eyes glow.

Elizabeth sat on the end of the bed and watched Isabelle apply a coral shade of lipstick and lightly fluff her long chestnut hair in its carefully styled feminine pompadour that left the front section of her hair rolled back in a wave and the rest artfully falling down her shoulders in the back in loose waves. It was a hairstyle that Elizabeth never had the patience for herself.

"Go put on that gown I laid out for you. I swear, if I see one more gingham-print dress on you, I shall die," Isabelle declared with her usual drama, but it only made Elizabeth laugh.

She did as Isabelle ordered and slipped into the dark-blue princess gown with capped sleeves and a sweetheart neckline. It was embroidered with silver flowers, and it draped dramatically over her body. The gown was too glamorous for her, but Aunt Isabelle was right in one respect. A gingham dress simply would not do, not for the sort of party they were attending this evening. A wealthy brigadier-general and his wife, who had recently returned from abroad in Ceylon, had settled in a large house in Chelsea and were reacquainting themselves with friends old and new.

"Ready?" Isabelle appeared in the doorway, striking quite a figure in her black velvet evening gown. She was willowy, with the perfect figure for fashion. She had been a model in Paris for a year before winning Norman Hartnell's eye with her natural talent for design.

"I'm ready." Elizabeth joined her aunt as they took a cab to the party.

"Now, when we arrive, I must speak with everyone. You may stay at my side or go about the party as you please." Isabelle leaned forward to peer at the row of cars along the street a few minutes later. "It's just there." She pointed out the townhouse to the cabdriver.

"Here we are, loves." The driver smiled broadly at Isabelle, who slipped him his fare before they left the vehicle. They both stood facing the door to the home.

"Chin up, my dear," her aunt said. "No worlds were ever conquered by a woman who stared at her feet."

Elizabeth lifted her chin, more than ever aware of how much she and Isabelle were alike, forging their own paths away from convention. Yet for the last month Elizabeth had felt adrift upon a vast sea, rudderless, unable to get her bearings. She knew what she wished to do, but she had no idea how to do it.

She followed her aunt into a glittering home full of classical music and exquisitely attired party guests. Everywhere Elizabeth turned, there were people happy to be alive. It was as though everyone could sense the coming darkness, and they were desperate to create as much light as they could for as long as possible before they lost it.

"Come meet the brigadier and his wife." Isabelle pulled her along to meet a commanding man in his late fifties and his wife, who were holding court by the entryway. They were a fine set, he in his formal army dress uniform and his wife in a white-and-gold ballgown.

"Isabelle! Glad you could come!" The brigadier's booming voice carried all the way across the room.

"Brigadier Byron," Isabelle greeted. "Mrs. Byron." Isabelle then nudged Elizabeth forward. "This is my niece, Elizabeth Mowbray."

"Charmed." The brigadier shook Elizabeth's hand, his grip firm and precise in a way that Elizabeth immediately liked. She nodded and smiled at the brigadier's wife.

"Come in and have a drink." The brigadier smiled broadly, surprising warmth coming from a man whom Elizabeth had expected to be cool and brusque. "We ordered far too much champagne." He and his wife shared a chuckle before she rolled her eyes.

Isabelle made a slow round of the room, clearly acquainted with most everyone in attendance. Elizabeth was happy to stay on the fringes, taking it all in. Her eyes were drawn to a stunning blonde woman by the fireplace. She wore a deep-gold evening dress that clung to her skin and flowed like watered silk every time she moved. Confidence and vibrancy emanated from her, yet Elizabeth saw minute fractures in the façade of the woman's gaiety that likely went unnoticed by those around her. Her dark blue eyes would briefly flash then fade as her false joy vanished.

When she moved away from her crowd of admirers and stepped out alone onto the balcony, Elizabeth followed. The woman lit a cigarette and leaned on the railing to gaze at the perfectly tended garden. When she noticed Elizabeth, she half smiled.

"You can join me. I don't bite." Her husky voice, combined with her looks, made her a fascinating subject to study. Elizabeth

did like to people-watch, and she learned much from her obser-
vations. This was one of the reasons why Uncle George had
believed she had a talent for matchmaking.

Elizabeth smiled and stepped up beside her.

"You're a new face," the woman observed dryly.

Elizabeth chuckled. "I suppose I am."

"I know almost everyone here, all old friends of my parents."

"Your father is the brigadier?"

"He is."

Elizabeth was a little stunned. Isabelle hadn't mentioned that
the family had a daughter.

"Were you with them in Ceylon, or . . ." Elizabeth halted as
she realized the inquiry might be rude.

"I was. We've only just moved back. They threw this party
for me—unofficially, that is." The woman didn't seem pleased
about it at all, despite the fact that she looked like the sort of
woman everyone would want at the center of a grand gathering
such as this.

"You're not happy about that, are you?" Elizabeth guessed.

"My mother believes my spirits need lifting, and she also
wishes for me to remarry. A bloody nuisance, that." The woman
took a drag on her cigarette, then held the pack out to
Elizabeth.

She waved the offer away. "No, thank you. Do you mind if I
ask you a personal question?"

"Not at all. I'm feeling generous tonight."

"You were married before?"

At this, the woman held her cigarette away from her as
though the taste no longer appealed to her. She tapped the ashes
on the railing before stubbing it out in a nearby standing ashtray.

"I was. I met him in Ceylon. He was one of those dashing

young men under my father's command. A girl can make a fool of herself for a man in uniform, can't she?" She offered Elizabeth a rueful smile. "But one day, you wake up and realize that the glowing bubble of desire has popped and all that is left is . . . nothing. We had not one thing in common. We didn't even like each other. So we divorced."

"Desire can be fleeting. Truly *liking* a person lasts far longer." It was something Elizabeth had noticed in India when she'd paired together two friends, Miss Palmer and Mr. Elliott. They had genuinely enjoyed each other's company in a platonic sense too, not just physical desire. The pangs of desire only lasted so long, and someday a man and a woman had to be able to enjoy each other's company when not blinded by youthful lust.

"It's easy to think you're in love when the world lies at your feet and all about you is an exotic, sunlit land. I was worshiped, but worshiping is not the same as loving, you know." She turned around to lean back against the balcony railing, her eyes drifting over the exuberant crowds just inside. This woman understood loneliness. She understood the mistake a person could make when marrying without thinking it through and learning about the other person. Elizabeth felt an instant kinship with this woman she didn't even know.

A sudden idea struck Elizabeth. What if she had a business partner, someone to do the matchmaking with her? It would be brilliant. It would be fun and . . . But how to ask her?

"Wouldn't it be rather lovely to meet a man who was clearly suited to your needs?" Elizabeth asked, keeping the rush of excitement out of her tone. There was something about this woman that drew Elizabeth to her, wanting to be friends with her. She was someone who had everything she could ever dream of, yet she hadn't found the one thing she wanted—real love.

"It would be rather nice to meet a man who truly suited *me* and not what everyone else wants for me." The woman's face softened as she watched her father twirl her mother about on the floor. "I want a partner in life, not someone to command me about like a foot soldier."

"I know exactly what you mean. I escaped the prospect of a wretched marriage to a man everyone else adored. He was a tyrant, and I didn't even realize it until it was almost too late."

The two women stayed quiet a long moment, and then Elizabeth held out her hand.

"I am Elizabeth Mowbray. Lizzie, if you prefer."

The woman shook her hand. "Henrietta Byron, I didn't keep my married name. Everyone I adore calls me Hetty. And I think I might like you enough for you to do the same." She chuckled as if at some private joke. "Do you live in London?"

"I do for now. I'm living with my aunt Isabelle until I sort out what I want to do. Once I have gainful employment, perhaps I'll be able to afford a flat on my own."

Hetty leaned toward her a little. "What do you wish to do?"

"Well, that's just it. I have a rather mad idea, you see."

"Do tell. I *adore* mad ideas." Hetty said this with a mischievous grin.

"My uncle George . . . Oh, you see, this is a rather long story. I was in India when I broke off that engagement I mentioned."

"Good for you." Hetty gave her a mock salute. "Another liberated woman joins the ranks."

A blush rose in Elizabeth's face. "Yes, well, my dear uncle . . ."

"George?" Hetty supplied with a wink.

"Yes, Uncle George had this rather striking idea that I should become a matchmaker."

"A matchmaker?" Hetty didn't laugh at this, which Elizabeth saw as a small victory. She was taking her seriously.

"Yes. You see, I'm good at reading other people. Certainly not when it comes to my own romantic affairs, but with others, I have rather a knack for pairing people off. I matched a few of my friends to good success, and, well, isn't that something that matters?"

"Marrying people off, you mean?" Hetty chewed her bottom lip in thought.

"No. It's not about simply marrying them off. It's about building a bridge that connects two people in harmony. If there had been someone to speak to me and my ex-fiancé when we were apart from each other and get a better sense of what we both wanted in a marriage, there might never have been an engagement, you see? Someone could've warned me that we would not have suited."

"But isn't that the sort of business spinster great-aunts deal in?" Hetty teased. Elizabeth knew that she wasn't being taken seriously anymore.

"When you were in Ceylon, you came back on a ship. Don't you remember what it was like? Barely any girls spread out among the masses of men. And those men were all bound for home, desperate to find a wife, lonely, sex-starved, and forlorn. I'm not half so pretty as you, and yet nearly every man aboard was giving me the glad eye. I could have gotten engaged half a dozen times before we even made it into port."

Hetty was listening now, really listening, so Elizabeth continued. "These men returned to England to visit their families, but they're really on the prowl for a girl to marry. They have only a few months before they must return to Ceylon or India or wherever, and they won't leave for home again for a long time."

"Most of the men in Ceylon have no hope in hell of finding a wife," Hetty added thoughtfully. "They outnumber the eligible girls by thousands."

"And," Elizabeth continued in excitement, "most will marry whatever halfway presentable girl who comes along, and we both know how terrible that will be. So my idea is that we introduce them to *suitable* girls while they are on leave. I have quite a few girlfriends who would be happy to be introduced to eligible men. Think of it—so many men coming home, so many women here seeking husbands, yet they never meet. We can make a business of it—a marriage agency."

"You're serious about this, aren't you?"

Elizabeth reached into her purse and produced a slip of paper. "I am, and I would love for you to join me. I think we'd deal well together as business partners."

She hastily wrote down her address and phone number. Hetty accepted the card and opened a silver card case engraved with her initials and gave Elizabeth her own information.

"I'll think on it," Hetty promised.

"Good." Elizabeth noticed Isabelle was waving at her that she was ready to leave. "Well, it was lovely to meet you." Then she dashed off to join her aunt.

HETTY WATCHED THE LITTLE AUBURN-HAIRED YOUNG WOMAN walk away. She couldn't get the thought out of her head. *A marriage agency* . . . It was a truly novel idea—either a mad one or an utterly brilliant one. She lit a new cigarette and turned her focus back to her parents. The brigadier was still regaling his eager audience with tales from Ceylon.

A pang of longing struck Hetty's heart. She missed the golden sun and the promise of endless adventures there. She had been the toast of every young man, adored and desired. It had been an addictive feeling. But she was not the silly young creature men believed her to be. It always amazed her how often men assumed the loveliness of one's face accompanied a lack of intellect or fortitude.

This wasn't true for Hetty. She was organized, thorough, calculating, and a clever strategist. Her father had often remarked how those qualities would have a served her well in the armed forces had she been a man. He'd spoiled her, giving her money and a nice little flat upon returning to London so she could enjoy a life of parties, gossip, and flirtations while she pursued employment as an actress and model. He'd guessed she would miss the life she'd had in Ceylon, and he'd been right. Still, she couldn't have stayed there forever; she'd always known she would come back to London and get on with life.

Her father's gift of a lavish lifestyle had been enough to get her by until tonight. Until she met Elizabeth Mowbray. They were around the same age and faced the same diverging path in their lives where they must choose between doing what society expected or defying convention completely. Hetty liked to think she was brave and bold enough to defy those conventions, but without a plan, she didn't know where to begin.

Elizabeth clearly knew what she wanted to do. The light in her eyes as she spoke of matching up lonely people had touched Hetty at a time when she believed herself to be too jaded to feel inspired by life ever again. Hetty wanted to feel that same spark of self-discovery that burned so brightly inside Elizabeth. She was imaginative and romantic, while Hetty had always been practical and logical.

Her petite new friend had impishly good looks and a quick mind and tongue, all things that Hetty respected. Lizzie would be an equal both in friendship and business. But could she, a woman determined to be on the silver screen, abandon such plans to chase an idea like this? Hetty took in the night air and exhaled, a hint of smoke winding up in the air as she let the cigarette calm her thoughts.

Three hours later, she'd made her decision and rang the phone number Elizabeth had given to her. Isabelle answered.

"This is Henrietta Byron. May I speak to Elizabeth Mowbray?"

"Yes, yes, one moment."

A few seconds later, Elizabeth answered.

"Hetty?"

Hetty paused briefly before responding. "I've given it some thought. You know it's a lunatic idea, quite *simply* batty. However . . . I've decided I'll join you and give it a whirl. But I don't like the word *agency*. Let's call it the *Marriage Bureau*."

CHAPTER 3

Elizabeth sat in a tea shop near Paddington station, fretfully twirling a handkerchief between her fingers as she waited for Hetty. Each time the tea shop door opened, a brass bell tinkled, and she would look up hopefully only to be disappointed by the appearance of someone else. One minute before their agreed meeting time, Hetty strolled boldly in, wearing a striking red-and-black-plaid two-piece suit and black peep-toe mesh heels, a small red hat perched at a jaunty angle on her golden hair. She looked like she'd just stepped off a movie set and was ready for her publicity interviews.

"I was worried you wouldn't show," Elizabeth confessed as the other woman sat down.

At this, Hetty smiled. "Never fret. I'm here, aren't I?" She then waved over a waitress to order tea and sandwiches. "I thought we could discuss the particulars of the business."

Elizabeth nodded and pulled out a small leather-bound journal to take notes. "We will need to do this aboveboard and

give no one a reason to doubt or defame us." Elizabeth considered this one of the most important aspects of their business, to
be fully legitimate and trustworthy. "I thought, once we have our
ideas formed and our rules laid out, we could practice interviewing our friends and build a small group of clients until we
can open to the general public."

"That sounds reasonable enough," Hetty agreed.

A waitress brought them a tea service and two plates of
cucumber sandwiches.

"Where to start?" Elizabeth nibbled on her sandwich. "A
category to match the prospective couples on?"

"Yes." Hetty added a sugar lump to her tea and stirred it, her
gaze distant as she considered the matter. "We don't want to
match anyone with too much disparity in their backgrounds,
whether it's money, social circles, or religion. No pairing
mechanics with wealthy heiresses—at least, unless we have
reason to believe such a match would actually work for the
couple."

Elizabeth began jotting down notes. "We could make
notes on the client's file if they are open to different backgrounds and religions, of course, but I think you're right.
We can begin our matching by looking at similar backgrounds and circumstances. The last thing we need is to
become a haven for fortune hunters who are digging for
money."

"Agreed. I've seen my fair share of those, and while they are
fun to be chased by, you must never let them put a ring upon
your finger."

Hetty studied Elizabeth's notes and frowned ever so slightly.
"We had better have proper forms drawn up. Forms with questions, but also basic information such as height, general looks,

and age. We'll need a quick reference for when we begin the mating."

Elizabeth couldn't help but laugh. "The mating?"

"Well, it's rather fitting, don't you think? We are mating two profiles together. I thought you would appreciate the romanticism of it."

"I do," Elizabeth assured her, then leaned in to whisper, "but we ought not to let the clients hear that's what we call it. It would be far too scandalous."

A little smile escaped Hetty. "I don't mind the scandal, but you're right. It will be a private term just for us. Now, what else . . . ? We interview them and make notes in addition to the information on their forms. Then we mate them to a suitable candidate. We reach out to our female client first to see if she wants to meet the man."

"Do you think we ought to have them start a letter correspondence as the first step when communicating with their matches?" Elizabeth bit the end of her pen, mulling it over. "People tend to be more honest in writing than in speaking—at least in circumstances such as these, I think."

Hetty nudged a cup of tea toward Elizabeth, who drank it gratefully. She could easily get lost in a project and quite forget to eat or drink sometimes.

"Now, about the money," Hetty said. "What do you think of a modest fee that a client pays upon registration to cover a year's worth of introductions? Then, if one of our clients marries someone we've introduced them to through the bureau, they pay a more substantial after-marriage fee to the bureau. That way, we will be able to remain a viable business."

Penning notes regarding fees, Elizabeth nodded.

"What about the legalities?" Elizabeth asked. "I spoke with a detective at Scotland Yard this morning. He could not say definitely that this was illegal, but he told me to consult a solicitor and obtain a permit from the London County Council."

"You went to Scotland Yard?" Hetty giggled, the girlish sound revealing a softer, younger side to the beautiful model. "What on earth did the detective think of you?"

Elizabeth giggled in return. "He didn't know what to make of me. I quite baffled him. I don't suppose they receive many inquiries of a non-criminal nature."

"I should imagine not." Hetty finished her tea. "But it is a fair point. We definitely should see a solicitor. That would lend us some much-needed legitimacy." She collected her purse as Elizabeth finished the last bit of her tea and tucked her notebook in her small portfolio case.

"My father knows nearly everyone. I remember a law firm he's mentioned, Driscoll and Marley. We ought to start there."

❧❦❧

THEY TOOK A CAB TO THE WEST END AND CLIMBED THE STEPS to a brick building with a gold-plated sign with the name of the firm on the outside door. They were ushered into a waiting room by a pretty receptionist near their own age. Hetty gave the woman her name and asked for Harold Pennworth. They were soon escorted to a corner office, where a middle-aged man greeted them with a fawning smile reserved especially for Hetty.

"My dear Miss Byron, how wonderful of you to visit. How is your father?"

"Quite well. He's recently returned from Ceylon, but I'm sure you already know," Hetty said.

"Oh yes, quite so, quite so. One always keeps abreast of the news of one's friends." He went around the edge of his monolithic desk, which was polished to such a striking sheen that Elizabeth could see her reflection in it. Hetty shot her a significant look, which Elizabeth understood at once. This man, with his overly friendly manner, clearly believed that Hetty would give him a positive reference to her father that would result in business from the brigadier coming his way.

"Please sit." He waved at two expensive-looking armchairs, and they sat down. "Now, what may I help you with?"

"We wish to start a business and want to make sure we go about it properly," Hetty said primly, which secretly amused Elizabeth. Hetty was many wonderful and striking things, but prim was not one of them.

"Wonderful. What sort of business is it?" The solicitor collected a pad of paper and a pen and set them on his desk.

"Well . . ." Elizabeth explained their idea for the Marriage Bureau. The man's jowls slowly dropped in horror.

"Ladies, you cannot expect to run such a service! Why . . . It's unsavory at best, and at worst . . . it's most egregiously uncivil and against the laws of God and man. Prostitution—"

"*Prostitution?*" Hetty cut in sharply. "We didn't say anything about that."

The man arched a brow. "Bringing men and women together, taking money for matching these men to your ex-debutante friends in need of stable income, all under the charming guise of two well-bred ladies who run a brothel as madams? Oh yes, I'm sure some wealthy men would find that most amusing, but it doesn't change the fact that it would indeed be a brothel." By this point, the man's face had turned a frightening shade of red, and his breathing had grown harsh.

Elizabeth inched forward in her chair, her own body reacting with sudden panic. Was that what people would really think about them? That they were madams running a brothel? She'd never imagined for a single moment that what they'd planned would be seen in such a light. The shock and disappointment left her chest hollow.

"Well, it seems we didn't quite explain ourselves," Hetty countered. "We are not planning to open a high-end brothel. We simply want to create a service that helps lonely couples match based on personalities in order to create lasting marriages, not brief dalliances." Hetty gave the man such a strong glare of disapproval that he calmed somewhat, but he obviously remained unconvinced.

"Assuming this is even legal, do you have enough capital to make a proper go of it?" He crossed his arms over his chest and lowered his brows, still clearly judging the pair of them. It was obvious this was not the man they should work with. It was time to find a different solicitor.

Elizabeth raised her head, making herself appear as innocent as possible before speaking to Hetty.

"I don't believe we have enough capital to pull this off. What do you think?"

"I think you are right. We are in over our heads," Hetty replied with a perfect look of disapproval. "Perhaps we ought not to waste Mr. Pennworth's time further."

"I quite agree." Elizabeth stood. "Thank you so much for your time, sir."

The man sputtered for a response, but they left his office so quickly he didn't have time to form words.

As they exited Pennworth's office, the young receptionist rushed after them.

"Oh! Please, I didn't mean to overhear," the girl said with a blush. "It's just . . . I think your business is a wonderful idea . . . and I would very much like to be contacted. That is . . ." She cleared her throat. "If you end up starting it, would you reach out to me?" The woman held out a cream-colored card with her name, address, and telephone number.

"You want to be a client?" Elizabeth asked, barely able to contain her excitement.

"Yes." The woman grinned sheepishly. "I haven't had much time to go out to parties and meet men. With my workload, I stay busy and am simply too tired in the evenings to go out searching. It would be ever so much better if I had someone to help me find eligible men."

Hetty took the card and tucked it safely in her purse. "Not to worry, we will be opening soon, and I'll send you our client questionnaire once we're all set."

"Thank you!" The woman smiled again before hastily ducking back to her desk.

Once outside Driscoll and Marley's office building, Hetty and Elizabeth paused on the top step to collect themselves. Hetty frowned.

"Well, that wasn't what I expected, with Pennworth at any rate. The brigadier certainly won't bring any clients to him. But at least *we* have a potential client."

Elizabeth laughed. "Perhaps we need to find a solicitor who is a bit more modern in their thinking? Surely you know someone younger?"

They went across the street to sit on a park bench. Hetty removed a little black book from her purse. As she opened it, Elizabeth saw that hundreds of names and addresses filled the pages. The names, all crafted in Hetty's elaborate penmanship, were quite illegible to Elizabeth.

"Let's see . . . Oh no, not him." Hetty traced a finger down the page, muttering to herself. "Too nervous . . . too overeager . . . not eager enough . . . Oh, Humphrey! Yes, he's perfect. Quite the one to understand what we're about."

"Humphrey it is, then."

Elizabeth felt more encouraged when they arrived at Mr. Humphrey's office.

"You'll like him, Lizzie. He's a wonderful chap. A bit cheeky, perhaps, but brilliant. His father is an earl, but he's not stuffy like some of those people can be. I should know, since I run about with that set."

"What set?"

"Oh, there's a group of young men who were always up to trouble, but the fun kind. And there was a group of us ladies who loved to tag along when we were younger. We're all adults now, supposed to be respectable." Hetty grinned. "But what's that saying about a leopard and their spots? Anyway, my point is, I think Humphrey's our man."

"I trust you, but why didn't you consider him before?" Elizabeth asked as they stepped into the small reception of the new firm.

"He's only just recently become a solicitor. I wasn't sure if he'd be comfortable handling something a bit off the usual pace, but he's infinitely clever and won't lead us astray, even if he might not know the answers." Hetty moved to speak to the secretary at the front desk.

They were shown into an office and saw an attractive man with flashing gray eyes scribbling furiously on a sheet of paper. His hair was the color of burnished gold and fell into his eyes as he bent over his desk to work. He, like Hetty, was a snappy dresser and looked quite handsome in a double-breasted pinstriped suit. Half a dozen dusty, fat tomes with legal titles on their spines cluttered his desk, creating a small wall around him. He glanced up and smiled broadly at Hetty. He practically leapt to his feet to offer his hand to Hetty.

"Sorry, Hetty, I was deep in a case. It's quite the case, you see . . ." He shook his head in a charmingly bashful way and sat back. "What can I help you with?"

"Charles, I'd like you to meet Elizabeth Mowbray."

Elizabeth shook the solicitor's hand and then exchanged a look with Hetty. "Should I tell him our scheme?"

Hetty nodded, and Elizabeth began to explain the idea of the Marriage Bureau.

Charles listened intently, not speaking or interrupting to ask questions. By the end of her explanation, Elizabeth became nervous about his silence.

"Well? Are we mad or brilliant?" Hetty asked him.

"Mad? Certainly not." The solicitor steepled his fingers. "Brilliant? Most definitely. It's just the sort of business we need. If you do this properly, well . . . it should succeed beyond measure. I might even register myself once you're ready for clients. My one recommendation is that you establish your rules clearly and have registration forms with concise terms and conditions. I'd be happy to draw them up, assuming you'd like me to."

Elizabeth liked this man, and her instincts urged her to trust him. "We'd love that."

He produced a clean sheet of paper and began to write. "Let's see. Client interviews should be free. No clients currently married, and you should require proof of divorce for divorced clients—otherwise, we'd be opening you both up to a legal liability, not just a moral issue. I'd limit your acceptance of clients until you believe you have proper numbers to match them with, but you can make a waiting list and keep them on there until you have suitable matches."

"We were thinking of charging fees . . . an initial registration fee and another fee after marriage," Hetty added.

Charles nodded. "Keep the registration fee affordable for everyone, and the after-marriage fee can be set at your discretion, based on the income of the clients. Don't send out lists to clients like a phone book, nor collections of photos. You don't want this to become a mail-order bride enterprise, if you understand my meaning. You want these matches to be genuine and based on one-on-one interactions."

"That is definitely our intention," Elizabeth replied.

The solicitor sketched out a brief registration paragraph that covered much of the company's mission and registration requirements.

"I'll finalize this in a few days and send you a copy. Do you have a business address yet?"

"Not as of yet," Hetty said. "It was to be our next stop after meeting with you."

Charles beamed at her. "Well, where do you wish to look?"

"Bond Street," Elizabeth answered at once, and then the heat of embarrassment flooded her face. "I mean, if that's all right with you, Hetty."

"It might be hard to find an open storefront, but perhaps you'll get lucky." Charles made another note on the bureau's terms before setting his pen down.

"In the meantime, send everything to me," Hetty said. "As for now, we are bound for Bond Street." She winked at Charles as she and Elizabeth left on their next mission.

HETTY WAS A LITTLE MORE ENCOURAGED AFTER THEIR meeting with Charles. He was a far better choice than Mr. Pennworth, the old undertaker. He'd only needed a black top hat and a cold body on a slab to perfect the grim image. She'd felt rather foolish for taking Elizabeth to him when she should have gone straight to Charles. She'd known him for years—her parents and his were old friends—but having moved to Ceylon at sixteen, she'd lost touch with her usual crowd and was only just getting back to her old circle of friends.

As she and Elizabeth headed toward Bond Street, Elizabeth spoke up. "You don't mind Bond Street, do you? I shouldn't have blurted it out like that."

"I don't mind, Lizzie. I was actually thinking the same as you. It's a well-known street, with lots of wealthy people visiting the shops. We're more likely to find clients able to pay for our services."

Elizabeth's face brightened. "Once we get underway, perhaps we could develop a fee payment schedule for those who aren't able to afford the after-marriage fee all at once."

Hetty was beginning to realize that she could not deny her new friend anything. "You know you have too big a heart," Hetty sighed with a smile. "It's a good thing I'm here."

"I'm sure you'll keep me from being too soft," Elizabeth laughed before she returned to the subject of where to look for offices. "Anyway, bond Street is likely to have all those young men on leave who are shopping. We'll have visibility for one of our biggest potential client bases." She paused on the pavement to draw out a bit of newspaper from her jacket pocket. It was a clipping she'd taken from the advertisements the day before.

"The location for this one is Piccadilly Circus, near Bond Street. It says, 'Comfortable office facilities. Twelve shillings and sixpence per week.' I have twenty pounds; we could set up for a week and see what we think of the location."

Hetty nodded. "Let's go have a look, then."

By the time they'd located and visited the "office," Hetty's frown was so deep she feared it would leave permanent wrinkles upon her brow. *Office* wasn't quite the term she would have applied to the room they were shown. Several men milled about a collection of desks scattered throughout the room. They wore dark suits, most of them ill-fitting, and carried the air of casual desperation that could only belong to traveling salesmen. One man leaned back in his chair, his muddy boots resting on the edge of his desk as he guffawed with laughter at whatever his companion had said. Cigar smoke created a gray cloud above the heads of the men.

"Are you coming in?" the property manager asked them.

"Lord, no," Hetty said, just as Elizabeth moved into the hazy room and the crowd of men.

She headed for the only empty desk at the back of the room. She looked so petite in her thin scarlet coat with a black velvet collar, a look that was in complete opposition to the mass of salesmen around her. Elizabeth reached the desk, completely ignoring the men who had already started to toss out suggestive comments that made Hetty's blood boil.

Elizabeth studied the desk a moment longer, as if the desk was all she cared about, then beat a retreat toward Hetty and the door, though not so fast as to appear she was fleeing. When she got to the door, she inhaled the clearer air and turned to the property manager, thanking him for his time.

"I'm sorry, that won't do. Imagine us listening to a client pour her heart out and having those men leer and throw out suggestive comments. No, it won't do at all."

A sudden idea occurred to Hetty. "Never mind the advertisement. We should consult an estate agent." If they looked at properties of a different nature, they might have better luck.

"Oh, Hetty, you are a genius!" Elizabeth exclaimed in delight. "That's it." She started to dash down the street, leaving Hetty behind. It took her a moment to catch up, though her friend was oblivious to the effort required to keep pace with her.

"What is it? You seem possessed by something."

"I have an idea. When I first came to London, I was afraid Isabelle would want me out of her house as soon as possible, so I was watching the boards of a few estate agents. I remember reading about a place on Bond Street. We had better hurry!"

By the time they reached Bond Street, Hetty couldn't believe how excited Elizabeth was as she rushed into a women's lingerie store like an eager schoolgirl. Above it, a small sign in faded letters said, *Small Office to Let.*

They went into the lingerie shop, where a woman in her sixties was delicately wrapping up a silk nightgown for a customer.

"Excuse me, who do we speak to about the small office?" Elizabeth asked.

"Pardon? Oh, that would be me, Edna Meriwether." The woman blushed. "It's rather a small place, I'm afraid. Just upstairs. I have the key if you still wish to see it." The woman seemed a bit baffled that anyone had come into her shop to ask about it, but Elizabeth's enthusiasm left the woman all smiles as she called for one of her shopgirls to watch the register while she took Hetty and Elizabeth upstairs.

It was a dusty old place, with one smaller room off the main one. A fair amount of dirt had collected on the floor and windowsills over the years.

Hetty arched her brow as she studied the room. "Is there a lavatory?" It was nothing like the nicely furnished flat her father had acquired for her when they'd returned from Ceylon.

"Upstairs. There's a small attic and a little stairwell that takes you up to the roof." The woman smoothed her hair nervously. "I didn't think anyone would ever want to rent it, what with a war coming. I'm tempted to move my shop out of London entirely."

Hetty coolly appraised the woman, while Elizabeth fluttered about, smiling to herself and sighing with a girlish romantic look upon her face. Her red cape flared behind her like butterfly wings as she drifted around the empty little office. What did she see in the dusty, dim set of rooms that Hetty couldn't? Elizabeth seemed to ignore the remark about war and appeared entirely unconcerned about being on a street like this if any air raids began.

"How much is the rent?" Hetty asked the shopkeeper.

"Twenty shillings a week," the woman replied. "But I could let you pay eighteen if you stay on for six months and pay the first two months in advance."

Hetty continued to gaze about the shabby room. The floor would need to be replaced because she highly doubted they could hide the ink stains forming blots on the linoleum near the two battered old desks that stood against one wall. Two swivel chairs were stacked atop each other in the corner by a teetering old bookshelf. There was a telephone with a frayed cord, along with a flickering bulb concealed by a ratty lampshade, which hung precariously from the ceiling. Hetty guessed the two-bar electric fire heater would offer little warmth in the winter.

Elizabeth turned to Hetty. "I'm thinking new paint, clean the floors, add a lovely carpet, perhaps a new lampshade, some varnish for the desks . . . I think it's brilliant. What a cozy place we could make it. What do you think? A place of our very own." The bright light of hope and romantic imaginings glowed in Elizabeth's eyes, and something inside Hetty filled with a matching warmth.

A place of our very own.

Had any place ever truly been hers? Even the flat she lived in belonged to her father. But here she could put her occasional earnings from her modeling and acting toward this little office. *Her* office. Suddenly the dim little set of rooms seemed to glow, and a giddy feeling grew inside her chest. She couldn't help but smile back.

"I think it's perfectly *splendid.*"

Elizabeth spun to the woman still hanging by the door. "We'll take it."

"You will?"

Hetty and Elizabeth both nodded.

"And what sort of business will you be running?" the woman asked.

"The Marriage Bureau," they replied at the same time.

The lingerie saleswoman's nose wrinkled in confusion. "The what?"

"It's a matchmaking agency for men and women who are in search of suitable marriage partners," Elizabeth explained with a gentle politeness. Hetty suddenly envisioned it to be the tone she would use when dealing with potential clients. By the look on the shopkeeper's face, it was clear that Elizabeth's approach was working.

The woman tilted her head. "Oh? Well now, I might just register. I could certainly do with a decent husband. I don't suppose you take widows . . . as clients, I mean?" The woman's voice was so full of hope that Hetty finally understood Elizabeth's excitement about this venture. They wouldn't just be offering a service to people—they would be doing much more.

Elizabeth's natural cheerfulness filled the room. "I believe you will be one of our first clients."

Already three potential clients and a place of our own.

It was a brilliant, beautiful light shining against a dark, looming horizon, and Hetty clung to the image with all of her might. The inevitable war was drawing ever closer, and yet she now saw what Elizabeth had seen all along. Making matches under the cloud of war might be the hope everyone needed to fight, to hang on—to not only survive but to *live*.

CHAPTER 4

A*pril 1939*

ELIZABETH SET THE BUCKET OF BRIGHT-YELLOW PAINT DOWN on the old canvas tarp that covered the office floor—not that the old linoleum needed protecting when she planned to rip it up soon. She placed her hands on her hips and studied the office walls. Yellow, such a cheery color, would brighten the moods of visiting clients. Their new office would look smashing when they were done fixing it up.

The door opened behind Elizabeth, and Hetty stumbled in, wearing an old pair of slacks and a loose masculine shirt, gripping a heavy paint can.

"You know we look positively ridiculous in these clothes," Hetty said.

"You're welcome to splatter paint on your best dress if you wish," Elizabeth teased. Nothing could ruin her good mood today. They were setting up their official office, and it felt like the world around her was as bright and cheery as the paint she was about to use.

"Ha, ha," Hetty snorted. "I am just glad that's the last of it. I don't want to run into anyone I know on the street and have them see me like this."

"Well, let's go to work, and once we're done we can change." Elizabeth prepped a station for them to dip their brushes in the paint and handed one to Hetty.

They worked in a long moment of silence, neither of them wanting to break their concentration as they brushed clean paint lines upon the wall. But after a while Elizabeth couldn't help but hum. The tune was one that had gotten stuck in her head these last few months. It was "Where Are the Songs We Sung?" by Noël Coward.

Hetty began to sing the words, her lovely voice carrying the song effortlessly. After that, their work moved even more quickly, their spirits buoyed.

A familiar masculine voice intruded on them. "That's lovely, Hetty. I didn't know you could carry a tune."

Elizabeth and Hetty turned to see Charles Humphrey lounging in the doorway. He wore a gray wool herringbone suit and a smart hat tipped rakishly over his eyes. He had his hands tucked in his trouser pockets, and only the middle three buttons of his coat were fastened. At his feet was a wicker picnic basket. He looked every bit the part of a handsome, leisurely aristocrat rather than the busy young solicitor Elizabeth had first seen him as.

Hetty scrambled to put her paintbrush down and frantically

smoothed her hands over her work clothes before touching her hair to see if her coiffure was still perfect. "What are you doing here?"

Elizabeth didn't miss her friend's blush and wanted to laugh, but she knew Hetty was a bit too serious when it came to Charles for anyone to giggle.

"You telephoned a few days ago with the new address, and I thought, as your solicitor and also a future client, I ought to come and see the bureau for myself." Charles removed his hat and brushed his hair out of his eyes with one hand as he surveyed their office. Then he retrieved the picnic basket from the floor.

"What's that?" Hetty asked suspiciously as he moved over to the pair of desks they had put in the center of the room and set the basket down.

"*This* is lunch." Charles grinned. "Consider it part of my payment for being a client." He unfastened the top of the basket and began removing carefully wrapped sandwiches. "I don't suppose you have a place to put the kettle on?"

At this, Elizabeth leapt into action to give Hetty and Charles a moment to themselves. "Yes, of course we do. In the other room." They had a small stove in the second room, which they planned to use as their private office. She left Hetty and Charles alone while she prepared tea for the three of them.

Isabelle had given them a blue-and-white-patterned tea set to congratulate them on their new venture, and this would be its maiden voyage. As Elizabeth heated the water in the kettle, she listened to the low hum of voices from the other room and tried to hide a smile.

Hetty had no idea why Charles was really here, but Elizabeth did. It was clear the handsome solicitor had a fondness for Hetty.

It made sense, really. The two of them had known each other for years, and they had the natural ease of old friends, but Hetty's time in Ceylon had changed things between them. There was an electric charge in the air now that Elizabeth felt even when she was in the other room.

I shall take care with them.

As Hetty was independent and headstrong, she would not want to have her own match made with a man. But Elizabeth feared Hetty had no idea that Charles was interested in her. So she would be clever in bringing them together.

The moment the tea was ready, Elizabeth carried the tray into the other room and halted as she found Charles on his hands and knees. His hat and coat were tossed over a chair. Hetty hovered beside him, one brow arched as she watched him adjusting the legs of the desk, which tended to rock slightly as one leaned upon it. It was something they had been trying to fix most of the morning when they weren't painting.

"Another moment and—yes, that should do it." Charles climbed out from underneath the desk and stood, brushing his palms on his trousers before he pressed down on the edge of the desk. It didn't budge even an inch.

"Oh, I say, bravo, Charles!" Hetty's apprehensive look vanished, and she beamed at the solicitor.

"Yes, thank you, Mr. Humphrey. That was driving us quite mad." Elizabeth placed the tea tray down, and the three of them began to have lunch.

"I suppose others have come around to see your office?" Charles asked them as they finished eating. The sandwiches were egg salad with cress, and they were quite delicious; only empty packages were left behind in Charles's basket.

"Only Aunt Isabelle," Elizabeth said.

"Not the brigadier?" Charles asked Hetty.

"No, not yet. I haven't . . . er, told them yet. It will be quite a feather ruffler, especially when my grandmother finds out. The old dragon has the most traditional notions, and her divorced granddaughter marrying other people off for money will *not* be acceptable." Hetty sighed, and she shot Elizabeth a look of mutual commiseration.

This was a topic that had come up frequently between them over the last few days. What would they tell everyone? And would they react with enthusiasm or derision? Elizabeth knew her parents would be outraged and horrified, but they never came to London. It would take them a while longer to discover what she had been up to. Alan and Isabelle, on the other hand, already knew and thoroughly approved of all of it but kept mum to protect her from her parents' wrath.

"I could bring a few lads by once you're ready for interviews." Charles stroked his chin as he leaned back in the rickety chair. Elizabeth tensed, praying the chair wouldn't topple over or give way beneath him. It creaked ominously but didn't break.

"We'll need them," Hetty confessed. "Lizzie and I went to every advertiser in town, but none will take us. They all think the bureau sounds suspect. Half of them think we're running some type of brothel." She rolled her eyes.

Charles chuckled but quickly covered his smile with a cough when Hetty narrowed her eyes at him.

"Will the newspapers be interested?" Elizabeth asked. "With all the doom and gloom, we thought perhaps that a positive story might give us a bit of good publicity."

She'd thought it would be perfect for the papers to have a happy story to focus on, but lately she'd been wondering if she was the only one who wanted to focus on positive thoughts.

Everyone else seemed to want to discuss nothing but Germany.

"I can ask around for you. I know a few journalists," Charles offered.

"Thank you. You can give them our address and this number." Elizabeth wrote down Isabelle's phone number on the slip of paper and handed it to Charles.

Charles gathered up the remnants of their luncheon and put it back in his basket. "Well, I'll leave you both to it, then, shall I?"

Elizabeth saw one more opportunity to push Hetty and Charles together, and she took advantage of it.

"Hetty, why don't you walk Mr. Humphrey to the door. I'll freshen up the paint for us."

Elizabeth gave her friend a gentle nudge out the door and closed it behind her. She waited until she heard their voices fade, then rushed to the window facing the street and watched them appear on the steps below. Charles leaned against the bricked railing on the steps and spoke to Hetty for another minute before Hetty bid him goodbye and came back into the building.

Small steps, Elizabeth reminded herself. *I shall get them there, but I must be patient.*

Her gaze lifted from the street to the vast city of London, far beyond their little rooms on Bond Street. The city had grown almost greedily in the last several years, stretching its borders beyond its earlier limits.

Everything seemed to be here in one place. A quarter of the country's imports arrived at the sprawling London docks, and the Square Mile dominated the world of banking and insurance. Academics filled the halls of the University of London, Imperial College, and the London School of Economics. Theaters thrived in colorful clusters around Shaftesbury Avenue. Ballet companies, opera houses, and art galleries opened the city's eyes to a vibrant cultural world.

London was a city where anything was possible. Despite the belching smoke of coal fire and the Dickensian poverty that existed in some parts of the grand old city, Elizabeth still felt like this place was the center of the modern world. It was a place that would give her and Hetty a chance to choose their own path in life and make a difference. She picked up her paintbrush just as Hetty came back into the room.

"We had better get the phone working." Hetty studied the phone; it had a long cord that was a bit frayed in places. "I want to be able to take calls here at the office as soon as we can." She set the phone down on the desk nearest her. As she lifted the cord a little, the phone suddenly rang loudly.

Elizabeth and Hetty stared at each other, and then at the phone, before Hetty lifted the receiver and answered.

"Hello?" She waited a moment. "Hello?" she repeated before replacing the phone in its cradle. "There was no one on the line." She reached again for the cord to move it and again the phone rang, and yet no one answered when Hetty spoke.

"Must be faulty wiring," Elizabeth guessed as she played with the wire. Whenever it was pulled slightly at the end that connected to the phone's base, it would ring.

"Must be. What a nuisance." Hetty sat down at her desk and began making a list of what they needed. The words *new phone* were at the top. Below that were items like a wireless radio and other things that would give them a bit more creature comforts.

"Hetty, we have access to the roof, don't we? I wonder if we ought to make it a bit more of a second waiting room in case we have a crowd?"

While they painted this morning, Elizabeth had been trying to imagine what a typical day would be like in their new office. One of them would need to greet clients. The other would need to be taking down information, but it would be so much better if they could both listen to the interviews together.

"We could, but I doubt we will ever have a full office." Hetty bit her lip and then stood and collected the teacups to wash them.

Elizabeth ventured up the stairwell and set aside her paintbrush just outside the door. Then, with the help of a broom, she cleared dust off the stairs all the way up to the roof. It was only a two-story building, and the roof didn't make her edgy as heights usually did. Rather, it felt cozy, as though she were in a garden park . . . or it would, once she put potted plants up there and a chair or two. A pigeon landed on the roof. It cooed and waddled its snow-white body along the raised brick edge of the roof that came up to Elizabeth's chest.

"Goodness, you're brave." Elizabeth laughed as the pigeon poked at the handle of the broom with its beak.

She wished she had something to feed it, but she hadn't thought of that when Charles had packed up the remnants of their lunch. Elizabeth stared at the skyline of Bond Street for a long moment, enjoying the feel of being an outside observer of the shops and the shoppers below. Her chest tightened with a sudden love for the city and the people in it.

That elation was swiftly followed by fear. She didn't want to think of another war or what could happen; it seemed an unimaginable thing after the Great War. The world could not go through that again. She couldn't let her brother go off to fight halfway around the world. She felt *helpless*. She was helpless to stop what was coming, and it terrified her.

Don't think about it. Don't, she reminded herself. It was becoming a daily mantra to keep herself sane.

"You up here, Lizzie?" Hetty's voice echoed from the stairs.

"What? Oh yes, I'm coming down." Elizabeth wiped at her eyes, surprised to find her fingertips wet. She hastily pulled out a handkerchief and dabbed away the evidence of her tears. Then she headed back down to the new headquarters of the Marriage Bureau.

❧

HETTY WAITED AN ENTIRE WEEK BEFORE SHE SUMMONED THE courage to tell her parents about the Marriage Bureau. She invited them to lunch at one of the Lyons Corner House restaurants. The place was packed with people, and the Nippies were dashing about the room, seeing to the diners. These waitresses were given their nickname because of the way they nipped about the dining room. The Lyons Corner House was a perfect place to meet for a decent luncheon without paying too much, not that Hetty was usually worried about expenses like that, but she felt the busier the place the better if she had to deliver news that might result in disgruntled parents.

Hetty wore her favorite red-and-green-plaid three-button suit with a pleated skirt and black pumps as she paced anxiously in the entryway of Lyons. When she spotted her father striding toward her, his hand lightly placed on her mother's back as he ushered her inside, Hetty tensed even further.

"Hetty!" Her father's usually booming voice, so often full of natural command, was softer than she'd expected.

"Hello, Papa." She bussed his cheek and then embraced her mother.

"You had us all dreadfully worried," her mother said in a gentle tone. "You've been so quiet the last few weeks since we returned from Ceylon. We worried . . ." Her mother shared a look with Hetty's father. The brigadier's gray mustache twitched as he studied Hetty's face intently, but Hetty let nothing show. She was as good as him at masking her emotions when she needed to be.

"Shall we sit?" She turned toward the host at the counter in charge of seating.

"Yes, but we must get a table for four," her mother insisted.

"Four?"

"Yes, your grandmother decided to join us." Her mother's face reddened slightly at the mention of the old dragon.

"Grandmama? Whatever for?" Hetty and her grandmother didn't always get on. They were as different as oil and water. If anyone would be angry about the Marriage Bureau, it would be her grandmother.

"I know you haven't seen her since last Christmas, and it would do you good to visit with her."

Hetty let out an aggrieved sigh and told the host they would need a table for four and left the young man staring agog when she told him to expect an old battle-ax to show up looking for their table. If there was one person in all the world who disapproved of her, it was her grandmother.

"Really, Hetty," her mother admonished.

"Well, she is. Heavens, Mother, you don't even call her by her name, or even say that she's your mother. It's always *Hetty, your dear grandmother* this or *Hetty, your dear grandmother* that."

At this her father coughed and hid a chuckle, which earned him an arch look from his wife.

As they took their seats in the main dining room, the public atmosphere with the white tablecloths and brown leather-back chairs that creaked as people moved and talked between meals provided Hetty with a strange reassurance. She always felt better in the midst of activity; besides, it would reduce the odds of any of them making a scene.

"Well, what's this news of yours?" her father prompted as he picked up his menu and perused it.

"Hadn't we better wait for—?"

"For me?" An old woman approached the table, her eyes still bright with awareness, even for her age of ninety-six. She wore a long dress of dark plum, and a hat a decade out of fashion was perched on her head, but Hetty couldn't deny that the outfit suited her grandmother. Lady Agnes Allerdale, the daughter of an earl and mother to five daughters, was indeed an ancient fire-breathing dragon, and even though she and Hetty didn't get on, Hetty did grudgingly admire the woman. In another age, this woman had been the ruler of London ballrooms.

"Mother." Hetty's mother leapt to embrace Agnes, and the brigadier pulled out a chair for her at their table.

"Thank you." Agnes offered Hetty's father a nod of acknowledgment. "Now, what's this I hear of news?" Agnes demanded with far more command than even the brigadier could muster.

Hetty's throat ran dry, and she swallowed hard and licked her lips as she did her best to quell the sudden flutter of nerves in her belly. It was as though a fleet of butterflies had set sail inside her.

"Right, well, I've started a business."

"A business, you say?" Her father's face lit with interest. Her mother remained quiet, and her grandmother waved to a passing waitress, who rushed over to them. The waitress stretched a hand up to her white starched cap embroidered with a red *L* atop her head, as though to make sure it was securely in place. Once she reached them, she smoothed a hand over the black alpaca dress. The double row of pearl buttons down her uniform caught the light and flashed with a watery iridescence. The little apron tied around her waist and the cuffs and collar completed a look that most maids would envy in its simplicity and class.

"Yes, ma'am?" The girl curtsied to Agnes.

"I believe we are in desperate need of tea."

The girl bobbed and dashed away to fetch a tea tray.

"*Business*." Agnes drew out the word slowly, and Hetty prepared for battle. There was no possible way her grandmother, the queen of traditional values, would approve of the Marriage Bureau.

"Yes, what business is it, dear?" her mother cut in diplomatically.

"Well, it's a matchmaking business. You see, at our welcome home party, I met this sweet little creature, Elizabeth Mowbray. She had this mad idea about helping match up people and charging a fee for a successful marriage. It's rather genius. We interview men and women and take notes, then suggest pairings and so forth. If they wish to meet any of the matches we suggest, we arrange a letter correspondence and then a meeting in person as the next step. We believe we can do a tidy business once the papers run our interviews in a few days."

"Leave it to you, my darling, to make money on the natural course of nature. Bravo." Her father laughed, and Hetty knew he approved of it.

Her mother, on the other hand, was a little apprehensive. "Is that . . . legal?"

"Of course. We spoke with our solicitor, Charles Humphrey. You remember him, don't you, Mama?"

"You mean Lord Lonsdale's boy?" Agnes asked. Her eyes sharpened on Hetty's face.

"Yes, Grandmother, he's a solicitor."

"Is he?" The two words were not quite a question. "I suppose he needed something to occupy him. Lonsdales never die. Like as not, he will be well into his graying years before he gains the title."

Her grandmother spoke so dispassionately of death, but Hetty supposed that made sense. At ninety-six, she'd lived through so much and lost practically everyone of her generation. Perhaps that was what made her so bitter at times. Hetty didn't like to think of what the world would be like for her someday, when all those she'd loved were gone.

"Mr. Humphrey said this was legal?" her mother clarified.

"Yes, quite so. It hasn't been done before, but there are no laws against it." She briefly laid out their business plan and told her family the address of their little office on Bond Street.

"Well . . . that's something, Hetty my girl." Her father beamed at her.

"So you see, I wished to tell you this since Lizzie and I will be in the papers tomorrow morning." She finally met her grandmother's gaze, expecting an outcry.

Her grandmother regarded her with a stoicism that sent a curl of dread through Hetty's abdomen. Lord, they were about to do battle, weren't they? She steeled herself for the coming fight.

"When I was a young mother, doing my best to marry off my daughters, I had a dreadful time of it. I didn't even succeed in marrying all of them off—not that I didn't try, of course, but parties and balls and everything that goes with it cost us dearly, far more than your Marriage Bureau fees, I expect. If you can help ladies and gentlemen successfully pair up and make a go of it, I will be heartily glad for you, my dear."

Hetty's lips parted in shock as her grandmother stared at her from across the table. There was no thunderous cloud in her eyes, just quiet approval.

"You aren't upset?" she asked.

"What? By this? Certainly not. This is the twentieth century, after all. We had best adjust to changes, hadn't we?" A rare smile stole across Agnes's face. "I'm already planning on who I will send around to be matched."

Utterly stunned by her grandmother's response, Hetty actually enjoyed her lunch with her parents and her grandmother. By the time she found Elizabeth at their office, she was bursting with the good news.

"They weren't at all upset." Hetty set her handbag down on her desk and told Elizabeth of all that had transpired over luncheon.

Her friend clapped her hands together. "Oh, this is splendid. You've settled things with them, and I won't worry about my parents. They never take the paper." Elizabeth's tone was light, but Hetty didn't miss the look in the other woman's eyes. *Pain.* She couldn't begin to imagine how much it would hurt to be cast out by one's family. She'd never been more aware of how lucky she was compared to other girls, to have a doting father who saw her as brilliant, a mother who supported her in any endeavor, and apparently a grandmother who approved of her entrepreneurship. Elizabeth, meanwhile, was fighting for her independence and security entirely on her own.

"This is all you, Lizzie," Hetty said more quietly, her heart full of respect for her friend. "You're the one who dreamed this up. I don't know where I'd be if not for you." She did know, though, and it wasn't something she liked to think about. She would still be attending parties and lingering on the shadowy verandas, puffing clouds of cigarette smoke above her head as she considered why life felt so unsatisfying.

Elizabeth laughed, the pain in her eyes fading a little. "Only give me credit if it isn't a complete and utter failure."

"I have a good feeling," Hetty insisted as she carefully sat in her creaky old office chair. "A very good feeling indeed."

"At least one of us does." Elizabeth set about polishing every wood surface, and a short while later, Hetty went down the street to collect their new sign to hang up on the brick wall by the door leading to the upstairs rooms. It was all rather enterprising. She had no trouble at all nailing the beautiful new brass-plated sign into the wall. She deliberately ignored the occasional whistle from men on the sidewalk as she perched on the stepladder clad in her suit and heels.

"Excuse me, miss?" a man spoke up, and Hetty gritted her teeth, prepared to face a man who would likely say something unpleasant, which would then make her very cross. But when she turned, she found a man in a white florist's uniform, holding two large bouquets of red roses.

"Are you Miss Hetty Byron?"

"Yes, I am."

The young man grinned. "These are for you." He handed her the two bouquets.

"Thank you." Hetty stared at the roses, baffled. By the time she looked up to ask the man who'd sent them, he was too far down the street.

She carried the flowers upstairs, and when she bustled into their reading room, Elizabeth glanced up, a dust rag in her hand.

"Oh, lovely. Who sent them? Charles?" There was a teasing

glint in Elizabeth's eyes as she tossed her rag onto the desk and went to fill two vases with water.

"I'm not sure . . ." Hetty noticed a small white card tucked among the sprigs of baby's breath. She retrieved the card and read it aloud as Elizabeth set each bouquet in a vase.

"Hetty, darling, these are for you and Miss Mowbray. I wish you both good fortune. Make me proud. Agnes."

"Agnes. That's your grandmother, right?" Elizabeth concluded.

"Yes, and one of these is yours." Hetty placed one of the two vases on Elizabeth's desk and set the other on her own.

With the new paint, the old linoleum replaced by a fine cream-colored carpet, and watercolor paintings of flowers and pastoral scenes on the walls, the Marriage Bureau agency felt ready for business.

Elizabeth plucked one rose out of her vase and inhaled the scent, and then she giggled mischievously. "What if we gave a rose to every woman who first interviews with us? The rose will be a tangible promise to them that love will come, and we'll be here to help find it for our clients."

It was romantic and so very Elizabeth, which meant it was perfect, Hetty decided.

"Yes, I think that's a lovely idea." Hetty brushed her fingertips over one of the crimson blooms and silently thanked her grandmother. Tomorrow, the news of the Marriage Bureau would flood London and the countryside. Then they would see what their future would hold.

CHAPTER 5

Their faces had been everywhere in the previous week. The photos Elizabeth had sent to the editors of several newspapers have been printed, along with cheerful articles about the Marriage Bureau. Even Godfrey Winn, one of the *Sunday Express*'s most popular journalists, wrote an entire column about the Marriage Bureau and the two young women running it.

Elizabeth dashed up the steps and paused only long enough to smile at seeing the sign that read *Marriage Bureau: Private and Confidential* before she continued in to the front room with a stack of newspapers from last week that she'd been collecting. It was only half past eight, but Hetty was already at her desk, a cup of tea cooling there while she sorted out a set of knitting needles, a large ball of blue wool, and a pattern book.

"What's all this?" Elizabeth nodded at the knitting kit.

"I've always wanted to try knitting. Been too busy with traveling with my parents to learn before now, but if things are slow

today, which I fear they might be, I could knit someone a scarf."
Hetty flipped through the pattern book to the pages that
covered scarves.

"You think things will still be slow?" They hadn't had any
appointments yet or anyone showing up at their door for the last
four or five days despite the newspaper coverage. It was more
than a bit depressing.

"One should always be prepared," Hetty said with a slight
frown as she stared back down at her knitting patterns.

Elizabeth tried to cheer herself up.

"I think you should knit Charles a scarf. He's been so helpful,
and we haven't even discussed his fees," Elizabeth suggested
casually, hoping that Hetty wouldn't sense a matchmaking
attempt afoot.

"Hmm, do you think he'd take a scarf instead of money?"
Hetty asked, as though she completely missed Elizabeth's teasing
intent.

"Most definitely. A good scarf is worth its weight in gold,"
Elizabeth said, matching Hetty's serious tone.

"What have you got there?" Hetty glanced at the newspapers
in Elizabeth's arms.

"The papers from last week." She placed the papers before
Hetty. "I was able to find them all and thought I should bring
them in for you to see." She eagerly watched her friend, hoping
to see the excitement and pride she felt reflected on Hetty's
face.

Hetty briefly set aside her knitting to look over the articles,
while Elizabeth put her coat away and set her handbag down.
She had a small book about learning to play bridge in case things
were exceedingly slow. It seemed she and Hetty had had the
same idea about possibly needing entertainment. Everyone

played bridge, but Elizabeth had never seemed to be able to sit still long enough to learn.

"Well, they're all good," Hetty acknowledged as she finished perusing the last of the papers. "None of the articles makes us sound too fluffy, so that's something. I wonder why no one has shown up yet?"

"I thought so too." Elizabeth, too nervous to sit, paced around the room a bit before going upstairs to the roof and arranging the potted plants she'd brought up the day before. They'd acquired two chairs and had a little folding table that could be moved downstairs in case of foul weather. With the green plants in the pots surrounding the little roof, it felt cozy yet open to the air.

After a bit, she headed back down to the rooms below. It was as she reached the last step that she heard the metallic clink of the mail slot in their front door.

"Is that the post?" Elizabeth reached the door at the same moment her friend did.

A handful of letters had fallen to the floor. Hetty retrieved them, and with a beaming smile she showed Elizabeth that the top one was addressed to them: "The Marriage Bureau."

"Oh, how wonderful—" Elizabeth halted as the mail slot clinked again and a dozen more letters fell to the floor. Then more and *more* fell. After four packets of letters had dropped through the slot, Elizabeth opened the door to find a ruddy-cheeked postman on his knees, attempting to shove handfuls of yet more letters into the slender slot.

"Goodness." Elizabeth covered her mouth with one hand as the postman got to his feet.

"I'm right glad you're here, miss." He handed her a large canvas mailbag. "Every one of them is for you. We didn't know we'd get so many last week for this address, and we ended up putting 'em all in a bag and forgot to bring them to you." He tilted his cap back on his head and wiped a thin sheen of sweat upon his brow.

Elizabeth blinked with wide eyes at the heavy bundle of mail in her arms before she carried it to the two desks and emptied it. Hundreds of letters spilled out and cascaded onto the floor. In a daze, Elizabeth held out the now empty mailbag to Hetty, who returned it to the postman, who peered inside the doorway with curiosity.

"Thank you," Hetty told him.

"I say . . ." The postman cleared his throat and hooked a finger in the collar of his uniform nervously. "This is the place where you help people find someone, right?"

"Yes, this is the Marriage Bureau," Hetty replied at once, taking on a tone of polite warmth that Elizabeth knew would make all their future clients feel welcome.

"Is it very much? Your services, I mean?" the postman began uncertainly. "I lost my wife two years ago, still have two little'uns to raise. I was hoping . . . to find them a good mother."

Elizabeth turned from her letter collecting to see Hetty retrieve one of their newly printed business forms and hand it to the postman.

"It's not very much at all. We work with clients on all income levels. If you would like to fill this out and return it when you have time, we'll set up a day for your interview."

The postman's eyes widened. "Interview?"

"Don't be nervous," Elizabeth said as she joined Hetty. "It's only for us to become better acquainted. The more we know about you, the better we can help find a woman who would suit not only your children but also you."

"Me?" the postman echoed as though the thought of finding love again simply had not occurred to him.

"Yes. A good marriage is made up of two people who suit each other and enjoy one another's company. We also hope that love comes with that mutual liking," Hetty added.

At this, the postman removed his cap and bowed his head bashfully. "Thank you. I'll take this home and bring it with tomorrow's mail."

Elizabeth and Hetty watched him carry his few remaining letters away to the building next door.

"Oh, Hetty," Elizabeth sighed in dreamy delight. "We have to find him a wife." The look in the postman's eyes had captured her heart. *Hope.* Hope for love, for a family, for a sense of not being alone in the world. It was a powerful thing to hope for love.

"He's not the only one," Hetty announced. She began to collect the tumble of envelopes on the desk. "There are at least a hundred letters here."

"At least," Elizabeth agreed. "Why don't we separate them into two piles? Men here and women there." She indicated places on Hetty's desk. "Then we can begin making notes and sorting them based on other categories. I'll fetch some index cards." Elizabeth took her copy of the book about learning to play bridge and moved it into a drawer of her desk, and Hetty did the same with her knitting needles and pattern book.

For the next three hours, they sorted the letters into male and female candidates.

"Oh, look at this one. Man or woman? They didn't say." Hetty passed a piece of paper to Elizabeth. Elizabeth scanned the contents. There were plenty of personal details but nothing that could identify the writer as a man or woman. Even the handwriting offered no clues.

"We had better make an uncertain pile." Elizabeth handed the letter back to Hetty. The place where their desks were pushed together became the uncertain territory. Elizabeth retrieved a letter from the stack nearest her and opened it. She unfolded the paper, and an old photograph slipped out. She couldn't help but giggle as she took a closer look at it. A plump-cheeked baby lay sprawled naked on a tiger-skin rug, and on the back of the photo was scrawled, "Me at seven months."

"Look at this." She passed the photo over to Hetty, and Hetty snorted as she tried not to laugh. "Man or woman? I can't tell," Elizabeth admitted. "We had better write back to all of the uncertain letter writers and obtain some extra information."

Hetty folded the letter and the photograph back into its envelope and placed it in the middle pile.

"I have an idea." Hetty sat up suddenly. "We need a little black book. Or rather, a *large* black book."

A flash of memory of sitting on a bench with Hetty after that first disastrous solicitor meeting came back to Elizabeth. Hetty had carried a little black book in her handbag that listed all her friends and their relevant information.

"Oh?"

"Yes, one with our clients, the ones unmatched. It must be a big volume, something like a ledger where we can record their name, religion, age, income, where they live, and so forth. We can sort them alphabetically by towns and even use a system to record when they have already met people."

"That sounds perfect." Elizabeth's mind was already spinning with the possibilities. "Once they pay their small registration fee and become an official member of the Marriage Bureau, we shall put their names in the book and assign them an official number."

She shuffled the blank index cards and bit her lip, thinking a moment before continuing. "Then we must also put their information on a card with details about them and what they are looking for in a partner. As we match, we can pair cards up together. We can also record the assigned numbers of the people they've met, so we don't fear introducing them twice to the same person."

Hetty nodded. "I'll start on the men, you start on the women."

They both turned at the sudden sound of a knock on the door.

"Do you think it's a client?" Elizabeth asked at the same time Hetty exclaimed, "I bet the postman's back."

"Quick, toss you for it." Hetty pulled a sixpence out of her handbag and tossed it. Hetty won.

She opened the door, and a middle-aged man in an officer's uniform, hat tucked under one arm, studied Hetty uncertainly. He was a handsome man in his forties, and his hair was lightly streaked with gray. He had a regal bearing that likely came with years as a commander of men, not unlike Hetty's father. Elizabeth decided she liked this man at once.

"This is the Marriage Bureau, is it not? My name is William Taylor."

"Yes, please come in. I'm Hetty, and this is my partner, Elizabeth."

Elizabeth took the man's hat and hung it on their spindly coatrack in the corner while Hetty gestured for him to sit in the nice chair that Charles had brought in a few days before for their clients. Hetty had tried to decline it, but Charles had insisted that his office had no need for a third chair for clients and it was getting in the way of the boxes of his current client work. Therefore, the beautiful leather-backed chair was now a permanent part of the Marriage Bureau office as the client interview chair.

Neither Elizabeth nor Hetty wanted to risk putting a client in one of the two rickety desk chairs until they could have them fixed. It was only a matter of time before a screw turned itself loose and a chair broke.

"Please, have a seat and we shall get started." Hetty was all calm politeness, but as she reached for the letters on the desk, her hands shook. Noticing this, Elizabeth hastily collected the piles of envelopes for her and took them to the inner office, where she set them on the small table out of sight. Even though she was not the one asking questions, she was nervous as well.

Their first client! And so soon! It was rather remarkable. This was one of the most important moments in their lives. The destiny of this man and those whose words filled the hundreds of letters in the other room hung on the bureau's ability to match them with the person who could fill the rest of their lives with joy. Every moment of this process with a client had to be handled with thoughtfulness and the utmost care.

Hetty collected an interview questionnaire and a pad of paper with a pen, and then, with a little initial awkwardness, she prompted the officer, a major, to explain his history and personal information. A few times Hetty froze, completely at a loss for what to ask him next.

"Now, I suppose you want to know what I'm looking for in a wife?" he volunteered gently.

Elizabeth watched the major from the doorway, careful not to intrude on the intimacy of the interview. It was clear he was a good man, quite kind and effectively able to lead Hetty through questions whenever she got a bit stalled.

"Yes, do tell me, what qualities, both physical and mental, do you require in a partner?"

At this, the major leaned forward a little, as though a tad embarrassed.

"She does not need to be a great beauty, but she does need a great heart. In my life, with what I've seen . . . I long for someone with compassion, someone who will care for others as I wish to." The frankness of his response made Elizabeth's throat tighten. A good man like this deserved a good woman, and someone out there—perhaps one of the women in their letters today—was *the one* for him.

Elizabeth glanced over her shoulder at the stack of envelopes safely tucked in their private back room while the interview slowly came to an end. Her fingers practically itched to tear into the envelopes and discover which woman might be the right one.

"Well, this is a good start, Major Taylor. If you don't mind filling this out for the rest of your contact information." Hetty presented him with the official registration form, and he dutifully filled it out.

"How much is the registration fee?" He slid the completed form across the desk and got to his feet. "I read something about ten guineas in the paper?"

"Oh, please, no fee today. You were very helpful to us, and . . . ," Hetty stammered.

At this, a small smile curved the major's lips. "I was your first client, wasn't I?" There was no judgment, only bemusement in his kind eyes.

Hetty's face turned as red as a radish. "Oh, but . . ."

He only continued to smile and shot a glance at Elizabeth. "It is ten guineas, isn't it?"

"Yes, but . . . ," Hetty said. "You really mustn't . . ." She tried to push away the guineas he held out.

"There." He placed them on the desktop next to his completed form. "It's ten guineas to register?"

Elizabeth nodded, her face heated with embarrassment. She agreed with Hetty that the major shouldn't have to pay for teaching them how to interview. But it was clear they would not win this battle of honor, not with the major still smiling with that gentleness that deserved to be given to a woman as darling as he was.

"Yes, that's right. Thank you so much, Major Taylor. We will be in touch soon with several promising matches," Elizabeth said as she regained herself.

His eyes, once so kind yet serious, now held a hint of mischief. "I imagine you will be. Goodbye, ladies." He bowed politely, put his hat back on his head, and saw himself out.

"Lizzie, be honest. Did I make an utter fool of myself?" Hetty collected the guineas and put them in a black leather envelope before she picked up the major's form.

"No, you didn't. It was your first time; I would have been as flummoxed as you. We'll both be far more relaxed next time." Elizabeth gave her shoulder a sisterly squeeze.

"Yes, we will. Oh, it was just so intimate, hearing what he wanted in a person. I hadn't thought about that part, about how much our clients will open their hearts and minds to us. They must have to trust us very much to do such a thing." Hetty's eyes grew round. "Heavens, we haven't any friends to introduce him to! He's much too old for our set, but oh, we must match him. He's absolutely wonderful, isn't he?"

Hetty was nearly swoony, and Elizabeth felt the same. He was rather the perfect client, and for him to be their very first, they were quite lucky. Elizabeth would do everything in her power to find him the perfect wife.

"The letters! There must be someone in there we can introduce him to." Elizabeth took the major's form and retrieved a blank note card to start their first entry in the catalog of men. "If none of these fit, we could send his money back in a few days."

"We'll find someone," Hetty vowed with such determination that Elizabeth beamed with pride before they spread the letters out on the table again.

Half an hour later, they had six very good candidates for Major Taylor.

"This one is the best so far. She says—" Hetty's excited words were cut off by another knock upon their door.

"Your turn," Hetty insisted.

"All right, but once we get better prepared, I believe we should do the interviews together." She had been thinking it over while watching Major Taylor's interview. Two minds were better than one when they both worked together. There would be a lot of questions that they could cover, which one person alone might forget.

Elizabeth opened the front door and came face-to-face with a tall, dark-haired, handsome man. His slightly hawklike nose and the lift of his chin gave off an air of haughtiness, however. As he stepped into the room, wearing a well-tailored suit, his movements were smooth and confident as he spoke. His voice was pleasing to the ears, but his abrupt manner of conversation left Elizabeth unamused.

"This is the matchmaking service, isn't it?" His brown eyes

swept over her and then moved to Hetty, lighting up with recognition. "Hang on, I've seen you before."

"Well, yes. I'm sure you have. We have had our pictures in the paper about the bureau—

The man shook his head and waved a hand. "No, I've seen you in the *Tatler*. You're some brigadier's daughter or some such thing. You wish to be an actress." His tone wasn't condescending but rather a tad smug, as though he was proud of himself for making the connection.

Hetty's previously demure compassion that Major Taylor had engendered faded, and she narrowed her eyes.

Oh dear. Best to intervene, thought Elizabeth.

"Please have a seat, Mr. . . ."

"Frank Malcolm," he supplied and seemed to expect a response of *"Ah, yes, the famous Frank! How could we not have recognized you?"* Elizabeth almost laughed, and she shot Hetty a look that made her friend roll her eyes.

"Well . . ." Elizabeth sat down beside him and pulled a clean pad of paper toward her. "Let's start with your likes and dislikes—"

"Who do you know *socially?*" he cut in.

The rudeness of the question caught Elizabeth off guard. "I beg your pardon?"

"Who do you know in the highest social circles? I must only be introduced to young, beautiful ladies in *the Book.*"

The Book? Lizzie had no idea what *the Book* was. She peeped quickly at Hetty, who mouthed the word *Debrett's* silently with raised eyebrows.

Ah, yes, Debrett's. It was the ultimate book, published each year, with information about all of England's wealthy and titled people. Elizabeth had never seen a copy before. She was a girl from Cambridge, after all. But Hetty must know about it.

"Well, who do you know?" Mr. Malcolm asked again, his gaze moving between Elizabeth's face and the rolled-up canvas by the door where they had hidden the mostly empty paint cans. Admittedly, it didn't present a professional portrait of their offices, but they hadn't had time to put it all away. Neither of them had imagined anyone would come knocking today.

"I see. If you don't have anyone . . ." His tone suggested they had *no one* . . . and he wasn't entirely wrong. They hadn't yet had time to sort through all the letters they'd received that morning.

"We do. It's just that we don't offer anyone up as a possible candidate until we've finished the interview." Elizabeth was making this rule up as she went along, but it was a good one.

Hetty sat down at her desk across from them, looking quite busy, when suddenly the phone rang. She answered immediately.

"This is the Marriage Bureau, Hetty speaking . . . Oh? Yes, of course, let me take down some information. An heiress? Oh, lovely. How much a year do you . . . That much? Why, of course, we would have a list of excellent gentlemen who— Yes, most definitely." Hetty gave Mr. Malcom a look of consideration as she listened to the woman on the phone while she also scribbled notes on a pad.

It took Elizabeth a moment to collect herself, and she turned back to Malcolm as Hetty ended the call, only for the phone to ring again. And again. The entire length of Mr. Malcolm's interview, Hetty took a staggering amount of phone calls, all from young women of means and with connections.

"Please fill out the rest of this form, Mr. Malcolm, and if you wish, you may pay your fee. Then we will contact you soon about potential matches."

He filled out his form, frowning occasionally as he answered the questions about his future wife's requirements of height, religion, figure, income, and other topics.

"My income is eight hundred pounds a year. It's best to marry someone already out in society, you see. Back in Calcutta, there are *expectations*, and I shouldn't like to disappoint people. My wife will need to impress my set back in India when we return."

"Yes, yes, of course," Elizabeth murmured as though she cared, but in truth, this man wasn't that likeable. He didn't seem to be a fortune hunter, but his hunger for glory was less than inspiring. It would make it all the more difficult to find a wife for him. Fully aware of and frankly embarrassed by her own bias against Mr. Malcom, Elizabeth tried to smile and nod as he continued to talk about his friends back in Calcutta.

Elizabeth accepted his form and fee, a cramping sensation developing in her stomach at the thought of finding a woman who would tolerate Mr. Malcolm from Calcutta. She didn't want to send any nice girl out to dinner with him. She'd likely toss a bowl of soup over his head once he dared to open his mouth. But perhaps she could find a woman who didn't mind his desire to social climb, and they could make the precarious journey up the ladder together?

Once Mr. Malcolm left the office, Hetty leaned back in her chair and smirked.

"What was that all about? Would any of those women really make a good match for him?"

"Oh, come now," Hetty snickered. "There *weren't* any women. I could see him putting together that we had only just started, and I'm not interested in matchmaking him. But we don't want him spreading the word that we have no prospects for matches on the books. So . . ." She kicked the phone cord on the desk, and the phone rang.

Elizabeth burst out laughing. "Every single call?"

"Every one. That will give him something to think about besides getting himself photographed in the *Tatler*, the *Daily Sketch*, or the *Bystander*. Christ, what a man. He's a true schemer. I didn't think we'd have any of those so early."

Elizabeth hadn't thought they'd have gotten anyone like that at all. She'd spent the last few days rehearsing a dozen types of conversations in her head to coax shy Londoners out of their shells to discuss their romantic needs. But the Calcutta man, Mr. Malcolm, was entirely unexpected.

She placed his form and matching index card in a new pile in their private back office and had just settled down, only to jump to her feet when there was yet another knock.

"Together this time?" Hetty asked.

"Together." Elizabeth smiled and opened the door to find a trio of young working-class girls near their own age.

"Welcome to the Marriage Bureau."

CHAPTER 6

J *une 1939*

"ISABELLE?" ELIZABETH CAME DOWN FOR BREAKFAST AND halted as she saw two men out in her aunt's back garden. Each man had a shovel, and they were digging up Isabelle's best roses. The blooms and their leafy branches had been tossed into a messy pile a short distance away.

"Isabelle?" she called again, more deeply concerned than ever.

"Yes?" Isabelle swanned into the room. She'd pulled her hair back in a loose knot at the nape of her neck and looked ready to go on a picnic on the Amalfi Coast. The dark-green dress she wore was more sedate than her usual fashion.

Elizabeth pointed toward the kitchen window that over-looked the garden. "What are those men doing?"

Isabelle peered out the window. "Oh, good, they're here. They've come to put our Anderson shelter in."

Elizabeth shot her aunt a glance. "Do we need one?"

She and Isabelle stared at each other a long moment. "All the neighbors on our street are putting them in. I thought it was best while they still have enough. We don't know what will happen to supplies when the fighting starts."

The fighting . . . Elizabeth closed her eyes and tried to take a deep breath.

For a long while, she and Isabelle studied the men digging. Elizabeth tried not to think about what it would mean to stay all night in a shelter while a cold wind howled and rainwater collected in puddles at her feet. The men had finished digging and were now moving six sheets of curved metal into a position where they were half-buried in the earth.

"Mrs. Potts, who lives two doors down said it would hold four adults and two children. We should have plenty of room if . . ."

If . . . The single word hung in the air, like a dark, choking cloud.

The corrugated iron roof was a harsh metallic creature that stood out amongst the wild glorious flowers Isabelle had worked hard to cultivate in the garden. It was silly, but Elizabeth wanted to cry at the sight of those roses that lay dying upon the gravel path. Some of the blooms had been so perfect. Without a second thought, she rushed outside, ignoring the confused stares of the two workers.

Her hands dug frantically around in the discarded blooms. Most were crushed, ripped apart, the petals ravaged and scattered upon the gravel path. Elizabeth swept up the few fallen roses that still held their glorious shape. Carrying them back to the house as though they were more fragile than spun glass, she fought back tears.

"Lizzie, what on earth are you doing?" Isabelle asked as she retrieved a vase and filled it with water before she took the stems from Elizabeth.

Once the blooms were safe, they both noticed the blood that had dripped on the kitchen table. Little crimson droplets covered the wood surface. Elizabeth found dozens of little pricks in her palms and arms. Blood welled up in several fresh places, ready to fall to the table below.

Isabelle gasped and began dabbing at the cuts with a clean cloth. "Lizzie, are you sure you're all right?" Her eyes were shadowed with worry.

"Yes, of course." Lizzie's breath was a little faint. "I just . . . Something came over me, and I couldn't . . ."

She didn't dare finish her thoughts. It sounded mad to say that seeing those roses, innocent creations of nature, being tossed so carelessly away to die so that something so ugly, so unnatural as a bomb shelter could take their place felt wrong. It was as though the laws of nature were being overturned in the name of war.

Isabelle finished cleaning Elizabeth's arms and dabbed some ointment on them to protect the wounds.

"I don't like it either, but we must be practical." Isabelle tapped her chin with a manicured finger. "Perhaps we can plant things over the top of it. I've heard of others trying it. Some have even put wood around the outside to make it look like a garden shed."

"Shouldn't a shelter be buried deeper?" Elizabeth asked. The curved metal roof looked so vulnerable to any threat from above.

"Apparently it's supposed to be like that. They don't work unless they're halfway buried. It's something to do with the corrugated roof. It allows it to survive a nearby bomb blast."

"What about rain?" Elizabeth cringed to think of how wet and cold they would be huddling in such a thing at night.

"Mrs. Potts is putting in two sets of bunk beds. We could do the same, and make sure they're high enough up off the ground to stay out of rainwater." Isabelle turned away from the window and checked the slender wristwatch she wore. "I'm running late. You're off now too, aren't you?"

Elizabeth fetched her handbag. "Yes, I've got to meet Hetty early. We're reviewing letters from applicants for the secretary position."

Isabelle gave a proud smile. "Are you? Business that busy?"

"Yes, we're getting about three hundred letters a day. The poor postman has to make a second trip back by our office in the evening to deliver the rest of the letters for us. My hand was fairly cramped yesterday, so Hetty is buying a typewriter and we're looking for a secretary."

"Marvelous. Good for you, Lizzie. See you this evening at the Astoria?" Isabelle put on her ladies' fedora hat that had a dark-green scarf banded around it to match her dress.

"Yes."

Her aunt rushed off and left Elizabeth to lock up. By the time she reached the office, Hetty was inching the new typewriter into the right place on the third desk they'd recently added to the office.

"Oh, there you are. Did Mrs. Meriwether, the landlady speak with you on the way up?" Hetty asked.

"No, I came in through the back door." Elizabeth and Hetty had found that it was easier to use the entrance in the small mews beside the lingerie shop that belonged to Mrs. Meriwether so as not to disrupt her store during business hours.

"Well, she's selling the place—the bottom half, anyway."

"What? Oh no, she can't. What if whoever buys the bottom won't lease to us?" Panic rose inside Elizabeth with a swiftness that startled her. This place was more than just an office; it was a part of her now, and the thought of leaving made her ill.

"Oh, we'll be able to stay," Hetty assured her with a devious chuckle as she moved to study her reflection in the little mirror hanging on the wall. She smoothed her hair into place as she met Elizabeth's gaze through the mirror's reflection.

"What? How can you know?"

Hetty turned and placed her hands on her hips. "Because *we're* buying it. We need a decent waiting room below for customers to gather and a central front desk to check in. That way, we have these two rooms up here for more private inter-views and our own inner sanctum, where we may have a minute alone to do the mating of the cards."

Elizabeth noticed that a new table had been brought in, one that had been polished to a shine and was perfect for conducting interviews. Hetty had put their desks in the smaller private room where the kitchen was.

"Where did you find that?" She nodded at the table.

"It's a gift from Charles. Apparently, the man is remodeling his office space and he didn't need this old thing."

Elizabeth hid a smile. The desk was clearly brand-new.

"We'll have the new space below ready in a week, just in time for us to find a secretary. And I was thinking, we need curtains, and more flowers . . . It should feel like a proper drawing room."

It was a good idea. They wanted everyone who came in to feel comfortable.

A knock on the door came a moment later, preventing either of them from putting the kettle on or even settling down for the day.

"That must be our first official appointment!" Hetty hastily checked her hair again in the small mirror hanging on the wall before she answered the door. It always amused Elizabeth how much Hetty fretted over her hair. It was such a beautiful natural blonde, and Elizabeth wasn't sure she'd ever seen a strand of it out of place.

When Hetty opened the door, a tall man with dark-red hair came into the room and removed his hat. He was handsome, perhaps almost too much so, and there was a playful glint in his hazel eyes that warned her he might be quite a charmer.

"This is the Marriage Bureau, correct?" He glanced between them. "I was recommended to visit here by a friend."

"Oh? Who?" Elizabeth asked.

"Charles Humphrey."

A faint blossom of color darkened Hetty's cheeks. "Oh? How lovely. Charles is such a darling. Please come in and sit down. We'll begin our interview shortly."

"My name is Damien Russell, age twenty-five, fifteen thousand pounds a year in income . . ." He recited several more particulars of his person. "I've been in India for two years. Now I have a post here in London and plan to stay. I thought it was time to settle down."

He gave Hetty plenty of time to write notes on a sheet of paper. "I have a small house in the country, and I enjoy outdoor sporting life."

"And what is it you are looking for?" Elizabeth queried. "In a wife, I mean."

"Someone attractive, well bred, someone who can be a proper hostess. That being said . . ." He paused, his face more open and honest as he relaxed. "I don't wish to marry simply for the sake of being married. I would rather remain single than make a regrettable mistake. I've no use for a loveless marriage."

"Does the money a woman brings to the marriage matter?" Hetty asked.

Elizabeth read her mind. They had met a lovely heiress last week who did not mind if her husband had money or not. They rather liked her and had been quite excited to match her up with someone proper.

"I'm not keen on marrying anyone too well off. I'm the second son of a marquess. It's unlikely at all that I shall ever see the title in my hands. I'm quite glad of that, I assure you, but I do not want a wife who will marry me with certain expectations. I've worked hard to obtain what I have, and it would be unfair to marry a woman who has her heart set on a title."

Drat! Elizabeth had hoped the heiress might be an option for him, but he might be put off by a wife who had too much money. Most heiresses had expectations for that money to buy a title, even if the man they bought it from was poor.

The three of them spoke at length about what he really wanted. He rubbed the bridge of his nose and smiled bashfully. "I desire a wife who's passionate. Someone who'll explore everything with me, indoors and outdoors."

Hetty nodded in understanding. "A woman who is ready to taste life."

"Exactly."

Elizabeth thought of a clever young woman who had written to them that first week they'd started the business. "Hetty, what about Miss Penelope Ford?" She was a journalist who wrote columns about arts and the theater. She lived in London but was more than happy to move to the country. Her current position at her magazine was entirely by correspondence and required no physical presence in London. She had no interest in titles or any social expectations, but she was quite happy to entertain and do whatever a husband who had connections might require of a wife.

"Penelope, oh yes." Hetty turned to Mr. Russell. "How do you feel about a woman with a career like . . . say, a magazine writer?"

"I'm here visiting you, aren't I?" He winked at Hetty; his clear approval of career women was obvious.

"We will speak to Miss Ford. If you would write her a letter and post it to our office, we will send it along. We will handle the correspondence until you are ready to meet."

"Wonderful. Would you mind if I wrote to her now? In the hope she agrees? I don't want to waste a moment if she's the woman I've dreamt of finding."

Elizabeth set him up with pen and paper before she and Hetty retreated to the inner office to allow him some privacy to pen his thoughts.

"Penelope would be perfect. She's clever, but not demanding. She has a good sense of humor, and she's very pretty," Hetty said.

Elizabeth made them a fresh pot of tea as they discussed it. "She's had a devil of a time finding men who would approve of her continuing to write for the magazine after marriage. Mr. Russell might be a good option."

"I have an excellent feeling about it." Hetty smiled. "Perhaps he will be the first successful match we make."

When Mr. Russell left, Hetty and Elizabeth sat down to review letters of reference for potential secretaries. The ever-growing stack of letters had somehow mated with another pile on the counter of their kitchen and produced a small litter of more letters. They needed someone fast to manage the office, sort letters, and help them draft replies.

"You're coming out to the club tonight, right?" Elizabeth finally pushed away the last letter of reference in the pile of secretary letters and stretched her arms above her in her chair. Lord, she was stiff. She checked her watch and saw that she and Hetty had been sitting for nearly two hours. It was a good thing they'd planned to get out tonight and dance.

"The Astoria? Of course. I desperately need to go out. We've been pushing ourselves hard the last month." Hetty leaned back in her chair and sighed.

When someone knocked at the door, Hetty got up to see who it was. Elizabeth took a moment to use their newly installed second phone in their private office to dial Charles.

Charles's distracted voice answered. "This is Humphrey."

"Charles, it's Elizabeth."

"Oh, hello, Lizzie. Everything all right?" he asked, his voice warming now that he knew it was her.

"Fine, but I wanted to let you know that Hetty and I will be at the Astoria tonight if you wish to drop by and see us."

"The Astoria, eh?" Interest colored his tone. "I might be free this evening. Thank you for the call."

"You're welcome. Now I suspect you're deep in a case. I'll let you get back to it."

His amused chuckle made Elizabeth grin.

Let the secret matchmaking begin.

HETTY STOOD IN HER BEDROOM, ADMIRING THE FINISHING touches on her appearance in the floor-length mirror in the corner of the room. Outside her window, the sun was sinking deep into the horizon. The peachy hues of the waning sun brightened the pale-yellow walls of the room and made the walnut wood paneling glow. Her flat was exactly what she'd always enjoyed in modern houses. It had none of the Victorian or Edwardian clutter typically found in older homes. Everything here was lovely, yet comfortable. Her grandmother's home was overcrowded with ornaments and sentimental pieces that left the home feeling musty and dim, a relic of a lost age.

Hetty wanted her home to feel bright and light, with the freedom to move about.

She left her bedroom and passed briefly into the kitchen to wash her teacup and a small plate that had held a sandwich she had eaten an hour ago. Once they were rinsed clean, she set them to dry on a wooden draining board and dried her hands on a dishcloth. The sight of her hands, bare of jewelry, caught her eye.

When she'd first moved in, she had felt lonely. She had left Roger back in Ceylon, and while she didn't miss him, she did miss sharing her life and space with someone.

Her romance with Roger had once been wild, exciting, all fire and passion beneath the hot exotic sun. But the man he was and the woman she now knew herself to be hadn't *fit*. They were like two opposite edge pieces of an elaborate jigsaw puzzle, and an ocean of other pieces had kept them apart. When she'd moved home to England, she'd wanted no more ties to the past and she'd changed her name back to her maiden name of Byron. She needed to feel like herself again.

She absently rubbed the place where her wedding band had been. The bright sunlight of Ceylon had left a pale band of untanned skin on her finger, but even that had finally faded.

Giving herself a little shake, she dried her hands and retrieved her handbag from the sideboard table by the front door. It was good to go out this evening and change things up from her normal routine. She had not done a single social thing since the Marriage Bureau had opened, and while she was surprisingly fulfilled by her daily work, tonight she wanted to dance, to sing, to remind herself she was alive.

By the time she hired a cab to take her to Charing Cross, night had draped a cloak of darkness over the city. The shadowy world was broken intermittently with the illumination of shop windows and corner streetlights. The haze of the Astoria's illuminated red sign on the white building corner stood out eerily in the growing gloom.

Elizabeth and her aunt Isabelle were waiting just outside the entrance and waved at Hetty as she quickly crossed the street to join them. Isabelle wore a gold dress with square shoulders that tapered to her trim waist, and sequins flashed on her skirt. Hetty was immensely relieved to see that Elizabeth had abandoned her plain frocks and was wearing a lovely rose-colored dress. It was not as fashionable as Isabelle's was, but Elizabeth didn't need flashing glamor. There was a freshness to her that made her sparkle without the aid of sequins or beads.

Hetty's own gown was a black dress with a silver bodice that nipped in at the waist. Normally she would've donned a slinky thing of silk or satin that accented every curve, but such a gown wouldn't do for dancing.

"Are we ready to go in?" Isabelle asked as Hetty reached them.

"Yes, shall we get a drink first?"

They passed through the doors into the reception. The Astoria's main business was a theater by day, but there was a ballroom in the basement that had a nice little dance floor. They headed down the stairs to the ballroom below, where strains of music wove between the dancers to reach them. Hetty took a deep breath and let herself relax.

They made a stop at the bar, and Hetty ordered a cocktail.

"My recommendation," the bartender said. "It's a Vieux Carré."

"What's in it?" she asked as the man passed her a stout glass with amber-colored liquid inside.

"It's the favorite of the night. Rye, brandy, sweet vermouth, Bénédictine, and both Angostura and Peychaud's bitters. It's American."

"Oh?" She took a sip, and her eyes lit up. "It's smashing. Thank you."

The bartender winked at her and moved down the line to the next customer.

"See anyone you know, Lizzie?" Hetty asked. She joined Elizabeth and her aunt just at the edge of the dance floor.

"Actually, I do—or rather, we do." Lizzie pointed out a man hovering at the opposite edge of the dance floor close to the stage where a band performed. The man's golden hair formed a halo from the nearby stage lights.

"Good heavens, it's Charles!" Hetty burst out without thinking.

"Why don't you go on and say hello for me? I think my aunt spotted a friend." Elizabeth pointed out a group of women that

Isabelle was walking toward. "I'll go join her. Find me if you need me." She vanished into the crowd before Hetty could drag Elizabeth back so she wouldn't be alone. She wanted to strangle her friend. It was so obvious now what Elizabeth was up to.

We matchmake all day. Does she ever rest?

Rolling her eyes, Hetty crossed the ballroom floor. Charles's searching gaze swept the crowd and their gazes locked. He gave her a crooked smile that, blast him, completely disarmed her. She forgot whatever witty thing she would've said to someone upon a chance meeting like this. He strode toward her, and her feet seemed to grow roots because she could not move.

"Hello, Hetty." Charles grinned. "Care to dance?"

She arched a brow. "You know the rumba?" The band had changed songs, and the sultry tones of one of Xavier Cugat's tunes filled the room.

"Naturally. One of the perks of being my father's son. He said the way to every woman's heart is by dancing. Therefore, I had lessons *all* the time." He winked at her, and all she could think of was the boy she'd grown up with, the boy who was so quiet compared to all the other young men she'd known. Quiet, kind, and always watching her as though she was the most fascinating thing in the world.

"And are you after my heart?" Hetty teased, but her voice was a little breathless. She wanted to flirt, she wanted to feel that rush of giddiness that came with dancing with a young man.

"I might be . . . if you wish to give it to someone when you're ready." He spun her out onto the floor just as the rumba ended and the band played a song suited for a box step dance.

"You like to box step?" he asked.

She was glad for the change of subject, since she was

honestly not sure what she was to do about him or any man at the moment.

"Of course I do." She grasped his right hand in her left, and they began to dance. She swayed her hips, slowly stepping forward and then sidestepping in a quick—quick—slow pattern. Then he pulled her around to face him, her right hand clasped together with his left. She settled her other hand on his shoulder, and he held her rib cage, enveloping her in a way that made her feel safe. She tingled with an unexpected excitement. It reminded her too much of that first flare of passion she had felt with Roger, but that passion had faded away and she'd been left with nothing but memories.

"You're thinking too hard. It's a *box step*, Hetty darling." Charles pulled her another few inches closer, and they danced toward the stage as the music swept over both of them. She had never had a hard time talking to Charles before. It shouldn't affect her like this. This was all Lizzie's fault.

They danced in silence until the song ended and Hetty tried to pull away. Charles kept a firm hold of her as he turned her back to face him.

"I know about Ceylon," he said, his voice hushed, like a man gentling a horse.

"*Do you?*" she snapped, her temper flaring. "Just *what* do you know, Charles?"

Damn those soft gray eyes of his. They were the color of mercurial clouds right before a winter storm. Her favorite thing in the world . . . winter storms.

"I know you've had your heart broken and that you need time."

Heartbroken. How silly and romantic he made her divorce sound. What could he know of the feeling? The hollowness that had settled in her chest, pushing out everything else that mattered until nothing was left but bleak empty space. What could he know of those moments when she'd said "It's over" to a man she had hung her dreams upon? Or the way the gold band that used to be on her finger, a thing so foreign while she'd been married, now felt like a crucial piece of her because it was gone.

"You can't know, Charles," she said. "You simply can't."

He let her go as the band struck up a new tune. "Oh, but I can."

She swore and burst into the stairwell that led up to the theater reception, frantically trying to remember where she'd left her bloody handbag.

"Hetty?" Elizabeth's voice halted her at the top of the stairs. She closed her eyes, trying to push away the flood of hurt and anger.

"I saw you leave, and I thought I should check on you and bring you this." Elizabeth joined her at the top of the stairs and held out Hetty's handbag.

"I needed a bit of fresh air." Hetty wasn't sure why she lied, but she took her purse and said softly, "I think I'll go home for the night."

"I'll see you tomorrow?" Elizabeth asked, her tone a blend of worry and hope.

"Yes." Hetty would be there tomorrow. The Marriage Bureau was a place where she could feel useful and have control. It was a haven in a world that threatened so much fear and heartache.

"Good night, Hetty."

"Good night, Lizzie." Hetty stepped into the reception and out onto the street. That was when violent shouts pierced the air ahead of her.

CHAPTER 7

Hetty halted on the curb outside the Astoria to stare at a trio of men. They were clearly drunk, judging by the way they were staggering about, but what stopped her was what they were focused on. The men were shouting at a young woman. A frightened boy clung to her side as she tried to walk down the street. But the drunks had noticed them and cornered them.

"Come on, lovey, don't be like that!" one man said with a laugh as he reached for the woman, and she knocked his hand away. He tossed a brown bottle at the woman's feet. The sound of the glass shattering echoed sharply down the darkened street, blending with the woman's sharp cry of alarm.

Fury roared through Hetty, and she stepped off the curb. Before she was even halfway across the street, another one of the drunkards let loose a string of anti-Semitic slurs at the young woman that sent Hetty over the edge.

"*Oi!*" she shouted at the men, who all turned on stumbling

legs to stare at her in confusion. Good, she had their attention now.

The young woman and the boy pressed flat against the old brick wall, doing their best to try to blend in and disappear. Stark terror flashed in their eyes, and Hetty wanted to tell them not to be afraid, but she couldn't lose focus on the danger.

"Well now, there's a pretty piece," one of the men chuckled and adjusted his pants crudely.

"Sod off, the lot of you," Hetty barked.

"Or what?" one demanded. His thick features and puffy, alcohol-reddened face looked like a nightmarish caricature.

"You don't want to find out," Hetty warned.

The temper that so often got her into trouble was her best weapon tonight. It was far safer to let her anger control her than her fear. In that respect, she was every inch her father's daughter. When she'd married Roger, he'd given her a few lessons in self-defense, seeing it as important that, living near or on military bases her whole life, she ought to be prepared. She'd thought it silly but hadn't protested the lessons. If Roger had been here now, she would have kissed him.

The woman and the boy had been forgotten as the three drunks advanced on Hetty, leers stretching their faces into ghastly grimaces in the dark. When the first man lunged at her, Hetty swung her heavy leather handbag and, with perfect aim, walloped him squarely in the face. He howled in pain. The second man reached her before she had time to swing her bag again. But his hands were clumsy, his fingers unable to find purchase on the silk bodice of her dress.

She swung a fist and felled the second man with a sound blow to the jaw. Ignoring the pain in her fist, she readied for the next attack. The third man launched himself at her, but someone suddenly stepped in his path and swung his leg under the man's legs, knocking him off his feet. He landed on his back with a loud *oomph*, then groaned and lay still.

Hetty had but a second to assess the new man involved in the fight. He was a tall dark-haired fellow in a dark-blue RAF uniform. The man Hetty had struck with her handbag now held one hand over his eye, and with a growl, he lunged for Hetty. The airman swung his fist at the drunk, and the man staggered back. He let loose a curse before running off into the night, leaving his two fallen comrades to moan and writhe in pain on the ground.

The pilot turned to Hetty. "Are you all right, miss?"

"Yes, thank you." She caught her breath, then turned to see the young woman and the boy trying to slip away. "Wait! Please don't go!" she called after them.

The woman's shoulders stiffened beneath the worn brown coat she wore, and the boy eyed Hetty fearfully as the woman he was with paused in walking away.

"Please, you're safe now. We don't mean you any harm," Hetty said as she glanced at the pilot. He agreed with her statement with a nod.

"Yes, please, miss, don't go. We mean you no harm," the pilot said.

The young woman turned to face them, and a nearby street-lamp illuminated her dark-brown eyes and her flaxen-colored hair. The boy's coloring was the same, and Hetty couldn't help but wonder if they were siblings. They carried a battered pair of large brown suitcases.

Hetty kept her tone gentle. "Please don't go."

"Do you have a place you're headed to?" the RAF pilot asked. "I would be glad to escort you both."

"I . . . we . . . no, we do not." The girl spoke English hesitantly, with a Polish accent.

"Are you visiting someone you could stay the night with?" Hetty hoped they did have someone they could stay with. The pair looked run ragged, and it was too dangerous not to have a place to sleep right now.

The girl shook her head.

The pilot cleared his throat and glanced at Hetty. "They can't sleep on the street."

"No, they can't," Hetty agreed, and she focused on the young woman again. "I have two empty rooms at my flat. It's completely safe, I assure you."

The boy spoke rapidly in Polish to the young woman, who studied Hetty for a long moment. Then she let out a weary sigh, nodded slightly, and spoke.

"Thank you. We have not stopped moving since we left Poland."

"Christ," Hetty murmured. "You both need a decent meal and warm beds."

"Let me call a cab for you," the pilot offered, and he put his fingers into his mouth and let out a piercing whistle. An idling cab down the street heard and pulled around and headed in their direction.

"Thank you, Mr. . . . ."

"Sheridan. Nathan Sheridan, miss." The pilot smiled warmly, and Hetty noted that he was rather handsome. Pilots always were, in her experience. But there was something about the compassion in his brown eyes that filled her with an almost desire to trust him.

She held out her hand, and he took it. "I'm Henrietta Byron."

"A pleasure, Miss Byron." The pilot turned to the Polish woman. "My sincerest apologies for such a dreadful welcome to our city."

The young woman's face went from white to red, and she nodded shakily and then nudged her smaller companion, who stuttered out a *thank you.*

Mr. Sheridan waited for them to get inside the cab and for their suitcases to be tucked in the boot before they drove off. Hetty and the young woman both turned to see Mr. Sheridan still standing on the corner beneath the streetlight as he watched them drive away. It didn't escape her that she'd been very lucky tonight with his intervention. Very lucky indeed.

By the time they reached Hetty's flat, she was exhausted. She couldn't imagine how the young woman and the boy felt if they had been traveling all the way from Poland without rest.

"Come on, this is my place." She hastened up the steps and unlocked her flat. After she set her handbag on the sideboard table and turned on a few lights, she found her new charges still standing in the doorway, eyes shyly darting about the room. What on earth had they been through aside from tonight?

"Let me show you your bedrooms, and then I'll make a plate of sandwiches for us."

Hetty had two slightly smaller rooms that were furnished for guests. When she'd moved in, she'd had a plan to turn one into a study, but she hadn't gotten around to it.

"Choose whichever rooms you like." She stepped back and watched in amusement as the boy chose his first and the young woman took the remaining room.

"Settle in for a few minutes. The water closet is here." She pointed over her shoulder down the hall. "Come to the kitchen when you're ready to eat."

Hetty left them alone and went into the kitchen. It was too late to make something proper to eat, and she was no skilled cook. Sandwiches would have to do. She cut several pieces of fresh bread and removed some sliced turkey and cheese from the small fridge. She hastily made three sandwiches and put them on plates. Then she poured three glasses of milk. The girl came into the kitchen first, pulling the boy along with her.

"I hope this is all right," Hetty said quietly. "I'll run to the grocer's shop tomorrow for more food."

"This is wonderful," the girl replied. "Sit and eat," she told the boy in English. He didn't need to be told twice. He collapsed in the chair and wolfed down the sandwich so quickly it was a wonder he didn't get hiccups.

"Thank you for this, Miss Henrietta."

"Oh, please, call me Hetty."

"Hetty." The girl smiled wearily. "I am Eva Wolman, and this is my little brother, Marcus."

"It's lovely to meet you, Eva." Hetty didn't press her for details, but she hoped with food and rest the young woman would trust her.

They ate in silence, but it was a nice sort of silence, Hetty decided.

"Would you like another sandwich?" Hetty asked Marcus. He swallowed the last bit of his milk and set his glass down before he shook his head and yawned.

"Well, it's time for bed. I suspect you both need extra sleep as well."

Hetty shooed them from the kitchen to their rooms and cleaned the dishes before she turned out the lights.

Marcus went straight to sleep and didn't even remove his clothes, turn off the light, or shut the door. He fell asleep face-down on his bed, dead to the world in the way only young boys ever seemed to manage. Hetty suppressed a chuckle, turned off the light, and then closed the door.

Eva was still up, the light on her nightstand still on and her door still open as Hetty walked past. The young woman was sitting at the foot of the bed, her gaze distant as she stared straight ahead. A tear crept down her cheek.

Hetty stepped in the doorway and whispered, "Eva?"

Eva blinked and hastily wiped her face, erasing her tears as she tried to smile.

"Are you all right? I know we are strangers still, but . . . you can talk to me." Hetty meant that. Normally, she would have left someone alone to handle their tears, but she'd changed in the last few months. She didn't want to be the person who didn't offer a hand to someone who needed it.

"Yes, I'm fine," Eva said, but it was a clear lie and they both knew it. "I am worried for my parents. They own a bookstore in Warsaw. My father didn't want to close it even though there was talk . . . that maybe it isn't so safe to stay. I didn't want to go without them, but they sent me and Marcus on alone."

She looked so unbearably young then, and frightened. But above all, she looked brave, and Hetty respected her for whatever she'd had to do to bring her brother all the way across Europe to keep him safe.

"How old are you, Eva?" Hetty was young too, she knew, but she'd seen much of the world while traveling with her parents.

"Nineteen. Marcus is only fourteen."

So young to be on their own and to travel so far. That protectiveness inside Hetty sharpened to an even deeper pang within her chest.

"You will stay here until your parents come to London, all right? I won't hear any talk of you leaving, otherwise."

Eva's eyes lifted from the floor to fix on Hetty. "Marcus will need school, and I . . . I must find work."

A brilliant idea leapt into Hetty's mind, making her feel as eager as a spaniel. "You don't happen to know how to use a typewriter, do you? And can you write English decently well?"

"Yes, I write English even better than I speak it. My father taught me both English and French."

"And can you type?"

Eva nodded. "We had just gotten a typewriter at my father's shop before Marcus and I left. I was learning to use it for our correspondence and invoices."

Hetty clasped her hands together. "Then I have a job for you. We'll discuss it in the morning. Now, no more tears. You're safe and all is well."

The girl chuckled. "You sound like my mother." The comment was said with gentle teasing.

"I sound like mine too," Hetty laughed.

As she lay in her own bed later, Hetty marveled at this sudden turn of her life. She was not the mothering type, yet tonight she'd become fiercely protective of two complete strangers. This was all Elizabeth's fault. But that only made Hetty smile even more as she closed her eyes.

CHAPTER 8

Elizabeth stood in the back office of the Marriage Bureau near the tiny kitchenette. Her hands twisted uncomfortably as she waited for Hetty to arrive. Last night, Hetty had been upset, and the stricken look on her face was burned into Elizabeth's memory. All because she and Charles had danced . . . and whatever had happened between them had caused her usually cool and collected friend to flee the Astoria.

It's all my fault. I shouldn't have meddled, but that's what I do. I'm a bloody meddler.

The sound of the office door opening and closing sent Elizabeth rushing into the other room.

"Hetty, about last night . . ." Her words died away as she saw Hetty wasn't alone.

Hetty was removing her hat. Behind her, a young woman and a boy of perhaps thirteen or fourteen stood wide-eyed just inside the door of the outer office.

"Lizzie, I believe I found our secretary. This is Eva Wolman and her little brother, Marcus. Eva, this is my partner, Elizabeth Mowbray."

The young woman blushed and managed a nervous smile as she glanced about the office.

"It's nice to meet you, Miss Mowbray," Eva said. Her voice was soft, lyrical, and soothing. Gentle . . . that was the word. Everything about Eva seemed gentle and beautiful.

Elizabeth took a moment to study Eva, noticing her worn clothes and simple style of dress. Eva was like her, a fish out of proverbial water, and she instantly liked the shy girl.

"It's lovely to meet you, Eva and Marcus." She noticed the boy shifting restlessly. "Marcus, would you like some biscuits?" She had just opened a tin of them in the kitchen, and the boy's gaunt face made her think of her own brother, Alan. Marcus needed to eat more, and she was happy to help with that.

Marcus glanced at his sister, who nodded in approval. He followed Elizabeth back into the kitchen, where she sat him down at the table with a cup of tea and a tray of biscuits.

"Thank you," he murmured. His Polish accent was a little heavier than his sister's.

"You're welcome." She joined Hetty and Eva in the main room, where Hetty was setting up the third desk that Charles had given them for their new secretary.

"Eva and her brother came all the way from Warsaw, Lizzie. Their parents are still in Poland running a bookstore. I thought since Eva needs employment and she knows English well enough and can type . . . she could be the perfect secretary. What do you think?" Hetty rarely sounded tentative about anything, but now she did, and Elizabeth sensed she wanted to help Eva and her brother.

"I think it's a wonderful idea, Hetty," Elizabeth assured her, giving Hetty the approval she seemed to need in that moment.

Hetty's features softened in relief and her confidence returned. "I told Eva everything about the business of the Marriage Bureau. I believe she could start by writing back to the potential clients where we need more information."

"I agree, and when we're waiting for appointments to arrive, she could work at the desk downstairs now that the lingerie store is closed and she could bring the clients up to us." It was perfect, Elizabeth realized. They didn't have time to conduct interviews for a secretary when they barely had time to conduct interviews with their clients.

"Oh . . . I think I found a possible match for Mr. Malcolm, by the way," Hetty announced.

"*Mr. Calcutta?*" Elizabeth giggled as she used their nickname for him. "How can you be sure?"

Hetty removed a rolled-up copy of the *Tatler* from her handbag and set it on the table. She flipped through the pages until she found several pictures of the same woman at a charity event in Sussex.

"Goodness, she's in nearly all of these," Elizabeth said as she noticed the woman's face in each of the groups of society girls posing cheekily for the camera. She wasn't particularly beautiful, but that wouldn't matter to Mr. Calcutta.

"This is Madge Wilson, daughter of a baron. There's no real family money anymore, but she has a knack for being in the right place at the right time. I think we should write to her and see if she'd be interesting in becoming a client."

Eva peered at the photos, shyly asking, "Who is Mr. Calcutta?"

Elizabeth filled Eva in on this particular client, wanting her to know she was a part of the Marriage Bureau's business now.

"He really wants a wife who appears in magazines because he wants to be seen in society as important?" Eva asked.

"Yes, you'll find many of our clients have unique requests." Hetty chuckled. "Eva, why don't you write to Miss Wilson and see if she is interested in an introduction to Mr. Malcolm? I'll fetch you the note cards with his information."

Eva's dark eyes brightened with excitement. "Let me set Marcus up with something to read to occupy him until I can find some schoolbooks, and I shall begin at once." She left to see to her brother in the other room.

"I hope you're all right with this, Lizzie. She's a dear girl. I found her and Marcus wandering the streets last night after I left the Astoria. It was dreadful. Some drunks were harassing her. She's Jewish. Not everyone respects that. It's awfully dangerous right now . . . with things, *you know*," Hetty finished in a grave whisper, and Elizabeth nodded in understanding.

They had both seen the anti-Semitism in England, Jewish-owned businesses looted, shop windows smashed, slurs painted on doors. Adding that to the rumors of what was happening in the eastern part of Europe, it was even more unsettling. There was talk of Germany eyeing Poland with hungry eyes.

It was unfathomable to think that a country could simply invade another, sow death and destruction, and expect no one to protest. Yet Elizabeth feared that was exactly what would happen. No one would protest . . . simply to avoid another war themselves.

The scars of the Great War were still raw. No one wanted to see the fields bathed in blood or clouded with poisonous smoke. Certainly no one in England wanted to send men and boys away to die. Boys like Alan . . . Her brother had joined the navy last week and mailed off one last letter to her to inform her that he was going to training. Elizabeth's stomach turned each time she thought about it.

When Eva returned, Elizabeth and Hetty walked her through the standard introduction letter to send to Miss Wilson and then left her alone to conduct her first task of being the bureau's official secretary. It was unusual for them to approach someone who hadn't registered, but they believed in this case it was worth sending a brief letter to see if Miss Wilson might be interested in registering and receiving an introduction to Mr. Malcom.

"I believe we have an appointment in five minutes," Hetty announced as she checked the appointment book on her desk.

Elizabeth collected her pad of paper and a pen. "Man or woman?"

"Woman . . . a Miss Erica Hanley."

Precisely five minutes later, Miss Hanley entered the office. Right away, Elizabeth took stock of the woman's attributes, cataloguing them mentally. Her dress was an unattractive putty color, and it did nothing to enhance her appearance. She was in her middle thirties with clear skin but unremarkable features.

She nervously touched the old hat she wore, which rather reminded Elizabeth of something she might see in a *Punch* cartoon. A pair of glasses were perched on her nose—a nice, neat pair not at all out of date and style, but Elizabeth knew that men, foolish creatures, often made fewer romantic passes at women in glasses. Heaven knew why, but it was a fact. As she came toward Elizabeth and Hetty, Elizabeth saw that Miss Hanley's stockings matched the awful pudding-colored dress, and her pointy-toed shoes were far too British to be considered fashionable.

"This is the Marriage Bureau, isn't it?" Her voice, though hesitant, was soft and soothing, which made her far more appealing than her unfortunate choice in clothes.

"Yes, it is. Are you Miss Hanley?" Hetty gestured for her to take a seat at the desk Hetty had ready for the interview. Miss Hanley sat on the edge of the seat, now nervously playing with the hem of her skirt.

"We have the form that you mailed us." Elizabeth pulled out the filled-out form, showing her the information. "It says you live in Somerset?"

"Yes, it's a small little village—you wouldn't know it." She tried to hide her embarrassment with a smile.

"And what do you do there?" Hetty asked.

"Social work, mainly." Miss Hanley paused. "I visit the chronic invalids and manage the flowers in the church for the vicar and a few other things." She tried to put excitement in her tone, but Elizabeth knew exactly how prisonlike that sort of life could be. She could picture Miss Hanley spending hours at the rectory perfecting floral arrangements that would go unnoticed and unappreciated by some stuffy old vicar.

"How did you hear about us?" Elizabeth asked. She could tell that Miss Hanley had taken a brave step in coming here. Most women in her situation did not take the initiative to free themselves of such domestic captivity.

"The village doctor's wife brought me some flowers to display in the vestry, and when I unwrapped the newspaper they were in, I saw a column about you. After I read it, I thought perhaps . . ."

Miss Hanley's face turned completely red, her gaze dropped

to the floor, and her head slightly bowed, as if she regretted even thinking they could do a thing for her.

Elizabeth's heart swelled with compassion for her. Miss Hanley was exactly the sort of person the Marriage Bureau was designed to help. She could only imagine what it must be like, to take such care with chronic invalids and with the flowers in the church every day and her hard work going endlessly unnoticed and then . . . unfurling a paper to find their article. It must have burned inside Miss Hanley like a beacon of hope.

"So you came to us because you'd like to get married and your current choices are few to none in your village?" Hetty surmised.

"Yes, is that . . . I mean . . . is that what you do?" Miss Hanley's fear was not unusual. Elizabeth and Hetty had grown used to reassuring new clients during their first interviews that coming to the Marriage Bureau was smart and sensible rather than a mad thing to do.

"Yes, that is exactly our forte, Miss Hanley. We are quite excited to help you."

Elizabeth was ready to get the important details written down. "I expect you have a type of man who appeals to you? Tell me as much as you can. And please share your view on children. Do you want any? Do you wish to live in town or in the country? Would a widower with a ready-made family suit you, or do you want a bachelor?" They hit her with all the important questions to get started.

"The city would be lovely . . . and I rather like children and would be happy to take on a husband's current children so long as they are good-hearted."

Elizabeth made notes on the note card with Miss Hanley's name printed at the top. "And your ideal man? His manner, his looks? What matters to you?"

Their client bit her lip, thinking. "I don't suppose his looks matter overmuch so long as he isn't too unpleasant to look at. And I would like a man with a good nature, someone who likes to laugh, but not at my expense."

At this Elizabeth paused in her note-taking to consider Miss Hanley. Had some gentleman made fun of her in the past? If so, Elizabeth wished she could find the man and slap him soundly across the face.

As Miss Hanley talked, Elizabeth's view of the woman as a poor lonely spinster was quickly fading, and instead she saw a woman who had a chance to make her life the best it could be.

What if they could re-create this woman so she could be the best version of herself? Many women didn't know what clothing looked best on them or that their hairstyle could be improved. Hetty was a genius at hair, clothes, and makeup. Miss Hanley had clear skin, a decent figure beneath the shapeless putty-colored dress, and a delightfully pleasant voice. She could be very appealing.

Miss Hanley's face had lost its blush, and she was speaking smoothly and confidently. The frightened dormouse was now gone, and in her place was a woman with confidence whose smile illuminated her face.

"Miss Hanley, what would you say if I suggested some changes? Particularly those relating to your appearance? I don't think you're at your best, but I believe with a bit of coaching, you'd be incredibly attractive."

"I . . . ," she began, but Elizabeth stood up.

"Hetty, we have a few hours before our next appointment, don't we?"

"At least two," Hetty said as she rose and grabbed her hand-bag. "I take it we're bound for the shops?"

"Yes, it's quite the emergency," Elizabeth teased gently. "Let's start with the undergarments."

⁂

HALF AN HOUR LATER, HETTY AND ELIZABETH STOOD OUTSIDE the dressing room of a lingerie and clothing shop while Miss Hanley tried on her new undergarments and a new outfit.

"Toss your old pieces to us," Hetty said.

Petticoats flapped over the top of the door, and a heavy pair of cotton stays followed. Hetty grimaced at them in horror.

"I think this is strong enough to make a parachute for the troops. We ought to mail it to the military," Hetty whispered. She attempted to pry the stays apart, but the ironlike fabric didn't stretch a single inch.

Elizabeth snorted and covered her mouth, her eyes twinkling.

"Do they fit?" Elizabeth asked Miss Hanley.

"Yes, but I feel rather *exposed*," the muffled reply came back.

"I do believe the word you're looking for is *freed*." Hetty collected the rest of Miss Hanley's undergarments, along with the putty-colored gown, and balled them up. "May we dispose of these old clothes?"

"Oh . . . yes, I suppose so. I'm coming out now," Miss Hanley announced.

Hetty was itching to see how her reimagining of Miss Hanley was going. They had purchased a new wardrobe of dresses and shoes, and it should have completely changed the woman's look.

When Miss Hanley emerged from the dressing room, she looked smart in a new dark-blue wrap dress and a white-and-blue polka-dot scarf. Her tan suede pumps added to the elegant vision. Miss Hanley's hands fluttered nervously about her waist. It was clear she wasn't used to wearing a dress that hugged her curves. But her figure was trim and had a nice hourglass shape that made her look rather stunning.

"Do I look all right?" she asked fearfully.

"Miss Hanley, you are an entirely different person." Hetty pulled their new client out of the small dressing room and toward a bigger mirror in the shop.

"Should I be different, though?" Miss Hanley asked. "I mean, the point is to be myself, isn't it?" The woman stared at herself in the mirror, and Hetty wanted to hug her.

"Miss Hanley, you have lived too long as someone else. This . . ." Hetty placed her hands on Miss Hanley's shoulders. "This is the real you. She's beautiful, confident, classy, and anything she wants to do, she can. She is *you*."

Hetty meant every word. She wanted Miss Hanley to understand that this step toward her new life was the most important decision she could ever make.

Elizabeth smiled, and Hetty felt a little delighted and even embarrassed. She understood now that at the Marriage Bureau they weren't simply arranging marriages. They were helping people make their lives the best they could be.

Miss Hanley touched the top of her head and smoothed a hand down over her hair, suddenly more decisive.

"Should I have a new hairstyle, do you suppose?"

"Definitely." Hetty played with a lock of Miss Hanley's hair. "Natural waves. Try that. Your hair has plenty of volume. Show the hairdresser a picture of Lauren Bacall. That's the look you want."

"Lauren Bacall?" Miss Hanley's eyes widened.

"Yes. Now I think you're ready." Hetty left her by the

changing room with Elizabeth, and she paid the bill for the new clothes. It felt good to use her money to the advantage of someone else for a change. She wouldn't make a habit of doing this for every client, but Erica certainly needed the help and didn't have the confidence on her own to make the changes. Perhaps there would be a way to work in a consultation fee for clients interested in such a process in the future, but she'd have to talk to Elizabeth about that.

With Miss Hanley's wardrobe settled, they returned to the bureau and finished conducting her interview before they planned for Miss Hanley's introduction to a man named Mr. Sessions. He was a retired civil servant who came across as polite, reliable, and kind. Everything would work out splendidly —Hetty was certain of it.

CHAPTER 9

 *ugust 1939*

EVERYTHING DID NOT GO SPLENDIDLY WITH MISS HANLEY'S
first introduction, as it turned out.

Hetty answered the phone at the Marriage Bureau a week
later. Miss Hanley's frantic voice was on the other end of the
line.

"Miss Byron? It's Erica Hanley."

"Yes?" Hetty thought she had recognized Miss Hanley's
voice.

"May I come visit you and Miss Mowbray?"

Hetty shot a look at her business partner, who was seated on
the floor with hundreds of note cards spread out around her in a
chaotic arrangement that only made sense to Elizabeth. Eliza-

beth looked up when she realized Hetty was watching her. Her dark brows rose in silent question. Hetty covered the mouth-piece of the phone and mouthed, *Miss Hanley.*

Elizabeth gave a shake of her head and gestured at all the note cards around her.

"We're awfully busy today, but you could tell me on the phone," Hetty suggested.

"I couldn't possibly. Oh dear, please let me come see you," the client begged.

"Very well, come straightaway." Hetty hung up and then rubbed her temples.

"What's the matter with Miss Hanley?" Elizabeth abandoned the scattered index cards and got up off the floor, smoothing her skirts.

"I can only assume something terrible happened with her and Mr. Sessions." Hetty felt ill thinking over what it might be. "Mr. Sessions is so wonderful. I would trust him to look after a mere babe."

Elizabeth bit her bottom lip. "We both did. Perhaps it's nothing so terrible . . ."

"Perhaps . . ." Hetty paced the length of her office until Miss Hanley arrived. Eva escorted her directly into the back room.

Despite Miss Hanley's frantic expression, her appearance reflected her new positive attitude. No one would ever look at her again as a quiet church mouse of a woman.

"What's happened?" Hetty asked, placing a hand on Erica's shoulder to calm her. She was fluttering about the room like a peahen with ruffled feathers.

"I . . . oh dear . . . he kissed me! Can you believe it?" She exclaimed this with such drama that she might as well have been shouting for the entire street to hear.

Elizabeth sought to clarify. "Who kissed you? Mr. Sessions?"

"Yes. It all happened so fast. We were in a taxi after dinner."

Hetty nearly laughed. All this fuss over a kiss?

"If you don't want a man to kiss you, don't let him. A good slap or an elbow to the ribs—" Hetty mimed jabbing an elbow into an invisible man.

"*Ahem.*" Elizabeth cut Hetty off and took Miss Hanley by the arm, directing her to sit in the nearest chair. She immediately relaxed at Elizabeth's intervention. Hetty frowned and waited for Elizabeth to work her magic.

"Do I . . . ? I mean, should a woman let a man kiss her on the first date?"

Elizabeth sent Hetty a look, and Hetty perched on the edge of the desk close to Miss Hanley.

"It depends on three things: you, the man, and how much you like him." She ticked these three things off on her fingers as she spoke. "I don't recommend a kiss on the first date. No, not even if you want to. Men often get the wrong impression. So I would advise you to wait, at least until the second meeting," Hetty said firmly.

"Hetty's right," Elizabeth assured her. "It's best not to go about kissing men until you're certain of your feelings."

Miss Hanley folded her hands in her lap, a woeful expression wilting her features. "I don't know the first thing about men—what to do, what to say, how to be around them."

Hetty understood then what their client faced. She lacked the instinctive knowledge that many women were born with. Hetty had always assumed most women were like her, confident in flirting and reading men's body language.

But the piles of letters delivered to their desk every day clearly showed that men *and* women had poorer instincts toward courtship than most animals did. She nearly laughed, but she didn't, because she assumed Miss Hanley would believe the laugh was directed at her.

"A man will usually approach you and start things," Elizabeth said. "Like Mr. Sessions, did he look deeply into your eyes before he kissed you? That's usually what men do."

Hetty's mind suddenly filled with the memory of Charles at the Astoria, holding her close as they danced, his gaze locked on her. A flutter shot through her belly, and she tried to shove the thought away.

Focus on work, not Charles. Work.

"Listen, Miss Hanley," Hetty said. "You want the man to do most of the work. *You* are the prize. You are the thing he earns after time and affection are given. If a man sees you as too eager for his attention, there's no attraction there. Despite men saying otherwise, they do like challenges. You don't want to marry a man who will never notice you or value you for who you are."

Miss Hanley sniffed. "No, I don't want that. I want . . . I want someone to value me and the things I do."

"Good." Elizabeth patted her hand. "So start with gently rebuffing an advance, even if it comes from a man you like, especially if it comes too soon. Make him take the time to get to know you. Don't be overeager to please. Choose what you like from the menu at dinner; don't let him order for you. Be the woman you want to be, and the right man will put in the effort to win you."

"Bravo, Lizzie, well put." Hetty couldn't agree more. "Now, let's put you in touch with a few other men."

Hetty and Elizabeth spent the next hour coupling several more matches and giving Miss Hanley the instructions to write to each of the men. Like many clients needing initial privacy when first corresponding to new introductions, she used their office as her return address to avoid her elderly aunt intercepting the mail. Apparently, the aunt wouldn't take kindly to losing her caretaker and would be rather unpleasant about it.

When they were alone in the office again, Hetty sank into her chair, exhausted. Elizabeth was back on the floor, idly moving index cards about, pairing them up.

"I never thought we would be advising on *that* level of intimacy," Hetty admitted with a weary chuckle.

"Neither did I, but it does make me realize how much more we must discuss things with our female clients than our male ones."

"Agreed. Dating advice should be included with our initial interviews." Hetty closed her eyes a brief moment, and then the phone rang and she and Elizabeth both started to laugh. If there was one thing to be said about the Marriage Bureau, it was that they never had a dull or slow day.

THE NEXT FEW WEEKS WERE A BLUR FOR ELIZABETH, HETTY, and Eva. A large number of aristocratic girls had joined the bureau's list of clients. It was not possible to match them up with the batch of working-class men who had flooded their books recently, so they were forming a client waiting list to handle the matches that couldn't be made until appropriate numbers of eligible parties joined the registry.

"What of the widows?" Eva asked one afternoon as the three of them sat on the floor sorting letters. "I have several asking for middle-aged husbands, 'no confirmed bachelors.'" Eva pursed her lips in concentration, forming the expression "confirmed bachelors" over and over, as if the act of repeating the phrase would reveal its meaning to her.

Elizabeth held her hand out for the letter that Eva was reading, and Eva passed it to her. She scanned the page, searching for the reference, then read aloud, "*I wish for a man who was previously married or widowed. No confirmed bachelors please, as I won't have the energy to please them or the desire to conform to their rituals.*"

Hetty chuckled. "*No one* wants a confirmed bachelor."

Eva looked between them, still confused, so Elizabeth handed her the letter back and explained.

"Confirmed bachelors have lived a long time on their own. They are set in their ways. They run their homes to their own liking. They spend much of their time out at gentlemen's clubs away from the house, and to them, a wife is an accessory. Something they engage with on their terms at a time of their choosing. It's not a man we would willingly introduce to our female clients. There is nothing wrong with a confirmed bachelor. They are often nice enough. But we want marriages where a man and a woman see each other as partners, as people of value to each other that they want to spend time with."

"Ah, I see." Eva nodded. "A man like that is set in his ways and expects the woman to work her life around his routine."

"Yes, that's it exactly." Elizabeth was pleased that Eva grasped the English phrase with such proficiency.

Eva looked over at her brother, Marcus, who was completing an assignment that Eva had given him. She'd managed to find schoolbooks in the last few days and set up a schedule for him. It was as though if she were to get him focused on schoolwork, he might for a time forget that they'd had to leave their parents and their home behind. He was such a quiet boy, but under Hetty's care he had started to lose the gaunt features and the haunted look in his eyes. Elizabeth met Eva's gaze when she turned her focus back to the letters, and they shared a smile.

"You know . . . ," Hetty began, tapping her pen lightly on a blank notepad in her lap. "We may want to consider a secondary headquarters for the bureau at some point."

"What?" Elizabeth glanced up, startled.

"Yes, I've been thinking. We need a second secretary down below in the reception now that we have a proper reception on the ground floor. That way, we'll have a proper reception area and Eva can handle the correspondence up here without worrying about the client flow if she has someone downstairs to manage appointment check-ins."

Hetty set her pad aside and stood, looking out the window onto Bond Street. Her tone now more serious, she continued, "And I've been thinking . . . if war ever comes and, well, we are bombed, I want copies of our client records somewhere safe."

"But where?" Elizabeth asked.

"The country—somewhere just far enough away that there wouldn't be bombs dropping on it."

A chill rippled up Elizabeth's spine. *Bombs.* Lord, how she hated the word. If only war wasn't an ever-growing certainty.

"Yes, I'll give it some thought over the next few weeks." Hetty reached for her purse and retrieved a few pound notes. "Marcus, would you mind running down to the market and buying some sandwiches for us? You may use the change to buy any sweets you like."

The young boy abandoned his schoolwork and took the money from Hetty with a grin. His mop of blond hair fell in his eyes, and Elizabeth was reminded of how very young he was. A place in the country would be far safer for Marcus, and she imagined Eva would feel better with her brother away from the city as well.

After Marcus was gone, the three women shared a quiet, worried look.

"It seems we cannot run far enough from danger," Eva murmured, her eyes full of fear. "Will we ever be safe?"

"You will," Hetty said with confidence, but Elizabeth wasn't so sure.

Something inside her warned her that this war, if it came, would be far worse than anything they could even imagine. In the Great War, the fighting had been on the fields of France, but now . . . now the war could not only touch but *obliterate* everything here with ease.

"Right, well . . . back to work. Eva, who is coming in today for an interview?"

Hetty attempted to distract them all from negative thoughts, and Elizabeth was grateful. What would she have done if she had never gone to the party with Isabelle and seen that mysterious woman smoking on the veranda?

Eva went back into the main office and retrieved the appointment book she had overseen since starting work at the bureau. She set the book on the small kitchenette counter and tapped through to the present day, her blonde hair shadowing her face as she peered at the names written down.

"Mary Midland should be here soon." Eva closed the appointment book. "I'll go downstairs to the reception and watch for her."

"Thank you, Eva," Elizabeth said. She headed toward the filing cabinet in the corner of their office and dug around a bit in the ladies' section under the letter *M* until she found Mary's card.

"Who's this one?" Hetty put a kettle on to heat water for tea and then sat down at her desk, waiting for Elizabeth to fill her in on the pertinent details of their new client.

"She's a young woman from Yorkshire who now lives in London. Oh yes, she's sent such lovely letters. Do you remember? She is an excellent writer and rather humorous, but not overly so."

Hetty's face brightened. "Is she the one who wrote about the sheep and—?"

"Yes." Elizabeth laughed at the memory. Mary's letters made Yorkshire sound idyllic and amusing.

Eva peered in the half-closed doorway. "Er . . . Miss Midland is here early."

"Show her in." Elizabeth collected her interview materials, and she and Hetty left their inner office and stepped into the outer room. It was a marvel how much the rooms had changed since they'd opened in the spring. Now it was cozier, and the lovely desk that Charles had given to them was for their clients to sit at rather than the two old desks they'd started out with. Those had been safely hidden from view in the inner room of their private office.

Hetty and Elizabeth sat down behind the large desk and waited. A moment later, Eva ushered in Mary Midland. Elizabeth felt Hetty stiffen beside her, and when she lifted her own gaze to their new client, she just barely prevented herself from making a sound.

Mary Midland was a thin woman with a delicate bone structure that leant itself to beauty, but her manner of dress did not work well at all with her looks or coloring. Her dress was black and long, almost to the floor and clearly an evening gown, yet she was wearing it in the middle of the day. She also wore a black fur stole despite the summer warmth.

She strode toward them and slid into the chair facing their desk with such a languorous movement that Elizabeth was reminded of any number of Hollywood actresses who would swoon into chaise longues on screen. Draped around her neck were at least six different necklaces, some beads, some pearls, all at various lengths. It was as if she had worn every bit of jewelry she owned to this meeting.

Hetty cleared her throat. "Miss Midland?"

Mary wove her fingers anxiously through her necklaces, making the beads and pearls click together. This vamp was not the woman Elizabeth had expected from her letters.

"Miss Byron and Miss Mowbray?" Mary's voice was soft and breathy, as though her nerves had a strong grip on her vocal cords. Elizabeth wondered if Mary had put on a costume for the allure of being seen as mysterious or if she was just rather eccentric in her tastes, which they hadn't been able to predict from her letters to them.

"It's lovely to meet you." Elizabeth tried to steer her mind away from the need to rush Mary out to the store for a new wardrobe the way they had Miss Hanley.

"We've reviewed your matches, and here are the names of six men we believe you should consult with." Hetty passed her copies of introductory letters from the men, which Eva handed to her before retreating to her desk near the door.

Mary took the letters and briefly glanced through them.

"Now, you can write to them through us, and when you decide who you wish to meet with, we'll arrange a place for you to have your first meeting."

"After I meet someone, when I like . . . or don't like the man, what do I do?" Mary asked. Her face was pale, and she looked a little ill. Elizabeth wondered if the poor girl had a terrible case of nerves.

"You will let us know. Give us a full report. The gentleman you meet will do the same about you."

"Oh, heavens!" The idea of a man reporting his thoughts on her clearly distressed her by the way she gripped her pearls and beads at her throat, her eyes going wide. "What if he doesn't like me?" Her hands continued to flutter around the necklaces, and Elizabeth's heart tugged for her. This woman wanted to be loved, it was written all over her face, but like all of their clients, she was at a loss as to how to manage it.

"If he doesn't show interest, he's not the right one for you," Elizabeth said.

"You know, Miss Midland, red is a fetching color, something dark and merlot-colored perhaps, or cranberry. With your light-brown hair and gray eyes, it would be very fetching, far better than black."

"Red?" The woman glanced down at her black evening gown, and a blush highlighted her cheekbones. "Yes, I believe I have a red frock or two."

"Remember to wear a shorter skirt for luncheon. Show off your legs," Hetty added a tad more bluntly.

"Oh, but I don't have a decent pair of stockings . . ." Miss Midland's voice trailed off, her face reddening further.

So that's why she wore the long dress, Elizabeth realized.

"Take these." Hetty pulled a box of new stockings out of her desk like a magician and slid the box across the surface toward Mary. The woman's eyes went round.

"Oh, but I can't possibly afford—"

"Consider this a client privilege," Hetty assured her and nudged the stockings another inch closer to Mary.

"Oh, thank you, truly." Mary accepted the box, clutching it to her chest. Then she folded the letters from the gentlemen. "May I take these home?"

"Yes, those are copies we've had made for you." Elizabeth smiled. "Look them over and write any letters and send them to us so that we can forward them on to the men who pique your interest."

"Thank you." Mary stood up, tucking the silk stockings and the letters safely in her worn leather handbag.

"I'll see you out, Miss Midland." Eva took the woman downstairs. For a long moment, Hetty and Elizabeth were quiet.

"Sometimes I forget how important what we're doing is," Hetty murmured. "That poor woman, wearing a black evening gown and fur stole in the summer."

"I believe it was because she didn't have any stockings, so she wore the only dress that wouldn't be an issue. It was kind of you to give her a pair."

At this, Hetty grinned and opened the drawer. Several boxes of various sizes and colors sat inside. "I bought a few last week. I've noticed more than one client needs a bit more guidance on such crucial pieces of their wardrobe. I spoke with some of the shops on our street about our situation with clients, and they are interested in giving us a private discount for clients on stockings and other clothes."

Eva came back into the interview room and sent Hetty a curious look. "Hetty . . . there's a Mr. Humphrey here to see you."

"Charles is here?" Hetty's voice pitched up an octave.

Hetty and Charles hadn't spoken since that night at the Astoria.

"Hetty, you must speak to him," Elizabeth gently urged.

"I will." Hetty's voice softened. "I shall be right back." She rose, hastily checked her appearance in the mirror, and left the room. Eva sidled over to Elizabeth and took Hetty's vacated seat.

"Who is Mr. Humphrey?"

"A childhood friend of Hetty's. He is also the official solicitor for the Marriage Bureau, but more importantly, I think he's in love with her."

Elizabeth explained the events of the night at the Astoria to Eva. It was so easy to speak with the Polish girl. In just a short span of time, Eva had become almost as close to her as Hetty was.

"He's a very pleasant man to look at." Eva smiled. It was a rare thing to see the secretary grin like that, and Elizabeth knew Eva worried greatly about her parents back in Poland.

"Charles is an utter darling. I honestly don't know what is holding Hetty back."

At this, Eva looked down at her hands in her lap. "She was married before, yes?"

"She was. To a naval officer in Ceylon. She was very young and got divorced after a year." Hetty rarely mentioned her ex-husband to them. But Charles wasn't like him. He was very different from what Elizabeth had heard about Roger.

"It is hard to trust your heart when you have been hurt before." Eva's sage words hit Elizabeth far more closely than she expected.

Memories of Algernon . . . of India . . . of all that she had left behind came back. A wave of homesickness for Aabha and dear

Uncle George washed over her, like a tide pulling her out to sea. Algernon had at one time been her future and a way to stay with her uncle in India, but she'd had to be free of him or else she would have died inside one day at a time until nothing of who she had been was left and she was simply Algernon's obedient shadow.

It still woke her up at night sometimes when she thought of how blind she had been when it came to Algernon. She hadn't seen his dark side until it was almost too late. She didn't trust her judgment, let alone her heart, when it came to any man for herself, even if she easily read the intentions of other men for her clients. It was possible Hetty felt the same.

And here I am shoving her at Charles, and she's terrified of getting her heart broken again.

Elizabeth cleared her throat and focused on work. "Eva, let's look at what's next on the appointments for tomorrow while Hetty's busy. I want to see if we can find some matches in advance for whoever is coming in." She would let Hetty handle Charles and she would not interfere . . . no matter how much she itched to.

CHAPTER 10

Hetty came down the stairs into the new reception and found Charles standing by the door. He had his hands in his trouser pockets and his hat tipped rakishly over his eyes.

He wore a dark-blue two-button single-breasted model coat with a snappy sports back. As he turned, she noted the elegant five-button double-breasted waistcoat with modified lapels. His trousers had full frontal pleats. It was a suit designed for everyday wear, but seeing it on Charles made it all the more appealing to her. The man knew how to dress, and that was one more reason to stay away from him, yet she couldn't. She moved toward him as if he had his own personal field of gravity.

"Hello, Hetty," he said in that deep, seductive voice. He removed his hat, letting his tawny gold hair fall into those eyes that held her in rapturous fascination.

How had it all changed after a single dance? It made no sense. She wasn't a silly romantic. She was practical. She was . . .

Lord, she was letting herself get swept away. Hetty gave her head a little shake.

"Charles . . . I . . . it's good to see you." The dozen other words she wanted to say were trapped on her lips.

"We should talk . . . about the night at the Astoria." He traced the brim of his hat with long, elegant, but strong fingers. As he spoke, Hetty's eyes were drawn to the movement of his hands, and she had the desire to feel him touch her like that. But then his words sank in. She glanced away.

"Please, let's not talk about it. It doesn't matter."

His eyes lifted from their focused look on his hat to her face. "Doesn't it?"

She saw it in his gaze, the words he wanted to say, but they both knew if he did, she would run again.

"Maybe it does," Hetty admitted softly, her heart beating a little out of sync.

"Then we'll talk about it another day. Why don't you and Elizabeth come down to the river with me soon? The summer is ending, and I'd like to take the yacht out once more before I put it up for the winter."

It had been ages since she had been on the river. And if she brought Elizabeth, she couldn't exactly get into trouble, right?

"Let me see if Elizabeth wants to go, and I'll call you. We could use a brief respite from work."

At this, Charles smiled more broadly. "Any luck with finding a secretary?"

"As it happens, I rescued a secretary the night I left the Astoria."

"Rescued?"

She chuckled at his bafflement. She told him the story of

finding Eva and Marcus and how a pilot named Sheridan had aided her in fending off the drunks.

"Sheridan? You don't mean Nathan Sheridan?"

"Do you know him?" She had been wanting to write him a thank-you note and let him know that Eva and Marcus were well.

"I do. He is an old schoolmate of mine from Eton and Cambridge. Nice fellow. Our families go a long way back. I knew he'd joined the RAF, but haven't spoken to him in a few months. I should give him a ring."

"If you do, please get his address for me. I wish to let him know Eva and Marcus are doing well."

"And you will let me know about the river?" Charles asked as they moved to the front door.

"Yes, I promise I will."

He opened the door and put his hat back on. Hesitating a moment longer, he reached up and brushed the backs of his knuckles over her cheek, the simple touch sending ripples of delicious fire through her. Then, as if he had to remind himself to leave, he let out a soft sigh and flashed her a wry smile before departing.

Hetty watched him from the doorway, and once he was out of sight, she headed back upstairs. She hesitated just outside their office. Her hands trembled as she touched the door. It wasn't possible to postpone that conversation with Charles forever, but she wasn't sure what she could say.

She cared about him. She felt . . . *alive* when he was near. It was such an odd thing . . . She'd known Charles for most of her life. He'd always been there, even while she'd been pining after other young men. Then she'd gone off to Ceylon and married Roger. Now she was back in London, and Charles was there for her again, as steadfast and reliable as ever. Yet something had changed between them.

Perhaps it was the looming fear of war and the changes she'd made to her life, but she felt she was seeing him for the first time, truly *seeing* him. She caught herself watching him more, hungering for each sight of him and fearing it at the same time. Every time they met, he found a way to touch her, just a brush of his fingers on her skin, his hand on her lower back, the way he seemed to pull her toward him with that magnetic smile that offered warmth and a hint of passion if she but opened herself to it. It was so much more than she'd ever had with Roger.

The thought caused an ache in her heart. Hetty was not a woman who liked to regret anything or look back on past decisions, but she wished she had known then what she was coming to learn now about passion and love.

She pressed her forehead to the closed door and drew in a deep, steadying breath. It was time to get back to work and forget the conversation with Charles until another day. As she opened the door, she heard the comforting sounds of Elizabeth and Eva speaking in the private back office. Something inside her went still, burning this moment into her mind, a moment when they were all together and safe.

She had a strange premonition that someday the three of them would no longer be like this, safe, happy, together. Hetty shook the maudlin thought away and headed toward the back office.

When she rejoined Elizabeth and Eva, they were preparing for interviews for the following week by laying out client index cards with potential matches to suggest to them. She sat down on the floor and helped them. Dozens of cards were arranged in various patterns, forming a lovely paper mosaic on the carpet.

"How are you pairing them up?" Hetty asked the other women.

"By personality first," Eva explained.

"Then by social status and type of employment," Elizabeth added.

Hetty studied the layout for a minute, taking the measure of Lizzie's system, and then nodded.

Half an hour later when the downstairs bell rang, Eva got up to see to it.

When they were alone, Elizabeth caught her gaze.

"Is everything all right with Charles?"

"What? Oh yes," Hetty replied, not daring to let her focus on work slip away again.

When Eva returned, she was escorting a middle-aged woman up to the outer office. She was not in the appointment book, but no one wanted to turn a potential client away.

"I'll interview her," Hetty volunteered. "You and Eva keep mating the cards."

"All right," Elizabeth agreed, and she and Eva stayed in the back office while Hetty prepared to take notes for the new arrival. The woman carried her handbag over one arm and surveyed the room like a woman shopping in a high-end store.

"I'm Julia Sykes," she announced. "I must speak to you about my daughter." She settled into the chair opposite Hetty with calm and ease, as though she were about to try on shoes. The woman had a natural grace, and her dress and shoes were expensive and well paired. Hetty hoped the daughter might have similar good looks and taste in clothing. She'd have to meet the young woman, of course, before making any true first impressions.

"Let's start by getting a bit of information about your daughter. Age, eye and hair color, general shape of her figure, her likes and dislikes, and what she is looking for in a partner."

Mrs. Sykes provided her daughter's details before adding, "I want her to marry someone with means and connections and a good deal of friends."

Hetty frowned slightly. Such men were not in abundance, and it sounded like Mrs. Sykes had a particular vision in mind for her daughter's life. Hetty couldn't help but worry that the daughter had no control.

"Is your daughter fond of entertaining?" If the daughter married a man who had many friends, entertaining would be a necessary skill for the girl, and if she didn't enjoy it, life would be utter torture.

"She'll learn to like it. Now, who do you have to match her to?" Mrs. Sykes's brisk shopping tone made Hetty wince inwardly. Did the poor girl have any say in her own life, or did this woman run her daughter's life completely?

"Mrs. Sykes. It's best if we know our clients on a more personal level." Hetty tried to imagine how gently Elizabeth would say this. She couldn't tell the woman they were not the local butcher and she couldn't simply ask for the choicest cut of beef to be slapped down on the scales to be weighed and packaged. That would not go over well.

"We should have plenty of eligible men," Hetty continued. "But I cannot say which ones are best until I meet your daughter and talk with her. The key to our business is the *matching* part of matchmaking. If we simply toss her together with random men, who is to say whether she would like any of them? You don't want her to be in an unhappy marriage." Hetty left that as a firm statement.

They were not in the business of selling daughters off to

spare their parents the inconvenience of having them at home. Elizabeth had shared much about her parents' disdain for her choosing not to marry Algernon in India and moving home. It was a fate Hetty and Elizabeth wished to prevent for other girls.

"I don't want her to be unhappy," Mrs. Sykes agreed. "Perhaps you should meet her, but she mustn't know I've hired you. She'd be dreadfully upset with me."

Hetty was not about to match a woman against her will, but she could understand that perhaps the daughter would not like the idea of her mother hiring a matchmaker. So if she had a chance to meet the girl and get a sense of her, she might be able to privately convince the daughter of her goal and see the girl's real interests in marriage.

"What if we met for tea this afternoon? We could run into each other as casual acquaintances, and I could bring up the subject of men and see what she says."

The woman nodded eagerly. "I was actually going to meet her in half an hour at Rules restaurant. If you're free, we could do it now?"

Hetty normally liked to expedite all things in life, when possible, but rushing the process of matchmaking wasn't one of these things. However, she could slip away and meet the poor girl and find out what she was really dealing with.

Hetty saw Mrs. Sykes out of the office and then offered a report to Elizabeth and Eva about the situation.

"Do you think it's a terrible idea for me to meet this girl under false pretenses?" she asked them. "I plan to tell her the truth the moment I have a chance."

"I don't think so," Elizabeth said, her brow furrowed. "I mean, if the mother has such control, marriage might be an option to escape, assuming we help choose the right man for her."

"I agree," Eva said. "Once she is more aware of our purpose, she might be excited to participate in the hunt for the right man."

"Very well, then. I'm off to Rules to meet the girl for tea." Hetty retrieved her hat and handbag and then paused by the door. "Lizzie, Charles has invited us to the river to sail in his yacht. Eva and Marcus have also been included. Would you like to come?"

"We'd love to," they both said at once and then laughed.

Hetty left them to meet Mrs. Sykes at Rules restaurant in Covent Garden. Rules was one of London's oldest establishments, and it was rumored to have been there since 1798, just as Napoleon was invading Egypt. Hetty always liked the comfort of places that had been standing for more than a hundred years. Perhaps it was her English blood, but she trusted a place that could stand the test of time in an age when everything seemed to be changing. The warm velvet padded booths were full of people dining.

Hetty spotted Mrs. Sykes at a booth near the back. It wouldn't be too hard to feign running into the mother. She spoke to the waiter, telling him she saw her party at the back. Then she strolled through the tables, and with a gasp of surprise, she halted in front of Julia Sykes.

"Julia!" she exclaimed in pretend delight.

"Miss Byron! Oh, Sarah, this is Henrietta Byron." Mrs. Sykes gestured toward Hetty, and Hetty had her first decent glimpse of her newest client. Sarah Sykes was a slim girl, very attractive, and she had the most enormous gray eyes Hetty had ever seen. Sarah was twenty-one, and yet when she turned her gaze upon Hetty, it was as if she were being looked upon by a goddess of old, one both innocent and wise beyond imagining.

"It's lovely to meet you, Sarah. Please call me Hetty."

"Oh, do join us, Hetty." Julia waved at the empty space in the booth opposite her and her daughter.

"I'd love to, thank you." She slid into the booth, and a waiter took their order after they'd had a chance to look over the menu. Hetty was famished and decided to forgo the light tea for real food.

"Steak and kidney pie, please." Sarah ordered the same with a shy smile at her. Julia chose a salad and then spent the next fifteen minutes discussing friends in common, of which they had none, but Hetty played her part as if she were auditioning for the silver screen.

"Clarissa Fleming has remarried, you know, to that diplomat fellow."

"I heard. That's an interesting match," Hetty lied smoothly. She had no idea who Clarissa was.

"Isn't it?" Julia stirred a spoon in her tea, mixing the cream before she blundered into the discussion of marriage again. "It's important, don't you think, for a woman to consider getting married and running her own household?"

At this, Sarah's face began to slowly turn pink, and Hetty did her best not to stare at the girl while she tried to read her better. Sarah twisted her linen napkin on the edge of the table between her fingers, clearly distressed.

"I mean, a woman has so many more wonderful things to do when she's married and her home is full of babies. She really needn't bother with a career or any other silly distractions. Why would anyone want to delay marriage and motherhood when they are so wonderful?"

In that moment, Hetty's silent allegiance solidified with poor Sarah Sykes against her mother. "Sometimes it's wiser for a woman to meet a good deal of men before making such a life-altering decision. In fact, a career could be a very decent way of giving a woman a chance to meet men as they truly are and not as they pretend to be when they show up with flowers and chocolates."

Sarah stopped twisting her napkin, and her gaze lifted to Hetty's in silent question.

Julia's tone turned a little harsher. "Nothing could be better than a career as a wife and mother. Matrimony is crucial for a woman's happiness. I think you, Hetty, of all people, would agree, given that your own career is making romantic matches for other women."

Hetty wanted to tell Julia just how complicated and rewarding it was to run a business as a woman, but now wasn't the time for a lecture on the value of careers.

At that moment the food arrived, and she excused herself from the table to find the ladies' room.

The instant they were alone, Sarah sat up a little straighter, and the wisdom in her gaze outweighed the innocence.

"I hope Mama didn't trick you into coming out here to meet me without properly paying for your services."

Hetty smiled. "She paid my fee. Now, we have a brief minute to discuss you and what you really wish for in a man and your future before your mother returns."

Sarah's gaze floated about the room. "I've been engaged before. Twice. My mother frightened both gentlemen away. Not intentionally, mind you. But she can be a bit overbearing. I've given up, not that I was particularly keen to marry. I am a secretary working for a bank, and I adore my work. I don't wish to leave it."

"And your mother has convinced you that marriage and a career cannot dwell in the same sphere of a woman's life?" Hetty guessed.

"Yes, exactly." The tension in the other woman eased as she seemed to realize Hetty was on her side.

"Well, I believe if you put your faith in me, I could find a man you like and a man your mother won't be able to scare off. And he will be someone who will respect you and value you."

Sarah smiled a little, and Hetty had the sudden idea that perhaps a man a little older would suit her, someone wiser, someone to match the woman Hetty sensed Sarah was.

"Come visit me tomorrow. There is a most charming major who might suit you."

Sarah's brows rose hopefully.

"Come alone. Send your mother on some other mission for you," Hetty suggested quickly, just as Julia returned to the table.

"Well, I believe that we have everything all sorted out for your daughter, Julia." Hetty smiled sweetly at Mrs. Sykes.

"Sorted? Oh?" She looked hopefully about. "I assume that means she's finally come to her senses?"

"You could certainly say that." Hetty winked at Sarah when Julia focused on her meal, and Sarah bit her lip to hide a smile.

⚜

ELIZABETH BID GOODBYE TO HETTY AND EVA THAT EVENING and left the Marriage Bureau's offices feeling more buoyant of spirit than she had in months. They had received a letter that morning from Madge Wilson that her lunch date with Frank

Malcolm—or Mr. Calcutta, as they called him—had gone well. She said she had liked him quite a bit and had arranged to see him for dinner in a few nights.

If she tolerates him enough for lunch and wants to see him again so soon, then we must have made a successful match, she thought.

The street shops were closing earlier and earlier these days, but Elizabeth found one still open on her walk home. It was a corner shop that carried a bit of everything. She selected a few magazines, ones with hairstyles and fashions featured prominently. They would be a nice touch on the reception coffee tables for clients who were waiting to be brought up for interviews. As the cashier rang up her items, she noticed a set of maps of the nearby areas outside of London just behind him.

"Could I have one of those, please?" she asked the young man who was ringing up her items. He glanced behind him to where she pointed.

"The maps, you mean?" he asked.

"Yes." She thought it would be smart for her and Hetty to have a decent set of maps while they were looking for a secondary headquarters for the Marriage Bureau.

"Do you have a license?"

Elizabeth felt a bit silly as she stared at him. "A what?"

The young man blushed. "Er, yes . . . a police-issued license. We can't sell any maps unless you have one."

"A police-issued license . . ." She echoed the words faintly in confusion. "Why would they require that?"

The young man leaned over the counter, his gaze darting around at the other customers before he spoke in a lowered voice.

"It's the Germans . . . They don't want any maps falling into their hands. They could be out there right now, planning how to roll tanks through the streets. We can't make it easy for them, you know."

"Good heavens," Elizabeth murmured. "No, I don't have one." She wasn't sure what shocked her more, that such a simple thing as a map was now restricted or that the Germans might be among them already with ill intent.

"Sorry," the clerk said, and she thanked him for the magazines before she left the shop.

She looked at the street around her and shuddered. The glow of her good mood faded again. The closed signs hanging from the windows too early and the empty feeling of her little corner of the world seemed far more significant and far more sinister than ever before.

By the time she arrived home, Isabelle was in the drawing room listening to the wireless. On the nearby coffee table in front of her were two boxes.

"Oh good, you're home." Isabelle stood and turned off the radio before she picked up one box, holding it out to her. "This is for you."

Elizabeth took it. It was slightly larger than a shoebox. Curiosity made her smile a little as she uncovered the present. But a moment later the smile vanished, and she dropped the lid to the floor in horror. A gas mask lay in the box.

"Isabelle?" Elizabeth's voice escaped in a frightened whisper. "What on earth . . . ?" She couldn't finish the sentence.

"They brought them to the office in a large batch. I took one for you and one for me. We'll all need them. There will be a requirement to take them with us everywhere soon, I suspect." Isabelle sighed, the sound world-weary. "I'm worried, Lizzie. This isn't like before. The planes, the gas—it's not a war on French soil we'll be fighting this time. The war will be here in

England. Women and children will be victims as well, not just soldiers."

Isabelle's words tolled like bells of doom. She'd always been positive, always smart, and yet here she was, unraveling with worry in front of Elizabeth. It made Elizabeth feel very small and alone to know that even the strongest people in her life were crumbling. It was even stranger to be talking of war, bombs, gas, and death when everything still seemed so normal outside their door in some ways.

"Take it to your room. Keep it by your bed at night." Isabelle nodded at the gas mask. Elizabeth stared down at the frightening thing. It reminded her of those raven-beaked masks that medieval plague doctors wore several hundred years ago.

She did as Isabelle said and placed the mask on her nightstand, but as she lay in bed that night, the moon illuminated the mask's grotesque shape in the darkness. She had heard a man yesterday on the bus cursing the full moon. He had called it a "bomber's moon" because the brightness of a full moon offered light for German bombers to see the city by.

The thought left Elizabeth bleary-eyed until well past midnight.

When sleep finally claimed her, she dreamt of India—of Uncle George and coming home to find the plantation house empty. There was no one to be found. She ran from room to room, calling for him, for Aabha, for anyone.

She stopped when she reached the courtyard. The only sound was the wind whistling through the empty corridors. It was a wind without a name, a wind that stole memory itself as it blew past. It ruffled the petals of the foxtail orchids and rippled along the once mirrorlike surface of the old stone fountain that no longer poured water from its sides. All was empty, all was still.

Everything bright and beautiful that had made this place feel like home to her was gone. There was nothing left but moonlight and shadow.

"Uncle George, I want to come home to you," Elizabeth whispered to the vast emptiness before her. The dream faded, and she finally slipped even farther into the abyss of sleep.

CHAPTER 11

S eptember 3, 1939

HETTY WALKED DOWN THE DOCK TOWARD THE BLUE-AND-white-painted yacht. Behind her, Elizabeth, Marcus, and Eva followed.

The other three were talking excitedly about the trip down the river today. But Hetty was overcome with a wild fluttering in her chest that sent invisible starlings to flight inside her. Charles stood at the edge of the dock, slowly uncoiling the length of rope from the nearby post that kept his ship moored. He turned to face them, and when he saw her, a smile broke out across his face.

"We are ready to board," he called out with a laugh as a

strong breeze buffeted them all and they nearly toppled over on the dock.

Charles caught Hetty's elbow, steadying her, and she leaned into him briefly, the warmth of him seeping into her and chasing away the chill that had lingered in her for the last few days. Lord, it was so good to see him again. The wind ruffled his golden hair, and the bright September sky made his gray eyes far more blue.

"Steady on, Hetty, my girl," he teased and gave her waist a playful squeeze before stepping back and focusing on the others.

Steady on . . . It was such a simple command, yet her heart was anything but steady at the moment. The last few nights she'd had terrible dreams, dreams that left her cold and weary come morning, and yet she had no memory of what she'd actually dreamed about . . . only the vaguest sense that it was about Charles and losing him.

Seeing him now so very much alive left her confused and unsure of herself. Part of her wanted to blame it all on the news of Germany invading Poland. Eva had been a ghost of herself for the last three days, and Marcus had fared no better. It was only today that they had managed to bury their worries, thanks to Charles's outing.

Hetty watched Charles help Marcus aboard first, and then he lifted Eva and Elizabeth onto the ship next.

"Your turn," he called out, and Hetty stepped toward him. He grasped her by the waist, lifting her easily over the short distance between the dock and the boat. Then he vaulted onto the deck beside her.

"Charles, she is a beauty!" Elizabeth announced as she ran her hand over the polished walnut deck railing.

"Thank you. My father had her made by Philip & Son in

1930. She's not bad for being almost a decade old. She can host six passengers and six crew, but we won't need any crew today. I can manage her for a simple river cruise."

Hetty took the measure of the yacht. It was nearly one hundred and twenty feet long, with a beam of almost eighteen feet.

"How fast can she go?" Hetty asked.

"Twelve knots. Not terribly fast, but she's a stately beauty, aren't you, girl?" Charles patted the side of the cabin, which was a bright white, a lovely contrast to the darker blue hull of the ship. "Shall we get her out on the river and throw the anchor before we have luncheon?"

"That sounds lovely." Hetty lingered close to the bow of the ship as Charles set the yacht away from the docks and headed into the main part of the river. Many other boats were already out enjoying one of the last few days of good weather. Hetty wondered if these other voyagers had the same feeling that she did, that something was coming and they must cling to these last beautiful days of sunlight.

The River Hamble wandered through South Hampshire and reached the sea by way of the waters of Southampton. The warm sun beat down on Hetty's face, and she closed her eyes, letting the light burn against her eyelids. The wind increased as the yacht entered the river and picked up speed.

After a quarter of an hour, Charles located a quiet part of the river where the water was slow-moving and little inlets offered a place for people to swim. He anchored the yacht, and Elizabeth and Eva retrieved the picnic baskets from the cabin in order to set out their lunch.

Hetty, not nearly so domestic, kept out of their way, as did Marcus. The boy sat on the nearest chair by the bow and stared at the water. The wind played with his pale hair, and Hetty, without thinking, reached out to brush it back from his eyes. He let out a soft sigh.

"Are you all right?"

Marcus stole a quick glance at her before focusing on the water ahead of them again.

"Do you ever feel . . ." He spoke slowly, as though choosing his words carefully. "Do you ever feel like you are a moth in the dark and you see light and you fly toward it, but you crash into glass? It stops you from reaching the light. Instead, you stay outside, beating your wings uselessly against the glass."

His words painted such a visceral image in Hetty's mind, she shivered. It was such a strange way to describe the feeling, yet Hetty knew exactly what he meant. It was a feeling of *hopelessness.*

"I do, Marcus," she replied. "I do."

She looked away from the river to where Charles leaned against the doorway of the cabin, watching her. His khaki slacks and the white shirt he wore molded to his frame, reminding her he was a powerful, muscled man, not just a charming solicitor. This was a man capable of going to war. That meant he was also able to die on a field far from home.

She thought of all the young men she had grown up with who might leave England to fight, letting a cold, creeping fear steal into her. She tried to brush away the maudlin thoughts.

"Lunch is ready. Come and eat," Elizabeth announced.

"Hear that? Food's on," Hetty teased Marcus and gave him a playful push on his shoulder.

The boy went ahead of Hetty toward the back of the ship where a little table had been set up and laden with finger sandwiches and lemonade in a pitcher. They all ate and talked about friends they had in common and things they wished to do before winter came.

Marcus was given command of the RCA portable radio. He bent over it, turning the dial indicator, which was a green plastic disc with a white stripe painted down the center. The little beige box sent music into the air.

Charles lowered the small ladder off the back of the yacht, and everyone took turns in the cabin changing into their swimsuits. They had managed to buy Marcus a pair of blue swim trunks the week before and had even found a swimsuit for Eva. By the time Hetty changed and emerged from the cabin, she heard Eva and Elizabeth splashing about with Marcus in the water.

"My turn," Charles said, and Hetty stepped back, letting him pass by her into the cabin. His eyes swept over her, heat filling the look he gave her before he slowly closed the door between them.

Hetty knew she looked stunning in her rayon taffeta two-piece suit, but she felt unusually vulnerable. She liked Charles looking at her, but rather than making her feel desirable and confident, the way the attention of men usually did, she felt *uncertain*. About what, though, she couldn't say.

"So, how are the matches coming?" Charles asked through the closed door. Hetty heard the rustle of clothing as he changed. She tried not to think of Charles without clothes. For some reason, that made her flush all over.

"Good. Very good. We just introduced a charming major to a beautiful young woman with the largest gray eyes I've ever seen. She's rather like a dove, soft and sweet, but she's also smart and intuitive. I think she will be a good match for him."

"I love that," Charles said.

"Love what?" Hetty leaned against the cabin door to hear him better, but suddenly the door opened, and she tumbled into Charles. His bare upper body pressed into hers as he deftly caught her in his arms. How did he always do that? Catch her when she fell like some distressed damsel?

"I love that you care so deeply about your clients, and you know them so well. It's rather magnificent, what you and Elizabeth do."

"You really think so?" She liked Charles's compliment far more than was wise.

Charles's eyes were deep and endless as he replied softly, "I do. Things are changing, Hetty. The world is shifting, and someday soon all that we'll have to hang on to are those we love. You are giving these people a life raft for the coming storm."

Hetty cleared her throat and pulled free of his gentle hold. Turning her back on him, she crossed the deck toward the ladder. He came up behind her, following her down the rungs. Thankfully, he didn't say anything else as they both entered the river.

The crisp, cool feel of the water made Hetty feel more alive than ever. She swam a short distance away from the yacht, stretching her limbs. Music from the wireless floated on the water around them as the sun climbed toward its zenith. It wasn't even noon yet. Still, Hetty had the strangest sense that the day would slip away from her if she did not hold on to each minute as it passed.

As the water flowed around her, Hetty felt a wildness stir in her blood. It was a wildness born of a longing to never be tied to one moment or one place. Until today, she'd felt like a caged wild creature that had thrashed against the bars of its prison so long that she'd forgotten what freedom felt like.

Charles swam toward her, his hair wet and slicked back on his head, gleaming a burnished bronze in the sunlight. As they reached the shallow part of the river, he caught her waist and held her close, their toes just touching the bottom of the river and allowing them to stand. The sun beat down on their heads and shoulders above the surface, and for a long moment, they simply stared at each other.

Time stilled then, and only the water and wind around them seemed to move. Spellbound, Hetty couldn't look away from his eyes. Things she had never thought she'd find again burned in their depths. Promises of passion and vows of forever. Things that she wanted with such a desperation it frightened her.

He moved his head a few inches closer, his lips parting, his gaze dropping to her lips. She knew what was coming, knew it the way she'd always known when a man meant to kiss her. But this time . . . this time she wanted it more than just for the pleasure of knowing a man's kiss. She wanted to feel his mouth on hers and feel a connection, one that went beyond her body.

Their lips brushed softly once, a kiss that asked the question, *What if?*

What if? The words echoed until they became a rumble as deep as the shifting of the plates that formed the very continents. That wild creature inside her crept farther out of its cage and stretched its wings. Could one remember how to fly if one had never flown before?

Hetty curled her arms around Charles's neck and pressed herself against him. He moved his mouth over hers gingerly, slowly, as if he had all the time in the world to kiss her. She lost herself in him. Even in her most passionate moments with Roger, she'd never felt *this*—as if one kiss had set her world on fire. Yet it was so much more than lust. It was everything in between and beyond.

It was only a distant cry from Elizabeth that broke them apart. Charles pressed his forehead to hers, their breath mingling as the water lapped at their shoulders.

"Hetty, Charles! Come quick! The prime minister is about to come on the wireless." Elizabeth waved at them frantically from her place at the base of the ladder.

Hetty tried to catch her breath before she and Charles swam back to the boat. Marcus had climbed back aboard the yacht and brought the radio to the railing so the others could hear. Neville Chamberlain's reedy voice came over the radio.

"I am speaking to you from the Cabinet Room at 10 Downing Street. This morning the British ambassador in Berlin handed the German government a final note stating that unless we heard from them by eleven o'clock that they were prepared at once to withdraw their troops from Poland, a state of war would exist between us. I have to tell you now that no such undertaking has been received, and that consequently this country is at war with Germany."

Hetty reached for Charles's hand under the water as they both gripped the base of the ladder at the back of the boat. The prime minister continued to speak.

"You can imagine what a bitter blow it is to me that all my long struggle to win peace has failed. Yet I cannot believe that there is anything more or anything different that I could have done and that would have been more successful.

"Up to the very last it would have been quite possible to have arranged a peaceful and honorable settlement between Germany and Poland. But Hitler would not have it. He had evidently made up his mind to attack Poland whatever happened, and although he now says he put forward reasonable proposals which were rejected by the Poles, that is not a true statement."

Eva covered her mouth to stifle a cry, her eyes wide with fear. Elizabeth pulled Eva toward the ladder to help her get back into the boat, where she put her arms around her brother's shoulders.

"The proposals were never shown to the Poles, nor to us, and, though they were announced in a German broadcast on Thursday night, Hitler did not wait to hear comments on them, but ordered his troops to cross the Polish frontier. His action shows convincingly that there is no chance of expecting that this man will ever give up his practice of using force to gain his will. He can only be stopped by force.

"We and France are today, in fulfillment of our obligations, going to the aid of Poland, who is so bravely resisting this wicked and unprovoked attack upon her people. We have a clear conscience. We have done all that any country could do to establish peace, but a situation in which no word given by Germany's ruler could be trusted and no people or country could feel themselves safe had become intolerable. And now that we have resolved to finish it, I know that you will all play your part with calmness and courage.

"At such a moment as this, the assurances of support that we have received from the Empire are a source of profound encouragement to us.

"Now may God bless you all and may He defend the right. For it is evil things that we shall be fighting against, brute force, bad faith, injustice, oppression, and persecution. And against them, I am certain that the right will prevail."

There was a brief silence before a series of announcements came over the wireless. All places of entertainment were to close with immediate effect, and people were discouraged from crowding together, unless it was to attend church. Details of an air raid warning were given, and people were advised not to use tube stations as shelters. After the broadcast ended, everyone climbed aboard the boat and changed out of their swimsuits in silence.

"We need to get back to the city," Charles said as he went to turn the yacht engine on and head back toward the docks.

Hetty stood at the stern, watching the wake ripple out behind the yacht, and she knew that this was the last hour of innocence for England. This war would come to English shores and leave behind death, pain, and sorrow. The despair of such thoughts was strong enough to strangle the breath out of her.

She closed her eyes. A moment later, a slender hand tucked into hers, and she found Elizabeth gazing at her, her blue eyes bright with determination.

"We will survive this, Hetty. I know it," she said.

"How can you know?" Hetty asked in a half whisper.

"Because good always wins. Even with great sacrifice, we cannot give up. We *won't*."

Hetty squeezed her friend's hand tight, thankful more than ever that fate had set them on the same path together. She'd always heard her father say that courage wasn't the absence of fear, but that courage existed in spite of it. Seeing Elizabeth's face in the noonday sun, full of undaunted courage, she *believed*.

We will win this war. We have to. And I shall do my part.

PART II

CHAPTER 12

Elizabeth halted in the middle of the train station at the sight before her. Hordes of children of all ages were clustered in the station. Each child held a bag or satchel of belongings and had a tag with their name printed on it attached to their coat. All the children carried gas masks, and the youngest—under four years—had theirs tied to their bags by string or rope. Many of them were entirely alone and faced their situation bravely, as only children can in times that frighten even the strongest of adults.

Mothers wept as they hugged their children, possibly for the last time. Elizabeth sucked in a breath at the heartbreaking sight. She knew with a terrible certainty that some of them would never see each other again.

Since the declaration of war a week ago, children had been leaving for the countryside en masse, but Elizabeth hadn't seen it for herself. It was far worse than she could have imagined. Lines and lines of children, mothers bravely holding their tears at bay until the little faces vanished behind train windows obscured by smoke and steam.

Elizabeth's body was taut with inner pain as she witnessed parting after parting, an endless stream of love and sacrifice from both mothers and children. This was the heart of the English spirit, the mothers who chose safety for their children, and the children bravely facing their new lives for however long they must before they could come home.

Elizabeth had come down to the train station for the first time in weeks so she could meet one of her clients for his first in-person introduction. Mr. Damien Russell was coming in from the country to meet another Marriage Bureau client, Penelope Ford. They were to have tea this afternoon, and Elizabeth wanted to make the introduction between her two clients personally.

She moved carefully around the groups of children, trying not to separate them from their mothers as the mothers bid them goodbye. One of the trains rolled into the station, a puff of steam escaping from the front of the engine with a loud hiss. As the smoke cleared, a familiar red-haired man leaned out of the train carriage doorway, spotting her. She waved at him. He waved back before he leapt onto the platform toward her.

"Miss Mowbray!" he called out.

Elizabeth had forgotten how striking Mr. Russell was. His ready smile slipped as he noticed the children all around him. Some of them stopped and tilted their little heads up to look at him, hoping to find direction, protection, anything that would make them feel safer.

"Christ," he muttered. "I had heard the trains were taking them out of London, but I hadn't expected so many . . ." He didn't finish and gave his head a small, sad shake.

"I know, the poor little dears." Elizabeth shivered. "I wish we could help match them with families in the country the way we do adults."

"My home is far enough away from the city. I could take a handful. I'll see to it after our meeting today."

At this, Elizabeth gasped. "You would take in children?"

"Why not?" He shrugged. "I have nearly a dozen rooms available at my manor house. My butler will have a fit, but I think the old boy could do with a bit of a change. Taking care of a boring old bachelor must be damned dull work."

Elizabeth laughed. "Children would certainly change that."

At this, Mr. Russell grinned again. "Perhaps I'll have a wife soon as well, if all goes to plan." He waggled his brows mischievously at her.

"I hope it does. Penelope is a wonderful woman."

They left the train station and passed more parents who were sending their children away to the country. Neither of them spoke again until they had left the sorrowful scene.

"Penelope sounds quite lovely from her letters," Mr. Russell added, continuing their previous conversation.

"I think she'll be a good match for you. Her ambitions are related only to her article writing. She doesn't care at all about titles or having a grand social status or lack thereof."

A tiny bit of tension in his face faded at her words. "I'm glad to hear it."

"How have things been in the country so far?" Elizabeth asked. "Is it like here? All gas masks and blackouts?"

"A little," he admitted. "But we do worry far less. It stays darker at night, and what little light we might let show is not as noticeable as it is here."

They walked to a Lyons Corner House not far from the train

station. A young woman in a dark-red knee-length dress accented by a thin black belt was waiting outside the restaurant. Her shoulder-length hair fell in long waves and was left uncovered by any hat or scarf. A breeze ruffled her hair and rippled her skirt as she turned their way, making her look like the heroine of a moving picture. Mr. Russell halted abruptly.

"Mr. Russell?" Elizabeth whispered worriedly as she caught the look on his face. He looked as though he had seen a ghost.

"It's her . . ."

Elizabeth shot a glance between him and the stunning woman who held his attention. "Who?"

"The one that got away," Mr. Russell murmured in a daze as he gazed at Penelope.

It struck Elizabeth then in a flash of excitement that her two clients had met before.

"Mr. Russell, have you met Miss Ford before?"

At this, Mr. Russell blinked, some of his stunned reaction fading. "That . . . *that* is Miss Ford?"

"Yes, the woman we've matched you with. Do you know her?" Clearly there was a piece to this puzzle she was missing.

"When I returned from India a year ago for a brief holiday over Christmas, I met her at a holiday party. We never introduced ourselves, but . . ." His face became a little ruddy. "She was utterly perfect for me, and then I lost her and never could find out her name. She's the reason I wanted to settle down. I wanted to find a connection like I had that night with her. My God . . ."

He started walking again toward Miss Ford, and Elizabeth rushed to catch up just as he stopped in front of Penelope. Her green eyes widened as she recognized him.

"The man from beneath the mistletoe."

"Hello," Damien replied, still a little stunned.

"Elizabeth," Penelope began uncertainly. "Is he the man who . . . ?"

"I'm Damien Russell." He held out his hand to Penelope.

A smile broke out on her face. "Penelope." As the two of them stared at each other, Elizabeth's heart began to hum with joy. They were lost in their own world, just the two of them. She had done it. Elizabeth had always believed in fate, and this was one of those moments that proved to her it was real.

"Well, I see you two have met, so I'll leave you to your lunch," Elizabeth said, but she highly doubted either of them was listening to her. She didn't mind in the slightest. She turned around when Mr. Russell called to her.

"Thank you, Miss Mowbray. Thank you for everything."

With a smile, she nodded and walked away. Her steps were light, and her spirit was not constrained by the darkness that had befallen so many people of late.

As she rounded the corner of the train station, a dozen young men in uniform marched past her, their gear bags slung over their shoulders. She slowed her steps as they walked by. Something in their faces . . . something strange about their expressions, puzzled her. It was as though each of them had seen something that she could not. Elizabeth had the sudden mad need to rush up to them and ask what it was they had seen. The faraway look was a blend of sorrow, hope, and resolve.

Once, many long days ago in Assam, she had asked Uncle George what the Great War had been like, and he'd grown quiet, his face so very much like these young boys as he witnessed a vision in his mind that he alone could see. He had reached for his cigarette and puffed the smoke about his head in clove-scented clouds before he spoke again.

"There is a moment when you realize that words and prayers

will not save you from the evil in another man's heart. You have only your bones and blood between you and the devil. You either surrender or you fight to your last breath with everything you've got. You hold the line with the man on either side of you. That's what makes the difference. The person who stands tall in the face of danger while others cower, that one person is brave enough to save the world sometimes. The fields of Europe were full of such heroes. Someday I fear we will forget how to be brave, and that's the day we will *lose*."

Elizabeth hadn't fully understood what he had meant then. Yes, she'd understood bravery, understood standing up to the evil in others. But now she felt like she was close to understanding what it meant to put only yourself between evil and everything you love, even knowing you might well lose the fight. These boys . . . these mere boys had the look of doomed heroism in their eyes, and she wanted to hug each of them, but she dared not intrude upon their march to the trains.

She nodded solemnly at each one and resolved in that moment to do more, to do whatever she could to help these young men who were going off to fight.

So few, yet so brave to fight for all of us . . .

The need to do something, to help those young men with distant gazes, was overpowering. Elizabeth's hands shook a little as she glanced about the street, watching more soldiers and sailors heading for distant ships and shores. Their faces began to blur with the tearstained faces of mothers and the brave little children who boarded trains.

She had to do something, anything, to help. It wasn't enough to be in London. She had to contribute *more*. She believed in England, believed in what it meant for her country to go to war against a nation who believed they could own the world. This fight, it needed heroes of every age, gender, and size. She wasn't a good cook or a talented knitter, but if she visited the Women's Voluntary Services, she'd find something to do.

Thankfully, the Marriage Bureau's appointments that afternoon were light, so she visited the nearest WVS headquarters, which was only one street away from the bureau.

The WVS had been founded the previous year to provide welfare services in the event of war. Much of their work consisted of making clothes and blankets for the evacuees, as well as swabs, pajamas, and other supplies for hospitals to cope with wounded civilians once gas and bombing attacks began.

The volunteer center was full of tables crowded almost uncomfortably by eager volunteers. The energy in the room spurred Elizabeth onward, fueling her resolve to commit to working each week to help the war effort. Huge stacks of wool covered every table, and Elizabeth joined a group of women closest to her.

She stood out a bit from the ladies who wore the standard WVS uniform dresses, but she was welcomed with smiles and nods as she took a seat. It amazed her to see a blend of classes in the room, highborn women with perfect coiffures down to women with weary faces and hard lines etched in their skin. There was a unity of purpose here that destroyed class divides.

"All right, ladies." A matronly woman in a standard two-piece herringbone tweed WVS uniform marched through the room, her voice carrying in the sudden stillness. "We are knitting bedcovers today. These will be quilts for the hospital cots. Just take your cues from your table leader and work as long as you can. Someone will take your place when you leave."

Elizabeth carefully studied the rhythmic flow of the other women at the table and tentatively joined in stitching double rows on the quilts. Electric sewing machines began to hum like the roar of distant planes. No one spoke at first, each woman bent silently over her fabric as she worked, but after an hour, talk began to creep back in at the tables. Soon, people were sharing stories and soft whispers with little chuckles and smiles.

The feel of connection in the volunteer center was almost overwhelming. None of the women seemed to know each other's names, yet in this simple act, they came together as one, working, talking, reminding each other that life wasn't over, that the fight for *this*, for each other, had only just begun.

It was nearly night by the time Elizabeth pulled herself away from the table and whispered a few goodbyes to her sewing mates. Her fingers ached and her eyes burned with the strain of peering down at the stitches, but her heart was full.

When she stepped out of the center and onto the street, she halted at the sight of the darkened city surrounding her. For a moment, she panicked, unable to breathe at the vast blackness that had enveloped everything. She'd always made it home before dark since the blackouts had begun, but not tonight. She was too late. Every streetlight and every car headlamp had been extinguished. Every window was shuttered or curtained with black material or black paper. No manmade light escaped into the endless night.

The sound of the silence and darkness was deafening. The violent roar of blood in her ears nearly brought her to her knees. Someone had said that the blackouts turned London into "a city of dreadful night." At the time, she hadn't quite grasped the depths of what they'd meant, but now she did. Not even the stars dared to shine brightly. In the distance, she glimpsed beneath the muted starlight the monolithic shape of barrage balloons. The hulking silver airships protected strategic areas of

London from low-level bombing. Elizabeth prayed they would never see if the balloons worked.

The city felt empty at night. Nearly one and a half million people had left England's major cities, including London, to seek the safety of the countryside. Elizabeth clutched her handbag tight, a gas mask inside, ignoring the prick of pain on her bruised fingertips from the sewing. Pressing her palm flat on the wall of the nearest building, she started the walk home. She knew where she was now, but if she wasn't careful, she could get turned around. With each step, she grew more aware of the shapes of buildings and her eyes adjusted to the dark.

She finally found Isabelle's townhouse, climbed the steps to the front door, and fumbled around in her handbag until she found her key and slipped it into the lock. When she entered the townhouse, Isabelle came toward her in a fluttering panic.

"Where have you been?" her aunt gasped and threw her arms around her, hugging her so fiercely Elizabeth choked for air.

"I'm sorry, Isabelle. I stopped by the WVS center near the bureau and sewed quilts for the hospital cots."

Her aunt's face was pale and her eyes were red-rimmed, as though she had been crying.

"Isabelle, what's the matter?"

"You mustn't scare me like that. I thought something had . . . I . . ." Isabelle covered her mouth, choking down a little sob. "What if they had started the bombing? You were out there all alone . . . No one should be alone." She wiped her eyes, smearing a delicate line of makeup until she looked a bit like a beautiful badger. It was so easy to jump at shadows, even though the bombing hadn't even started yet.

Elizabeth swallowed down a lump of guilt. She'd been so lost in her own mind these last few weeks, a ghost of her usual self. It was as though she had lived forty years in a single day, her body and mind weary with the ever-growing gloom that layered London, yet each new morning she found but one day had passed for the city of dreadful night. Wars lasted a long time, and if this was anything like the Great War, they would be facing years of darkness. How could they possibly survive like this?

"I'm sorry. I'll call before I disappear again."

"Good." Her aunt flashed a falsely bright smile, as if everything was fine again. Perhaps that was the only way—to sally forth as though the world was not on the brink of war.

"Well . . . let's see what we can scrape up for dinner," Isabelle said.

They raided the larder in the kitchen and found enough ingredients to make a potato and leek soup with roast chicken. As they cooked, Isabelle shared the latest drama in the fashion world, and for a moment, things felt blissfully normal.

"Did you match anyone today?" Isabelle asked as she placed their plates on the table and added two glasses of water.

"Oh yes! Do you remember Mr. Russell?" Elizabeth had shared many stories about her clients in confidence with her aunt.

Isabelle nodded. "The dashing redhead?"

"Yes, that's the one. He came into London today to meet Miss Ford, a stunning young woman who writes magazine articles." Elizabeth took a bite of her roast chicken and sighed in pleasure. She hadn't realized how hungry she'd been until now. It had been more than half a day since she'd bothered to eat anything.

"Well, do you think they'll end up married?" Isabelle asked.

"I hope so. It turns out they've met once before, last Christmas at a party, but they never knew each other's names.

Such a chance meeting, and then today . . . to meet again, it was fate." Elizabeth closed her eyes, replaying the moment in her head.

"You really love it, don't you?" her aunt asked, a soft smile on her lips.

"What?"

"The matchmaking. You truly find pleasure in it."

"I do," Elizabeth agreed. "I'm frightfully good at matching people . . . just not myself."

Her aunt raised a brow. "Well, you might if you went out a little more. Several gentlemen you met that night at the Astoria last summer have been asking me about you when they drop by for their modeling fittings."

"I don't want to date a model. I want . . ." Elizabeth honestly didn't know *what* she wanted. She only knew she wanted to be with someone who thought so much of others that he didn't have the self-obsession of a man like Algernon. She wanted someone who inspired her and made her a better person, not someone who wanted her to be his shadow.

"No models . . . Well, perhaps you ought to put Hetty on the case of your own marriage prospects."

Elizabeth laughed. "Hetty is far too busy matching our real clients to match me."

After dinner, Isabelle poured them each a glass of sherry.

"It feels a bit like Christmas," Elizabeth said as she sipped the dessert drink and relished the way it went straight to her head. For a moment she forgot about gas masks, and anything that made her think of war, and the young men with their distant gazes as they saw what she was too afraid to see.

There was only the murmur of Isabelle's voice and the way

the sherry made her nose tingle. She thought back to what one of those women had said while knitting at the women's center.

"You must grasp on to the little everyday things—hold them tight and they will keep you sane. For me it's my chickens. Every morning I retrieve two lovely brown eggs from the coop, and at least I know that I have breakfast."

Elizabeth knew her everyday things were small, yet they grounded her to the earth, pulling her feet safely back down when the winds of war threatened to blow her far away. Isabelle's leather handbag by the door, always toppled over because she entered the house in such a flurry of activity. The smell of freshly cut roses in the bureau's interview room. Hetty's clever smile as she mated client index cards. Marcus's youthful laugh and Eva's steadfast tenderness.

They were such small things, yet they had become Elizabeth's whole world. She could rely upon these things each day to find joy and comfort. Within her mind, she twisted each one of these small but precious things around each other, forming a glowing rope of memories that mattered. She would wrap her hands around that rope and hang on to it when the world crumbled around her.

CHAPTER 13

D*ecember 18, 1939*

"WE MUST DO SOMETHING," HETTY MUTTERED AS SHE STARED at the account balance that the bank employee had written down on a slip of paper for her.

Elizabeth leaned from her perch on the edge of one of the old, battered desks in their private office. "Is it really that bad?"

"Lizzie, we have seven pounds and six shillings in the Marriage Bureau's accounts. *That's all.* I can fund next month's rent and Eva's salary, but we'll need a steadier income like we had before September or we're finished."

Hetty folded up the bank letter and was amazed at her own self-control not to tear it up in frustration. They had worked too hard for the business to fail now. Things had been booming, with money rolling in from registrations, until the war started.

Then people stopped calling, the letters dwindled to a stop, and the postman no longer had to make two trips, which suited him fine since he now had a wife to go home to . . . a wife they'd found for him. They needed a way to generate interest in the Marriage Bureau again, or else they would be in dire need of a miracle to stay in business.

Elizabeth took a seat at her desk and began to sift through the letters that had been delivered half an hour ago.

"We could start collecting our after-marriage fees. We're owed quite a bit," Elizabeth suggested as she opened one of the letters and began to read it.

"We are, but it's still not enough." Hetty tapped her fingers on her chin, brooding as she tried to come up with a decent plan.

"Oh goodness!" Elizabeth leapt out of her chair and waved a letter in the air. "Mr. Russell has done it!"

Hetty wasn't following her friend's train of thought. "Done what?" She grasped the letter and read the news for herself.

"My dear matchmakers, it is my sincerest delight to inform you that Miss Penelope Ford has accepted my proposal of marriage. We are to be married on Christmas Day at my house in the country. You and your staff are invited to join us for the wedding and the Christmas Day feast afterward. I have reviewed my contract, and the proper fee is enclosed, along with a little extra because I cannot imagine living one more day without Penelope in my life. We might never have found each other again had it not been for the efforts of the Marriage Bureau."

"Seventy-five pounds." Elizabeth waved the banknotes about

with childlike glee. "We did it! Oh, I'm so happy, Hetty. Isn't this wonderful?"

Hetty read the letter again, feeling that same joy sweep through her too. It wasn't the first letter bearing such good tidings, but it was a rather important one. He'd paid one of the higher after-marriage fees.

"We are going to the wedding, aren't we?" Elizabeth asked.

"Absolutely." Hetty decided in that moment they could all do with a bit of a holiday.

Eva's head appeared around the office door as she lightly knocked to get their attention. "Er . . . sorry to interrupt, but two clients are here. They have a few things to say to you." Eva bit her lip, and Hetty's joy evaporated.

"Which clients?" she asked, trying to think of anyone who might be unsatisfied with their business.

"Oh, just come and see," Eva said, and this time she was smiling. "You will want to, I promise."

Hetty followed Elizabeth into the interview room and saw Major Taylor in the open doorway that led to the reception downstairs.

"Major Taylor," she greeted. "Is everything all right?"

The solemn, handsome major smiled as he removed his cap and tucked it under one arm.

"I have come to tell you in person nothing is all right. Everything is rather *perfect*, actually." He reached behind him to pull someone into view who had been hidden behind his muscular frame. Sarah Sykes, who looked stunning in a cream-colored day dress, held a small bouquet of lilies. She was a breath of springtime in the midst of a bitterly cold winter.

"I would like to introduce you to my wife, Sarah Taylor. As of nine o'clock this morning, I am a happily married man."

Sarah beamed up at the major's face, and a deep blush spread across her cheeks.

"Isn't it wonderful?" Sarah asked. "My mother couldn't scare him off," the young bride added proudly.

"I admit, she was a formidable opponent, but we won in the end." He smiled down at his bride, and Hetty wanted to clutch her chest and swoon, as Elizabeth would often do. This truly was a love match, just like all the others, but Major Taylor would always be special to her and the Marriage Bureau. He had been the very first client on their books and the first to be interviewed. She'd often spent time the last few months dreaming of finding him that perfect woman, and now she had.

"All he had to do was say '*Madam*' in his wonderfully deep voice, and my mother all but snapped her heels and saluted him." Sarah giggled. "And my father simply adores him." At this, the major blushed like a schoolboy.

"We came to say thank you and pay our after-marriage fee." He cleared his throat, and Eva collected the money and wrote him a receipt.

"Oh, Major, we are terribly happy for you both," Elizabeth said, wiping tears from her cheeks. "And we desperately needed good news today."

A sharp, disciplined look becoming of his rank came over his face. "What? Has something happened? Tell me and I shall endeavor to help at once."

Hetty jumped in before Elizabeth said too much about their situation. "It's just a little slow at the bureau, that's all. It seems war is consuming everyone's minds and not love."

"It's been like that for many businesses," the major added thoughtfully. "Have you reached out to the newspapers? That was how I found you, and they are hungry for good news right now. Ever since we lost the HMS *Courageous* off the coast of Ireland, it's been one bit of bad news after the other. England needs help. Remind everyone what we are fighting for. It's not just the ground beneath our feet. It's the people fighting beside us, the ones we *love*."

As he spoke the word, he directed his gaze at his wife. Hetty saw the fear and pain in his new bride's eyes beneath the flame of love. Major Taylor was going to fight, and there was always the chance he could be lost. No, Hetty would not even think it.

"You're right. We will contact the papers this afternoon."

The loss of the HMS *Courageous* to a U-boat had been a huge blow to England's sense of safety. It was the first ship to be lost, but it would not be the last. People would need to be reminded that love gave them everything to fight for.

"We had better get home," Major Taylor said. "I have only one week before I ship out, and I wish to have as much time as possible to enjoy my honeymoon."

He pressed a kiss to Sarah's cheek, and the young woman's eyes half closed as she briefly held on to his arm.

"We're so happy for you both," Hetty said in the best imitation of her father as she saluted him. He winked at her before he and Sarah took their leave.

"England stands a chance with men like Major Taylor," Eva said, her voice soft and hopeful.

"Yes, yes it does." Hetty swallowed as a wave of emotions rolled through her. "Lizzie, let's go pay a call on those newspapermen."

"Good idea." Elizabeth plucked her red wool coat off a rack and adopted a serious expression that matched Hetty's determination. They set off to save the Marriage Bureau and hopefully do their part to save England.

AS LUCK WOULD HAVE IT, EVERY SINGLE NEWSPAPER WAS QUITE excited about revisiting the Marriage Bureau story. Now that the bureau had so many success stories to share, the journalists leapt all over the tales of the recently engaged or married couples. Hetty had contacted several of their newly married clients and obtained permission to share their stories with the papers.

By Christmas Eve, the bureau was seeing clients come in again, and the mailbag once more grew full of letters. Hetty felt as though she could relax a little. They were to leave for Mr. Russell's home later that afternoon. She was all packed up, as were Marcus and Eva, and ready to leave for the station.

The front doorbell rang. Hetty answered and was stunned to see Charles. They had spoken often since September and shared biweekly lunches, but he hadn't brought up their kiss that day in the river. The magic that had dwelt in the water of the River Hamble had been overshadowed as pressing ration concerns and blackouts consumed so much of everyone's thoughts. Here he was, standing at her door, his charming grin gone. He was serious, his eyes full of a depth of emotion that worried her.

Charles removed his hat and managed a rueful smile. "Hetty, would you take a walk with me?"

"A walk? Charles, I must catch a train soon . . ."

"Please. It will not take long." The intensity in his gaze sent a ripple of apprehension through her. "Please."

If there was one thing in the world Hetty could not resist, it was a gorgeous man who said the word *please*.

"Eva, I'll be back soon," she called out before she retrieved her coat and followed Charles down the steps and onto the street. He crooked his elbow out toward her in silent offering. She tucked her arm in his, and they walked a moment in companionable silence before they reached the nearest street corner.

"War is here, Hetty, and I have a duty to my country. I've decided to enlist. I wanted to tell you before I leave."

"Enlist?" Hetty choked on the word as terror tightened her muscles and her stomach roiled.

"Yes. My father fought in the Great War . . . I must honor him and his service with my own."

"No," Hetty said, her tone heavy with a natural command that came from being a brigadier's daughter.

Charles's lips twitched as though he was almost amused. "Hetty, this is *my* choice."

She pulled her arm free of his, frowning.

"So you enlist and go to war in France, fight the Germans, and *die?*"

"I should hope you have a fair bit more confidence in me than that." He was half teasing, but her fury was building, and she was in no mood for his gallows humor.

"Charles . . . you can't," she whispered. "You *can't.*"

"I have to. They'll need men like me over there. I'm a crack shot, and I don't fear much."

Her voice pitched up a desperate octave. "You should be afraid of *dying!*"

This time, his smile was sad. "I'm more afraid of losing you and England to the Nazis. I would die a thousand times if it meant protecting you and our home." She let him pull her into his arms, but she balled a fist and smacked him in the chest.

"And then you go and say a bloody awful romantic thing like that," she gasped and buried her face in his chest. She inhaled, taking his scent so deep into her that she vowed she would never forget it.

"I know we said we would talk about this another time. But that time is *now*." Charles moved one hand up her back to cup her neck. She lifted her head to stare at him.

"Don't you dare," she warned.

His gaze intensified on her face. "*Marry me*, Hetty. Send me off with your love, and I promise to come back alive." He cupped her cheek, his thumb stroking her skin and making her shiver as she longed to agree, to give him anything he wanted in that instant if only he'd stay. He made her want to break all the rules she'd made against falling in love again after her failed marriage to Roger. Charles made her believe that happy endings and fairy tales weren't just for young children and dreamers like Elizabeth.

When he held her like this—his warm, hard body pressed to hers, the strength of his arms about her, and his eyes so full of promises she knew he'd keep—it made her want to cry. Cry for everything she'd wanted in life and love, cry for the thought that she'd lose herself if he didn't come home. It made her weak at the knees and damned light-headed. She didn't want to feel like this, to feel vulnerable and raw.

Tears stung her eyes, but Hetty shook her head. "No. You come back alive and then I'll marry you. Damn you . . ."

She pulled away without a backward glance and rushed away from him.

ELIZABETH SAT ON A BENCH IN THE TRAIN STATION, HER battered suitcase at her feet as she held the latest letter from her little brother, Alan. She had heard from him, but after the HMS *Courageous* was sunk, he had only scratched a few hasty lines on the paper. *"I'm safe. Don't worry. I'll miss you at Christmas."*

She desperately wanted to read the letter, but she was so afraid that it might be the last words she would ever have from him. If she didn't read them . . . maybe that would keep him safe. It was ridiculous and made no logical sense, but with everything around her feeling like it was a dark storm gathering upon the horizon, she found herself more superstitious than she'd ever been in her life.

"Stop being such a ninny." She slid a finger around the seal to open the letter. It wasn't long, but it was far more than his last cryptic missive had been.

My dearest Lizzie,

We will be at sea again by the time you read this. I cannot share more details than that, but there's talk of someone being assigned to the HMS King George V next October. I rather hope it's me. The ship is a beauty.

When I was last at home a few weeks ago, I went home to see Mother and Father. They know about you and the Marriage Bureau. Father was quite angry at first, but Mother was a little intrigued by the idea. She said that at least you are supporting yourself, and that seemed to ease Father's tensions a bit. Maybe someday they will see you for what you are and love you as I do. Never let the world change you, Lizzie. By the way, I'm sending several of my shipmates to the Marriage Bureau's address. We sailors need lovely ladies to fight for too.

She read the letter three more times, savoring each word from her little brother. She decided to send a letter to

Uncle George for Christmas. Isabelle, Alan, and Uncle George were everything to her, and she would see neither Alan nor Uncle George for a long time. She could feel deep in her bones that the war would take those years from her.

"Lizzie?"

She sat up straighter at the sound of her name and glanced about the busy train station. She spotted Eva coming toward her, Marcus right behind, and a short distance beyond him was Hetty. It was Eva who had spotted her and was waving.

Elizabeth hastily folded Alan's letter and slipped it into her coat pocket. Then she got up and embraced Eva and Marcus just as Hetty caught up with them. Hetty looked ready to step onto the set of a moving picture. She wore a dark-purple dress with a cornflower-blue collar and a jaunty little cornflower-blue fedora on her head. But the spectacular effect was dulled by the unnatural pallor of her face.

"Hetty?" Elizabeth said in a soft question.

"It's nothing. I'm a bit under the weather is all."

"Will it be a long train ride?" Marcus asked as they all showed the conductor their tickets and boarded the train carriage that would take them northwest into the countryside.

"Perhaps four hours or a little more." Elizabeth had never been to Mr. Russell's village before, but she was excited about the journey.

They settled in for a long ride. Hetty was quieter than usual. Marcus kept his youthful questions going the entire time, with Lizzie and Eva taking turns to answer and keep him entertained. Eva smiled with such motherly affection that it reminded Elizabeth that Eva had to raise her little brother and how much the girl must worry about their parents.

It was very close to midnight when the train stopped at the

station close to Lavenham, but they still had an hour-long ride in the car before they reached Mr. Russell's home. As they wearily exited the train, Elizabeth spotted Mr. Russell waiting on the platform for them. He was leaning against the wall, his fedora tipped over his eyes as he read a newspaper. At the commotion of passengers leaving the train and coming toward him, he folded the paper and glanced up, spotting them.

"Ah, perfect timing. How was the ride down?"

"Fine, quite fine," Elizabeth replied.

"Excellent. This way." He led their party outside, where two cars were waiting for them.

"These are yours?" Marcus gasped as he saw the elegant pair of BMW 335s.

"Lizzie and Hetty can come with me. Eva, you and Marcus can travel with my driver, Mr. Gardner."

A middle-aged man with a kind face stood behind the second BMW. He waved at them, and Marcus bounded toward the expensive car with a puppy's exuberance, which Elizabeth envied. He began tossing dozens of questions at the chauffeur about the car.

"Lord, to have a child's energy," Elizabeth sighed as Eva joined her.

"He is so much better here, but I worry . . . when the bombing starts . . ."

There was no *if*—it was simply a matter of *when*. No matter how many air-raid drills they had or how much they had tried to prepare, no one knew what that first bombing would feel like. They only knew that it would happen.

War like this had happened before. Germany had stretched its fingers across the land, driven by power-hungry overlords. History seemed doomed to repeat itself, but on a much more devastating scale. This time, Elizabeth knew, there would be bombings in England.

"We will have a good time," Eva said, her tone brighter, but Elizabeth heard the note of dread buried beneath the excitement.

She put her arm around Eva's shoulders. "Yes, we will." Not even war could cancel Christmas in England.

CHAPTER 14

C *hristmas Day 1939*

MR. RUSSELL'S COUNTRY ESTATE, BARROW HOUSE, WAS buzzing with excitement Christmas morning. As Elizabeth came downstairs, she had to dodge a pair of footmen and a few upstairs maids. All of them were flustered but smiling as they continued to prepare the house for the wedding and the holidays. Last night Damien had explained that they'd received permission to have a local Anglican minister perform the ceremony in the grand hall of the house rather than at a church, and they would have a late luncheon following the wedding.

As Elizabeth reached the bottom of the stairs, she soaked in the festive glow of the hall. Evergreen decorations hung from every mantel, railing, and doorway. Someone had brought in an entire hothouse of flowers in every color imaginable. There were bouquets of lunaria, their purple petals brilliant amongst the white lilies. Dried cape gooseberries accented the wilder looking floral arrangements, which lent the room a wintry feel without the cold.

Damien was speaking to his butler, and two young children were with him. He had his hand on the shoulder of a boy who looked to be about six and held a little girl of four in his arms, balancing her easily on one hip. The children seemed to be glued to his side. When Damien noticed her, he waved Elizabeth over.

"Did you rest well?" Damien asked.

By the time Elizabeth and her party had reached the estate, the sun had been long past the horizon.

"Oh yes, and we can catch up on sleep tonight." She nodded at the children. "Who are your young friends?"

At this, Damien's face turned ruddy. "This is Nella," he indicated the little girl. "And her older brother, Cliff."

"Hello, Nella and Cliff." Elizabeth smiled at the girl and held out a hand to the boy, who shook it solemnly. His large blue eyes were taking in all the decorations around them.

"Are they . . . ," Elizabeth whispered to Damien, and he answered with a slight nod.

They were children from London. So he had done as he'd said he would and rescued the poor lambs. And lambs they were; their hair had been shorn close to their heads. She'd heard that some of the children were in a bad state, and measures had to be taken to care for them. Many had lice, and it often required a close haircut and a dozen baths and new clothes to get rid of them.

"Mrs. Danby is working to fatten you up, right?" Damien

teased the little girl, who kicked her legs and giggled as he tickled her. "Now, Cliff, why don't you run and find Penelope for me? Do you remember the way to her room?"

The boy nodded.

"And take your sister." Damien set the girl down, and Nella scampered after her older brother toward the stairs.

"How long have you had them?" Elizabeth asked once the children were gone.

"Since the day I met you at the station. Penelope and I had a wonderful tea that afternoon, and when I came back there were so many lost little souls boarding the outbound trains. Nella and Cliff's mother couldn't afford their tickets. She was trying to raise money in the train station. I agreed to pay for their passage and promised to escort them safely. They were bound for my part of the country, and I just . . ." He shrugged. "All of those children needed safe homes and warm beds. I ended up taking these two home that day. The woman who was originally assigned to take them was glad because she had four other children who were bound for her house already, and she was worried about having six mouths to feed. They've brought my home to life, and Penelope is already in love with them. I dread to think of the day when we have to send them back." He cleared his throat and glanced away. "I want them to be with their family, but damned if I haven't gotten attached to the little darlings." Where most men might have been awkward with his own children, let alone strangers, Damien seemed to take to his position of temporary fatherhood with dedication and warmth.

"When you do have to send them home, they will have been safe and loved here, and that will have made all the difference in the world," Elizabeth promised him. "Instead of memories of terror and hiding in shelters, you'll be letting them have their childhood, as much as you are able."

His face softened with a rueful smile. "How is it that one so young as you is so very wise?"

She blushed. "I'm only wise when it comes to the lives of others. I make a dreadful mess of my own."

"Sometimes life is a complex tapestry of events that illustrates your destiny, one that isn't always clear at the outset. Sometimes you need to give it time before the image reveals itself. Whatever brought you to this moment, to be here at my home attending my wedding, *that* is a beautiful outcome of your life. I know you have many more moments like this ahead. You and Hetty . . . what you do matters. You are uniting the people of England during a time when we most need love and hope."

Damien's praise made her heart quiver, and she felt what songbirds must feel right before they open their beaks to sing—that joyous sense of self at knowing they are doing what they are supposed to do. That lighthearted feeling continued as she met with the other guests before taking up her spot in the crowd once the ceremony was ready to begin. Hetty, Eva, and Marcus joined Elizabeth as the rest of the guests filtered into the hall.

Damien took up his position at the front of the hall with the clergyman. A few minutes later, a footman with a violin began to play a beautiful classical piece of music. Penelope and her father appeared at the top of the stairs. She wore a knee-length white dress trimmed with pale-blue flowers embroidered on the sleeves. She carried a bouquet that cascaded down from her arms.

Elizabeth felt a sudden longing for India as she remembered the foxtail orchids hanging from the pots in a similar way as these beautiful flowers draped down over the bride's arms. Penelope passed by Elizabeth, her eyes glowing with happy tears.

"We did it," Hetty whispered to Elizabeth.

Those three little words seemed so simple, yet at this moment their meaning was infinitely profound for the both of them. The scheme planted in her mind by Uncle George in Assam was truly real in this moment.

"We did," Elizabeth agreed.

At the front of the room, Penelope kissed her father's cheek, and he left her with Damien before retreating to join the rapt audience. The couple spoke their vows, and the clergyman spoke his parts of the ceremony, but it all seemed such a blur to Elizabeth. She tried to imprint a thousand details in her mind at once, which was impossible.

After the ceremony, the bride tossed the bouquet. A stunned Eva caught it reflexively as Hetty dodged the flowery projectile.

"Do you know the tradition behind throwing the bouquet?" Elizabeth asked.

Eva buried her face in the flowers, smiling softly as she breathed in their floral scent. "No. Is it a normal custom?"

"Quite normal—for us Brits, anyway. In the barbaric times of the fifteenth century, it was a tradition for wedding guests to tear off bits of the bridal dress, flowers, and even her hair, believing it would bring them good luck."

Eva's jaw dropped.

"As I said, *barbaric*. But some clever young bride decided she would rather not be stripped naked on the way to her wedding feast, and instead chucked the bouquet at the mob and ran. Thus, a far better tradition was born."

"Oh my," Eva murmured.

Hetty, who had been close enough to overhear this conversation, chuckled. "Better not tell her about the threshold tradition. You'll frighten the poor girl."

At this, Eva glanced between them, curious and wary at the same time.

"Well, that's a Germanic tradition. In old Germanic tribes, the groom would hoist his bride over his shoulder and carry her into his hut. It supposedly made the bride look less than excited about her wedding night, which was supposed to signify her chastity."

Eva's grip on the bouquet loosened, and Hetty caught the flowers before they fell to the ground.

Hetty rolled her eyes with an amused smile. "I told you not to tell her."

"Everyone, please follow us to the dining room for the wedding feast." Damien escorted his new bride into the large, high-ceilinged dining room. Elizabeth could barely contain her joy at seeing the newly married couple together and happy. *As long as we can love, there's hope,* Elizabeth thought as she watched Damien kiss Penelope's cheek and pull her close to whisper something in her ear that made the new bride blush furiously. Elizabeth diverted her focus to give the couple their privacy.

The long dining room table had been turned into a buffet, with every kind of cake and sandwich available on its surface. Everyone began to pile food on their plates, and soon the table was full of occupied chairs.

For the next two hours, it was possible to forget they were at war and that the hardships were only just beginning. Elizabeth counted the boughs of holly and lost herself in eating cinnamon buns and Christmas pudding. Everyone gathered around the piano and sang carols and other songs that made them feel like the world was just beginning and not on the verge of ending.

They told old jokes, and Elizabeth shared stories from India that she'd forgotten.

Everything came back to her as though she'd stumbled upon a diary in her mind where she'd recorded each moment perfectly. She entertained the guests, as did others with tales of their own. For a brief time, everyone's memories were sharper, as though some ancient magic allowed them a clear view of their past days, past loves, and past holidays.

Elizabeth wished Alan and Isabelle were there to celebrate with her. She even missed her parents a little.

"Let's have a toast," Damien announced.

Glasses of sherry were raised all around, and Elizabeth's lips trembled as Damien spoke again. "To everyone we've loved and lost, and to all those we might lose. May we forever preserve this moment in time in our hearts. Be not afraid of joy or grief in the days to come, for what is joy but newly born love and what is grief but love surviving?"

Someone sniffed, and more than one person drew in a steadying breath.

"To all those we love," Damien finally said, his deep voice resonating across the dining room.

"To all those we love," everyone echoed. Elizabeth meant those words more than she had anything else in her life. The sherry in her glass tasted a thousand times sweeter on her tongue as she drank her toast.

HETTY CARRIED AN ARMFUL OF WRAPPED PRESENTS TOWARD the group of people gathered in the great hall that evening. The tall Christmas tree stretched up to the ceiling of the second story of the manor house. Glittering baubles and shiny tinsel winked beneath the glow of the electric lights.

Little Nella and Cliff clung to Penelope and eyed the staggering pile of presents beneath the tree with shock and longing. Hetty's chest tightened at the thought that the little ones might not have had anything like this in their past. They likely had no idea that the bounty beneath the tree contained several presents with their names on them.

Marcus was also watching the tree, his longing only slightly less obvious than the younger children. He would be quite surprised to learn he had presents underneath the tree too. Hetty set down her armful of gifts by the others and retreated to where Elizabeth stood watching the guests mingle by the fireplace.

The wildness Hetty had felt that day on the River Hamble was back. That need to be free was as strong as ever, yet this place and these people were answering the call.

The hint of woodsmoke from the fire in the grand marble fireplace teased her nose. A thin, sweet winter wind crept into the hall, mixing the floral scents of the wedding flowers with the cooking spices from the kitchens below. These swirling scents and others wrapped around Hetty, becoming a siren's call to her wild heart. She breathed in deep and was satisfied. She was free here, in this moment. Free as she could be. Yet like any creature born to fly, she sensed a closing cage. How many days like this were left to her? To any of them?

Penelope herded the two little children toward the tree and announced they would be opening gifts. Little Nella leaned back to take in the full sight of the glittering, towering tree. Her eyes grew wide as Penelope sat on the floor beside her and handed her a present. Nella peeled away the wrapping paper with clumsy fingers before revealing a Shirley Temple doll.

"Mine?" Nella asked in a soft voice that made Hetty think of a delicate songbird.

"Yours, my darling," Penelope assured the child.

Nella closed her eyes tight and squeezed the doll fiercely against her chest before barreling into Penelope's arms and cuddling in her lap. Penelope kissed the girl's short, lamblike curls and shared a warm look with Damien.

Hetty missed nothing between the couple. Penelope and Damien were taking to their ready-made family so well, but what would happen when they had to send the children back to their mother after the war ended?

"Cliff, come here." Damien pulled a large object from behind the tree and set it down before the boy. The box was larger than Cliff was tall. "Go ahead, lad, unwrap it," he encouraged.

Cliff, eyes round as saucers, tore the wrapping paper away and gasped. A Chrysler pedal car, black and shiny, was ready to be driven. Damien picked Cliff up and set him down in the driver's seat, showing him how to pedal.

"Now, only one rule—no running anyone over in the halls." He winked at Cliff, and the boy laughed.

Marcus watched the younger children, his face falling slightly.

"Eva," Hetty whispered. "I think it's time for Marcus's gift."

Eva, her smile lighting up her face, nodded and rushed from the room to retrieve it.

"Marcus," Hetty said, "I believe it's your turn."

"Mine?" The boy stared at the tree expectantly, but Hetty grasped his shoulders and gently turned him toward the hall, where Eva emerged. She wheeled out a shiny new bicycle, and Marcus gasped. His eyes shot between Hetty and Eva.

"A bicycle?"

"It's from your sister, Lizzie, and me. We want you to have an easy way to get around the city when you run errands." The look of pure joy on his face was one of those things that etched itself forever into Hetty's memory.

"There's no snow on the gravel road outside if you wish to give it a try," Damien said.

Marcus gripped the handlebars and rushed outside with his prize. With the children having been seen to, the adults were left to open their presents. Hetty and Elizabeth had pooled their money to buy Eva a fancy dress and shoes, along with new stockings for her to wear when they went out to nightclubs.

"You didn't need to do this," Eva said as she held the blue-and-silver dress against her body, admiring the way the sequins sparkled. Hetty knew every shilling spent had been worth it. "I wish our parents were here," Eva added in a low voice so that the other guests didn't overhear.

"I know . . . ," Elizabeth said. "Is there no way of contacting them?"

"No. I sent letters two weeks ago, but none have been answered. I sent them to our neighbor as well, but if the Germans have taken Warsaw . . ." She didn't finish. The possibility was not one anyone wished to say aloud, in fear that the universe was listening.

"Let's enjoy Christmas," Eva said, trying to bury her own worries. "It is our first, after all, and I am most anxious to learn more about how the English celebrate it."

Eva and Marcus had celebrated Hanukkah earlier that month. Elizabeth and Hetty had thoroughly enjoyed celebrating with them and had managed to acquire a spare menorah from a wonderful Jewish family who lived not too far from the Marriage Bureau's offices. Now Eva and Marcus were embracing Christmas wholeheartedly.

"Yes, let's enjoy the holiday. We have so much work to do when we get back," Elizabeth announced.

Hetty nodded, but her thoughts were miles away, wondering about Charles and whether he had enlisted.

Damned brave fool . . .

She would have to find a way to stop him. It was selfish, of course, but she would not let go of him, not even for the sake of England.

⚜

TWO DAYS LATER, HETTY KNOCKED ON HER FATHER'S STUDY door and held her breath so long her lungs burned.

"Enter," her father called out. She turned the knob and clicked the door open enough to peer inside.

He was seated at his desk, a paper spread out in front of him. He looked perfectly content there in the winter sunlight, enjoying a private moment, and Hetty knew that she was going to devastate him with her request, but she had to do it.

"Father." She slipped into the room, closed the door behind her, and leaned back against it.

"Father? Oh dear, what have I done now for such seriousness?" he teased. She tried to smile, but her stomach turned.

Her father stood, his mustache twitching as his smile faded. "Hetty, what's wrong?"

"Nothing," she assured him. "I must speak with you about Charles Humphrey."

"Lord Lonsdale's son? How is the boy? I haven't seen him since we've been back in England."

"He is well, Father. You know he's the official solicitor for the Marriage Bureau now."

"He is?" Her father's warm chuckle almost melted the icy layer of fear around her heart.

"Yes, he's been wonderful. So wonderful, in fact, that we cannot do without him."

She could not do without him, not anymore. Somehow in the last year, the man had crawled beneath her skin and burrowed into her heart where she'd never be able to get him out.

"Do without him?"

She nodded and stepped closer to her father's desk. "Charles told me right before Christmas that he plans to enlist in the army."

"He is, is he?"

Hetty clasped her hands together, her fingers twisting tight as she fought to control her pain and fear.

"What are you telling me? Do you want him assigned to a commander I know who will watch out for him?"

"No . . ." The word was a bare whisper, but he heard her. She drew air into her lungs and spoke again. "I want you to stop him. Don't let him qualify for service. Keep him here—keep him *safe*."

The look on her father's face would haunt Hetty for the rest of her life. It was a look of hurt and deepest betrayal. She knew he had every right to feel this way. She was asking him to do something no soldier would ever do. He would think it cowardly not to fight and cowardly for her to ask him to stop someone from fighting who clearly wished to.

"Everyone must answer the call of duty. If he wishes to enlist, then you must let him. We need every man fighting for our home." He turned away from her, his eyes going distant as he looked out on the sprawling back gardens. "You were a child, a mere infant, when the last war started. I left your mother to fight on the western front."

Hetty's gaze strayed to the nearest bookshelf, where a dark-blue box lay open, its red velvet interior faded from two decades of sunlight on it. A small Victoria Cross medal lay inside. That bit of metal was the only physical evidence of her father's valiant service in the Battle of Arras in France. The British had lost 160,000 good men, and 120,000 Germans had been killed. Most men who were awarded that medal didn't live to receive it.

As a child, she had loved to see the cross pinned on her father's uniform on those rare occasions when he wore full military dress. He had told her that the cross was rumored to be made from the metal of two Russian cannons captured by the British during the Crimean War in the mid-1800s.

As she'd grown older, that cross had changed in her eyes. It became an outward manifestation of Britain's grief, as though the tears of every wife and mother who'd lost someone had been turned into metal and forged in a blacksmith's fire until they made those dark crosses.

Now, as she stared at the cross, she could hear the cries of men, feel the cold chill of death and the bite of the razor wire lining the trenches. The fog of war surrounded that tiny adornment, and it made her even more determined to save Charles.

"SOLDIERS ARE CITIZENS OF DEATH'S GREY LAND,
    Drawing no dividend from time's tomorrows.
    In the great hour of destiny they stand,
    Each with his feuds, and jealousies, and sorrows."

. . .

HETTY QUOTED AN OLD POEM FROM THE GREAT WAR. IT WAS one her father used to recite when he'd had too much whiskey on long winter nights and old memories and the ghosts closed in around him.

Her father turned, eyes sharp with pain. "Then you know how it ends." He cleared his throat and, in a quiet voice, finished it for her.

"SOLDIERS ARE SWORN TO ACTION; THEY MUST WIN
  Some flowing, fatal climax with their lives.
  Soldiers are dreamers; when the guns begin
  They think of firelit homes, clean beds and wives."

"ALL I'M ASKING IS FOR YOU TO GIVE CHARLES HIS DREAMS OF tomorrows. *Please . . .*"

For a long moment, her father didn't move. He was so still that she felt his stillness to the deepest part of herself.

"Why him? You have many gentlemen friends you've grown up with. Why this man?"

Man . . . no longer boy.

How things change so quickly, she thought.

"Hetty, you can't ask me this and not tell me why."

"Because I'm in love with him. And if I lost him . . ." The admission to her weakness, to be in love with Charles, threatened to destroy her. She, who needed no man to survive, could not afford to lose him.

Her father's hard gaze softened slightly. "You've known him almost your entire life. What's changed?"

She met her father's gaze unflinchingly. *"Everything.* I've never asked you for anything. But now, now I am. I would take his place in the trenches if they would let me."

Her father crossed the space between them, grasping her shoulders as he gazed at her with fierce pride.

"I know you would, my girl. I know you would be brave and strong, and you'd be the last to hold the line."

Pain tightened her throat. He understood. He knew that she would have taken Charles's place in this fight, but destiny had given her the life of a woman. She could not take any man's place in this war, no matter how brave or strong she was.

"Someday, they may let women fight alongside us . . . and someday, men will see women like you for what you are. Damned strong and fierce," her father murmured proudly.

"But until then, I'm *helpless* to protect him."

They stared at each other a moment longer before her father spoke. "If, and I mean *if*, I can keep him safe in London, you had better bloody well marry him and give me a dozen grandchildren."

Most of the tension that had been coiled dangerously tight inside Hetty ebbed away like a retreating tide.

"I thought only Mother wanted grandchildren."

Her father gave her a bittersweet smile. "All parents long for them. It's the way we recapture the magic of our own children as little ones."

Hetty lowered her head, her mind buzzing with the relief and warmth at the thought of a child she might share with Charles. She'd never imagined herself as the motherly type, but now she felt a desperate need to combine her life with Charles's to create a new one.

"*Marry* him," her father reminded, and kissed her forehead before he turned away.

Hetty left him alone and stood in the hall, trembling with relief. If anyone could stop Charles from leaving for France, it would be her father. He could do anything. He'd already helped save England once. All he needed to do now was save one man.

CHAPTER 15

L *ate January 1940*

As it turned out, Major Taylor's suggestion continued to be a huge success. Every paper continued to feature the Marriage Bureau again and again, but this time dozens of couples came forward, happy to report weddings or pending nuptials in the newspaper articles.

It was a positive boost for Londoners since food rationing had been announced. Elizabeth had been floating on clouds since Christmas and was determined not to let the new restrictions affect her mood.

Eva read the latest rationing announcements in the paper. "Four ounces of bacon and butter per person per week . . ."

The three of them were sitting in the back office enjoying a quiet moment and a spot of tea before their appointments began for the day. Elizabeth had been daydreaming.

"Only four? It's not nearly enough." She sighed dramatically and spread more butter on her sliced toast.

"Twelve ounces of sugar," Eva continued.

"And there goes St. Valentine's Day," Elizabeth groaned. "No more chocolate."

Eva and Hetty laughed at her, but she couldn't help but mourn the loss of her favorite dessert. "What? I have a sweet tooth. To think of no chocolate, especially on Valentine's Day, seems particularly cruel."

"Cruel indeed," Hetty agreed.

"Does it say anything else?" Elizabeth asked, trying to ignore the prickle of dread at the thought of any more restrictions.

"Er . . ." Eva continued to read. "It says something about digging for victory? What is that?"

"It's a campaign to encourage us to grow our own vegetables," Hetty explained. "I suppose we ought to start planting tomatoes on the roof."

"Too bad we can't plant cacao trees," Elizabeth muttered.

The phone rang in the outer office, and Eva rushed to answer it. Elizabeth and Hetty overheard the conversation as they finished their toast and tea.

"This is the Marriage Bureau. How may we assist you? Yes, I'm sure we can find someone suitable for you. Let me take down your information . . . What's that? You want someone who enjoys fellatio?"

Elizabeth, who was in the middle of sipping her tea, choked on it and coughed as she hastily set her cup down, causing tea to splash onto the desk.

"Oh, of course," Eva replied eagerly. "We have several people who enjoy stamp collecting. I'm sure we can find someone . . . Hello? Hello?"

Elizabeth wiped the tea off her desk and ignored Hetty's chortle as they rushed into the room. Eva was putting the phone down on its cradle with a disappointed look on her face.

"He ended the call. I'm so sorry I lost him."

"No, it's quite all right. We don't want any clients asking about that particular *hobby* he mentioned."

Eva's brows drew together in confusion. "Stamp collecting?"

Hetty leaned down and whispered in the poor girl's ear explaining that philately was the hobby of collecting stamps where as fellatio was something entirely different. Eva's face was as red as the tomatoes Elizabeth had no intention of planting on the roof.

Eva covered her cheeks and shook her head. "Oh my . . ."

"Yes, we would prefer it if clients did not bring up such matters."

The bell downstairs rang, and Hetty went to answer it. When she returned, she was followed by a demure woman in her midforties.

"This is Miss Plumley, the new downstairs secretary."

Elizabeth greeted the woman. Hetty had mentioned she had conducted interviews last week, and Elizabeth trusted her to hire someone who would suit them.

"I'll settle her in, and then we can get to work," Hetty said, then escorted the other woman downstairs.

"It will be nice to have extra help," Eva admitted.

"Agreed," Elizabeth said as she retrieved the appointment book for the day to see what lay in store for them.

"Looks like we have a man named Mr. Warner. He should be here any moment."

Ten minutes later, a man entered the outer office for an interview. Elizabeth and Hetty took the task of interviewing the stout but well-dressed man together. He held out a hand in greeting. Elizabeth shook it, wincing at his hard grip.

"I am Mr. Warner." He handed over a registration form that had already been filled out in bold, scrawling handwriting.

"Where are you from, Mr. Warner?" Hetty asked, a little wariness in her tone. He had an American accent, but there was a hint of something to it . . . possibly German?

"I am from New York, but I was born in Germany. I live in America and run an insurance company now."

He fired off his information so rapidly that they could barely get it written down fast enough to keep up with him. He was fifty-six and had immigrated to the United States as a child and had spent most of his life there. In the early 1930s, he'd returned to the land of his birth for new business opportunities and then left again for America in 1938 to work on transferring his business to Europe.

"I left Berlin at the urging of my English friends. I love England and would very much like to work and live here, and naturally I want companionship . . . An English wife would be most perfect."

He moved deeper into the room, and his panther-like grace became unsettling. He swept his gaze over Elizabeth and Hetty before landing on Eva, who was staring at him from her chair, utterly still, like a rabbit frozen in the face of an approaching wolf.

Elizabeth had been around a few sinister and dangerous men in her many travels between India and back, and she recognized the danger that emanated from this man. As he spoke, answering the carefully worded questions Hetty posed to him, Elizabeth was memorizing every detail about him. The way he almost clicked his heels together in a militaristic fashion, the little lightning bolt silver pin on his lapel that winked in the light, and the ominous note of German in his mostly American accent. It was all too . . . *something* . . . Like she was watching an actor in a role.

"And where are you currently staying? We'll need an address to direct letters to from your potential matches."

"This is my address at the Hampden Club in Marylebone. I'm in the midst of purchasing a flat in Knightsbridge."

"Thank you," Hetty murmured as she copied down the address he'd shown her on a business card. "What sort of woman are you interested in?"

"An attractive woman. She must have a good income, a good figure, and a very good family. I will insist on this last part. She must also have been previously married."

"Naturally," Hetty agreed, as if what he was asking for made entirely too much sense. "You need an experienced wife to handle your complicated business life."

"Yes, exactly." Mr. Warner lips curving beneath his dark mustache. The look he gave her was dazzling, but Elizabeth knew even snakes could smile.

"We'll be in touch soon. Let me see you out." Hetty smiled back smoothly, but Elizabeth saw her friend's grin for what it was—a lioness baring her teeth in subtle warning.

The moment he and Hetty left the outer office, Elizabeth let go of the knot of tension inside her. It was only when Hetty returned that Eva seemed to resume breathing.

"*Hetty.*" The name was spoken so tremulously that both Elizabeth and Hetty turned abruptly toward Eva.

"What's the matter?" Elizabeth asked.

"That man . . . You must go to the police. He is a bad man."

"There was certainly something off about him." Hetty shuddered. "He was very *oily*."

"No, I mean very *bad*. The pin he was wearing, the little *S*." Eva drew the shape with her finger in the air. Elizabeth recognized it as a lightning bolt.

"What is it?" Elizabeth asked her.

"It's the Schutzstaffel—or rather, half of the design for it. I've seen two of the same symbols together before in the same style."

"What is the Schutzstaffel? I've never heard of it," Hetty said.

"The German soldiers who wear this symbol were in Warsaw before we left. They called my family a problem. One of these men came into my father's bookstore and said that someday there would be no more Jews left in Warsaw or all of Poland. That we would be dealt with. He was the reason our parents convinced me to take Marcus and leave. They belong to a group led by a man named Heinrich Himmler."

"Himmler!" Hetty hissed the name so harshly that it stung the air. She spun to face Elizabeth. "We have to go to Scotland Yard at once. I must call Charles. You stay here with Eva and Miss Plumley. When Marcus returns from his errands, keep him here. I do not want him out alone right now with men like Warner hanging about."

"Yes, of course," Elizabeth promised. They had allowed Marcus to handle more and more of their deliveries and errands now that he had his new bicycle. But whatever Hetty knew about this Himmler man, he was clearly dangerous.

Hetty put on her coat and grabbed her handbag from the side table by the door. "I'll be right back." She left in a flurry of skirts, leaving a cold wind to trickle up from the downstairs reception.

"It's not the first time we've had to go to the Yard," Elizabeth mused.

The police were tightening up investigations of foreign nationals due to the sudden influx of people into England. Their primary concern was false marriages, which meant the Marriage Bureau had to be very careful. But so far, all the individuals they'd provided information on to the Yard had been approved and cleared for marriage. Hetty, Elizabeth, and Eva had gone about arranging matches for them with a rather high success rate.

"This man is different than the others," Eva insisted. "He is dangerous."

"Then let's pray Hetty can convince Scotland Yard to look deeply into his background."

HETTY STOPPED OUTSIDE CHARLES'S OFFICE. PENNY, HIS secretary, beamed at Hetty and nodded at her to go on in. Penny had recently married a young banker named Raymond Baran and was quite happy with the Marriage Bureau's work.

Baran had been looking for a wife who had an occupation and didn't mind working. He liked having someone to come home to discuss work with and worried that a housewife wouldn't enjoy listening to him ramble on about banking. He wanted someone who also had a profession so they could share stories together. He was an excellent conversationalist when he'd interviewed with Hetty and Elizabeth, and they'd felt he'd make a good match for Charles's charming legal secretary, who was very clever.

"Go on in," Penny urged. "He's always happy to see you, Miss Byron."

Hetty pushed the door open and had a brief moment to enjoy the sight of Charles at work. His head was bent and his brow furrowed as he focused entirely on a case. Few people could fall so deeply into their work like that. It was something—rather, one of the many things—she admired about him.

"Knock, knock," she teased, saying the words aloud rather than actually knocking on his door.

His focus lifted from the papers in front of him and onto her. The expression that struck his features was one of sunny illumination.

"Hetty." He shoved his chair back and got to his feet. She hadn't seen him since Christmas. She'd been too afraid. But now, seeing him again, every feeling that he aroused in her sharpened. She'd hated that they hadn't seen each other since their quarrel before Christmas.

"It's so good to see you. Did you have a happy Christmas?" he asked.

"Yes, and you?"

He chuckled. "Yes, I went home. The old lion can still roar, but he was in a good mood." Charles adored his father, and Hetty knew he was only teasing.

"I hate to disturb you at work, but it's rather urgent."

"What is it?" He pulled her gently toward one of the chairs in front of his desk. She removed her gloves and fiddled with them in her lap.

"We've just had the most peculiar visitor at the office . . ." Hetty explained the mysterious German man and went into detail about Eva's violent reaction to the stranger's little silver pin on his suit.

Charles agreed with her proposed course of action when she explained her intentions. "We need to go to the Yard at once. I'll come with you."

"Do you mind?" She bit her lip, hating how much she'd come to rely on him, even in small ways.

"Not at all. In fact, let me make a call." He pulled his phone toward him on his desk and waited before he heard the dial tone. Then he contacted the operator.

"Scotland Yard, please. Inspector Talmudge Crumholt."

Charles looked up at her, his gray eyes full of storms.

"Crumholt? Yes, Charles Humphrey. Could you meet me at the following address?" He stated the address of the Marriage Bureau, then hung up.

"We aren't going to the Yard?"

"I want Crumholt to hear every detail from all of you in a private place. If your German fellow is a spy, there could be ears at Scotland Yard." He reached for his coat. "Let's return to the bureau."

They met Inspector Crumholt at the front door to the Marriage Bureau's reception. He was a tall man in his late forties with kind but serious brown eyes.

"Charles, it's good to see you, even under such circumstances." Crumholt then turned toward Hetty. "Miss."

"This is Miss Byron, my friend," said Charles.

Hetty shook the inspector's hand. "Let's go upstairs and speak with my friends."

"After you." He waited for her to show the way.

Hetty introduced the inspector to Elizabeth and Eva as well as Marcus, who had returned and was eating a sandwich while working in his schoolbooks in the corner.

"Now . . ." The inspector swept his gaze over the office,

taking everything in. "Tell me everything that each of you remembers about this man."

"I drew this." Elizabeth produced a sheet of paper with a detailed pencil sketch of their German man. Then each of the women shared what they remembered of the encounter, including the address he'd supplied them with where he was staying.

"I'll be in touch with anything I uncover once I do some digging." The inspector carefully placed the sketch in his coat pocket, along with his small notebook.

"I'll see the inspector out," Charles said. Hetty followed him down the stairs and caught Charles before he left.

"Lunch soon?" she asked, her heart hammering.

"Tomorrow?" he replied with that charming smile that made her knees wobble in a silly damsel sort of way that she hated, and also liked—not that she'd ever admit that to a single soul. She wanted to tell him how glad she was that he'd decided not to be angry with her about what she'd said. But she dared not.

"Tomorrow," she agreed, and rushed back up the stairs, grinning like a silly girl . . . a silly girl in love.

⚜

THREE DAYS LATER, INSPECTOR CRUMHOLT CALLED THE Marriage Bureau's office, and Hetty took the call.

"Inspector, how are you?" she asked.

"Well enough. I have news about your German man. Turns out he is a German count. We arrested him yesterday."

"Arrested?" Hetty echoed. Eva and Elizabeth both rushed over to hear the conversation better.

"Yes, apparently he has spent more time in Germany than he

led you to believe. He is also a member of . . . What did Miss Wolman call that thing?"

"The Schutzstaffel?" Hetty asked.

"Yes, the SS is what our ministry calls it. Bloody bad set of bastards, the SS. They are considered Hitler's personal body-guards, but the rumors . . . Well, I don't want to burden you with such grim tales as what we're hearing out of Europe. But Miss Wolman is right. He's a damned spy. The last thing we need is any woman who's well connected to marry him. It could put him in the middle of conversations happening in the drawing rooms of members of our government."

Hetty met Eva's gaze as she spoke.

"He won't be let out of prison?" she asked Crumholt.

"Not for a very long time. We found certain things hidden in his residence that give us enough to throw away the key to his cell for a long time. Thankfully for us, the man wasn't that talented at hiding his connections to the German government. Interestingly enough, the Germans aren't too pleased with him either. Perhaps that's why he came here. Thought he could marry an Englishwoman and gain intelligence to get back into the good graces of his own country. Either way, he's not going to cause any trouble now."

Tension bled out of Hetty. "I'm glad to hear that, Inspector."

"You did a fine job alerting us as you did. The boys at the Yard will be watching for more names from you in the future. You can always call me on my private line at this number."

He gave her the number, and they said their goodbyes. When she hung up the phone, Elizabeth, Eva, and Marcus were watching her.

"Well?" Elizabeth prodded.

"He was a spy. They've arrested him, and he won't be let out anytime soon."

"A spy . . ." Elizabeth's eyes were wide. "We caught a spy? All because he wanted to marry an Englishwoman." The fact of that took a minute to sink in for all of them.

"We had better watch out for men like him, possibly women too. We must be on guard for anyone who comes to us with a mercenary eye toward marriage."

Elizabeth sighed. "Here I was thinking the worst clients we'd face would be merciless fortune hunters. But spies? Good Lord."

Good Lord indeed, Hetty thought. Matchmaking now had a more official part of the true war effort. Perhaps they would have to update their sign outside. *The Marriage Bureau: Matchmakers and Spy Catchers.*

CHAPTER 16

A*pril 1940*

THE SPRING RAIN SHOULD HAVE MADE ELIZABETH SMILE. IT misted and coated every bit of soil in the gardens and the fresh flower boxes. She'd even glimpsed a row of fine crocuses that had bloomed on the Marriage Bureau's rooftop in the half dozen pots that Marcus had been charged with tending to. Snowdrops had grown lazily on the patches of grass along the pavement outside the bureau's headquarters, as though spring was desperately trying to show it was here and that the bitter winter had finally ended.

But the appearance of early flowers wasn't enough to warm Elizabeth's heart. Today she felt the cold down to her very bones.

She stood on a train station platform with Hetty and Charles, far from everything beautiful and flowering in the world that made her feel hopeful. Instead, she was trapped in a prism of metal and glass, inhaling the stale scents of the train station.

They had come to see Major Taylor off. He had been home for a brief period of time to see his wife and his other friends in London. Sarah had sent a note asking if Elizabeth and Hetty wouldn't mind coming to see them off at the station. She said she felt the bureau was good luck and didn't want to tempt fate by not having them there.

"Where are you bound, Major?" Charles asked as a train pulled into the station.

"Some little coastal town. Dunkirk, I believe. We need reinforcements for the British Expeditionary Forces. Our fellows are outmanned now that Germany's invaded Denmark and Norway, and they're pushing toward the coast. We've got to beat back the panzer divisions before they pulverize every village in France."

"Major, could you make an inquiry for me?" Charles asked. "I put in my application for military service just after Christmas, but I haven't heard back yet."

Hetty stiffened the slightest bit as Charles spoke, and Elizabeth shot a glance between her and Charles.

The major nodded. "I'll certainly ask around. We could do with a man like you."

Sarah glanced at the train and its departing passengers. When the major noticed the flood of people emptying the newly arrived train, he sighed.

"Well, that's me, isn't it?"

"Yes, I believe so," Sarah replied in a faint voice, her skin pale as she looked between him and the train. All around them, soldiers, sailors, and airmen were going off leave and returning to the fight in France. Friends and family gathered around them, wishing them a safe journey.

"You'll be careful?" Sarah placed a hand on her abdomen in a protective way. Elizabeth wondered how far along in her pregnancy the quiet, dove-eyed beauty was. Sarah looked so terribly young and frail as she fixed a happy expression on her face for her husband.

"I always am, my darling. I'll be back so soon that you won't have time to miss me," the major promised.

Elizabeth looked away as the couple shared a kiss and a tight embrace.

The light rain steamed off the train station roof, drowning any light with mist and smoke, making it feel like a graveyard. Everyone around Elizabeth seemed colorless and more like ghosts than flesh and blood. The thought sent a queer feeling through her that left her on edge. She had the sudden dreadful thought that if she closed her eyes, the souls lost in the war would crawl up from the train tracks, haunting her with the last sight they beheld before death.

She'd had more than one nightmare about those poor young men who'd perished since the sea battles had begun a few weeks ago. She dreamt of cold green water closing over her head, swallowing her in blackness. The feel of little rescue boats smacked about by the hard winds, men praying for calm seas but knowing their fate would likely be to drown in a cold numbness. Her fears for Alan had magnified, and she was having to let other men she cared about leave for France. Was she now to have nightmares of these men, these fresh-faced boys, brought down by enemy fire on a French coastal town, their last moments brutal, terrifying, and brief?

"Lizzie? Are you all right?" Hetty murmured. "You look ill."

I am ill, Elizabeth thought.

"Bit of bad tea this morning," she said instead.

The major hugged Hetty, then Elizabeth, before shaking Charles's hand. Then he shouldered his gear bag and walked the remaining steps to his train with Sarah at his side.

"I have a terrible feeling about this," Hetty whispered.

"So do I," Elizabeth confessed. "So do I."

Near them, a single young man in an army uniform watched the goodbyes of others around him with a forlorn expression. He couldn't have been more than twenty, barely a year or so older than her brother, Alan.

Driven by some need to care for the young soldier, Elizabeth walked toward him. He blushed a little when he noticed her heading in his direction.

"Excuse me, but are you all alone?" she asked.

"Yes," the young man admitted. "My parents are in Yorkshire. They couldn't follow me to London to see me off."

"I'm Elizabeth." She held out her hand, and he shook it.

"Wyatt Harding."

"Well, Mr. Harding, you will be careful over there, won't you? You will come back to us safe and sound." She spoke to him like any good mother hen would to a chick. At this, his lips twitched in a ghost of a smile, and he nodded respectfully.

"I will, ma'am."

She retrieved one of the bureau's business cards and held it out to him. "Write to me here."

"The Marriage Bureau?" he said with amusement.

"We'll find you a nice girl when you come home. So your duty is to return to London safe and sound."

He tucked the card into a pocket of his uniform. "You promise to find me a nice girl?"

"I promise." On impulse, she hugged the young man and kissed his cheek. "Now off you go. Ask for Major Taylor on the train. He'll look out for you."

"Major Taylor, I'll remember that," the soldier said. "Thank you, ma'am."

Wyatt headed for the train, his head held the slightest bit higher.

When Elizabeth turned back, she saw Charles and Hetty had been watching her the whole while.

"That was a kind thing you did," Hetty said.

Only then did Elizabeth let her resolve and strength go so she could crumble. Hetty put an arm around her shoulders. "There, there, my dear, chin up. The rest of those darling boys are watching."

Elizabeth lifted her head, sniffled, and tried to smile at a few of the concerned young soldiers nearby. They nodded at her in silent greeting as she passed by.

"I just keep thinking of Alan. What if he never has *anyone* to say goodbye to and tell him he'd better come home? Oh, I can't bear to think of anyone leaving to fight and facing that last moment at a train station alone. They all need to know that someone is waiting for them. They—"

Her words stuttered to a stop as the pain in her chest became too much to bear. She wiped furiously at the tears spilling onto her cheeks instead of speaking. There was nothing worse than feeling helpless and having one's emotions on display without being able to control them.

"Come on, Lizzie, dry your eyes," Hetty said, but her voice was also rough with emotion. "Do stop that or we'll all start crying too. We need to be strong for Sarah."

When Sarah returned to them, they all faced the train, seeing

Major Taylor's face in the window. Smoke and mist rose up from the train as it moved out of the station, obscuring the faces of the servicemen. A terrible stillness overcame Elizabeth.

When she was a child and passed by an old churchyard, she would try to whistle to disrupt that eerie, deathlike stillness. She felt that same stillness now. The train whistle shrilled into that void of sound, and the wheels screeched as the train backed up, carrying the brave men of England away with it to the coast.

They parted ways with Sarah at the edge of the station, and then Elizabeth and Hetty bid Charles goodbye not long after. Once it was just the two friends, Elizabeth gave voice to something that had stuck in her mind.

"Hetty, why hasn't Charles heard back on his enlistment? Surely they would want him to serve, wouldn't they?"

Hetty bit her lip and glanced away, her face draining of color.

"What is it? You know you can tell me anything." They walked back down the street toward the bureau's office.

"It's . . . Oh Lord, you'll think me the worst sort of person, Lizzie." Hetty tried to shy away from the subject.

"I would never," Elizabeth promised.

They walked another minute in silence before Hetty halted abruptly.

"I spoke to my father. I asked him to keep Charles from being accepted into service."

Elizabeth gasped.

Hetty continued, her voice weak. "Whatever he did, it must be working."

Elizabeth pitched her voice low. "If Charles finds out you meddled, he will be *furious*, Hetty."

"I know . . ." Hetty sighed miserably. "I'll have to tell him soon. Better he hear from me than find out some other way."

They finished the walk back to the bureau. As they reached the top of the steps, Elizabeth caught Hetty's arm.

"I don't blame you for keeping Charles here. I wish I could keep every one of those men home. This war . . . it isn't a fight we should even have to fight. But if we don't, the evil that's crossing the Continent will continue to spread." England had fought this battle once before and won, but at such a great and terrible cost. Now they were here, fighting all over again. But this time it felt different, more desperate than before.

"I know," Hetty whispered. "If you don't stand up to bullies when they hurt others, there will be no one left to stand up for you when the bully turns your way. Christ, it reminds me of finishing school. Those girls were vipers. If we had any good sense, we would send them after the Germans. Just suit them up and let them parachute down into Berlin. The Germans would be crying before lunch, and the war would be over."

Elizabeth laughed. "I didn't know you went to finishing school, Hetty."

Her friend shuddered dramatically. "My grandmother insisted. It's not something I enjoyed. It was worse than the Dark Ages."

"And here I was thinking that being a farm girl was rather unpleasant." Elizabeth laughed.

Hetty sighed in exaggeration. "I would *much* rather muck stalls and chase chickens about any day before going back to that den of jackals."

With their moods boosted a little by their humor, they walked up the stairs to the office and found Eva on the phone with someone. She glanced up and waved them over.

"Here they are now. Let me see if they can speak with you." She covered the phone's receiver. "It's a young woman who wants to come to see you in half an hour about a man she's interested in."

"She already knows the man she wants?" Hetty asked. "What the devil does she need us for?"

Eva waited for Hetty to decide what the potential client should be told.

"Well, have her drop by, and we'll see what she wants us to do," Hetty said.

"Yes, have her come see us." Elizabeth needed a good match to get her mind off the memories of the misty train station goodbyes.

Eva gave the woman instructions and hung up. "How were the major and Sarah?" she asked while Hetty hung up their coats.

"Well enough, given the circumstances. Sarah is with child, I think," Hetty said.

"I had the same thought," Elizabeth added. "Can you imagine, having to watch your husband leave while your family is only beginning? It must be terribly frightening." Her solemn words left them all rather subdued, and it was only the thought of their new client arriving that rallied Elizabeth's spirits.

The young woman who walked in was stunning, with bright-red hair and a genuine, ready smile. She was slender, and her purple-and-cream frock looked expensive. Her natural radiance brightened the dreary day.

"Hello. I'm the rather mad woman who called on the phone." She laughed softly, her Scottish accent lending her an extra air of charm. She held out a hand to Hetty, who was nearest to her.

"Yes, do come and sit, Miss—"

"Fiona Storey."

"I'm Hetty, that's Eva, and this is Elizabeth."

Fiona nodded at them in greeting. "Well, I read a wee article in the paper, and I thought you might be able to help me." She paused. "I wish to meet . . . to see if . . . Well, I wish to see if a man might take a liking to me."

"We provide introductions to men currently registered with our bureau." Elizabeth was already stringing together names of men in her mind who would fall madly in love with this woman. "We have plenty of gentlemen we could introduce you to."

"Oh no, I don't need anyone else."

"But that's what we do," Hetty said slowly. "We make matches."

"That's just it. I have someone in mind already, but, well . . . we don't actually know each other."

"I'm afraid we're not following," Eva said.

Fiona blushed. "There is a man who lives three doors down from me on the same road. He is simply the *most* handsome man I've ever seen. He lives alone, a bachelor, but he's not old, and he seems so delightfully pleasant to everyone he meets on the street."

She gushed about this mystery man, and her interest in him was infectious. Elizabeth imagined Fiona peeping at him from behind her curtains each day as he walked by and swooning as he passed.

"We have lived near each other for three years. I've seen him play polo—there's a field near where we live. I can even see his garden wall from my backyard and see the tops of his trees just over the top of the wall. He grows the most lovely apples that . . ." Her voice trailed off, as she was clearly lost in her memory. "Yes, sorry. Well, I always thought we would meet, that we would have a mutual acquaintance, but no one I know seems to know him even after three years."

"You've never passed him on the street?" Elizabeth asked.

"Yes, I have, but I tend to look away, only because I'm afraid he'll see how badly I wish to know him. It's positively ridiculous, I know."

"Not that ridiculous," Hetty said. "You aren't the first person to be shy to talk to people."

Elizabeth ran through meeting scenarios in her head as options. "Fiona, do you have a dog you could walk? One who could tangle its leash about the man's legs or something? You could fall into each other, and well . . . off you go, then."

"No," Fiona shook her head. "No dog. I have a plump old cat named Neville, but all he does is watch the pigeons grow fatter in the tree out front of my window. Well, what do you think, ladies? Is it a lost cause, or is there any way you could arrange for us to meet?" Her eyes were so bright with hope that Elizabeth had to come up with something.

"What's this man's name? Perhaps he has registered with us and we can make a formal introduction?"

"His name is Robert McKinnon."

"Eva, would you check the registry for Mr. McKinnon?" Hetty asked.

"Yes, of course." Eva retrieved the large leather-bound ledger and set it down on the interview desk. She flipped through the pages, and then her shoulders slumped. "He's not listed."

"Drat," Elizabeth sighed. "If he's not on the books, I'm not sure what we can do."

Eva sat up in her chair. "Wait. I might have an idea."

Fiona's face brightened with hope. "Please, do anything you can."

Fiona signed her contract with the Marriage Bureau and paid her registration fee with a hopeful shine in her eyes. Eva saw

Fiona out, and then she came back. Elizabeth and Hetty were waiting for her.

"What's this plan?" Elizabeth asked.

Eva retrieved a telephone book from her desk and carefully thumbed through the pages until she found Robert McKinnon's phone number.

"One of you should call him in this evening, and here's what you should say . . ."

❧

ELIZABETH DIALED MR. MCKINNON'S PHONE NUMBER AND tried to calm her rapidly beating heart. *This is no different from any other interview,* she tried to remind herself. The line connected, and a deep voice answered.

"Is this Mr. Robert McKinnon?"

"This is McKinnon," the man replied.

"This is Miss Elizabeth Mowbray. I am one of the owners of the Marriage Bureau. I'm so sorry I missed your previous call when you invited me to lunch tomorrow. I just wanted to let you know I'd be so pleased to meet you. Could we make it noon rather than eleven thirty?"

Hetty and Eva watched her, both of them leaning closer to try to overhear what was being said.

"The *what* bureau? I'm sorry, there must be a mistake. I don't —" He sounded amused instead of irritated, so Elizabeth continued.

"Oh goodness, I received a message from you . . . Perhaps it was a joke? Could one of your friends have called and left your information for me?" She feigned surprise at the realization. "I must admit, this is terribly embarrassing."

His laugh was warm and infectious, and it was easy to imagine how Fiona would have fallen for this man if his face matched his voice and manner.

"Perhaps we ought to meet anyway? Then we could solve this little mystery?" he suggested.

"If you would like to, I would be glad to meet."

"Would today work for you? I'm actually free in an hour, if dinner this evening suits you."

Elizabeth checked the clock on the wall. "Yes, I believe it does."

"Perfect." He provided the name of a coffeehouse close to Bond Street, and then Elizabeth hung up.

"Well?" Eva asked. "Did it work?"

Elizabeth grinned. "We're meeting for dinner tonight."

"Good, now the trick will be convincing him to sign on as a client for the Marriage Bureau," Hetty reminded her.

"Right."

An hour later, Elizabeth stepped into the coffeehouse, which also served sandwiches. She searched the crowd until she saw a tall, dashing man checking his watch, not in an important way, but as though he was focused on the passage of time and wanting something to begin. He was an attractive fellow, with dark eyes and an easy smile. He glanced up when he saw her and the small rose tucked in the breast pocket of her suit coat. It was the signal that she was from the Marriage Bureau.

He strode toward her. "Miss Mowbray?"

"Mr. McKinnon?"

"Wonderful to meet you. Thank you for coming tonight. Shall we?" He waved a waiter down, as they claimed a nearby table, where they ordered sandwiches and coffee.

"So, tell me, what is this Marriage Bureau of yours, exactly? I admit, after your telephone call I'm very intrigued."

"We arrange introductions between people based on a set of detailed criteria to match them." She went into an explanation about their matching process and provided him with some of their success stories.

"So it must've been one of my friends who called you. I wonder which one?" Robert mused. His good-natured response to the situation made Elizabeth relax and play more into the clever plot Eva had constructed to bring Robert into the bureau.

"I'm afraid I haven't a clue. Are you single?"

He chuckled. "Not by choice, I assure you, but I've been rather busy the last few years. I work at the ministry of Defense. It hasn't left me much time to meet anyone."

Elizabeth tried to stay calm and not seem too eager.

"*Well*, if you might be interested, we would be happy to put you into our books. It's rather an easy process. You need not be flooded with dozens of women—you may send a few letters off and see what happens. We'll only match you with some select women who truly fit your needs." She pulled an interview sheet out of her handbag. "We can do your interview here, so you wouldn't have to worry about stopping by the office for that part of the process. We'll mail you a questionnaire and fee information in a day or two."

Robert contemplated this. "All right . . . Why not? You really do this daily? Make matches like this?"

"Yes, we certainly do. We get hundreds of letters a week, and we have appointments and phone calls every day."

"That's simply incredible," he said with a laugh. "Well, let's put me down on your books. I have to see how this match-making works up close."

As they ate their dinner, Elizabeth ran Robert through the usual questions and was quite secretly pleased that he seemed like a good match for Fiona. She also explained how they worked with interviews, questionnaires, and the standard registration fees and after-marriage fees.

"Offhand, I would say there are several wonderful women we can introduce you to. There is a most darling woman named Fiona I think you'd do well with. I'll send you her information tomorrow, if she sounds interesting to you. We'll connect you both via written correspondence, and then you can meet her in person when you're ready."

"Excellent. I can drop by your office and fill out my paperwork and pay my fee."

Elizabeth thanked him. After dinner, she went straight home and dialed Fiona's number.

"Fiona? It's Elizabeth Mowbray." She played with a pen and doodled on a pad of paper while she talked.

"Miss Mowbray, how are you?"

"Good, I have excellent news for you. I've just had dinner with Mr. McKinnon and convinced him to register at the bureau. I will be officially matching you tomorrow. If you want, you can go ahead and write him your first letter."

"Thank you so much. This is wonderful," Fiona said in her charming Scottish accent, and then she laughed. "Oh Lord, I'm so terribly nervous."

"Don't be. He's quite open to the idea of being matched. Just be yourself."

"Yes, myself," Fiona echoed with resolve. "Thank you, Miss Mowbray."

Elizabeth set the phone in the cradle, smiling.

"What are you up to now, Lizzie?" Isabelle asked.

"Our new client asked us to find a way to match her with a man she likes who lives three doors away from her. It's rather funny they've never officially met, isn't it?"

"Indeed. I wonder if they will end up working out together?"

"I honestly think they will."

"Well, you do have an instinct for such things. Come on, dinner's ready," Isabelle said. "We're having cabbage soup tonight. I added a bit of shredded carrots and leeks from the garden. Our second course is a toast with scrambled eggs and diced rabbit leg."

"Rabbit? Where on earth did you find a rabbit?" She'd never been one for game meat, but chicken and beef were getting harder and harder to come by.

"Mr. Fleming down the street caught one this morning in a snare. It was eating his lettuce. I told him we'd take the meat if he didn't want it," Isabelle said. "We ought to practice economizing when we can. The rations have tightened up what the butchers have available to sell to us."

"Perhaps we ought to set up a few traps in our garden? I could have Mr. Fleming show me how to set snares," Elizabeth said. She'd always been rather handy at making things and wouldn't mind learning to catch rabbits.

Isabelle nodded. "Good idea. If you catch them, I'll cook them."

That night, they ate and talked of all the men they knew who had left for Europe in the last few months.

Isabelle got up and went over to the stove. "Your father said one of the boys who lived near you enlisted and shipped out last month."

Panic prickled beneath her skin as she thought of all the nice young boys she'd grown up with. "Who was it?"

"Louis Sbardella." Isabelle ladled more soup in her bowl before returning to the table.

Elizabeth's heart sank. "Louis? But he's only nineteen . . ."

The Sbardellas were local dairy farmers in Elizabeth's tiny village outside Cambridge. She had grown up exploring the creeks and woods with Alan and Louis as children. He was a quiet young man with kind eyes. While most little boys collected tacks to put on the chairs of older sisters, he was always nursing some sick animal he'd found back to health. He was a healer, a *gentle* soul.

Now that kind boy would be asked to kill and possibly be killed. It was against everything that young man was. To think of him trapped in a place ruled by such senseless cruelty . . .

Something crumbled inside Elizabeth. She imagined the worst that lay ahead for all those young boys. "Poor Louis . . ."

Isabelle cleared her throat. "One of the designers in my department, Gerald Schaefer, announced he's leaving tomorrow for France. He was barely able to focus on work. I saw him sitting at his station, staring at the same page designs for more than half an hour. It seemed like his mind was miles away." Isabelle swallowed hard. "It makes me think of the last time, of all those boys who set off so light of heart, so determined to do their duty . . . and didn't come back."

Elizabeth's throat was so tight that she wanted to scream, to do anything to release the fear and pain that she couldn't save any of those boys. They had been here before. They knew how this ended. With *millions* dead.

"Do you remember that poem? The one about the boys?" Isabelle asked, her gaze distant. "I always forget how it goes."

Elizabeth knew that poem—so many of them did.

· · ·

"*They shall not grow old, as we are that left grow old:*
  Age shall not weary them, nor the years condemn.
  At the going down of the sun and in the morning
  We will remember them."

Elizabeth couldn't remember the middle of the poem, but the last part was etched in her memory.

"*As the stars that shall be bright when we are dust,*
  Moving in marches upon the heavenly plain;
  As the stars that are starry in the time of our darkness,
  To the end, to the end, they remain."

"Do you suppose that's true?" Isabelle asked. "That the stars will still be shining when this is all over? I know it's silly to ask such a thing, but I feel so maudlin of late."

It frightened Elizabeth to see her strong, capable aunt like this. Isabelle was afraid of nothing, or so it had seemed. Even if the worst happened, there would have to be someone left to see the stars that did not fall from the sky.

"I think the stars will still be here." Elizabeth turned her gaze toward the blacked-out windows. "Even if we won't see them for a while."

CHAPTER 17

M *ay 1940*

"Do you think he ate a heavy lunch?" Eva nodded at the middle-aged man fast asleep on the settee in the interview room of the Marriage Bureau's office.

"That or he had a bit too much brandy at his club," Hetty whispered back.

Despite the ever-growing sense that something bad was on the horizon, Hetty realized it was easy to spend days lost in her work at the bureau. Between client meetings and the rather interesting and unplanned events that occurred in the bureau's offices almost daily, she could forget the country was at war.

Now, for example, was one of the more bemusing moments of running their office. Mr. Garfield, a retired former diplomat, had entered the outer interview office and checked in with Eva for his follow-up appointment to see how his first date with another of their clients had gone. But after he'd given his name to Eva, he'd promptly fallen asleep on the settee.

He was stretched out in an almost funereal fashion. All that was missing was a bouquet of daisies between his clasped hands. The only evidence that he was still alive was his rather florid face and a cigar that hung out of his mouth beneath his fluffy beard, which twitched whenever he seemed engaged in a particularly interesting dream.

Elizabeth was in the back room sorting the latest letters that had arrived with the post, and Hetty didn't wish to disturb her with Mr. Garfield's napping situation.

"Let's see if we can't rouse the old boy," Hetty said.

She went over to Eva's desk and expertly wiggled the cord of the phone with her foot, causing it to ring. They had never bothered to fix the faulty phone, realizing it had its uses for unusual situations like this. Sadly, it didn't work in this case to rouse their client. No matter how much the phone rang, the diplomat slept on.

Hetty puffed out a breath in frustration. "Bloody hell. We can't let him stay like that. He'll scare off any women who set foot in the door."

Eva picked up a stack of Marcus's schoolbooks. The boy was currently up on the roof tending to the plants. Eva decisively dropped the books upon the floor with a loud *thwack*. Still the man slept on.

Hetty bit her lip. They had to do something before—

The office door opened, and a man came in. He glanced at the man asleep on the settee but offered no comment. Instead, he approached Hetty with a look of determination. He removed his hat, an old beat-up thing, and gazed down at his scuffed shoes.

"I've come from Liverpool. I build boats," he said. "Hopefully you remember me? The name is Ernest Geraghty."

"Oh! Mr. Geraghty! Do come in." Hetty shot a glance at the sleeping diplomat, who had not stirred even an inch during this new intrusion. "Thank you for making the trip to see us in person." Hetty recalled the letters that they had received from Mr. Geraghty. He had mentioned desperately needing someone in his life.

Hetty directed him to their interview desk. "Yes, come and sit. Tell me, what made you write to us?"

He took a seat, resting his hat nervously on one knee. Behind him, Eva retrieved the heavy books she had dropped on the floor near the comatose diplomat. Her look of bafflement was so amusing that it distracted Hetty from whatever Mr. Geraghty was saying. Hetty forced herself to focus.

"I'm sorry. What did you say?"

Mr. Geraghty sighed. "I was saying . . . it's been a rather difficult year, and two of the most terrible things happened to me in the same week."

Hetty didn't interrupt him. She didn't dare move her pen on her pad as she waited for him to continue, as she sensed it was something serious he wished to tell her about.

"I have one *real* talent, Miss Byron. I build boats, beautiful ones, and Edna, my wife, was my passion. We had a terrible storm last fall, and my shed collapsed. The boat I'd worked on for three years was destroyed in an instant." The pain in his eyes deepened further still. "Then two days later my wife was walking home during the evening, and a car hit her in the fog—and I lost her too."

He swallowed hard and looked away, collecting himself before he spoke again. "My Edna, she was the color in my world, you see. She was the wind that caught in my sails and moved me. Without her, I'm drifting on a windless sea without even a rudder." His quiet desperation and heartache for more than just the loss of the love of his life made Hetty's hands tremble. This man had lost everything that gave him a purpose.

Hetty could envision this man working tirelessly on his boat, his every waking moment directed to his boatmaking. He would need a woman who would see him as a partner, a woman who did not need the entirety of his attention to feel loved. The perfect wife for him was a woman who was very much her own creature, someone who would want to take charge of things and would enjoy taking care of the absentminded boat builder.

"I think we will find the right wife for you. A woman who will make you want to dive back into the world."

She thought almost at once of a rather picky client who was a nurse. She'd found fault with most of the men the bureau had paired her with. Hetty secretly believed the woman simply needed a cause to fight for. As a nurse who treated those in need, she was accustomed to entering a home and taking charge. Mr. Geraghty was not unlike any other patient a nurse would take care of. If a nurse saw this distraught but kind soul, she might turn her practical friendship into devotion and romance.

"Let me take down a few more pieces of information from you, and then I want to write a letter of introduction to a woman I think you should meet." Once Hetty had squared away Ernest Geraghty and sent him off with hopes of a new love life, she turned her focus back to the sleeping diplomat.

"Eva, the tea tray, if you please," Hetty said.

Eva brought the tea tray out, and then Hetty picked it up

and dropped it loudly on the desk surface. The silver items rattled sharply.

"Tea sounds lovely!" Hetty nearly shouted.

The diplomat snorted as he flew upright, his cigar tumbling down the length of his three-piece suit and onto the floor.

"Good God, is that the time?" He stared at the clock on the wall a brief second before collecting himself and rushing out the door without a word to either Hetty or Eva about the appointment he had slept through. Hetty slumped in her chair, not sure whether to shake her head or laugh.

"Are there any other appointments?" Hetty asked.

Eva flipped through the appointment book. "Not this afternoon."

"Good. I think it's time Lizzie and I look for our secondary headquarters. Can you and Miss Plumley manage the office?"

"I think so."

"If Marcus is done with his homework, I should like him to come with us. We'll take the car, so we'll have plenty of room."

"He would love that." Eva beamed and rushed into the inner office to tell her brother. Last week Marcus had turned fifteen, and the little boy in him was already beginning to fade beneath a growth spurt of his youthful manhood.

Hetty had been around enough men in her life to know he needed more responsibility and activities as he grew older. Hetty collected her handbag just as Elizabeth and Marcus left the inner office.

"Is it true we're bound for the country?" he asked, trying to sound casual, more adult. He seemed to be glad to be included, and Hetty was happy to have the boy along.

"Yes, we're headquarters hunting. I thought you could be our map reader." She pulled out a map of the little roads and areas outside of London. She'd had to have Inspector Crumholt get it for her last week since she didn't have a police license. She passed the map to Marcus.

"Be careful," Eva said to her brother.

He was now taller than her by a few inches, and he kissed her cheek as he said goodbye, his face softening in a brotherly way that made Hetty's heart ache. Eva and Marcus had come so far together, and they had made a life for themselves here in a foreign city so well that Hetty sometimes forgot she hadn't known them for a decade, but rather it had been less than a year.

The three of them headed downstairs and piled into Hetty's car. Hetty's Morris Eight was a deep red color and decently comfortable to drive about the country in.

Marcus sat up front, his map spread out on his thighs as he read the road signs to get his bearings. Elizabeth sat in the back, and Hetty caught her up on the day's events, including the interview with Mr. Geraghty.

"So I think we could introduce him to Ethel Frost. You know, the nurse," Hetty suggested.

"Ethel? Yes, she'd take one look at Ernest and want to care for him," Elizabeth agreed.

"Turn left at the next bend in the road," Marcus interrupted as they headed in the direction of Aldershot.

Hetty took the left and continued her conversation. "We need to do something about that diplomat. He doesn't actually seem to like anyone we match him with. I picture him reading each letter with masculine glee and waiting to see if any of these women live up to his imagination."

Elizabeth folded her arms over her chest, frowning. "Yes, we'll have to do something about him."

The landscape gave way to lush fields of wildflowers and stone walls. Little homes, a bit like one might see in a Grimm's fairytale book, dotted the landscape with their cozy thatched roofs.

Marcus pointed to an estate agent's board. "What's that?" It was freshly painted, which likely meant whatever property it represented was newly to let.

"Good job, Marcus. That's a property for lease." Hetty checked the road. Seeing no one was coming in either direction, she stopped the car and backed up to the iron gates that marked the entrance of the high walled property advertised by the estate agent's board. She pulled up to the gates, and Marcus climbed out with her.

They stopped at the two rusty wrought-iron gates, and after exchanging a glance with Marcus, Hetty placed a hand on the gate, giving it a push. The gate creaked, and then the creak turned into a moan as the gate opened for them.

In the distance beneath the drive, shrouded from above with trees arching over the road, was a stone manor house. Ivy writhed against the surface of the house, the leaves undulating in the spring breeze. It seemed as if the house were breathing, like an old man asleep on a settee. Hetty found herself smiling at that comparison. Life had a way of mirroring itself in the oddest ways.

"Shall I open the other side?" Marcus asked as he lifted the metal pole, locking the second gate into place.

"Yes, and I'll drive the car through."

Hetty let Marcus handle the gates, while she and Elizabeth drove between them. They picked Marcus up and drove the rest of the way toward the manor house.

"Oh, how romantic," Elizabeth sighed. "Like something out

of a storybook. Do you suppose there's an enchanted princess asleep inside?"

"A princess?" Marcus echoed.

"You might have to wake her up," Hetty teased and nudged the lad with an elbow. He blushed deeply and focused on folding up the map.

Hetty parked the car in the driveway. The three of them climbed out, then walked up the steps leading to the immense oak door.

"Goodness," Elizabeth said as Hetty bravely pulled on the brass knocker and tapped it on the door.

"Do you think anyone lives here?" Marcus asked.

"I think someone must. The gardens in the front look like they've been recently tended to." Elizabeth nodded to the irises blooming beneath the windows and the almost perfect rows of poppies blanketing the space in front of them.

There was the scraping of a key in the lock, and the massive door opened to reveal a plump, pleasant-looking woman in a floral-patterned frock, complete with a white apron. She eyed them curiously, but Hetty's gaze moved beyond her to the high marble halls of the manor's interior. Old medieval crests were carved into the front frames of the doors and painted in an array of colors. Hetty recognized them at once as some very old heraldic emblems probably belonging to an ancient English family.

"What's this, then?" the woman in the doorway asked, not unkindly.

Elizabeth took over the situation with her usual sweetness and charm. "Oh, please excuse us. We saw the estate agent's board from the road, and well . . . is this lovely place still available to let?" Hetty was happy to learn that the manor didn't have some old bedeviled hounds to chase them off the property.

"Why yes, are you interested in the place?" The woman stepped back and let them into the entryway before she closed the door. "I can show you around."

Spanish chests and stained-glass windows spoke to the home's glory days, and while Hetty was not nearly so romantic as Elizabeth, she still appreciated this house and its aged splendor.

Hetty made the introductions. "I'm Hetty Byron, and this is Elizabeth Mowbray and Marcus Wolman. Do you mind if we cover the details of the property inside?"

"Yes, come on in. I was just about to put the kettle on. I'm Margaret Harrow."

"Tea sounds lovely." They followed Mrs. Harrow toward the kitchen.

ELIZABETH LINGERED IN THE ENTRYWAY AFTER HETTY followed the housekeeper.

"Can you believe this place?" she asked Marcus, who had stayed behind in the entryway with her.

"It's like a castle," Marcus replied in a similar state of wonder.

They wandered through the rooms. Dusty, embroidered velvet chairs, cloth-covered tables. and bookshelves teeming with ancient leather-bound volumes filled the house. Glass cabinets displayed military medals, snuffboxes, and collections of ancient coins. Paintings of men and women in elaborate silk frock coats and billowing satin gowns decorated the walls.

This slice of history had remained almost perfectly

preserved. Wisteria bracketed the windows of the ballroom, and the light filtered through the windows to catch and glint upon the crystal chandelier, sparkling in rainbow fragments on the walls.

She and Marcus continued to explore the parade of rooms, and she barely noticed the cobwebs in the corners or the faded furnishings. Instead, she marveled at the silent gazes of the occupants of the oil portraits and lost herself in the events she imagined could have happened at this house over the last several centuries. A pair of medieval suits of armor stood guard, their barely rusted metal bodies glinting in the corners of the ballroom.

"Could we really live here?" Marcus walked up to one of the suits of armor and gently blew on the breastplate, sending a cloud of dust up in the air.

"We might. I imagine Hetty could talk down the rent, whatever it might be." They wandered back into the main entryway and followed the sound of voices until they reached Hetty and the housekeeper in the kitchen.

"You dears want any tea?" Mrs. Harrow asked them.

"Yes, please, ma'am," said Marcus.

"Well, Lizzie, what do you think? I suppose you had a good look around?" Hetty gave Elizabeth a questioning look.

"Yes, it's simply magical."

Hetty chuckled. "I knew you would say as much. It has fifteen bedrooms. We could try it out for a few months and see if the drive from London is too far."

"Oh, please, Hetty, let's!" Elizabeth clapped her hands in joy. "You don't think it's too much space, do you?"

Hetty shrugged. "I think we could branch out and offer honeymoon rooms to any couples who end up marrying. It could be fun, perhaps even profitable. A safe getaway from London for couples. We could use the extra income in case things become slow again."

"It's twenty-five guineas for a quarter of the year," Mrs. Harrow said.

Hetty's eyes narrowed. "Twenty," she countered.

"Twenty? But—"

"We'll be putting our own money into the property to make some updates and repairs," Hetty added.

"Oh, well, perhaps . . . Let me contact the owner and see if he agrees to twenty." Mrs. Harrow poured Elizabeth and Marcus tea.

"Who is the owner, by the way?" Hetty asked casually.

Elizabeth sipped her tea and winked at Marcus, who grinned back at her.

"I doubt you know him, dear. He is some Italian chap. High up, mind you. One of those exiled monarchs, or some such thing. He's in America now, too afraid of the bleedin' Huns, he says. I told him I didn't see any of them clipping their heels and marching in the fields, but he didn't want to risk staying. So here we are . . . an empty house."

"An Italian chap?" Marcus echoed, clearly curious as he ate half a plate of biscuits in a matter of minutes.

Hetty turned to Mrs. Harrow. "We'll take it, assuming the owner agrees."

"I'll contact the estate agent this afternoon," the house-keeper promised.

After enjoying tea and biscuits, Hetty, Elizabeth, and Marcus headed toward the car. A sudden distant droning sound above halted them, and they cast their eyes skyward. Several large planes rumbled past overhead.

"Those are Hurricanes!" Marcus cried excitedly.

"What?" Elizabeth asked, her eyes still on the planes as they continued their progress across the sky.

"Hurricanes—they are RAF. They're on our side," the boy explained. "They have Rolls-Royce Merlin engines and—"

"How on earth do you know that?" Hetty asked, her tone sharp with worry.

"I met a few pilots last week. They were on leave and stopped for lunch at a café where I was getting sandwiches. I talked to them. Nice chaps. They said the Hurricanes can function as both fighters and bombers. They come in like hurricanes and wreck the enemy."

It amazed Elizabeth how *British* Marcus was becoming. He still had an accent, like Eva, but it wasn't as strong as it had been the year before. It had softened considerably. And his knowledge of the English language had grown by leaps and bounds.

Marcus watched the planes vanish on the horizon and sighed dreamily. "When I turn eighteen, I'm going to join the fight."

Elizabeth and Hetty shared a grim look as he climbed back into the car. If only the war would end before Marcus turned eighteen . . .

CHAPTER 18

O ne week later, the Marriage Bureau moved into its
second office at the country house.

Marcus had christened it Knight House due to
the two suits of armor guarding the ballroom. Elizabeth spent
the day directing several strapping young men from the village
nearby who'd offered to help. They moved throughout the
house, carrying furniture and boxes to wherever Elizabeth or Eva
wanted them to go.

Marcus was in charge of removing the white drop cloths
from the furniture in the primary rooms they planned to use. He
happily whipped them off with a flourish like a Spanish bull-
fighter. Clouds of dust soon sent everyone running outside in
coughing fits.

"Oh, for heaven's sake, open the windows, you daft lads. It's
only a bit of dust," Mrs. Harrow barked at the young men, who,
with proverbial tails tucked between their legs, marched back

into the house to open all the windows before moving more furniture.

While Marcus and the young men focused on the furniture, Elizabeth enlisted Eva in helping her set up the bureau's front office on the ground floor. They wanted to use the study as their private office, where they would match client index cards and review files. It would also serve as a file storage area. The adjacent drawing room would be the new interview room. The telephone lines were all in working order, and they dialed Hetty back at the Bond Street office.

"Marriage Bureau, how may I help you?" Miss Plumley asked.

"Miss Plumley, it's Lizzie. Put Hetty on, please."

"Yes, Miss Mowbray."

Hetty answered a moment later. "Are you all set up?"

"More or less." She watched two young men walk past the window carrying a heavy desk between them, arguing about who was carrying more of the load. Elizabeth almost laughed.

"Good. I'll stay in London this week and send you names of potential lessees for those other rooms. The estate agent adjusted the board by the road to reflect the spare rooms for rent, so you might get a few people coming to see the place. Let me know if you want me to handle interviews here or if you want me to send any clients out to the house."

"Let's try a few appointments here at Knight House. Call tomorrow's clients and see if they'll make the drive out." Elizabeth wanted to be sure no one minded the drive to Knight House from London, given the petrol rationing.

"I'll call them." Hetty said she would take care of it, and Elizabeth got back to work with Eva. They'd managed to re-create most of the filing system they had in London and should be able to operate here as seamlessly as they would there with complete sets of files in both London and the country. The difficult part would be for Eva and Miss Plumley to keep in close contact about any status changes with clients as they were matched or introduced.

Later that afternoon, Elizabeth was interrupted in her mating of client index cards by raised voices in the hall.

"I demand to speak to the woman in charge!" a voice growled from somewhere nearby.

"Not without an appointment you won't!" Mrs. Harrow growled right back.

"Bloody hell, woman, don't you know who I am?"

"Should I? All I know is that you're trespassing on this property!"

"Trespassing? That is my family crest above your head, *madam*. And that painting behind you is my bloody portrait."

Mrs. Harrow's voice cracked with a hint of confusion. "Your what?"

Elizabeth opened the study door and saw a man a few feet away from the housekeeper. He was silver-haired and had a salt-and-pepper mustache and beard. He wore a tweed suit and looked rather like he'd stumbled out of a colonial expedition to Africa. She then glanced behind the housekeeper's head at the portrait on the wall of a slightly younger man, but the resemblance was clear.

"May I help you?" Elizabeth asked.

His hazel eyes shifted from Mrs. Harrow to Elizabeth and narrowed. "Are you in charge here?"

The man sounded positively military, and from the intensity of his physical presence, she guessed he'd been a soldier at some point.

"Er . . . yes, I suppose I am." She closed her office door

behind her and drifted between the man and Mrs. Harrow, defusing the tension between them.

"Good." He grunted the word. "I'm here to rent a room."

"How did you—?"

"The estate agent called me. He knows I'm interested in this place." The man spoke abruptly as though annoyed.

"By *interested* you mean—?"

"He knows I want to move back in. I'll pay ten shillings a month, and I'll go to my room now, if you don't mind."

Mrs. Harrow began to mutter under her breath, and Elizabeth sensed another fight brewing.

"Don't worry, I'll handle him," Elizabeth said. She rushed after the older gentleman and caught up with his long strides as he reached the grand staircase.

"How do you know where the rooms are?"

The man laid his fingertips on the banister, his battlefield expression fading as he slowed at the top of the stairs.

"Because I *used* to live here."

He proceeded down the hall, his strides confident, as though he did indeed used to live there. He paused before one of the bedrooms, his hand resting a moment on the door latch. He drew in a deep breath, then opened it.

"You used to live here?"

"This is Cunningham House," the man said more softly. "I am Colonel William Cunningham." His gaze moved almost lovingly over the bedroom. "Thank God the bastard didn't change a thing."

"*Who* didn't change a thing?" Elizabeth couldn't help her terrible curiosity. Mrs. Harrow hadn't said much about the man who owned the house.

"Count Francesco Moretti," he said. "The man who stole my

bloody home from me while I was in France more than twenty years ago."

Colonel Cunningham walked into the room with a heavy sigh. He sank down on the edge of the large four-poster bed. The second he sat down, a cloud of dust billowed up around him. Elizabeth fanned the air in front of her with a hand, trying to dispel the dust as best she could.

The old oak bed suddenly groaned, and with a terrible crack, the legs at the foot of the bed snapped and the colonel was thrown forward. Elizabeth caught him as he stumbled. The back two legs of the bed followed the first as the bed frame slammed to the floor in a thunderous crash.

Elizabeth stared at the bed, unsure how best to react.

"Well . . . I'll have to fix that tomorrow," Colonel Cunningham said in a thoughtful tone. "I wonder what else that fool let fall apart?" He seemed not nearly as angry as she'd expected. He appeared almost cheerful at the thought of doing something in the house.

"Colonel, do you really wish to stay here?"

"Of course. This room is fine."

"I meant the house, and with us." Elizabeth wasn't quite sure he would be suitable as a lodger. If he marched up and down the corridor growling at clients, he'd scare away half of them.

For the first time since she had met him, he finally stopped to really look at her.

"Madam, this is my *home*. It's been in my family for two hundred years."

"So you said. But how did Count Moretti acquire it?"

"When I left to fight in the last war, my wife, bless her, wasn't good at keeping expenses paid. She ran into debt, and when I was declared missing, she assumed the worst and sold the house to Moretti. She died from the Spanish flu before I returned. When the war was over I . . . came home to find both her and my home were gone . . ."

He walked over to the bay window in the bedroom and traced the emblem carved into the wood above the sill. "I settled my family's debts and moved into a small residence nearby for the last twenty years, waiting to catch Moretti in a mood to sell it back to me. I've been out of the country for several months and only returned two days ago. Otherwise, I would have made an offer Moretti couldn't refuse before he decided to leave."

The colonel turned back toward her. "So let's hear it. Who are you, madam?"

"I'm Elizabeth Mowbray. I run the Marriage Bureau with my business partner, Henrietta Byron."

"Byron? She's not Brigadier Byron's daughter, is she? I remember hearing about her. He was damned proud of her, if I recall."

"Yes, that would be her. He quite adores her. We all do." Elizabeth smiled, recalling her first few moments of meeting Hetty on the balcony that night at the party, marveling at how much they'd both changed since then.

"Her father's a good man. Crossed paths with him during my European tour and then later on in Ceylon. Now what's this you said about a bureau?"

"The Marriage Bureau. We make matches for people."

His mustache twitched and he harrumphed, but it didn't seem all that negative of a sound. It sounded more like a disguised chuckle.

"Well, I suppose that sort of thing won't bother me too much. I'll go and fetch my things and be back in time for dinner." He strode from the room, and Elizabeth hastened after him.

Eva and Marcus were in the hall, and they stared at the colonel, who gave them both a brief nod before he left through the front door.

"Who was that?" Eva asked once he was gone.

"Our new houseguest, Colonel William Cunningham. Apparently, Knight House is actually *Cunningham* House."

"He's a colonel?" Marcus asked. His eagerness made his eyes sparkle.

"Marcus, you mustn't pester him," Eva warned.

"I won't," the boy promised, but Elizabeth guessed that Colonel Cunningham would soon have a second shadow.

"We had better have the movers put his bed back together before dinner, and the maids need to put fresh sheets on the bed."

Eva shifted the stack of bureau files in her arms as she followed Elizabeth toward the kitchen. "Put his bed back together? What did he do to it?"

"The poor man broke all the legs when he sat down . . ."

❧

Dinner that evening was a tense affair. Elizabeth felt like she was caught in a war between Mrs. Harrow and Colonel Cunningham. As it turned out, Mrs. Harrow had only been the housekeeper for a few months and hadn't run into Colonel Cunningham in the village as he'd been in Africa while she'd been taking care of the house. Neither seemed ready to back down as to who was actually in charge of Cunningham House.

The two did not have a good start, and the hostilities continued well past the first course.

"What on earth is this?" He spooned a bit of the soup up and let the contents slop dramatically back into the bowl. It was rather-unfortunate tasting, Elizabeth agreed, but one did not insult one's cook.

"Turnip and beetroot stew," Mrs. Harrow replied, her brows arched in challenge. "It was my mother's favorite recipe."

"Your mother must have had no sense of taste." The colonel sniffed and winced. "Or *smell*, for that matter."

The housekeeper bristled. "Why, I never—"

"Mrs. Harrow, I would love to cook tomorrow evening," Eva interjected sweetly. "I need to keep my own mother's recipes fresh in my mind. Would you mind terribly if I impose myself on your kitchen tomorrow for dinner?"

"Why yes, yes, of course, dear," Mrs. Harrow agreed and shot the colonel a quelling look.

The colonel seemed to sense this battle was best left for another day, and he retreated into safer discussion topics.

"Explain how this bureau of yours works, Miss Mowbray. I should like to know what to expect under my roof."

No one corrected him that he was *renting* his room. He was the house's former master, and Elizabeth felt compelled to respect that claim of ownership. Indeed, the house itself seemed to have welcomed him back. Dust no longer gathered on shelves or other surfaces, and the rooms somehow appeared brighter.

However, she would need to remove the drawn battle lines between the colonel and Mrs. Harrow if the house was to have any sort of real and lasting peace. In the meantime, she explained to the colonel how the bureau operated.

"Fascinating," he mused thoughtfully, his soup left untouched as he listened to Elizabeth and Eva as they shared some stories of their latest matches.

"And these clients of yours will come out to the house?"

"Yes, for interviews and consultations. Our primary office is on Bond Street, but if things become unsafe, we wished to have a secondary location."

"They'd better not bomb Cunningham House or there will be hell to pay," Colonel Cunningham growled.

"On that we agree," Mrs. Harrow said. She and the silver-haired colonel shared a reluctant look of respect.

After dinner, the colonel retired to his bedroom since his former study was now filled with file boxes of Marriage Bureau paperwork.

"He's rather something, isn't he?" Eva asked Elizabeth as they helped Mrs. Harrow clean off the dining room table.

"He is *something* all right," the housekeeper huffed as she bustled past them with a stack of dishes.

Marcus snorted and then coughed to cover his laugh.

"Perhaps he'll help us build an Anderson shelter in the garden," Elizabeth mused.

"I can ask him," Marcus volunteered.

"Tomorrow," Eva said. "Tonight, he needs some time to settle into his home."

"As do we," Elizabeth chuckled.

They had so much to do and so many clients on the books to meet. As much as she loved the Bond Street office, she wouldn't miss the constant threat of bombing that came with being in London. But until the bombing started, they planned to move between the two offices frequently.

Isabelle had taken a trip to Edinburgh and would be gone for a full month, so Elizabeth felt she had time to set everything up here without worrying about her aunt being alone in London. Once they were well underway, she would have one of the numerous spare bedrooms ready for Isabelle to come stay whenever they all planned to spend time in the country.

❧

HETTY CHECKED HER APPEARANCE IN HER MIRROR SEVERAL times, lost in her own world, before she realized someone was knocking on the door. She rushed to answer, knowing who it was.

Charles waited patiently in the doorway, his dark-blue three-piece suit accenting his gold hair, illuminated by the building's interior corridor's sconce lights. The blackout curtains allowed no light to escape, making this moment feel cozier, more *intimate* than she'd imagined.

She'd been alone with Charles many times before, but this time was different. There was an intensity to his gaze that made her wonder if something was the matter. It was rare for her to feel off-balance around men, but tonight, she was very aware of the physical differences between her and Charles. His height, the breadth of his shoulders, and that easy confidence of his. She'd always liked all those things, but again . . . tonight seemed different. For good or ill, she wasn't sure.

"All alone tonight? How scandalous," he teased as she stepped back to let him come into her home.

"Er . . . yes, can you believe it? Eva and Marcus are at our new house in the country." She hadn't imagined how lonely she would feel once they had left, but as evening had given way to twilight, she'd become all too aware of the stillness. There was no humming from Eva or chatter from Marcus, just the wind that whistled against the windowpanes and the occasional creaking of wood to break the silence. Now with Charles in her home, just the two of them, it seemed very much the opposite of lonely.

Charles removed his suit coat and tossed it over the back of her couch. "Where is the new house again?"

"Near Aldershot. Drink?" She retrieved two glasses from her wet bar by the door to the kitchen. She decided a bit of Dutch courage would do her good, since she was having an uncharacteristic fit of nerves.

"Scotch, if you have it." Charles sat down on the couch, stretching one arm over the back and letting his head fall so he could stare at the ceiling. Hetty poured scotch for him and herself before joining him on the couch. She slipped out of her tan pumps and curled her legs under her as she nestled in beside him.

"Here. It sounds like you might need it." She offered him his glass and then took a sip of her own.

"I most certainly do." His lips kicked up in a grin as he accepted the glass. "Been busy with cases, and three days ago I was invited into the War Cabinet."

Hetty blinked. "Not *the* War Cabinet?"

"Yes, it seems your attempt to keep me off the battlefield has instead landed me in the middle of cabinet affairs."

Hetty tensed, every muscle taut as her breathing stopped. The remnants of her drink tasted like ash upon her tongue. Dread drilled a bottomless pit into her stomach.

Charles didn't look at her. His gaze was focused on the wireless across the room, which played music softly in the background. The surrounding darkness from the blackout curtains and dim lighting suddenly felt terribly oppressive. It was as though the guilt she'd been trying to ignore was crushing her from all sides, drowning her in the London darkness.

"Charles . . ." Hetty closed her eyes, drew in a breath, and then decided she had to own up to her actions. "I'm sorry I intervened. I shouldn't have."

"No, you shouldn't have," he said, but his tone held no anger, only a firm reproach. Like she was a misbehaving child who'd been allowed too much and now she was being reminded of the rules. She understood. If anyone had meddled in her life like that, taken away her right to make her own decisions, she would have been screaming like a Valkyrie preparing to fight.

But not Charles. He was always gentle with her. She sometimes wondered why he didn't shout at her the way her ex-husband had when they'd quarreled.

"I met with your father this morning after Churchill himself explained to me how I ended up in the cabinet."

"You spoke to Churchill *and* my father?" She wasn't sure which meeting surprised her more.

Charles's eyes finally settled on her face. "Your father told me what it meant for you to ask him to intervene on my behalf. He said you know better than most young women what this war means. You know about his time served in the last great war . . . You know every terrible detail of his time there where most women your age have only a vague idea of the sorrow that war left behind."

Hetty's eyes blurred with tears. She turned her face away to hide from him, but he caught her cheek in his palm and gently turned her back to him.

"What those men . . . those *boys* went through," she whispered. "Pain, death, and endless darkness."

Charles searched her face. "It is all of that," he agreed. "But we can't stand by, or this evil will never stop until it consumes the world. I know you want me to be safe, but if Hitler and his armies march down the street, *none of us* are safe."

"I know." Hetty could barely speak. "I can't go with you to make sure you're safe. It isn't fair." She knew it was stupid, but she felt deep in her bones that if she was with him, no harm would come to him. She would throw herself in the path of danger for him. She'd never felt that way about any other man, but with him? She'd do it without a second thought.

Charles traced her lips with the pad of his thumb. "*Life* isn't fair." Heat flared between them wherever he touched her. If they weren't having such an important conversation, she'd lean in and demand more with a kiss. But this was something they couldn't avoid. It had to be discussed.

"That's why we need to strive every day to make it fair." Hetty didn't want anyone else telling her she couldn't help, that she couldn't do anything. "I want to help. I *need* to help, and I can't sit about and stitch blankets for hospitals or sort food. I need something *more* . . ."

At this, Charles's face turned pensive.

"What?" Hetty noticed the shift in him.

"There may be a way, but I fear your father might kill me if . . . and if anything were to happen to you, I'd kill myself. If you were any other woman, I would not even consider it. Hell, I feel like a damned villain for even thinking about it."

"What? Tell me?" The wildness inside Hetty began to stir, like a wind that traversed continents—ever restless, ever nameless.

"Our men, the British Expeditionary Forces, are retreating to Dunkirk, a small town on the coast of France, as we speak."

"Dunkirk . . . Wait, that's where Major Taylor was headed." Fear seized her heart, its icy claws sinking deep.

"The Germans are closing in; the French couldn't keep them out. Even now, the forces are divided. It will be a miracle if we can get even the smallest numbers of our troops safely to the beaches for evacuation. We're going to lose thousands of men. Possibly hundreds of thousands."

Hundreds of thousands. The terrible number echoed in her mind. She knew what that number meant, but picturing each single life lost as part of those thousands . . . it was unbearable.

"They have to rescue those men. They—"

"The cabinet has been fighting for several days. Ironside, our Chief of the Imperial General Staff thinks Dunkirk could be a trap. Major-General Dewing thinks the BEF ought to fight their way to Somme. But the forces are scattered. Reports are coming in, and it's clear that even the French and Belgian countrysides are in chaos. The cabinet finally worked up a plan for the twenty-seven-mile stretch of coast between Ostend and Dunkirk as the best bet for evacuation. But they're still fighting over the logistics. The admiral of the fleet thinks they only need a handful of naval vessels for the evacuation."

Charles sipped his scotch and cleared his throat. "An RAF group captain, some fellow named Goddard, well, he simply challenged the admiral himself. He told the admiral that the handful of boats selected to help the troops weren't enough. He said, 'You must send not only Channel packets, but pleasure steamers, coasters, fishing boats, lifeboats, yachts, motorboats, everything that can cross the Channel.' He was so overwrought that he had to excuse himself from the meeting for a time. I think the RAF has a better sense of what we're up against than the Admiralty."

Hetty's mind was spinning. "And they need every boat?"

"Every boat that's seaworthy," Charles said.

She clenched her scotch glass so tight her knuckles were alabaster. "Including your yacht."

"Including my yacht," he agreed. "I'm leaving in two days to get her out of the boatyard. I should be able to find an engineer and a sailor or two who can aid me in the crossing. I don't want any engine trouble stranding us halfway across the Channel. Not when we'll be slowed down and vulnerable with troops on board. We can't afford to lose anyone."

The fine hairs rose on Hetty's neck. "No, we can't. Very well, I accept." She threw back the rest of her drink, the burn of the scotch waking all of her senses.

Charles set his drink aside on a nearby table, his gaze locking with hers. "Accept what?" he asked.

"The *mission*. You would never have told me this if you didn't expect me to come with you."

"I couldn't stop you if I tried, could I?" he asked, his voice soft and low.

"No one can stop me." Her voice was hard. The wildness inside her began to hum a battle hymn. They would get to Dunkirk, and God save anyone who got in their way.

The Marriage Bureau was going to war.

CHAPTER 19

M*ay 29, 1940*

HETTY CALLED CUNNINGHAM HOUSE EARLY IN THE MORNING. A weary Mrs. Harrow answered the phone. Hetty's stomach knotted as she tried not to think about what she was getting ready to do. She had her hair pulled back in a band at the nape of her neck and wore comfortable trousers and a blue sweater, along with a pair of work boots that she had broken in ages ago. It was the best "rescue the BEF" outfit she could devise that would keep her warm and mobile while working on the boat.

"Mrs. Harrow, it's Hetty. It's rather urgent. Can you wake Lizzie up?"

"What on earth for, dearie?"

"Please, Mrs. Harrow. It's an emergency," Hetty begged her.

She twisted the cable of the phone between her fingers, anxiously waiting for her friend. She didn't have much time if she was to meet Charles at the boatyard. Despite his assurances he would wait, she couldn't risk that he might sail off without her.

"Hold on, let me fetch her."

Hetty held her breath until Elizabeth answered the phone. Her tone was a little breathless, as though she'd been running.

"Hetty? What's the matter, Mrs. Harrow said it was an emergency."

"I don't have much time. Charles and I are leaving for France."

"France? Hetty, what are you—?"

"The Royal Navy needs every boat, even yachts like Charles's since his has a motor, to rescue our forces at Dunkirk. Thousands of men are stranded there, men like Major Taylor. We must save as many as we can, and I won't let Charles go alone."

There was a long silence before Elizabeth finally spoke up, her voice shaky with emotion. "Be careful, won't you?"

"You know me, darling," Hetty teased in a bravado-filled voice. "I'll have the Germans running in fear. But you must keep the bureau running while I'm gone."

"Of course. I'll return to London at once, and Eva can stay at Cunningham House."

"Thank you." Hetty closed her eyes and pressed her head to the wall as she cradled the phone against her ear.

"You'll call me the moment you're both safe, won't you?"

"Yes, you'll be my first call. I'm not telling my parents. If I don't . . ." Hetty refused to give voice to dark *what-ifs*.

"I'll tell them," Elizabeth promised. "Take care."

Hetty could hear all the words left unsaid, and she wished

she was speaking to Elizabeth in person so she could embrace her friend. Despite what some might think, such a display of sentiment was not a weakness but a strength. If anything, it embodied everything they were fighting for—the ability to care for one another.

"Thank you, Elizabeth." She placed the phone in the cradle and collected her keys, then turned off the lights of her flat. She took one last look around before she closed the door and hurried down to the street to flag a cab.

The cab dropped her off at Charles's boatyard, and she found him waiting in a large queue of men who slowly proceeded into the boatyard. There had to be more than a hundred and fifty men there.

"There you are." Charles pulled her into his arms, kissing her hard before letting go. She immediately missed his warmth. He wore trousers and a fisherman's sweater and managed to look just as comfortable in those clothes as he did in his bespoke suits. Her attention shifted back to the situation around them.

"What's our plan?" she asked.

"Word's gotten out. Someone from the Admiralty called the Royal Ocean Racing Club, and every yachtsman for miles showed up. We are to take our ships to Sheerness and then on to Ramsgate. There we will meet a commodore and his crew, who will check our ship over. We have to be deemed seaworthy before they'll allow us to cross the Channel."

Over the next hour, the boatyard filled with lightermen, dockworkers, deckhands, and bargemen. The ship owners worked with the waterfront crews, setting boat after boat into the water and preparing them to sail. Hetty kept quiet, ignoring the frequent looks of confusion as she was the only woman there. When it came their turn, she and Charles got his yacht out into the water, with the help of a lithe yet muscled Italian sailor named Angelo Santoro and a blond-haired young marine engineer, Harold Dowdy, both of whom had volunteered to come on their boat for the rescue mission.

Santoro had been on many different ships, and at the age of thirty-four, he was well seasoned for the mission. Harold was far younger at only twenty-three, but he knew his way around almost every type of marine engine, and he promised Charles he wouldn't let them down. He could man the helm as well, should the need arise. Charles was happy to take them aboard, and so was Hetty. They'd need as much help as they could find.

They sailed the yacht toward Sheerness, following in the wake of the boats ahead of them. The harbor on the Thames was bustling. Ships filled every bit of water as far as the eye could see. Charles put his yacht in line with other similar vessels, and after an hour, they were boarded by a crew for inspection.

A young man wearing a naval lieutenant's uniform asked as he held up a clipboard to take down their information, "Who is the vessel's commander? And what is your vessel's name?"

Charles stepped forward. "I am the captain, sir. Charles Humphrey. This is the *Henrietta*."

"And who are your crew?" The man's gaze landed on Hetty, who had straightened up and looked at Charles when he'd said the name of the ship. The last time they'd been on the boat, she hadn't seen a name painted on it and hadn't thought once about what it was called. She couldn't help but wonder how long it had been named after her.

"This is Angelo Santoro and Harold Dowdy." The two men nodded at the lieutenant respectfully. "Santoro's an experienced sailor, and Dowdy's a marine engineer."

The officer nodded at Hetty. "And her?"

"Hetty Byron," Hetty said, raising her chin a little as she met the lieutenant's stare.

"Ma'am," the officer began, a scolding tone in his voice, "you should stay here—"

Hetty fixed him with her most baleful expression. "*Lieutenant*, you are wasting valuable time. Feel free to contact Brigadier Byron about me, but for God's sake, do not tell me to leave."

The officer blushed, and without another word, he and his crew proceeded to check the vessel's engine and cabin.

"Will we need weapons, sir?" Angelo asked the lieutenant.

"You might, but unfortunately, we don't have any to give. The escort vessels will take what few Lewis machine guns we have." The officer gave them all a sad smile. "Be careful of enemy aircraft. That will be the biggest danger to you."

When the inspection was done, the officer shook Charles's hand. "Proceed to Ramsgate to top off your fuel. We'll have provisions loaded on board, and you'll be assigned to a convoy. Do not lose your convoy if you need navigation assistance. It's the only way you won't get lost. Godspeed to you all."

The officer and his crew disembarked, and Charles turned his boat toward Ramsgate.

Hetty, Charles, and the others were quiet the entire twenty-eight nautical miles to Ramsgate. She imagined the others were lost in their own thoughts and worries, just as she was.

When they arrived, the port was teaming with vessels, everything from large merchant ships to little tugs, steamer paddleboats and sailboats with motors. Someone more critical might have turned away the smallest of the boats, but not today. Every vessel, no matter the size, held the weight of Britain's future on its decks.

As they refueled the yacht, stories began drifting back to them from other boat crews shouting across the water.

Men trapped on the beaches . . . Pinned down by German bombers . . . Terrifying . . . Ships sunk by bombers . . . Tens of thousands in need of rescue . . . More than we ever imagined . . .

"We're full up, Mr. Humphrey," Angelo said as the fuel ship moved away from the yacht. A tugboat came toward them.

"You the *Henrietta?*" a grizzled fisherman called out.

"Yes, sir!" Charles hollered back.

"Catch these and follow me. We're adding you to my convoy and heading out." The fisherman tossed a bundle onto the deck.

Harold retrieved the bag and opened it up to show a pocket tide table and a navigation chart with dozens of routes mapped in red, all headed toward Dunkirk. The yacht followed the tugboat called the *Auntie May* out of the port and joined several other vessels that had gathered together.

The *Auntie May* led the way out across the Channel, six boats following in its wake, two of which were naval escorts. Hetty joined Charles at the helm and slipped her hand in his as he held it out. Their fingers locked as they both looked toward the distant horizon in the direction of France.

⚜

ELIZABETH COULDN'T GET BACK TO SLEEP AFTER HETTY'S early call. She grabbed her dressing gown and wrapped it around herself before slipping her feet into her slippers and making the long walk from her bedchamber to the kitchen. She found the housekeeper up and brewing tea.

"What was all that about, dearie?" Mrs. Harrow asked. She

was also in her dressing gown, her hair bound up in a colorful scarf.

Elizabeth sank into a chair at the little table in the kitchen. "Hetty is on a boat headed for the coast of France. Our forces are having to evacuate, and they need every ship to help. She's gone with a friend of ours, Mr. Humphrey."

Mrs. Harrow's gaze widened. "Miss Byron's heading into danger?"

"It seems so. If anyone could get out of it, it's Hetty, but well, if the BEF are retreating, what does that say about the Germans? It . . ." Elizabeth swallowed and tried to control her fear for her friend. It was impossible.

"The best we can do for her is to pray and go about our day," Mrs. Harrow suggested.

"Yes, you're right. I need to return to London soon, but I want Eva and Marcus to stay here with you. Will you look after them for me?"

"Of course."

Elizabeth accepted the cup of tea the housekeeper held out to her, and then she ate a quick breakfast of toast and eggs before she went up to dress. She met the colonel on the stairs.

"Good morning, Colonel," she greeted as she brushed her auburn hair back from her face. It was always a bit wild in the morning until she had a chance to comb through it.

"Morning," he grunted and passed by her, but after she took a few more steps, she halted.

"Colonel? Where exactly is Dunkirk?" She turned around at the same time as he did at the bottom of the stairs.

"Dunkirk?"

"Yes, in France."

"I know where it is, but why do you ask?" the older gentleman replied.

She paused, but only for a moment. "I heard the BEF are attempting to evacuate from there." She came back down the steps. "One of my clients, a major, left for France only a month ago. And my friend and business partner, Hetty Byron, Brigadier Byron's daughter, is on a boat now headed for Dunkirk to help in the rescue. I'm terribly anxious about her going."

The colonel must have seen how shaken she was, because he let out an oath that made Elizabeth blush.

"Come with me." He headed for the library on the ground floor and turned on a few lamps, then dug around in a wooden chest of drawers that contained all sorts of odds and ends from his travels.

He retrieved a large map that had been folded up ages ago. Rather than put the map on one of the reading tables, he took it into the kitchen. When he caught sight of Mrs. Harrow, he made a growling demand for coffee while he unfolded the map.

"Oi! Watch out for your breakfast, now, or you'll wreck the table!" Mrs. Harrow swooped in to rescue a plate of bacon and a rack of toast she'd set down earlier for the Colonel.

The colonel spread the map out on the now clear table and picked up a nearby knife, pointing to a place on the map.

"This is the border between Belgium and France." He traced the map along the coast, moving inland. "And here is Dunkirk, just southwest of the border."

Elizabeth leaned over, peering at the map.

"You said the men are evacuating by boat?" he asked, his tone quiet.

"Yes. Hetty said they needed every boat they could find."

"The Royal Navy must be busy elsewhere, no doubt dealing

with U-boats in the Atlantic." He stroked his chin, staring at the map as if it would reveal its secrets if he glared at it long enough.

"What sort of boat is she on?" he asked.

"A pleasure yacht." Elizabeth described Charles's ship.

"They'll be damned lucky if they don't sink. That sort of ship won't have a strong enough hull. One good spray of bullets from the Luftwaffe and they'll be done for."

Elizabeth gasped, and the colonel looked up apologetically. "That being said," he admitted softly, "the Luftwaffe will probably focus on the beaches. That's where the majority of the men will be. Tiny boats on an ever-moving sea are much harder targets. The biggest danger your friend's ship will face is when they're trying to board troops. If there are any wharfs or docks, German planes will try to bomb them. And the men themselves will be a danger . . . They could swarm a ship in desperation and capsize it."

"Sounds like we'd better pray for fog," Mrs. Harrow interrupted as she set a poached egg in front of the colonel and a cup of coffee. "*Lots* of fog."

The colonel turned a thoughtful gaze to the housekeeper and accepted the coffee she handed him with a quiet thank you, to which Mrs. Harrow nodded back respectfully.

Elizabeth stared at the map and the tiny black dot with the name *Dunkirk* next to it and shivered. If there was any goodness left in the world, it would come from all those little English boats and the hearts of the people sailing them into danger.

"Be safe, Hetty," she whispered. "Come back home."

The smoke on the horizon was the first thing Hetty saw as the coast of France came into view. She rushed to the railing and stared toward the column of black clouds that rose up into the clear sky.

She covered her mouth as she saw the roaring flames. "Oh my God." As the wind changed, the sandy beaches with men waiting on them were revealed. There were thousands. *Tens of thousands.*

Hetty's knees buckled, and she had but a second to brace herself against the railing. Charles slowed the yacht as the other ships around them did the same. The tugboat leading their convoy angled toward a distant strip of land to the east. The mole, as it was called, was a vast, stony structure that stretched its arm out into the sea. Men by the thousands were standing on the unstable-looking area waiting to board boats that came up alongside it. Hetty rushed back toward Charles.

"Where are the docks? Why aren't they loading on them?" she asked, her gaze frantically searching the coast for any recognizable marine structure.

Harold pointed to the distant fires. "I believe those are the docks."

No wonder the men were stranded on the beaches. They had nowhere to board ships safely.

Hetty suddenly saw a dark, dangerous bulge of rocks in the water ahead of them. "Charles, watch out!" she shouted. He slowed the boat almost to a dead stop.

"What do you see?"

"Rocks . . . I . . ." Hetty leaned over the railing and got a better look, only to wish she hadn't.

They weren't rocks—they were bodies.

"Hetty?" Charles's voice sharpened with worry.

"It's m-men . . . ," she tried to call back, but her voice cracked. "Men," she repeated as she stared down at the lifeless forms. Some were bloated from hours or perhaps days adrift in the sea. Some were riddled with bullets, while others were . . . in pieces. Some were gray-haired, and others looked as young as Marcus. Every one of them had someone waiting for them back home, and they would never see them again.

"Poor souls," Angelo whispered beside her. He made the sign of the cross, and Hetty found herself saying a prayer along with him, as they both needed comfort from something greater in that moment.

She'd thought she was prepared for this, that she could handle what she was seeing, but this was everything from her father's darkest nightmares, the ones that woke him with hoarse screams at night.

Hetty had never told her father that she knew about his nightmares, or that she'd often wake and pace restlessly nearby until she heard her mother soothe him back to sleep.

Those nightmares had seemed such a foreign thing, a thing she couldn't fully understand. Her father was such a strong, brave man. How could simple dreams reduce him to such a primal state of fear? Now she understood . . . because now she would have her *own* nightmares.

"Hetty, are you all right?"

Startled, she turned to see Charles by her side. Angelo had taken over at the helm. His face was pale as he looked at the awful sight all around them. The stench of death came up from every wave lapping at the hull of the yacht, a stagnant, terrifying reminder of what they were facing.

"This isn't war—it's *murder*," she said. Her gaze swept over the beaches, seeing all the men waiting for rescue . . . or death.

"If we don't stop them, we'll all end up like this," Charles said. "Every last good man and woman on this earth are trusting their lives to us and what we're doing right now. Can you handle this, Hetty?" There was no judgment in his tone, no challenge, only compassion. How was he so bloody strong, stronger than her?

She looked out across the sea, toward the rows of soldiers waiting for help. *Her* help. There was only one choice—there always had been. She was a fighter, and she would not allow fear to send her cowering in a corner.

She could hear her father's voice in her head, the battle cry he screamed as he relived those darkest hours in the trenches as poisonous gas and machine guns had ravaged his countrymen all around him.

Hold the line . . . shoulder to shoulder . . . hold the line!

The internal battle cry kept shock from setting in. It put fire back in her blood. She would hold the bloody line. She would not fail.

"Yes. I can do this." She spoke the words with a steel she'd never before felt, as though her muscles and bones had become galvanized. She was ready to battle the gods themselves if she must.

Charles brushed a stray lock of her hair back from her face and tucked it behind her ear, his gray eyes deadly serious. "I love you to hell and back, Hetty."

She could only absorb his words, the light of them obliterating the shadows in her heart.

"What do we do?"

Charles looked back out over the water. "Check for survivors first. Many of them look as though they've drowned. Their gear will be deadly, weighing them down. Even the best swimmers won't last for long. If you see anyone moving, call for Angelo or Harold. I'll guide us toward the tugboat, and we'll wait for our turn at the mole."

"Why are we loading at the mole?"

"It's the only real place for the troops to reach the bigger boats like ours that can't get too close to shore since the docks are destroyed." He passed her a pair of field glasses. "And check the sky as well. We need to watch for German aircraft."

She pressed the field glasses to her eyes and scanned the sky before turning back to the water, but there was no movement among the bodies other than what their wake provided. She felt sick, and turned her attention to the shore.

Men were lined up, patiently waiting. It reminded her of the lines schoolchildren formed between breaks to return indoors. But these were men facing death, not children. Their faces, at least those close enough for her to see, were stained with tears and splattered with blood and mud. Each weary soul looked as though he'd survived a hell she would thankfully never fully know.

The boats ahead of them approached the mole one by one, and the men on the stony outcropping shuffled toward the wooden decking that covered parts of it. Waves crashed against the ships and the mole itself, sometimes knocking men into the sea. Screams echoed across the water and were quickly silenced as the men were either crushed or drowned.

Hetty gripped the field glasses, white-knuckled as she turned her gaze away from the awful sight and once again focused on the skies. A fleck of dust marred her lenses. She wiped at it with the sleeve of her sweater, but the speck only grew, and then she heard it—the hum of a plane engine.

"Plane incoming!" she screamed. A second later, the men on

the beaches of Dunkirk scattered. The perfect lines of waiting troops broke apart as the men ran for cover in every direction . . . some even into the dangerous swells of the sea.

"They're going to strafe the beaches! We're too close!" Harold bellowed. "Hit the deck!"

Hetty threw herself to the ground, covering her head as the German aircraft swept low over their boat like a black-winged raven of doom. Bombs fell from the sky in rapid succession.

Through the nearest break in the deck railing of the yacht, she saw the beach explode in clouds of smoke and sand. It looked like water dropping on the surface of a pond; the land rippled outward with the impact, and the dark dots of men lying upon the ground were either obliterated or buried in sand and debris. Then the plane moved on, almost disappearing on the horizon, only to arc back and rain hell down upon the beaches again before finally leaving.

Hetty's ears rang so loud she didn't hear anything else at first. She screamed in terror as she was pulled up on her feet and spun around.

It was Charles who'd grabbed her. His mouth was moving, but she could barely hear him over the ringing in her ears.

"Hetty? Are you all right? Hetty?" The words sounded as though they were coming through a watery tunnel.

She nodded, but her thoughts were scrambled and her vision dotted until she blinked it away.

"You're sure?" He still held her by the shoulders, looking over her for any injuries.

She drew a shaky breath and turned her face to the beaches. "Y-yes."

Men now climbed wearily to their feet and slowly moved back into lines . . . still waiting to be rescued. How many times had they done this? She couldn't fathom the strength they'd need to stay sane in the face of such relentless attacks.

The steamer ahead of them, filled to capacity with men, slowly drifted away from the mole and headed out to sea, leaving them up next.

"It's our turn!" Charles hollered to Angelo as the sailor steered the yacht toward the mole. An army major was shouting orders at the front, keeping troops in line as they prepared to board each ship. The yacht pulled up alongside them, and the major's face came into view beneath his helmet. Hetty's heart stilled.

"Major Taylor!" she shouted and waved at him.

The major glanced at her and then did a double take. "Miss Byron?" He approached the railing of the boat. "What the bloody hell are you doing here?"

She saluted him, and he managed a smile. "Proving my mettle, sir."

"How many men can you take?" the major asked.

"Twenty-five or thirty. I can't risk more," Charles said.

"Thirty it is. You lot." Major Taylor got the attention of the men in front of him. "You're up. I'll count you off." He began waving men aboard. Harold and Angelo were there to catch the soldiers and steady them so that none fell overboard. Hetty guided each of the men to the farthest end of the boat, directing them to sit, and she began handing out biscuits and cans of water.

"That's thirty," the major called out.

"What about you?" Hetty demanded as she rushed toward him.

Major Taylor offered her a gentle smile, the kind that had

won her heart over the first day he'd walked into the Marriage Bureau.

"I must maintain my position, Miss Byron. I shall be here when you return."

Hetty wanted to argue, but Charles caught her arm. "We have our duty to these men, Hetty . . . and he has a duty to those who are left behind. The faster we leave, the quicker we can return."

He was right. Major Taylor wouldn't leave anyone behind, and if she wanted to bring him home, she'd have to rescue every soldier she could.

Charles let her go and rushed back to the helm. As they pulled away from the mole and headed out to sea, Hetty saw the distant figure of Major Taylor standing resolute, until the smoke and fires of Dunkirk obscured him from view.

CHAPTER 20

The *Henrietta* was full of men huddled against each other for warmth as the sea breeze came across the bow of the ship. Hetty carefully rationed the tins of biscuits and cans of water they'd received from the Royal Navy at Ramsgate. She also brewed a pot of tea in the cabin and gave cups to the men who were wettest and in need of warming up. There weren't enough cups to give to all the men, so without a word spoken, they began to share.

A fine mist settled over the Channel, and Hetty provided blankets to the soldiers who'd been able to shed their wet gear. A young soldier sat on the floor of the cabin interior eating a biscuit, his deep-brown eyes miles away. Every now and then he'd sigh and take a bite, as though even the act of eating was tiring. A sense of helplessness stilled Hetty as she watched the young man.

There was so much she wanted to do to help these men, but it felt nowhere near enough. She wondered if perhaps just talking might bring some light back into the young man's eyes. He looked barely older than Marcus, and the thought made her heart twinge sharply with pain.

Hetty knelt in front of him. "What's your name, soldier?"

His dark eyes dilated as though she had startled him, and then he relaxed.

"Chester Kowalski, miss. Forty-Second Armored Division." His reply was automatic, clearly one he'd recited a thousand times.

"Where do you call home?" she asked.

"Manchester, miss."

Hetty smiled. "Rather good football teams you have up there." She tried to think of something that had no relation to the war or what he'd faced the last few days. If it had been her, she'd want to think about something that reminded her of home.

A timid smile flashed across the soldier's face. "We do indeed, miss."

"Eat your biscuits up now," she said, and she stroked a hand over the young man's head in a motherly way. Chester let out another sigh. She bit her lip as she watched him another moment before stepping back out on deck. When she paused by Angelo, she asked what their heading was.

"Toward Dover. The captain said he's following that ship ahead of us."

A small steamer was half a mile in front of them, laden with troops, and Charles kept right on their tail.

As France disappeared behind them, the men on the ship began, bit by bit, to come out of their shell-shocked silence. Their faces were burned into Hetty's memory—unshaven, hollow-eyed, their uniforms drenched with seawater, sand, and oil. There was an endless weariness to all of them, and Hetty knew that whatever these men had faced before they'd reached the beaches had been hell.

When Charles finally reached the port of Dover, they saw hundreds of men on the docks—soldiers, dockworkers, and Royal Navy sailors. It was a chaotic sight, and Hetty could see how frantic the rescue efforts were in bringing so many troops to the small towns and villages so quickly.

"This way, if you please," a stout fisherman bellowed as he caught the lines Harold tossed him and secured them to the nearest bollards.

Then the troops on the *Henrietta* stood. One by one, they stepped off the boat to the dock.

"Thank you, ma'am," more than one soldier said to Hetty as she saw each of them off. As much as she felt she'd barely done enough to help, she was reminded as each man departed the ship that they could have been still on the beach had Charles's ship not been there to rescue them. They had made a difference, huge to those men they'd saved, and she had to cling to that feeling of hope so that the despair for those still left behind wouldn't become too much to bear.

They refueled and loaded more biscuits, blankets, and cans of water, along with the other ships in their convoy. The tugboat *Auntie May* had done a fine job leading them all safely home.

"Those poor lads," Hetty whispered. Charles put his arm around her shoulders and pulled her back against him.

"You don't have to go back. You can stay here and help the men we've dropped off."

Hetty spun in his arms and frowned at him. "I'm going back if you are."

"I figured that would be the case." He leaned in and kissed her, tenderly at first, but his mouth turned rough as she tasted the desperation and fear on his lips. Then he released her, and they simply stared at each other before they both faced the sea.

"Ready when you are, Captain," Angelo announced.

"Follow the tug and head out," Charles commanded.

Within fifteen minutes, they were headed back to France.

The mist held up for the rest of the return journey, and it was dusk as they reached the waters off Dunkirk's coast. There were dozens of vessels in the water of all sizes, most of them clearly civilian. Hetty moved her field glasses so she could scan the beaches. A capsized ship hull loomed out of the water.

"Charles! A ship's capsized off the port side. Soldiers are in the water!"

Angelo and Harold joined her at the railing as they drew near to get a sense of what they were facing.

"Throw out the ladder on the back," Hetty told Harold.

"We don't have time! They're going under!" Angelo dove over the side of the yacht into the dark waters. Hetty leaned over the railing as she saw him splashing back to the surface, holding a drowning soldier up as he swam toward the ship.

"Give me your hand!" Hetty caught the soldier's outstretched hand, but his weight was so heavy she nearly fell overboard. Harold grabbed her waist, holding her safely on the ship.

"We've got him!" Hetty gasped as her muscles ached while she and Harold dragged the soldier toward the ladder a few feet away.

Shouts echoed across the water as other men sank beneath the churning sea. Angelo dove again and again, pulling man after man up and pushing them toward the boat. They eventually brought up seventeen men, but the last three they'd spotted sank and Angelo was unable to find them. Another body drifted past the boat, and Angelo caught the man, searching for signs of life.

He gave a shake of his head when the man he held didn't stir. Hetty couldn't stomach the thought of leaving the last of the men behind.

"Can't we bring him on board?" Hetty begged Harold.

"We need space for the living, lass," a middle-aged Scottish soldier said. He'd been pulling the last living man on board and now stood beside Hetty, staring at the body of the soldier floating on the surface.

Angelo murmured a prayer and let the soldier in his arms go. The body drifted a few yards away and then sank beneath the surface. No one on board said a word as they stared at the sea where the man had vanished. Angelo swam back to the ladder, and the Scotsman helped Hetty pull him aboard.

"Take us to the mole, Captain," Harold called out to Charles.

As they headed toward the mole, she saw that there were thousands of soldiers still queuing up to board ships. The Scotsman passed by the men on board, touching their shoulders and speaking softly before he approached Charles. Hetty followed him.

"Can ye tell the men manning the mole to grab any Bren guns on the beach? We'll need every bit of metal back in England." He showed Charles the light machine gun he had strapped to his back.

"That's a good point," Charles agreed.

"'Tis a good gun, if'n ye dinna fire too long an' too quick. The barrel heats up and ye lose accuracy." He removed the gun from his back and held it loosely, but ready to use.

"I'll pass that along," Charles promised.

The Scotsman nodded in approval.

At the mole, Hetty searched the faces in the growing gloom.

She cupped her hands around her mouth and shouted, "Major Taylor!"

"Who are ye looking for, lassie?" the Scotsman asked.

"Major William Taylor. He's a dear friend. He was in charge of the soldiers on the mole when we were here a few hours ago. I promised I wouldn't leave here without bringing him home to his wife."

The Scot nodded and bellowed to the men on the mole, "Listen up, lads! Find Major William Taylor! We need to speak with him!" The Scotsman's voice carried farther than hers, and word rippled down the line as soldiers passed on the message.

"If he's still here, they'll find him," the Scotsman said.

"Thank you . . . What's your name?"

"Angus Kincade, lassie." The Scot gave her a respectful nod.

"Thank you for your help, Mr. Kincade."

"'Tis my honor." He turned back to help the other men while they waited to leave.

In the meantime, another officer was counting troops to board the boat. Hetty feared they would leave before she saw the major again, but as another soldier leapt aboard, a familiar face broke through the waiting soldiers.

"Major!" Hetty called out in relief. Major Taylor's face was pale, but he smiled. Blood splattered his uniform, but it didn't seem to be his.

"I promised you I would still be here, Miss Byron." He saluted her and relieved the officer handling the boarding of troops.

"Make and keep that promise again."

He nodded solemnly. The soldiers they had rescued this time were in far worse shape than the first group.

"Ma'am?" Harold pulled her aside and whispered to her.

"We've got a man here with a bad wound. I'm not sure he'll make it." Harold indicated a man seated on a bench on the stern side of the yacht. Blood oozed from a shoulder wound, and the man's face was stark white, his gaze listless.

"Bring him into the cabin." Hetty rushed to find Charles's medical kit in the cabin and instructed Harold to put the injured soldier on the bed.

"Let's take a look at the wound." She got out the swabs, cleaning cloths, and medical alcohol, and Harold helped her remove the young man's coat and shirt. The gaping wound was far worse than she'd imagined. The man's teeth started chattering when he was exposed to the cool air.

"There now, we'll warm you up," Hetty promised as she wrapped a blanket around his shoulders, but she had to keep his wound visible, which left him still half-naked.

"C-cold—so cold." The young man, who couldn't have been more than twenty years old, started to shake.

"He's going into shock," Hetty gasped. The man convulsed violently, blood coating his lips as he coughed and struggled for breath.

"Try to hold him still." Harold helped pin the man down on the bed to keep him from hurting himself.

"Moth-mother . . ." He grasped Hetty's shoulder in an almost punishing grip, his eyes wide as terror seized him. "Don't—want to die." The words stuttered out of his bloody lips.

"It's all right, it's all right, you're *safe*." She stroked his wet blond hair back from his face. The man was shaking so hard that she couldn't look at his wound until he stilled.

"Mo-mother?" This time, the word was barely a rasp. "Scared . . ."

The fear in his eyes shattered everything inside her that had stayed strong until that moment, and she did the only thing she could. She wrapped herself around the man, hugging him to her body as he gasped and choked for air.

"I'm here. *I'm here.*"

With a soft exhale, the man went limp in her arms. She didn't let go, didn't open her eyes. She held the man, praying to feel him breathe against her neck, to feel some pulse of life within him. All she felt was stillness, that kind of stillness that swallows a person's soul. Somehow she'd managed to keep herself above the surface of despair, but this . . . this was too much. This boy she didn't even know lying dead in her arms. *It was far too much.*

"Please . . . no . . . *please* . . ." She wasn't sure who she was begging, a god who had turned His protective gaze away from England and her brave boys, or the young man who'd already passed on. She begged in a way she never had before. If she could just save him, just one more . . .

"He's gone," Harold said.

Her pleas turned to sobs, the kind that shook her so hard she'd ache for days afterward. She'd never been one to cry, but as the warmth of the man's body faded and the light in his eyes dimmed, she wept. The promise of youth and life had vanished from him as the mist did beneath the rising sun in the summer.

"There now, ma'am. You gave him comfort." Harold placed a hand on her shoulder. "You did all you could."

"He needed more. He needed . . ." She choked on her own words. "He needed his *mother.*"

She rocked on the bed, the lifeless soldier still in her arms. She closed her eyes, seeing Major Taylor's face on his body, seeing Marcus's face, her father's, and then Charles's. This man could have been any one of them. This man had been *someone* to others. A son to a mother and a father, possibly a husband or a brother.

Hetty slowly released the boy's body and laid him gently on his back on the bed. With trembling bloodstained fingertips, she closed his eyes. There was a light blanket that wasn't being used by the men above, and she drew it over his body, covering him as a death shroud.

She lifted her face and stared out the porthole window of the cabin at the gray sea. The rage and grief inside her were strong enough that if she faced down a division of Panzer tanks at that moment, she would show no mercy. It was a terrifying thing to learn about herself, that she was full of such rage.

The hum of a plane reached her ears, and she raced back up on deck. She snatched the nearest rifle from Angus Kincade. It was an M1 Garand, a standard infantry rifle that many of the men in the boat currently had strapped to their backs. She studied the gun, remembering what her father had taught her about the Garand. It had eight shots of .30-06 ammunition and was more powerful than the Bren guns. If she got lucky, she could bring the plane down, even if it was close to impossible.

She took aim as the German Stuka bore down on the beaches. She held her breath until the water ahead of them churned with the force of the low-flying aircraft.

"You won't get him, ma'am," Harold said. "The cockpit has armored glass four inches thick. Even if you aim for the fuel tanks, you'd need the devil's own luck to break through."

"I'll take it down if it's the last bloody thing I do."

The men on the beaches were running. Some had stopped and were firing their own guns at the Stuka because it had dipped low enough to make a decent target. Hetty ignored the chaos and shouting of men around her and stayed utterly still and focused. The men on the boat ducked for cover while she faced down the aircraft.

It was just like skeet shooting, she realized with a terrible coldness as she led the target the way she'd been taught. She fired off several shots in rapid succession along the side of the slender dark-green aircraft. It climbed higher and wheeled around the smoky sky for a second pass. Hetty reloaded the rifle. Harold appeared at her side, his own gun in his hands. The men on the decks glanced around, and then as Hetty prepared to fire, several of them scrambled to their feet, slinging guns off their backs. With a small army around her, Hetty steadied her breath and waited.

"Not yet!" she called out. "Wait for my signal!"

The Stuka bore down on them, the deafening rumble only driving her determination deeper.

"Now!" she shouted, and a volley of gunfire burst from the men aboard the *Henrietta* and straight into the oncoming plane.

A violent explosion tore through the air, knocking everyone off their feet and sending shock waves across the water, which rocked the boat violently.

Hetty scrambled to her feet, still gripping the semiautomatic rifle as she saw the plane smoldering in the shallows of the oil-slicked water while clouds of black smoke obscured the soldiers on the shore.

She slowly lowered the rifle, and Angus caught it before she dropped it in stunned horror at what she had done. Every soldier on board turned toward her with looks of amazement and admiration on their faces. They'd brought down a German aircraft and saved countless lives upon the beach.

Hetty glanced down at herself as her hands came away sticky with something. Her clothes were painted in crimson. It was only then that she realized her hands and chest were still covered with the blood of the soldier who'd died in her arms.

"Three cheers for the lady!" one of the men shouted, and the boys on the boat cheered with him.

Their cheers came to her as though through a dense fog. Hetty turned to Charles, needing in that moment to see him there. He was the one thing in this world that grounded her and made her feel safe.

His gray eyes were dark and fathomless as the sea, and she wondered if she'd broken something between them, never to be mended. Did he see a killer, a woman without a heart? She'd just killed two men in that plane. Would he ever look at her like he used to? It was not what a proper Englishwoman would do—it was barbaric, a *brutal* thing she'd done.

Their deaths didn't bring back the man who'd died in her arms. But those men would never hurt anyone else, and she clung to that cold solace.

She turned away, unable to bear the thought of what he must be thinking now. Instead, she watched the wreckage of the German aircraft burn in the shallows, black smoke billowing out from the flaming metal.

"I'm sorry," she whispered into the breeze. She was sorry that she'd had to kill, sorry that she'd lost the boy in the cabin below, sorry that any of them were even here fighting like this. Hadn't they all been through this twenty years ago? Why was this happening again?

They were underway for Dover when night fell. She found herself back in the cabin with the man they had lost. She stared at his pale face. How strange that he seemed to be unrecogniz- able in death. It was alien to her now in a way his living, breathing countenance had not been. She couldn't bear to leave him alone.

"I'm sorry," she whispered to him. "I'm sorry." The words would never feel strong enough or good enough, but they were all she had. She didn't know this man's name, but she would never forget him. His face would be there whenever she closed her eyes.

"Hetty . . ." She glanced up to see Charles lingering in the doorway. "I thought I'd find you here."

She turned her face away and discreetly wiped tears from her cheeks. "Shouldn't you be manning the helm?"

"The Scotsman took over for Harold and Angelo is at the helm. We have some time to rest, and I wanted to check on you." His gaze strayed to the dead soldier on the bed.

Without another word, he came over and put an arm around her shoulders. He seemed to do that a lot lately, wrap himself around her and hold her. Was he worried she would drift away? She'd felt as though she might until he held her like this. All the world could have blown away, and she'd stay rooted in that moment with him. Safe, cherished. She buried her face in his neck, and for a brief instant she forgot where she was and thought she was at home, curled up on the couch with him.

"Please don't hate me," she begged him.

"*Hate* you? Hetty, how could I?" he asked. His lips touched her forehead. She felt so cold inside and out, and Charles was pure sunlight, breathing warmth into her.

"I . . . I killed two men."

"I could never *hate* you. You are a fierce goddess of war. I only hate that you will carry this burden inside your heart. I wish I could take that from you and carry it upon my shoulders instead." He kissed the crown of her hair. "I hate that we all must fight, but hate *you*? Christ, woman, I'm *in love* with you." His wry chuckle made her lips flicker with a weak smile. "Nothing will ever change that. I'm *yours*, Hetty my darling."

She was his too . . . but the words were too new, too raw to be spoken just yet.

"Come up on deck when you're ready. We'll be in Dover in half an hour." He placed one more kiss upon her lips before he went back up on deck. He hadn't even noticed that some of the blood on her chest had transferred to his own.

She was dead on her feet but managed to find her way back up on deck and then marveled at the moonlight reflecting upon the water as white cliffs appeared in the distance.

This arrival at the port was harder than the first. The men on the deck were quieter this time. Perhaps it was the fall of darkness that made everyone feel the loss of their brothers more keenly. Hetty shook the hands of a few as they disembarked. The Scotsman, Angus Kincade, was the last, and he called out for a man stationed on the docks.

"We've got a lad on board who needs a few hands to carry him home with honor." Then Angus turned to Hetty. "I knew the lad who passed. Good man he was. Ye cared for him, lassie. His family will ken what happened, that he had a mother's love in the end."

"I'm no mother," Hetty said softly, wishing that she'd known what secrets a mother would have to help a child in his final hour.

"Mothers are *angels*, lassie, and ye were our *avenging* angel today. Ye may not have children of yer own yet, but yer an angel all the same." Angus bowed low to her before he and several soldiers retrieved the young man's body and carried him ashore. Hetty's hands fisted at her sides as she fought off fresh tears.

Charles sent a message with the dockworkers to call Elizabeth so she would know they had made it back safe again.

For the rest of her life, Hetty would never know where she found the strength to keep going after such heartbreak, but there were more men waiting for them. More men like Major Taylor who needed to be saved. She lifted her chin and faced the sea.

❦

"Nearly sixty men rescued in less than half a day," Elizabeth said softly as she hung up the phone. "So far, Hetty and Charles are safe, but they're headed back out again soon."

"Sixty men? For that ship, two loads, not bad," the colonel said. "Word is, there is a fleet of ships moving back and forth across the Channel." The colonel added this as they all sat down for dinner that night.

Elizabeth had decided to leave for London the following day. She'd been too worried about Hetty and Charles to get any real work done.

"Some ships are coming all the way down from Scotland," Marcus said. "That's what I heard when I biked to the village today. Everyone is talking about it. Someone said it's a *miracle*."

"It is," Elizabeth replied. "Civilian ships sailing into danger and successfully bringing men home *is* a miracle. I just pray that the German air force leaves the beaches and ships alone."

"I made a few calls," the colonel said. "I still have a few friends left in London who know what's happening. The French are keeping the German forces at bay. The French are buying our men time to evacuate. Never thought I'd hear a day when they'd defend us like that, at least not twice in one century. It's damned noble of them."

"Will we rescue the French too?" Marcus asked the colonel.

Colonel Cunningham's gaze lowered to the table, and he cleared his throat as though it was suddenly harder to speak.

"I—hope so, but some soldiers will have to stay behind and hold the perimeter as long as they can to give our men on the beaches a chance."

Marcus's face drained of color. "They'll be left behind when the Germans . . ." The boy didn't finish.

"Yes, I'm afraid so."

"Well," Mrs. Harrow interrupted, her tone falsely cheery. "Anyone want a cherry tart? I pulled a few from the oven. They're nice and hot."

Elizabeth and Eva both shook their heads. Marcus was the only one who had the heart to take the housekeeper up on her offered dessert. The others were thinking of those soldiers in France, the poor brave men left behind to keep the Germans from slaughtering the troops on the beaches.

The colonel muttered something about needing to see to things in his room. Elizabeth saw the older gentleman remove a brandy bottle from the cabinet and walk away with one of the glasses.

She wondered how this must feel to someone who knew the horrors of war, hearing about the next generation of young men facing it all over again and being unable to do anything about it. Elizabeth couldn't even imagine the toll that would take.

Elizabeth sank into her bed that night, listening to the old manor house creak and groan. As the wind blew against the gables, it whistled eerily through the tiny cracks in the doors and windows. Somewhere in the nearby forest, a fox screamed. The sudden sharp shriek made Elizabeth start, her fingers clenching the sheets.

Her dreams that night were full of men dying upon the beaches across the Channel, and her friends who were in terrible danger as they tried to help. England needed a miracle now more than ever.

CHAPTER 21

M*ay 31, 1940*

THE *HENRIETTA* REACHED DUNKIRK AGAIN EARLY ON THE LAST day of May, beginning their third day assisting with the evacuation. The growing light of dawn poured over the long stretches of sand dunes that dipped into gently shelving beaches. It was such a desolate, eerie place, made more so by the ruins of war scattered on the sand.

A dark line of men formed along the pale shores as they waited to take their chance at reaching the motorboats and other craft that were able to get closer to the beach than the destroyers and sloops. The burned-out remains of a paddle steamer named the *Crested Eagle* served as a fresh reminder of the dangers everyone faced.

A new wreck had joined the *Crested Eagle* since the last time they'd been there. It was another paddle steamer, the *Devonia*. Hetty and Elizabeth had been on the *Devonia* seven months ago in the Bristol Channel when they'd taken a brief holiday.

"Look." Angelo pointed out seven large lifeboats in the shallow water filling with men. The coxswains used whistles and called out orders sharply to keep the boarding soldiers from swamping and sinking them. The lifeboats were able to get close enough to shore that the men could wade waist-deep into the water before climbing aboard.

"Where did the lifeboats come from?" Hetty asked. They weren't lifeboats for many of the nearby ships that were aiding the rescue. These boats were much larger and more substantial. They could take well over a dozen men comfortably and a few more if necessary.

"They're probably from the Lifeboat Institution," Charles said as he joined them at the railing. "I heard some naval officers talking about it while you were sleeping during our last refueling."

"You'd better get some rest on the way back," she reminded him. "You've slept less than the rest of us." Hetty took Charles's face in her hands and studied the darkening circles under his eyes with concern. He closed his eyes at her touch.

"I'll sleep later, when the job is done," he replied.

She looked back at the beach. There were still too many men left. They would be coming back for days.

"You'll sleep on the way back, or else," she warned.

A mischievous twinkle lit his gray eyes. "Or else what?"

"Trust me, you don't want to know the '*or else*.'" She leaned in to brush her lips over his in a kiss. He caught her waist, his large hands spanning her body as he simply held her, his forehead pressed to hers. She hadn't realized until then that she needed to feel him *hold* her. She was barely clinging to sanity after all that they'd been through, and they weren't close to being finished.

"Ho there!" a man shouted. They broke apart as a lifeboat pulled up alongside them. It was full of men and headed back to Dover.

"Everyone all right?" Charles asked the coxswain who'd hailed them, his arm still wrapped around Hetty.

"Yes, sir. Our ship is full. But there's men that need to be picked up. They've been pinned down by the enemy and can't make it to the boarding areas with the others. They're over there." He pointed to a rocky part of the beach. Half a dozen army trucks had been driven into the sea, their tires shot out to make them of no use to the Germans, and they formed a barrier of sorts to give the men shelter from the aircraft that swooped down to strafe the beaches.

"I see it," Charles replied as he peered through his field glasses.

"There's about twenty or so men who need evacuation. Two of them are my boys. I was hoping you could pick them up?"

Charles's eyes widened. "Your sons?"

"I'm as shocked as you, sir. My lads were in different divisions, didn't even know they were both at Dunkirk. They ran into each other while helping to sink the lorries. My boys wouldn't let me take them on my boat, insisted the others go first."

The pride in the father's voice made Hetty's lip tremble. It was one of a thousand stories of bravery that would come from this week. They had to do something to help those men.

"We'll fetch them straightaway," she promised and looked to Charles. "Won't we?"

"Absolutely. Harold, set a course for that outcropping past the west mole." Charles pointed to the spot.

"Thank you, sir," the coxswain said.

"What are your sons' names?" Hetty asked, wanting to make sure they found them.

"Ralph and Lawrence Clement, ma'am," the coxswain answered.

"We'll see it done," Charles vowed and then went to work, readying the ship before they got close to where the men were hiding.

Masts of sunken ships filled the harbor, making navigation through the waters precarious. The beaches were filled with debris, evidence of aerial dogfights, including the bomber that Hetty and the other soldiers had brought down with their guns. She stared at the wreckage as waves lapped at the charred remains of the aircraft's tail. Her stomach pitched and she covered her mouth, swallowing down a rush of bile as she faced what she'd done. Thankfully, she didn't see the bodies of the pilots inside. That would have been too much for her.

"You all right?" Angelo asked.

It took her a moment to compose herself, and she gave a shaky nod. It was best to get back to work. Work would distract her.

As they drew closer to the beach, Hetty raised her field glasses, searching for the small band of men they were meant to rescue.

Hetty gasped as she saw the corpses of horses, their stomachs ripped apart and entrails scattered across the sand. Men lay in grotesque poses of violent deaths, their eyes wide, mouths open, a look of pain and horror in their sightless eyes.

"Oh dear God." She lowered the glasses and looked away for

a moment to catch her breath, but she forced herself to continue the search. An armored lorry that was hollowed out from a bombing run was half-sunk in the ocean. Huddled in the water beside it was a cluster of troops.

"Behind that lorry!" She pointed to the men, and the *Henrietta* angled toward the spot, going as far into the shallows as it could without getting trapped on the sand. Angelo cupped his hands around his mouth and called out to the men to come aboard.

One by one, the men began swimming out into the ocean in single file. They were up to their shoulders, rifles slung across their backs. Hetty guided them toward the ladder at the back of the yacht, where they were pulled up onto the ship.

"Do we have any Clements on board?" Hetty asked the dripping troops.

"Here!" Two young men so alike in features that they had to be brothers approached Hetty from either side.

"Ralph and Lawrence?" she asked.

"I'm Ralph," the older one said, and nodded at the younger-looking man beside him. "He's Lawrence."

"Thank God. We passed by your father. He was captaining a full lifeboat. We promised him we would bring you brave lads home," Hetty said.

"Such a dear old chap he is," Ralph chuckled, but Hetty heard the relief just below his laugh.

Lawrence smiled. "We told him to take the others first. Couldn't leave a man behind, you know."

Hetty retrieved an armful of blankets to hand out to the soldiers. "Let's get you all home."

"Wait! There's more men!" Angelo pointed to several

huddled figures farther back on the beach who were using a wrecked Stuka as a shield. "We can't leave them."

Hetty agreed, and rushed to the helm to show Charles where the other men were taking cover.

"They'll have to swim out to us like the others," Charles said as he maneuvered the yacht as close to the beach as he could.

"You lot!" Lawrence yelled to the men. "Drop your gear and swim to us!"

"Drop our gear, *monsieur?*" one man shouted back. He had a French accent, and there was a rush of muttering on the ship. The word *Frenchies* was mouthed several times among the recently rescued men on board.

"That's right. You'll drown if you don't. Drop everything you can," Lawrence called back. One by one, the men shed their gear bags and rifles before wading toward the *Henrietta*. The seawater frothed gray with oil and churning sand around the men who were making their way to Charles's yacht.

The drone of engines above them was their only warning as a trio of bombers blazed past overhead. Bullets peppered the beach and water. Everyone dove for what cover they could find. Hetty watched helplessly as the men in the water kept swimming. Their strokes were desperate, and terror filled their faces.

"Come on, lads, just a bit farther!" Ralph cried out. He leaned over the railing, waving at them. "Faster, now!"

As the bombers began to circle around on the beaches again, one of the men on board turned to Charles, raising a pistol. Hetty's heart dropped to her feet in fear.

"Leave the Frenchies behind! They'll get us killed!" the frantic soldier shouted. The gun in the man's hand trembled. The other men near him backed up.

"Easy now." Angelo tried to approach the soldier carefully.

The man shifted his aim toward Angelo, forcing the man to back up a step, then he aimed it back at Charles.

Charles released the wheel, his body rigid. His gaze flicked between the French soldiers still in the water and the German aircraft circling around for a second run.

The man brought his pistol closer to Charles's face. "I said get us the bloody hell out of here!"

Charles's hands twitched at his sides. Hetty guessed he was planning to reach for the pistol he kept near the helm, but he wouldn't get it out before the other man could shoot.

Hetty sank down to the deck, out of sight from the anxious soldier, and crawled along the wood planks past the others toward him. The majority of the men onboard were half-dead with exhaustion and just wanted to get home. She didn't blame them, but they couldn't leave those men in the water behind.

"I'll shoot!" the man with the gun shouted.

Hetty's heart was beating so loud that she could hear it above the German bombers overhead. Suddenly, a young officer inched his service weapon across the deck toward her. He nudged the gun into position so that Hetty could grasp it. She thanked him with the smallest of nods. Her fingers curled around the barrel, and a moment later she stood upright and aimed the gun at the back of the man holding a pistol on Charles.

"Here's was going to happen." Hetty's voice, to her own amazement, was firm and her hand didn't so much as shake. "You're going to sit down and wait for us to rescue the men in the water. Then I'll make everyone tea and biscuits. We'll all have a bloody nice trip back to Dover. Do you understand?"

The soldier tensed as Hetty pressed the barrel of her pistol against his back. His face turned the slightest bit in her direction, and it gave Charles the chance he needed. He knocked the other man's gun to the ground and rendered the man unconscious with a single punch to the face.

"Nicely done." Hetty's heart still battered her ribs even as she lowered the gun and gave it back to the officer who'd passed it to her.

"Boxing runs in the family. My father will be glad to know it saved our lives."

Hetty's shoulders sagged in relief as the first of the French troops climbed aboard. "And theirs."

"We've got to get them aboard and leave." Charles watched the bombers come in for another strafing run. They watched helplessly as men were mowed down by a hail of machine-gun fire. Everyone dove for cover as the bomber screamed past. One bomb blew up close enough that it showered everyone on board the *Henrietta* with sand and water. The sound deafened Hetty for several seconds, then her ears rang, and she blinked in a daze at the black dirt and sand that coated the faces of everyone around her.

"Charles, we still have to go back for Major Taylor!"

"We can't! Our boat's full, and they might come back. We can't give them a chance to sink us." Charles's eyes met hers across the deck, and she knew he was right. "We'll come back," he promised her. "He'll still be there. He wouldn't dare let you down."

Hetty turned her face toward the distant mole, glad that the sea spray masked her tears. "No, he wouldn't."

All she could think of as she wiped sand and sea from her eyes was that there were still too many men left on the shores of Dunkirk. Major Taylor was out there somewhere, hopefully still alive, but stranded on that beach. She felt a lump of dread that by the time they returned, it might be too late.

CHAPTER 22

J une 3, 1940

JUST AFTER MIDNIGHT, THE *HENRIETTA* MADE ONE FINAL TRIP
to the beaches of France. Seven hundred men in more than
twenty-four voyages had traveled from France to Dover aboard
the *Henrietta*. It felt like so many, and yet so few. The once-shiny
decks of the *Henrietta* were now covered in sand, dirt, and blood.
The cabin walls were lined with punctures from machine-gun
fire. During the day, the light had cut through the bullet holes,
leaving shining paths through the dark cabin interiors. It had
been eerie to see so many holes, knowing that each of these
bullets could have found places in the bodies of men instead.

Hetty thought of all the men who'd survived the trip back.

LAUREN SMITH

The endless procession of faces that had once seemed so different from each other now blurred together. She'd worn her fingers raw using fishing wire to stitch wounds, and her eyes hurt from squinting in the dark as she bandaged them. Every bone in her body ached so deep that she almost whimpered with every move she made.

But she couldn't rest, not yet. Major Taylor was still out there, waiting.

Hetty had to see the shores one more time and make sure there were no more men left to rescue. Major Taylor was there with another thousand or so men who'd emerged from the city of Dunkirk and the surrounding countryside in a frantic race to the coast.

The Germans were close now, and the British and French forces could feel something in the air, a desperation that had everyone on edge. During the last few trips they'd made, the men they'd rescued had been more haggard, more haunted than the others, as if they knew what was coming and couldn't leave Dunkirk fast enough.

All around them in the darkness to the east and to the west were flashes of light, flares and bombs and other artillery that lit up the night sky in an unnatural, eerie glow. The fighting was close now, slithering into the city, where before it had been a distant threat in the surrounding countryside. Now the Germans were in the city, no more than a mile or two from the shore.

The east mole was barely visible in the darkness. Much of it had been destroyed by bombing and strafing since their first visit. The remaining troops on this stretch were down to less than a hundred.

As the *Henrietta* reached the mole, Hetty searched the faces of the men who leapt onto the yacht. The major was not among them.

At the far end of the mole stood a man in an officer's uniform. His back was to her as he faced the city of Dunkirk. She recognized him, even under the fall of night.

"Major Taylor!" she hollered at him. The last of the troops on the mole had made it onto the *Henrietta*, and the remaining soldiers on the beaches were climbing aboard lifeboats and motorboats. The shore was nearly empty.

Gunshots echoed across the water with a distant *pop-pop-pop* that filled Hetty with primal dread. The French rear guard was fighting valiantly to the last man, giving England's forces a chance to escape.

"Major Taylor!" she cried out. "It's your turn!"

"Major Taylor, please! We must go!" Charles shouted.

The troops on the *Henrietta* stared at the lone figure of the major with weary respect.

A black pit opened in Hetty's stomach. "He's not going to come . . ."

"He wouldna leave a man behind," a Welshman said to Hetty. "He's damned noble, that one. I think he's waiting on the French soldiers, but they arena coming."

"Well, I'm not bloody well leaving him behind." She drew back and made the leap across to the mole, wobbling on the rocks a bit before she steadied herself.

"Christ, Hetty! Get back here!" Charles shouted, but she wasn't listening. She sprinted toward the major, shouting his name.

Major Taylor turned. "Miss Byron? You must get back on the boat."

"That's what I said." Charles gasped for breath as he caught up to them.

"We have to leave now. The beaches are cleared." Hetty nodded at the pale moonlit beach. The only soldiers left now were those who would never come home.

Another rapid succession of shots and a responding blast of something far bigger than rifles came from the city in the distance.

"If I can just reach the rear guard—" Major Taylor started toward the shore, but Hetty caught his arm, halting him. His once-crisp uniform was shredded in places. Blood and dirt covered much of him, and his hair was wild, as though he'd been driving his fingers through and pulling at it. He'd lost his officer's cap.

Hetty tried not to think of how clean and polished he'd looked when they'd said goodbye at the train station. He wasn't that man anymore. He was just a man, hurt and frightened and grieving like all the others.

"William . . ." She spoke his given name for the first time since she'd met him.

The sky above burst with light as enemy flares arced across the sky. They were out of time. The sight was haunting yet beautiful, so beautiful Hetty caught her breath as she watched the flares slowly fall near the dark shapes of Dunkirk. The report of rifle fire followed as the last of the French soldiers made their final stand. They were perishing in this little town for every life that was sailing away, including hers. There was nothing that could have prepared her for this, knowing that less than a mile away men were falling beneath the flares and moonlight, the bright lights of their lives extinguished so that she and all of England might live.

"We can't leave them . . ." Major Taylor's words broke like the waves upon the pale, shivering sands around them.

Hetty knew what her father would say, the words needed to convince a brave man to leave others behind.

"They are doing their duty. If you don't leave, their sacrifice will be in vain. Live now so that you might fight in their memory tomorrow."

Hetty held out a hand to the major as he slowly turned to look at her.

"Come home for Sarah, William. That is what those men are dying for. For the breath in all those who still live."

Major Taylor swallowed hard and accepted Hetty's hand, squeezing it once before he let go. "For them." They ran back down the rocky ledge of the mole and leapt onto the *Henrietta*.

The sounds of war chased them across the water as the *Henrietta* turned away from Dunkirk's lifeless shores.

As the *Henrietta* plunged toward home, the sharp staccato pulsing of gunfire was soon softer than the waves, and the flares became distant dancing lights upon a dark horizon. Everyone on board stared back toward the beaches.

It was a terrible thing to feel relief that one had survived at such a great cost. Hetty looked at the faces of the men around her. All silent, some streaked with tears, others gazing unblinking at what they'd escaped. No one said it, but Hetty could feel the unspoken question: Had they lost the war before it had even begun? Was Germany now coming for the beaches of England?

Major Taylor stepped up beside her. "To the men who stayed behind." His words echoed on the lips of every man aboard the ship as they faced the doomed French city. A barrage of shells exploded, lighting up the skeletal remains of the city like ghastly specters.

"I was never a very religious man," the major said quietly. "But something about what the last few men who reached the landing told me has a grip on my very soul."

He was silent a moment before speaking again. "They lost their division in the countryside and didn't know where to go. They were hopelessly turned around, and the Germans were closing in all around them. The SS were slaughtering anyone they captured. They crossed paths with a few French soldiers who were staying behind to make their final stand."

Hetty's throat closed as she tried not to cry.

"They asked the French soldiers where to go, they'd heard that the English and some of the French were evacuating. Bombs and flares were lighting up the sky around them tonight, and when they reached me, I asked them how they had found the beaches since they were so late and clearly lost."

The major closed his eyes for a brief moment before he continued. "The French soldiers pointed to the narrowing dark spot on the horizon ahead of them, the only place that wasn't being shelled. Above it was the brightest star any of them had ever seen. It glowed while all other stars flickered. The French soldiers told them to follow that star and they would find help." He turned to Hetty and smiled, but his expression was full of pain. "And here you are . . . the finest help anyone could ask for in their darkest hour."

Hetty felt unworthy of his words, of the depth of feeling behind them.

"We did what anyone would do." She checked on the men now settling down to sleep on the deck of the yacht, tucked up against each other for warmth. Blood, sand, and oil covered them, but on each face she saw the same expression.

Hope.

"By dawn, Dunkirk will be in the hands of the enemy and very few prisoners, if any, will be left alive. But not our men. It's a damned miracle." Major Taylor let out a sigh that held the weight of a thousand lives upon it.

"Try to get some rest, Major. Sarah will be upset with you if you don't take care of yourself." Hetty touched his shoulder with a gentle pat and then went to the cabin to try to sleep herself. Now that she'd found the major, the last of her energy was gone. She curled up in the cabin next to several soldiers and somehow managed to sleep for the first time in what felt like days.

She was shaken awake by Charles as he lifted her up by her hands and held her close, hugging her.

"We're here. We're in Dover. We made it, Hetty, with the last of them." He nuzzled her throat, and his warm breath felt like the kiss of a summer breeze in the midst of a long winter.

"It feels like a strange sort of dream, doesn't it?" Hetty confessed. She curled her arms around his neck and held on to him until she was grounded again. They were safe. They finally broke apart and walked out onto the deck of his yacht. Bullet holes covered part of the cabin walls, and shrapnel had embedded itself in the hull.

She touched the railing and spoke to the ship that had given so much to her and the men they'd rescued.

"You did well, my darling. You saved them." She patted the rail and managed a weary smile for Charles.

"She did at that, didn't she?" He looked exhausted, but his eyes were full of pride as he stared at the once-beautiful pleasure yacht. It bore worse marks of battle than they did.

"Well, I must report to the officers in charge and see what needs to be done," Major Taylor announced to Hetty and Charles as he joined them. He cleared his throat, and his mustache twitched as he seemed to struggle to control himself.

"Major?" Charles said with obvious concern.

The officer faced them, his eyes bright with tears. "What you did today—these last several days," he amended. "When I think of the risks and how many lives you saved . . . including mine . . ." He swallowed hard. "It makes a man realize how damned glad he is to be among friends." He held out his hand to Hetty and Charles.

Charles shook his hand first. "It was an honor, sir."

Hetty gently brushed the major's hand aside and threw her arms around him, hugging him. She ignored the burn of tears in her eyes as she leaned in and whispered in his ear, "You must call Sarah straightaway, do you hear? You can't have her worrying about you, not with the baby."

When they pulled apart, the major stared at her. "You knew?"

"Yes. I couldn't let anything happen to you. You were our first client, Major. You had faith in us when we feared no one would. That means more than you'll ever know. I'd fight beside you against anything or anyone."

The major's lips curved in that gentle smile she loved so well. But this time, he looked at Charles.

"You'd better watch out for this one. She's a damned brigadier in a skirt. Never let her out of your sight."

"I won't," Charles promised. "She's stuck with me, whether she realizes it or not."

Hetty managed a laugh, but her own exhaustion was catching up with her. The major bowed, and with one more smile, he departed the *Henrietta* to call his wife and report for further duty.

The docks were filled with soldiers as the last of the rescue boats arrived and released their troops. Blankets, food, and water were passed out by volunteers, and the grateful, battle-worn heroes vanished into the distance.

"Where will they go?" Hetty asked. Her heart was already missing every one of the men who had been aboard the yacht. They had become something more to her than strangers. They were *her* men, *her* soldiers. She would never see any of them again, but she'd never forget them.

"They'll go home, I expect. They'll be reassembled and then sent back to France once our military decide upon a new plan of attack. As glad as I am that we saved them, I fear we only delayed death for some of them. They'll all have to return and fight, and now we've lost France to the Germans. We need the United States to join in or we won't survive if the Germans push across the Channel."

It was something Hetty had thought of as well. The last war had been won when everyone had joined together. Without the United States, they had no chance of victory.

"Sir, permission to leave?" Harold Dowdy asked as he and Angelo joined them on deck, their few belongings packed up. They looked ready to collapse where they stood.

"Yes, yes, please go. You've performed admirably," Charles said as he shook their hands. "No man will forget what you did for them today."

Hetty hugged them before they stepped down to the docks and vanished into the crowds.

"And what about us? Where will we go?" Hetty asked.

"Back to London. We both need a very long night's sleep."

Hetty couldn't resist teasing him, even as tired as she was. "And then?"

"And *then?*" He rolled his eyes. "Christ, woman, I'm dead on my feet. I have no bloody idea what's next. I only know I want to be with you." He pulled her into his side with a rakish but weary smile and kissed her.

They left the ship after changing out of their bloody clothes. Charles gave the Royal Navy permission to use the *Henrietta* for anything else they might need.

They caught a train to London. Charles claimed a seat for them and put an arm around her shoulder before he promptly fell asleep, his head resting against the window glass.

Hetty watched the morning light illuminate his face. He was one of the most wonderful men she had ever known, and she decided in that moment she was going to marry him now, not later.

After everything she had seen in the last five days, she understood what she hadn't before. Life is precious and could be snatched away in an instant. Charles was her bright star in the dark sky, her compass pointing her home. She knew she couldn't stand in the way of him going off to war, not anymore. So she would marry him soon, before he left, and she would no longer have any regrets.

By the time they reached London, she and Charles were famished and bought several sandwiches as they left the station before heading to Charles's townhouse. His butler, Jarvis, greeted them at the door and took one look at their faces before nearly fainting dead away.

"Sir! What can I do? What do you need?" Jarvis asked.

"Tea, *lots* of tea, and then . . . Well, don't worry, old boy. We'll sort ourselves out." Charles slapped a hand on the butler's shoulder with an exhausted grin.

"Miss Byron," Jarvis greeted her with a warm and relieved smile. "You both look well."

"Hello, Jarvis, it's lovely to see you. Simply lovely. Yes, we're quite fine." Hetty hugged the butler, and the poor man blushed clear to his toes, but she didn't care. She and Charles were *alive*. All those darling soldiers they had saved were alive. Today was *glorious*. Positively glorious.

They headed into Charles's drawing room, and Hetty went straight to the sofa and collapsed on it, lying lengthways, propping her aching feet up over one armrest. Jarvis brought in tea and a stack of newspapers.

"It's all over the world, the news of the Miracle of Dunkirk." Jarvis nodded at the papers. "Even the Americans praised England."

Charles reached for the paper on top of the stack, and Hetty saw it was one of the American papers, the *New York Times*. He scanned the page until he found the article.

"So long as the English tongue survives, the word Dunkirk will be spoken with reverence. For in that harbor, in such a hell as never blazed on earth before, at the end of a lost battle, the rags and blemishes that have hidden the soul of democracy fell away. There, beaten but unconquered, in shining splendor, she faced the enemy. They sent away the wounded first. Men died so that others could escape. It was not so simple a thing as courage, which the Nazis had in plenty. It was not so simple a thing as discipline, which can be hammered into men by a drill sergeant. It was not the result of careful planning, for there could have been little. It was the common man of the free countries, rising in his glory out of mill, office, factory, mine, farm and ship, applying to war the lessons he learned when he went down the shaft to bring out trapped comrades, when he hurled the lifeboat through the surf, when he endured poverty and hard work for his children's sake. This shining thing in the souls of free men Hitler cannot command, or attain, or conquer. He has crushed it, where he could, from German hearts. It is the great tradition of democracy. It is the future. It is victory."

He slowly set the paper down, and his gaze turned distant. Hetty knew what he was seeing. The horrors and heartbreak that they'd seen on the shores. But they had given their all. They had brought as many as they could home. It was a victory, but at a great and terrible cost.

"Christ . . ." Charles approached the sofa. Hetty moved over, and he lay down beside her. He folded his arms behind his head, and she curled up against him and rested her head on his chest. Neither of them touched the tea.

"Charles," she murmured drowsily as she watched the steam rise from the teapot. She was so tired she knew she wouldn't stay awake much longer. It was as though her body knew on some animal level that they were safe. She could rest now, away from the German aircraft or the panzers that now prowled the shelled-out streets of Dunkirk. *Safe at last.*

"Hmm?" Charles's sleepy reply made her smile.

"I'll marry you."

"Will you?" His voice was still sleepy. "I'm not dreaming, am I? Perhaps I ought to get it in writing?"

"No, you're not dreaming." She playfully pinched his stomach, and he laughed.

"Good. Because after I'm done resting"—he yawned dramatically—"I'll prove to you how rather deliriously happy I am."

"I imagine you will."

She smiled and drifted to sleep, safe in his arms.

Elizabeth sat in the back office on Bond Street, reading through a stack of letters. Work was the only thing that offered any distraction from her worries about Hetty and Charles. News of Dunkirk had been all over the papers, and she'd devoured every article she could find. She'd still had no word from them that they were safe. Deciding work was the only thing she could do, she'd come here to answer letters and try to focus on anything but her fears.

She opened one and noticed it was a letter from Erica Hanley to one of the young soldiers who had come into the Marriage Bureau for an interview a few months ago. They had agreed to use the bureau as a point of contact to avoid Erica's elderly aunt snooping through her letters.

Elizabeth picked up the letter, attempting to tuck it back into the envelope, but there was something else inside preventing her from doing so. She opened the envelope further and found a pair of photographs of a lovely half-naked woman in a very elegant but risqué set of lingerie. She examined the woman's face more closely and gasped. "Good heavens!" It was Erica! Such bravado to pose for those pictures! To think their quiet country mouse was not such a country mouse anymore. Elizabeth couldn't wait to tell Hetty, but it also made Elizabeth hot all over in embarrassment for their client. She shoved the boudoir photos back into the envelope, along with Erica's letter.

She was about to reach for the next letter in the pile when Miss Plumley rushed into the office.

"Sorry, ma'am, but it's a Mr. Jarvis on the phone. He says he's Mr. Humphrey's butler and that you might expect him to call."

"Oh goodness, yes!" He must have news about Hetty and Charles. Elizabeth hastened into the front office and picked up the phone. "Mr. Jarvis?"

"Miss Mowbray."

"Tell me you have news?"

"I do indeed. Mr. Humphrey and Miss Byron arrived safely at the house ten minutes ago."

"May I speak to Hetty?"

"I'm afraid she's not able to come to the phone."

Elizabeth tried not to panic. "Is she all right?"

"Yes, it's just that they've fallen asleep on the sofa, and I haven't the heart to wake them. Not after all they've been through."

"Oh, I see." Elizabeth sighed, and the tension in her shoulders faded away. "They're really all right?"

"Yes," the butler assured her. "I will have her call you when she's awake."

"Thank you, Jarvis."

"It's my pleasure, ma'am."

Elizabeth hung up and then hugged a stunned Miss Plumley. "They're home and they're all right. Would you please call Eva at Cunningham House and let her know the good news?"

"Yes, of course." The secretary dialed the country house while Elizabeth returned to her desk. She couldn't stop humming as she sat down to read the remaining letters.

CHAPTER 23

J *une 7, 1940*

"*MARRIED?*"

Hetty covered her ears to dull the sound of Elizabeth's enthusiastic squeal.

"Don't act so surprised." Hetty shared a chuckle with Charles. He sat on the edge of Hetty's desk in the Bond Street office.

"When is the ceremony?"

"Next week," said Hetty. "We don't want to wait." She reached for Charles's hand, and their fingers laced together. He raised her hand to his lips and kissed it.

"No, I imagine you don't. Oh, this is simply wonderful!" Elizabeth was over the moon. She'd been afraid this day would never come, and now to see her friend safe, happy, and with a man who was good enough to deserve her was the most wonderful thing in the world.

"Yes, well, I thought we might as well marry, since we would eventually."

"Oh?" Charles chuckled at Hetty's matter-of-factness. "I distinctly recall *begging* you to marry me."

His gentle teasing was even more charming given how clearly besotted he was. Elizabeth could have danced at the sight of her two friends so happy together.

"Well, I didn't say I wouldn't, but I was . . . afraid," Hetty admitted.

Charles's teasing expression softened, and he pulled Hetty against him, nuzzling her cheek before kissing her forehead. "There's nothing to be afraid of now. We've proven that, haven't we?"

Elizabeth sensed that whatever they were talking about had to do with Dunkirk, and she wondered if she'd ever truly understand all the two of them had gone through together.

The office door opened, and Eva entered, pale as alabaster. She had come to London for a few weeks to work on copying new files for the country office.

In her hands she clutched a copy of the *Daily Mirror*.

"Eva?" Charles got to his feet, sensing the girl's distress as she held up the paper, her hands trembling.

"They . . . they are shooting men, women, and children in the streets. Thousands are dead in Warsaw. I've heard . . . they are rounding people up. There's talk of a ghetto being built. I don't know what to do. I still haven't heard from my parents . . ." She trailed off as Charles took the paper from her and scanned the article.

"Eva, write down your parents' names and their last address. I shall make inquiries on your behalf." He gave her a pad of paper and a pen. "If they can be found, I will do all that I can to bring them to London."

Eva wrote the names down and passed him the paper, then sat down at her desk, her gaze distant. Hetty and Elizabeth bid Charles goodbye and stepped into their private office.

"We must do something," Elizabeth said.

"I agree, but what? Perhaps we should insist she stay with Colonel Cunningham and Mrs. Harrow in the countryside. She'll hear less grave news there," Hetty replied.

"You aren't suggesting she bury her head in the sand," Elizabeth argued. "That's not wise, no matter how much any of us might want to."

Hetty sighed. "I know. But she is so fragile, and she's been through so much. She never speaks about leaving Warsaw or what she and Marcus endured on their trip here. But she does cry in her sleep. It breaks my heart."

"Perhaps Charles will be able to find her parents." Elizabeth prayed he would. If anyone had the ability and connections, it was him.

"Well . . . for now, let's get her to focus on work. Everyone is always better when they have something useful to do," Hetty suggested as she checked the appointment book.

Elizabeth agreed. They returned to the main interview room and had Eva prepare some response letters to potential clients while they waited for their next appointment to arrive.

Miss Autumn Joseph came two minutes early, her sparkling laugh instantly endearing her to Elizabeth. She was a tiny creature with bright-blue eyes and a sunny disposition that filled the entire room with energy.

"Hello!" She shook Hetty's and Elizabeth's hands before taking a seat at the interviewing desk.

It took Elizabeth a few minutes to realize their client wasn't exactly young, nor was she very beautiful. She was rather plain and in her forties, yet the joy so naturally on display in Autumn's features seemed to make her glow. She simply beamed and looked at the world in a perpetual state of awe.

"Forgive me, Miss Joseph, but you are so buoyant of spirit," Hetty said. Elizabeth guessed that Hetty feared the woman was perhaps a tad unstable. It was unusual to see someone so happy in the midst of a war, after all.

"Oh, I'm so sorry," Autumn replied, a blush staining her cheeks. "It's just that . . . well, everything is so wonderfully new, you see. For the last thirty years, I've been almost blind. Ever since I was a child barely under the age of ten, everything was a terrible blur. Shapes near and far were simply dark masses. I'd rather forgotten what so many things looked like. Even people," she confessed more solemnly.

Elizabeth was stunned at the woman's candor over something that was no doubt difficult to bear, and she wondered what miracle had changed all that.

"It's quite the most awful thing not to see. One's family finds you a terrible chore or an obligation. You have no friends and certainly no beaux. Men expect their wives to have some use. Even the women who can't cook or clean are at least very pretty. I'm not—no, please don't say I am." She held up a hand when Elizabeth went to correct her about her beauty. "I'm not unattractive, but I'm no beauty. I've spent thirty years as a burden to those around me. Then I learned of a doctor who specializes in eyes, and he suggested surgery. Naturally, I was quite nervous. What if he made a mistake and I became fully blind? It was a tough thing to decide, but finally I took the risk."

"So you had eye surgery?" Hetty asked, making a note on her pad.

"Three years ago," Autumn supplied.

"Three? So you have been able to see for—"

"No, not at all. After the surgery, it was as if nothing had changed. I wept for weeks, which made my eyes hurt more, of course." She chuckled wryly at some painful memory.

"But now you see?"

She nodded. "It came slowly over time. First, the hazy shapes began to sharpen slowly at the edges, like a blurry watercolor turning into a most brilliant oil painting. It's rather funny. One day I went to post a letter at the nearest pillar box, only it never seemed to get any closer." She paused to make sure they were ready for the rest of her story.

"Go on," Elizabeth said, raptly listening to Autumn.

"Well, I had my cane with me, you see, and I was practically chasing the pillar box about, trying to put my letter in the slot. I thought that on top of my near blindness my eyes were now playing tricks on me. Then suddenly I got close enough to realize why it had been moving. It wasn't a mailbox, but a Chelsea pensioner. The man stared at me and said, 'Madam, kindly stop trying to shove your letters in my stomach.'" She burst out laughing, and Elizabeth and Hetty shared a grin.

"I quite understand the mistake," Elizabeth said. The Chelsea pensioners were retired British Army veterans who typically wore uniforms very similar in color to the tall pillar boxes, and their army medals hanging upon their uniforms could be mistaken for a mail slot to someone who could only see vague shapes.

"I remember thinking how interesting he looks, because I could see his face once I got close enough. I suddenly looked all about me, squinting ever so slightly, and I could see so many things I hadn't seen since I was a little girl. Every day I had less and less of a need to squint."

Elizabeth couldn't help but feel a rush of joy for the woman who had been given back such an important part of her life.

"So I thought . . . Well, now I can see everything, and I should very much like to have a husband to look at, preferably one who is decently attractive, because I will quite appreciate the sight of him all the more. And someone with a sense of humor. My life has been hard at times, and I would like to have fun now."

"We can certainly find you a handsome, humorous man." Hetty made a few more notes.

"Wonderful." Autumn happily filled out her questionnaire and paid her registration fee before leaving the office.

"Oh heavens, I quite like her," Elizabeth confessed. "We must match her to someone immediately."

Hetty nodded. "I couldn't agree more."

They closed the office a tad early that day. Hetty was going to see her parents, and Elizabeth was to meet Isabelle for dinner at the Savoy. Eva took a cab to Cunningham House for the weekend to be with her brother.

"Are you all right to find Isabelle?" Hetty asked as they both shared a look at the darkening skies.

"Yes, I'll be fine." Elizabeth would take care to get to the restaurant quickly.

Hetty caught a cab and left Elizabeth to lock the office and head downstairs. Miss Plumley had taken the day off, so the main reception on the ground floor was quiet, and a strange melancholy came over Elizabeth. She straightened up the magazines on the coffee table in their sitting area and tidied up the desk a bit before leaving.

As she turned the key in the lock, she had a disquieting feeling she'd often had as a child when the breeze died yet the very air seemed charged with energy. It was an eerie feeling, one she did not particularly like.

She checked her handbag and made sure she had her gas mask. They'd had so few drills lately that it had become easy to forget to carry one's mask about. She rushed into the night, waving down a cab before it got too dark. Still, she couldn't shake the feeling that something terrible was going to happen, but in what way she didn't know.

🕮

HETTY WALKED UP THE STEPS OF HER PARENTS' TOWNHOUSE and knocked. Their butler, Mr. Russo, let her in.

"They're in the drawing room," he advised quietly.

Hetty found her parents both reading—her mother a novel, her father a newspaper.

She knocked at the open door in the habit she'd always had as a child. "Hello."

"Hetty!" Her mother beamed at her.

"Darling, give us a minute?" her father said to Hetty's mother.

"What, why?"

"*Please.*" Her father didn't explain further.

"Very well. I need to see when dinner shall be ready." She hugged Hetty before she left the room.

Hetty, sensing her father's grave attitude, closed the drawing room door.

"Papa—"

"I received a letter from the admiral of the fleet this morning." He held up the letter that he'd apparently hidden in the middle of the newspaper that he'd been reading. He stood and stared at her, then at the words as he started to read the letter's contents.

"'A woman was seen on a pleasure yacht at Ramsgate Port departing for the town of Dunkirk. She and the men on the yacht made more than a dozen trips in six days and rescued close to seven hundred men. The reports from the naval vessels in the area recounted a harrowing escape from machine-gun fire, bombings, and other dangers. A few men reportedly claimed the woman, assisted by other soldiers on the yacht brought down a German Junkers JU 87aircraft.' The odds of even achieving that . . ." Her father murmured the last, as it was clearly not part of the letter. "The admiral ended the letter stating that this rather remarkable woman told a lieutenant that she was Brigadier Byron's daughter, and if they had any issues with her, they could question me." He lowered the letter, and his eyes were solemn as he stared at her.

"I didn't want to frighten you, but—"

"You went to war." He spoke the words softly, proudly, yet they also seemed to break him apart. "You could have been *killed*." His tone hardened. "My only child. Did you think for one second that your mother and I could have survived *losing* you?" He sounded angry, but Hetty saw only fear in his eyes. Fear for *her*, something she'd never seen in him before.

She rushed toward him, throwing herself into his arms, and suddenly the emotions she had kept bottled up since returning from Dunkirk came crashing to the surface.

"My dear girl, it's over," her father soothed as he cupped her head and kissed her forehead as though she were a small child.

"I understand now," she whispered into his chest. "The things that we saw . . ."

Her father hugged her tighter and murmured in her ear, "Every night, you must picture the faces of the men who walked off your boat alive. Remember them above all."

They spoke no more of Dunkirk, but Hetty saw her father tuck the letter from the admiral into his favorite novel before sliding it back onto the bookshelf.

That evening over dinner, Hetty cleared her throat. "I . . . have some news that I hope will delight you."

Her mother looked up from her roast beef curiously. "Oh, what is it?"

"Charles has—"

"Oh! A wedding!" her mother cried with joy, and her father chuckled, his mustache twitching. Had it been that obvious?

"He's asked you to marry him?" her father asked, confirming the news that her mother had cut off so abruptly with her cry of joy.

"Yes, he asked me a while ago, and now I said yes."

"Finally! It's about time," her mother agreed, as if Hetty had taken far too long to come around to this decision.

"Mama, what do you mean, *finally?*"

"Well, Lady Lonsdale and I have been having lunch once a week for the past several months, plotting how to bring you two together."

"Plotting? Gracious, Mama." Hetty arched a brow. "Dare I ask *what* you were plotting?"

"Well, we thought Charles should take you sailing again. It is rather romantic. She suggested that he invite you on another outing. I'm assuming he did?"

"He certainly did," her father muttered.

Hetty almost choked on a bite of carrots.

"Well, when is the wedding?" her father asked with a twinkle in his eye.

"Next week."

"Next week?" her mother almost shrieked. "You're marrying into an ancient bloodline and becoming a future countess. You need *much* more time to prepare for an appropriate wedding befitting someone of your new station."

"You have *one week*, Mama. I'm not waiting another moment to be married to Charles." She shared a look with her father. "I don't want to waste any more time, not when I know what I can lose."

"What you can lose? My dear, what are you talking about? You're young, Charles is young, and—"

"Charles will be leaving for Europe soon. In the army," Hetty said more quietly.

Her father's gaze softened. He knew now what she wanted him to do. He was to remove any obstacles that would prevent Charles from joining up. There would be no more holding him back. She supposed, in hindsight, that was one of the reasons she'd gone to Dunkirk. She'd had to see him in the middle of battle and know that he could survive and come back to her.

Her mother gasped. "Oh, Hetty dear, I'm so sorry." Now her mother was the one who understood her. She was all too familiar with the dread of being left behind to fret and tear herself apart in fear for her husband's safety.

"It will be all right," Hetty said, but she wasn't quite sure if she was saying it to herself or to them. She wasn't sure who needed to hear it most.

It will be all right. It has to be. I won't accept any other outcome.

She was a brigadier's daughter, and she would weather this storm the way she had been raised to, even if her very heart would be walking onto the battlefields of Europe.

⚜

Elizabeth and Isabelle left the Savoy promptly at nine o'clock after they finished dinner. It had been so utterly strange to be waited upon by three waiters while dining upon Pimms, consommé frappe, and salmon and white-wine sauce. They'd even had potatoes and asparagus tips, praline ices, and coffee. So many people in London were facing ration tightening, and yet they'd eaten like queens. Elizabeth wouldn't have agreed to it, but Isabelle had informed her it was a very important work dinner and they'd needed another woman to even the numbers. So that was how she'd found herself dining at the Savoy among the glittering set of London's elite who pretended for much of the night as though they weren't in the midst of a war.

"That was certainly lovely," Isabelle sighed dreamily.

"You are used to dining like a queen," Elizabeth teased as they stepped into the dark night.

"Frequently," her aunt admitted, "but not all the time. This was rather special."

It certainly was. Elizabeth had been anxious to learn that she was to be dining with several gentlemen her aunt worked with.

But then she'd calmed when she'd realized that she would be able to recruit them as clients for the bureau if they were unattached.

"So, tell me, what did you think of Henry Goodyear?" Isabelle prompted.

"Mr. Goodyear?" He was a handsome man, with laughing gray eyes and a smile that promised delight in many forms. "He was perfect." He was perhaps a few years younger than Miss Autumn Joseph, but he had the same lively personality that could turn any glum-faced person into a laughing soul.

"So you wouldn't mind if I gave him a nudge, then?" her aunt asked as she waited for the Savoy bellman to flag down a cab so they didn't have to walk home in the dark.

"A nudge?" Elizabeth asked.

"To come and call on you. You haven't been on a single outing with any gentlemen since you moved to London. Hetty's getting married next week. She'll likely settle down, and you ought to be thinking along the same lines."

Settle down . . . Those words had always managed to send a current of fear through her. Life shouldn't be about settling down—it should be about exciting explorations and experiences. Life was meant to be an adventure with the right person. It was why she loved the Marriage Bureau. They weren't settling anyone down. They were matching soulmates, giving people a partner for whatever adventures life could offer them.

"Isabelle, Hetty isn't going to settle down. If anything, she's been more active than ever. She accompanied Charles on his yacht to Dunkirk. They rescued close to seven hundred men."

"She *what?*" Isabelle adjusted the glittering black wrap around her shoulders as the bellman of the hotel waved them over to a cab that had pulled up. The cab was fitted with slotted covers to deflect its front headlight beams downward in compliance with the blackout restrictions.

"Hetty went to Dunkirk. It was so heroic."

"Good God, she could have been killed," Isabelle muttered as they climbed into the back of the cab and gave the driver her address.

"Yes, well, Hetty has the devil's own luck, and I would never bet against her," Elizabeth said with pride.

"Humph," Isabelle said, then guided them back on topic. "So, Henry Goodyear. Should I tell him you'll accept an offer to go out?"

"What? Oh, no, Isabelle."

"Whyever not? You just said he was perfect."

"Not for *me*," Elizabeth corrected. "For one of my clients."

Isabelle let out a beleaguered sigh. "You'll help everyone else find happiness, but you won't look for your own?"

"Isabelle . . . I made the mistake once before of believing I knew what I wanted in a husband, and I barely escaped. No, I think marriage isn't for me."

"So you won't give Henry a chance?" her aunt asked.

"No, not for myself," Elizabeth said firmly. "But he's perfect for one of my most darling clients."

"You ought to try to date someone one of these days, Lizzie. Good men do not simply fall from the sky."

Fall from the sky . . . "Oh, pilots! What a splendid idea, Isabelle. I shall send Marcus around with some circulars to the spots where he's been meeting and chatting with airmen on leave. They would make wonderful clients. What woman wouldn't be proud to wear one of those sweetheart pins with the wings? Besides, airmen are always rakishly charming, aren't they?" Elizabeth's head was already spinning with ideas.

The cabdriver suddenly cursed, and the cab jerked sideways just in time for Elizabeth to see a bus bearing down on them in the moonlight. Everything happened so terribly fast, yet her mind recorded each second in slow motion.

The bus clipped the back of their cab on the passenger side where she was. Tires screeched and metal shrieked sharply as the bus knocked the cab around like a tin can. The car spun and collided with something. Pain exploded in Elizabeth's skull.

She blinked slowly as the car tipped on its side and then fell back on all four tires. She heard shouting in the distance, but her ears were ringing so terribly loud that she couldn't make out anything being said.

Had they been bombed? Where were the air-raid sirens? No, not a bombing, an accident. The bus . . . She tried to piece everything back together, but even thinking about it made her head throb hard enough to make her whimper.

She still tried to recall what happened. She had . . . She'd eaten dinner with Isabelle—Isabelle! Elizabeth tried to move as she turned to the right. Isabelle lay still beside her.

God . . . please no . . .

"Isabelle?" Elizabeth coughed and finally raised an arm to shake her aunt's shoulder.

"Oh . . . ," Isabelle moaned.

Elizabeth could have wept with relief.

"Ma'am?" The driver in front of her was trying to open his door. "Are you both all right?"

"I'm not sure," Elizabeth confessed. Panic rose in her as she saw blood trickling down Isabelle's forehead. "My head is killing me, and my aunt . . . she's bleeding."

"Are you injured?" A new voice came from outside the cab. The door she lay against suddenly gave way. She would have toppled to the ground if a pair of strong arms hadn't caught her. She gripped the man in return as he held her.

"There's a good girl. Get your feet under you," the man said. The light from a small personal torch flashed against the pavement and then moved up to her face briefly before swinging back down. The bloom of unexpected light blinded her, causing her to flinch.

"It looks like you hit your head."

"Please, *please* look at my aunt." Elizabeth tried to point behind her, but she felt far too weak. She sagged against the cab's boot.

"Let me check her over." The tall man moved into the cab and spoke to her aunt, his voice soothing and gentle.

"Come on now, there we go." The man carefully lifted Isabelle out of the car and cradled her in his arms like a damsel from an old Gothic novel.

"Can you walk?" he asked Elizabeth.

"Yes, yes I can." She would walk if it killed her.

"Let's set your aunt over by the curb for a minute, and then I'll come check on you in a moment. I need to see to the driver and the other passengers on the bus."

Elizabeth sat on the curb next to her aunt and put an arm around her protectively. She saw the flash of more torches, and several voices accompanied the play of shadowy figures briefly illuminated by the meager moonlight. As her eyes adjusted, she realized the bus and the cab had collided in the dark. It was a dangerous and all too common thing to happen.

Driving at night in a blacked-out city was a risk, but trying to walk home alone was even more so. As if the enemy across the Channel wasn't enough to worry about, the blackout rules had provided men who sought to harm women a perfect hunting ground. Women were being attacked at night on a large scale, and it was often hard to identify their attackers later because it was too dark to see their faces.

These grim thoughts were on Elizabeth's mind as the man who'd helped them escape from their cab returned to them. He crouched in front of her so that their faces were level.

"The ARP wardens are helping now. They heard the wreck. Do you mind if I look you and your aunt over more clearly somewhere inside?"

"Are—are you a doctor?"

"Er . . . sort of, yes," he replied evasively.

Elizabeth bristled. "Are you, or aren't you?"

"I'm actually a veterinarian, but I know almost as much about human anatomy as I do animals." He chuckled, and the sound was gentle, kind. Perhaps it was her trusting nature, but she wanted to believe in this man and that he would not harm her or her aunt.

"Very well, but where can we go? I'm not even sure where we are." She squinted in the dark at the nearest building, looking for the painted walls that were designed to show up in the dark. Most buildings on corners had the street names and even air-raid shelter directions painted in white to guide Londoners to safety. All she saw now was a distant pillar box that was smeared with a special paint that would change color if there was a gas attack.

"We're near Covent Garden. I live only a street away. If you like, we can go there and I can evaluate you both. Then I can see you home if you're both not in need of a medical doctor."

"Er . . ." Elizabeth glanced at her aunt, who seemed a bit dazed. "Very well, but I don't think my aunt can walk . . ."

"I'll carry her." The man bent and spoke to Isabelle. "Put your arms around my neck, darling." Isabelle obeyed. "That's it."

Then he lifted her up and adjusted her in his arms before starting to walk. Elizabeth kept up with him.

"My name is John Kirby, by the way," he offered as they moved down the street.

"I'm Elizabeth Mowbray. This is my aunt, Isabelle. Thank you so much for the rescue." Elizabeth couldn't admit how relieved she was to have someone who knew what to do in case Isabelle was truly hurt.

"It was no trouble. I'm often out late, and it seems I witness accidents like tonight almost every evening now."

She had to walk quickly to keep up with John's long strides. "What keeps you out so late, if you don't mind my asking?"

John chuckled. "I don't mind. I work after hours at an animal welfare charity. Thanks to a bloody Home Office pamphlet that suggested Londoners should send their pets to the country and if they couldn't it would be kinder to have them destroyed, we've been working after hours to save animals from being euthanized."

Elizabeth gasped. She loved animals. To simply end an animal's life out of fear of what the war would do . . . The very idea sickened her.

"It's all rot and nonsense, killing animals senselessly like that. If it wasn't for women like the Duchess of Hamilton, thousands of pets would be dead."

"What is the duchess doing?"

"Nina has turned her London mansion and her country estate into animal rescue sanctuaries. She's a saint."

"I didn't know about all those poor creatures. How could anyone do that?" When she'd been in India, she'd ridden upon the backs of elephants, and Aabha had her share of little monkeys that stayed in the house and were quite tame. There was something about an animal's eyes that always drew Elizabeth in. Even the more frightening creatures like king cobras commanded her respect.

John sighed. "People are frightened, and they make rash decisions when scared. If we get bombed and a pet owner dies, what befalls their beloved pet? They could be trapped, injured, or starving. I understand the fears people have, but that carelessly worded pamphlet has doomed more than half a million pets to death so far. We are trying to place animals in new homes, sometimes without the previous owners knowing. Most owners are taking us up on the offer of rehoming their pets in the country, but those who don't, well . . . I'm not about to put a decent dog or cat down. Animals may be legal property, but I'm not a killer of innocents. We vets have our oaths to heal, not hurt, just as physicians do."

If Elizabeth needed any further reason to trust John Kirby, she had it now.

"Ah, here we are." He paused in front of the building of flats. "I am on the ground floor. Would you mind retrieving my key in my right jacket pocket?"

Elizabeth found the key, and they entered the building.

"My flat is the first one on the left." He nodded at the closest door, and she unlocked it before holding it open. He passed by her and set Isabelle down on the sofa. Once he made sure his blackout curtains were closed, he turned on several lights and went into his washroom.

He returned with a first aid kit and gestured for Elizabeth to sit beside her aunt. They were both bloody, but Isabelle's head wound was far more severe than Elizabeth's few scrapes. Elizabeth had a chance to study Mr. Kirby as he sat down beside her aunt and opened the first aid kit. He was a very attractive man in his midthirties, perhaps, and incredibly tall. His large hands seemed infinitely gentle despite their obvious strength. That would come in handy with animals.

"Isabelle?" John spoke her aunt's name gently as he put his fingers under her chin and lifted her face so he could examine it.

"Yes . . . ," Isabelle replied, staring back at him in a daze.

"Follow the light with your eyes." He moved a very small torch in front of her. She obeyed. "Good. Now stare directly at the tip of my nose and tell me how many fingers you see." He pointed one finger at his nose while his other hand lifted up by his head to show three fingers.

"Three."

"And this side?" He switched his hands and held up one finger to the other side.

"One," Isabelle said.

"Good. Now, does your head hurt?"

"Yes, it's throbbing a bit." Isabelle let out a weary sigh, her hands fisting loosely in her black velvet evening gown.

John looked her over with a clinical eye. "Anything else hurting?"

"I feel very sore, quite battered, but better than I did a while ago." She yawned suddenly. "I really just wish to sleep . . ."

"Is she all right?" Elizabeth asked in a whisper.

"Yes, it is the adrenaline from the accident wearing off. You'll both be very tired soon. Her vision is good, and she isn't having trouble speaking or showing any other signs of brain trauma."

"Thank heavens for that." Elizabeth ran her hands through her hair and realized only then that she was trembling.

"And you?" John turned his attention to Elizabeth with the same concern. He removed several cloths and a bottle of antiseptic from his kit.

"Just a headache is all." She was still shaken by the incident, but not actually in pain other than her head. She wrapped one trembling hand over the other and held still for him.

John silently cleaned her wounds and placed a few bandages on her before returning to Isabelle.

"She lost a lot of blood. Is she really all right?" Elizabeth didn't like seeing so much blood on her aunt. It made her ill.

"Head wounds are damned tricky. They can bleed fiercely, but often aren't that serious. It's just that a lot of blood vessels are close to the surface."

Isabelle focused on John Kirby with wide eyes, obviously still slightly dazed. "You're quite a dish, did you know that?"

Mr. Kirby's face turned ruddy with a blush. "Er . . . thank you."

Elizabeth had never seen her aunt act so forward before. "Isabelle—"

"She has a concussion," John said. "It's normal to behave a little . . ." He waved his arms a bit as though drunk.

"Oh gracious, poor Isabelle. She always tries to act with the utmost dignity. This will mortify her." Elizabeth knew her aunt would feel embarrassed tomorrow.

"She probably won't remember much. She should rest. Where were you trying to go tonight?"

Elizabeth gave him the address of Isabelle's townhouse.

John's brow furrowed. "That's quite far. I wouldn't trust myself to put either of you in another cab after tonight, and it's too far for me to carry her in the dark. I have two clean beds if you wish to stay until morning. It would allow me to check on your aunt every few hours. She needs rest, but I want to keep an eye on her, nonetheless."

Elizabeth knew her aunt would say no, but Isabelle needed looking after by someone with a medical background.

"Thank you. We very much appreciate this."

"Let me prepare the spare room, and we can put your aunt there. I'll take the couch. You can have my bedroom."

"No, we couldn't—"

He chuckled. "Please, Miss Mowbray. I rarely have the opportunity to play the gentleman." He stood and left the drawing room before she could argue.

"Lizzie . . . ," Isabelle moaned. "I'm so tired. When shall we be home?"

"We're staying with our friend John tonight. Why don't you lie down?" She urged Isabelle to lie lengthwise on the sofa while John prepared the rooms for them.

"I'll carry her," John offered once he returned.

He took her aunt to the spare room and placed her on the freshly made bed. Then he laid out a pair of large nightshirts. "If you wish to be a little more comfortable, I can promise these are clean." Then he left them alone in the room, closing the door.

Elizabeth coaxed her sleeping aunt out of her black velvet dress, letting it pool on the floor. Isabelle grumbled as Elizabeth helped her into the large nightshirt. Then she tucked Isabelle beneath the covers and stepped into the corridor. With the second nightshirt draped over her arm, she turned to see that John was waiting for her.

"I'll check her pulse and blood pressure in a few hours. I shouldn't have to wake her for that," he promised. "My bedroom is here. Please come wake me on the couch if you need anything during the night."

"Thank you," Elizabeth said. "You've been so wonderfully kind."

His gentle smile was utterly charming. "I suppose I've always had a need to help."

Elizabeth grinned. "I think you have a soft spot for injured and stray creatures."

"I certainly do at that," he laughed. "Good night, Miss Mowbray."

Elizabeth closed the door to John's bedroom before she changed into the nightshirt, but she was already beginning to make plans, even as exhausted as she was.

Mr. Kirby wore no wedding band, and there was no sign of a woman in his life. It was possible he could be a candidate for the Marriage Bureau. She would ask him tomorrow morning. She wanted to reward his kindness with finding him the love of his life.

But that was a discussion for tomorrow. She sleepily giggled as she imagined explaining her business to him. He rescued stray animals; she rescued stray hearts. They weren't all that different in their missions.

Yes, John Kirby would be simply perfect for some lucky woman out there.

CHAPTER 24

The week that followed the announcement of Hetty's wedding and the unfortunate cab accident was a busy one for the Marriage Bureau. Elizabeth had convinced Mr. Kirby to come in for an interview and couldn't wait to introduce him to her friends, and Eva and Hetty lauded him as a hero for his rescue of the Mowbray ladies. The tall, well-built man had been adorably bashful under all the fawning attention.

Even Miss Plumley had pranced about the poor man, cooing over him. The middle-aged secretary had succumbed to the influence of the bureau and its tendency to make over ladies who were in need of it. She was dressing more fashionably, and her hair was no longer a dull gray but a vibrant red. Yet she seemed a bit desperate in her makeup and clothing, to the point that Elizabeth was starting to notice.

Miss Plumley had gone a bit too far in her duckling-to-swan transformation. After Mr. Kirby made his exit with the promise of lovely ladies soon to be sending letters his way, Elizabeth turned her thoughts to the secretary. They would somehow have to broach the delicate subject.

"Miss Mowbray," Miss Plumley said as she came up to her. "I wonder if I might have the afternoon off. I have a doctor's appointment."

"What? Yes, of course. I hope everything is all right?" Elizabeth asked. Ever since she and Isabelle had been in that accident, she was jumpy at the thought of anyone else coming to harm. It seemed like everyone she met these days had injured themselves during the blackouts.

"Oh yes, it's just a routine visit," the secretary answered with a relaxed smile.

Elizabeth let out a breath in relief. "Then we shall see you tomorrow?"

"Yes." Miss Plumley practically flew out the door. Elizabeth bit her lip in concern.

The time for appointments that afternoon had been booked full. The first was an attractive gentleman named Ralph Holtzclaw, who appeared in a perfectly tailored RAF uniform. His dark-blue coat, accented with the four bands of pale-blue stripes on his sleeves, indicated his status as a group captain.

Elizabeth had only just started to learn the various ranks of the Royal Air Force, thanks to Hetty, who'd insisted she learn in case they had clients come in uniform. A hint of gray showed at Mr. Holtzclaw's temples, but he was in his early forties, and Elizabeth suspected he would be as wonderful a candidate as Major Taylor had been.

"Mr. Holtzclaw?" Elizabeth asked.

"That's me." He had removed his cap and tucked it under his arm in that elegant fashion that military men of a certain age seemed to have mastered. Elizabeth thought the gesture was both courtly and romantic.

"This way, please." Hetty led him into the interview office.

He took a seat in front of the ornate desk and patiently waited for the romantic interrogation to begin.

"Your occupation, sir?" Elizabeth asked, even though she'd already guessed by his shoulder insignia.

"Group captain at the Royal Air Force base in Doncaster. That's South Yorkshire," he clarified.

"Age?" Hetty asked.

"Forty-two, ma'am." He supplied additional details about himself, and Elizabeth began to form an image of him in her mind, as she did with each of their clients. He was a man who had done his duty and had so far served twelve years in the RAF in various parts of the world. Now he was hoping to settle down.

"I'm teaching all these young pups to fly under such dangerous conditions," Ralph said. "The German pilots are older, more experienced, and they outman us. It's made me realize the seriousness of the situation we're facing, and it's only the beginning. If I have no one to come home to . . ." His voice softened. "Well, I suppose everyone needs someone. I love England, but I need *more* to fight for."

"I understand, Mr. Holtzclaw. What sort of woman are you interested in?" Hetty asked.

He placed his cap on his thigh and traced the brim with his fingertips. "Well, I would prefer a girl who enjoys dancing. I know that sounds like a rather odd request, but someone who loves to dance would be my choice. I have no other requirements. Someone in my line of work may not be alive long enough to enjoy a full married life. I just want to hold my wife in my arms and dance. That way, when I'm flying, I can remember that feeling."

Elizabeth's heart clenched at realizing how tragic his situation was. She couldn't begin to imagine what that must be like, to face death daily and want only a good memory to cling to. She'd give Captain Holtzclaw that if she could.

"We have quite a few women who enjoy dancing. Why, Hetty, what do you think of Evelyn Parrilli? You remember her? She's the American Red Cross volunteer we met with last week."

Evelyn was a pretty brunette with the most beautiful dark eyes and an irresistible smile. She adored dancing.

"Evie? Oh yes. She's a smart woman, but not an overly serious person. She also doesn't mind men writing to her directly rather than through the Bureau offices." Hetty went to collect Evelyn's address and provided a copy to Mr. Holtzclaw. "Please write an introductory letter to Miss Parrilli and mail it to this address. We'll inform her that you will be writing to her."

"Thank you, I certainly shall." Ralph held on to the paper with Evelyn's address and grinned boyishly.

"Oh, Mr. Holtzclaw, we forgot to ask, how did you hear about us?"

He was still smiling as he paused at the door. "Some cheeky young lad riding a bicycle was handing out pamphlets at the canteen a few blocks away. Several of my men took your pamphlets from him. The lad said this place had some sort of magic when it came to matches."

"Marcus," Elizabeth and Hetty said at the same time with a laugh. He'd been riding his bicycle all over London to spread the word. Although he spent most of his time at Cunningham House, Eva had been bringing him in every other week to London to get a bit of excitement of city life.

They finished the rest of the afternoon's appointments and had a brief break to enjoy a cup of tea. Hetty had just put the kettle on the stove when the bell rang down in the reception.

"I'll answer it," Elizabeth said, leaving Hetty to brew the tea.

A woman stood by the check-in desk, her finger hovering above the button that would ring the bell upstairs.

"May I help you?" Elizabeth asked. The woman's silvery hair was pulled back in a bright-red scarf, and her dress, a midlength blend of various patterns, made Elizabeth think of the Romani, or Travelers. The multiple silver rings that adorned her fingers and the heavy beaded necklaces draped around her neck added to the image.

She produced a card from her handbag with a magician's flair. "I am Madam Broadstone." Then she stroked the beads hanging from her neck as she waited for Elizabeth to respond.

Elizabeth read the card aloud. *"Madam Broadstone—Psychic Readings and Seaside Lodgings?"*

"Yes, I offer people readings on their future, and I also run a boardinghouse on the seaside. It's the most *darling* location." She drew out the word *darling* with a wide smile. "It's only a stone's throw away from the sea. Each room has a view of the ocean. Very romantic." The woman waited and stared at Elizabeth. *"Very romantic,"* she repeated, as if Elizabeth had missed some cue.

"And how may the Marriage Bureau help you, Mrs. Broadstone? Are you interested in being matched, or—"

"Heavens no," Mrs. Broadstone laughed. "My tea leaves have predicted three tall, dark men in my life, and each of them have been absolutely unsuitable. No, my dear, I thought I could help *you.*" She gave Elizabeth an exaggerated wink.

Elizabeth blinked. What on earth could the woman mean? "Help me?"

"Yes. You match people, and I predict futures. You make a tidy sum upon successful marriages, don't you?"

"Yes, I suppose, but I don't see how—"

Mrs. Broadstone waved a hand. "It's quite simple, my dear. You arrange a match between, say, a Mr. Brown and a Miss Jones and then urge them to visit me. I give a clever reading to them each in private, encouraging them to see that their new matches are, in fact, their *destiny*." She whispered the word *destiny* in a theatrical fashion. "Then it hurries the marriage up a bit, and I receive a small fee for my services."

"Oh, I see." Elizabeth was both stunned and a little offended by the woman's suggestion.

"And then when they wish to honeymoon . . . they can board at my little seaside cottage."

"I thought you said it was a boardinghouse." Elizabeth frowned.

Mrs. Broadstone waved a hand. "Cottage, house, it doesn't matter. You must come and see it. Stay the night for free," she offered. "This weekend I have rooms available."

"Er . . ." Elizabeth knew she did not want to be a part of any scheme that would defraud her clients, but if the cottage was lovely, it could be a nice place to refer clients. Therefore, she could justify visiting it to see what she thought.

"You have a business partner, yes? Go and speak to her," Madam Broadstone encouraged. "I'll wait here."

Elizabeth climbed the stairs and found Hetty in the back office. She explained the woman's scheme and the seaside board-inghouse as a possible place for clients to stay.

"I agree, we can't use her fortune-telling services, but

perhaps we could go see this boardinghouse, and if the place is up to snuff, we could refer clients. I'm not above playing along so that we might get a nice night by the sea," Hetty chuckled.

"True . . . you could bring Charles," Elizabeth suggested. "You won't have much time after the wedding before he must report for duty."

The laughter in Hetty's eyes dimmed at the mention of Charles's imminent departure.

"You're right. I'll telephone him. Would you ask her if we can come this evening?"

"Yes, of course."

Elizabeth returned to the reception, where she accepted Madam Broadstone's invitation. Eva and Marcus were to spend the weekend with Colonel Cunningham and Mrs. Harrow at the country house, and there were no more appointments for the weekend.

After they packed, Hetty and Charles picked Elizabeth up from her aunt's townhouse and drove east to the seaside village of Margate, which was on the south coast of the Thames estuary. The beaches they passed were clean, and the town of Margate was quite picturesque, right down to the old clock tower, which Charles explained had been built to commemorate Queen Victoria's Golden Jubilee in 1887. He read that from a travel book that he'd brought along, as Hetty navigated the streets.

"What's the address of this boarding house again?" Hetty asked.

Elizabeth read the address from the business card, and they drove away from the beaches and finally stopped in front of a little stone house at the end of the street. It had definitely seen better days.

"Oh dear," Elizabeth murmured.

"Perhaps its seaside charm is on the inside?" Charles said hopefully.

"I highly doubt it," Hetty grumbled as she parked the car, and they exited the vehicle. Madam Broadstone opened the door with a smile.

"Come in, come in. Let me show you to your rooms." She waved them inside, and Charles collected their bags from the car and followed them in.

The boardinghouse was dim and musty smelling. The clear air of the sea seemed unable to penetrate its walls. Every bit of the house was stuffed with antimacassar-covered furniture. The little needlepoint cloths decorated every armrest and headrest to the point that one could not see the original fabrics underneath. Stale smells hung ominously by the door leading to the kitchen, and Elizabeth feared that whatever they might be offered to eat tonight would perhaps be inedible. They were shown to a pair of rooms upstairs.

"Miss Mowbray." Mrs. Broadstone pointed to one door. "And for Mr. and Mrs. Humphrey, this one is yours." She nodded to a second door.

Charles's eyes widened at the pronouncement of a Mrs. Humphrey, but he didn't say anything.

"Settle in and come down for dinner in a few minutes." The fortune-teller left them upstairs.

When the three of them were alone, Charles looked at Hetty.

"One room?" he asked in a whisper.

Elizabeth hid a grin as she heard Hetty's reply. "I'm not sleeping alone in a place like this." As if that resolved the matter quite sufficiently.

"Well, I'll never argue for you to sleep alone, especially if *I'm* your roommate." Hetty jabbed an elbow into his ribs, and Charles leaned in and kissed her.

"See you down in a moment, Lizzie?" Hetty asked, not that she had much to "settle in" with. She'd only brought a small travel case with her. Elizabeth went into her room and set it at the foot of the narrow, metal-framed bed. Then she approached the window and pushed the blackout curtains aside to take in the view. All she saw was a building across the street.

She opened the window and craned her neck out. A flickering blue stripe between the two buildings on the left was her only view of the sea. So it was more *sea adjacent* than seaside, she realized with a bit of disappointment.

When she came back downstairs, she found Charles and Hetty seated at the small dining table with Mrs. Broadstone, who was pouring liberal amounts of gin from a bottle into some glasses.

"And then I told the man he was going to marry an heiress and have twelve children," Mrs. Broadstone was saying.

Hetty was staring at the gin bottle with no small amount of suspicion, while Charles was smiling and seemed perfectly content to listen to the fortune-teller ramble on.

"And did he?" Charles asked. "Have twelve children with the heiress?"

"Of course! Although I believe they ended up with thirteen children in the end. Busy man, that one," Mrs. Broadstone chuckled. "The handsome lads always are, aren't they?" She winked at Charles, who discreetly adjusted his tie and shot a quick glance at Hetty.

Dinner came half an hour later. Madam Broadstone served a burned beef Wellington and beetroot soup. It was a rather meager dinner, but Elizabeth imagined the poor woman had worked quite hard on the beef Wellington—not to mention she had used her precious meat rations on them—so Elizabeth vowed to eat every bite.

"Eat up, my dears, and drink your tea." Mrs. Broadstone fluttered her many-ringed fingers at their teacups. "I shall read your tea leaves while you dine." She smiled at them while they were all quickly drinking their tea. It wasn't the worst tea Elizabeth had ever had, which surprised her. She'd always thought tea for such fortune-tellings would taste terrible.

"Turn your cups over on the saucers," Madam Broadstone instructed. Charles did his first, and Elizabeth and Hetty followed.

"Good, good. Now, you first, Mr. Humphrey." She took Charles's teacup, while Charles sliced vigorously at his beef Wellington.

"Ah yes, I see." She turned his cup about, studying the dregs at the bottom. "I see fog . . ."

Hetty stifled a derisive snort.

"Fog . . . ," Madam Broadstone said again. "No . . . *gas*, not fog. You must take care, never leave your gas mask at home." She sent Charles a stern look. "There is a cross . . . a silver cross, but the metal is dark and something is engraved on it. I can't make out what." A furrow dented her brow. "But it's covered in blood. *Your* blood."

Hetty rolled her eyes, but Charles was staring at the teacup he'd given Madam Broadstone with an unusual stillness.

"Now you, dear." She leaned over and pried Hetty's cup out of her hands and then gave it a concentrated examination. "Hmm . . . I see a child. A little boy. But . . ." The fortune-teller's face fell. "He might not survive. You must not eat any onions for a year." She set the cup down and held out a hand toward Elizabeth.

When Elizabeth hesitated, Mrs. Broadstone wiggled her fingers. Hetty was staring at her plate of food as though checking for onions. She prodded her food this way and that way with a fork.

"Give it here, dear." Madam Broadstone took the cup, practically snatching it out of Elizabeth's hands. There was a long silence as she studied the leaves. Then she looked at Elizabeth, her face serious.

"The one you left behind wasn't a good man. But the next man will fall from the sky into your path. He will be everything that you could ever want or need. But you must trust him—or rather, you must trust *yourself*." She glanced down at the cup again. "He's your destiny, dear. You will recognize him by the way he befriends a lion tamer. He is fearless, and if you are brave enough, he can be yours."

Befriends a lion tamer? What did that mean?

Madam Broadstone blinked and cleared her throat. "Now . . . eat up, my dears. Your food is getting cold."

☙❧

HETTY, CHARLES, AND ELIZABETH CONTINUED TO EAT dinner, and Madam Broadstone regaled them with her triumphant predictions about the futures of many clients from the bureau.

"So you see, it would be an ideal arrangement to combine forces."

"We will certainly consider it," Hetty said with a polite smile. They were having dinner and staying here for free, so she wasn't about to tell this eccentric woman what she really thought of her plan to take advantage of Marriage Bureau clients.

"Well, shall we go to bed?" Hetty suggested and reached for Charles's hand.

He smiled politely at their hostess and winked at Elizabeth before he allowed his bride-to-be to drag him up the stairs to their small shared room. Hetty closed the door and locked it before she leaned back against it to look at Charles. He had his back to her, the single lamp in the room silhouetting him as he removed his suit coat. He was wearing a dark-blue suit, the color she fancied him in the most. It made his golden hair even richer, and it intensified his gray eyes to the color of winter storms.

Butterflies fluttered in her belly as he draped his coat over the nearest chair with casual ease. He was always so calm, so at ease with himself and her. She wanted to be that way with him, to be herself in a way she never had been with Roger. With any other man in the world, she was confident and self-possessed, because she didn't give a damn what those men thought. But this was Charles, and she felt like she was a schoolgirl again, her heart beating madly and her body wanting to swoon at his every smile. She'd thought this would be such a delightful weekend for the pair of them, but this hadn't gone at all as planned.

She glanced about their room and winced. This was far from the romantic interlude she'd hoped for. Instead, they were surrounded by blackout curtains and ridiculous knitted cloth coverings on all the chairs. The bed even had a knitted blanket covering it. Charles didn't seem to mind all this, however.

"I'm sorry about this. It's not what I had in mind for . . ." Her voice trailed off.

Charles came toward her, his gray eyes twinkling with mischief. "For our first night together?"

"Yes, it's a bit, well . . ."

"I think it's charming." He caged her against the wooden door, his hands on either side of her shoulders as he slowly leaned in and claimed her lips. The kiss sent her spiraling in a delight that would have had her grandmother calling her punch-drunk. He nibbled playfully at her lips, and she sighed, slipping into the heavenly feel of the moment. She had missed this, the intimacy of a man in her life, the knowledge that soon she would be drifting away upon clouds of pleasure. She was no stranger to lovemaking, she and Roger had been compatible in that department, but with Charles . . . everything was heightened, everything was somehow more intense. Every touch, every taste, every sigh and heated breath and kiss were sacred in a way she'd never imagined before she'd fallen in love with him.

She slid her arms around the back of his neck, trailing her fingertips into his hair. He groaned softly, pressing her harder against the door. She could feel his strength, the very power of his body, yet he was so gentle with her. Charles had a strange sort of magic that defied logic, and he pulled her into the moment of simply *being* with him.

When their lips finally broke apart, she was breathing hard and so was he. Hetty slid her hands down from his neck to his chest. She unbuttoned his waistcoat, sliding the mother-of-pearl buttons through the slits, and then peeled it off, letting the waistcoat drop to the floor.

Charles's eyes heated as he let her unbutton his shirt next. The moment her fingers lightly stroked his bare chest, he made a soft, possessive sound at the back of his throat before he scooped her up in his arms and carried her to the bed like a conquering warrior. She lifted her gaze up to his, feeling more vulnerable now than she had ever been in her life. She had faced

Dunkirk at this man's side and felt like she could do anything, but right now she felt as fragile as a butterfly in his arms.

"Henrietta Byron . . . I *loved* you from the moment we met," Charles said. His eyes, the color of a winter storm, held the answers her lonely heart had searched for.

"For that long?" she asked in wonder. They'd known each other half their lives.

"Yes," he chuckled softly as he laid her down on the little bed. He leaned over her as he removed his shirt and dropped it to the floor. "When did you decide you loved me?" He lay down on the bed beside her and slid an arm around her waist. Her skin felt too hot. She shifted restlessly beside him as he toyed with the snaps that closed the back of her black skirt.

"When did I know I loved you?" she repeated as he undid the buttons on her skirt. She gasped as his fingers grazed her lower back and he gently pulled at the blouse that was tucked into her skirt. "I fear you'll be rather upset with me. I've been such a fool when it comes to you."

"Will I?" He arched a brow, but his lips were still curved in a devious smile. He began to pluck at the buttons of her blouse until the silk fabric gaped open and allowed him a view of her breasts, barely concealed in lingerie. She rolled onto her back, and he slid closer, leaning over her, resting his head in his hand as he gazed down at her.

"*When?*" he asked again.

"When Lizzie and I walked into your office and told you about the Marriage Bureau. You didn't laugh at us—you *believed* in us. You believed in *me*. That was when I first suspected it. Then, when you asked me to go with you to Dunkirk, I was certain of it."

Charles gently pushed her blouse off her shoulders and

leaned in to press a kiss to the newly bared skin. A delicious shiver rippled through her.

"I will always believe in you, Henrietta. *Always*."

Somehow those words, murmured huskily in that dim little bedroom by the sea, were more powerful than any declarations of love or clever poems he could have recited.

"My grandmother once said that Lonsdales never die," Hetty said softly as their eyes locked and held.

"Did she, now?" His eyes held a hint of humor, even though the room was charged with the hunger and tension between them.

"Prove it to me. When you leave for the Continent. I need you to prove it, that Lonsdales never die."

He answered without a word as he lowered his head and captured her lips. She was swept away by him and everything that could be theirs if only they could just survive.

"Charles?" she murmured against his mouth.

He continued to steal kisses in all her forbidden places. "Yes, my darling?"

"Make love to me."

He looked at her and chuckled. "That's what I'm doing. I'm simply savoring it, and *you*, for as long as I can."

She pulled his head back down to hers, vowing to do the same. The time they had left was but sand pouring through an hourglass. All too soon, it would be over.

CHAPTER 25

L *ate June 1940*

IT WAS A BEAUTIFUL DAY FOR A WEDDING. EVEN HETTY, WHO didn't consider herself the least bit romantic, had to admit the weather was perfect. She stood in a lavish bedroom at the Lonsdale family estate and studied the grounds below through the window. Lebanon cedar trees planted more than a century ago edged the vast lawn of the estate like old guards. She placed her palm on the windowpane, soaking in the late spring sunlight through her fingers.

Hetty blinked and suddenly all of that beauty was gone, replaced with the beaches of Dunkirk strewn with dying men and bloody water. She blinked again, trying to erase the memories that had caused her so much pain of late.

"Hetty?" Her mother's voice pulled her out of her ruminations. The visions of dying men and bloody waters faded back into the rolling green life of Lonsdale Hall.

"Yes?" She turned to face her mother, whose eyes sparkled with tears.

"What's the matter?" Hetty took a step toward her. "Has something happened?"

"No, no, darling, everything is fine. It's just you look so lovely. I'm so very happy for you." Her mother came up to her and gently clutched Hetty's hands in her own. "This is the man you are meant to be with."

"Mama . . . ," Hetty began as her mother handed her a bridal bouquet. She then made a few adjustments to the floor-length satin gown Hetty wore. The lace sleeves came all the way down to her wrists, so thin that it looked as though it was made of spider's silk. A layer of cream lace dropped down the back over the satin gown to form a three-foot train behind her.

Hetty had worried it was all too much. She was no virginal new bride, after all, but a divorcée. It was scandalous enough for Charles to be marrying her given that fact, yet his family had wished to celebrate their wedding with all the fanfare due to a future earl and his future countess.

Hetty looked down at the bouquet. Elizabeth had insisted on the flowers, and now Hetty could see why. Among the white calla lilies, beautiful foxtail orchids spilled over and cascaded down as though the flowers were growing out of Hetty's hands from some ancient magic.

Elizabeth came into the room and halted, her eyes going wide. She wore a pale-pink bridesmaid's dress, and her own small bouquet was clutched in her hands. "Oh, Hetty, you look . . ."

"Suitable?" Hetty suggested.

"*Perfect*," Elizabeth corrected, and her eyes grew misty.

"Oh no, not you too." Hetty groaned at the sight of her mother and best friend crying.

Somewhere downstairs, music began to play. This was so different from the quick civil ceremony on the military base in Ceylon with Roger. Only her parents had been present, and she had worn a simple cream-colored day dress. Now she was draped in satin and lace and already feeling like she was in some sort of dream.

"Do you mind if I come in?" Lady Lonsdale stood in the doorway. Charles's mother was an auburn-haired beauty with kind eyes and a compassionate demeanor that always put Hetty at ease. She'd always made Hetty feel welcome, even as a young girl.

She waved for Lady Lonsdale to join them. "Yes, of course."

"I hope you won't mind, but I have something I wish to lend you. Something that will be yours one day." She held up a square black velvet box and opened it. The midday sun caught on the diamonds and pearls, causing them to glitter and glow.

"This is the Countess of Lonsdale's tiara, and it goes back more than a century. It was commissioned by the first Charles Humphrey in our family in 1825. He gave it to his wife, Lily, as an anniversary present. He and Lily had a long and happy life together, with children and love. It has given every countess since then the same fortunate luck. I wish for you to have all the luck in the world, my dear."

Hetty's mother held the box. The countess removed the tiara and placed it upon Hetty's head, securing it with a few hairpins until it rested firmly in her wavy golden hair. Then she, Elizabeth, and Hetty's mother all took a step back and stared at the final effect.

"Beautiful," Lady Lonsdale whispered. She wiped a tear from her cheek. "They are ready for you downstairs."

Elizabeth gave Hetty a wink and proceeded out of the room with both of the mothers. Hetty glanced at herself in the mirror once more, startled to see the beautiful stranger reflected back at her.

This was truly happening. She and Charles were to be *married*. A year ago, the thought would've terrified her, but she was different now. She wasn't a stranger to herself anymore. That night she and Elizabeth had met on the balcony had set her on a path to discovering herself. That simple chance meeting had led her back to Charles, it had sent her to Bond Street to start a business, it had put her in the path between Eva and Marcus and danger, it had sent her toward Dunkirk to save hundreds of men . . .

And now it led her here. Her heart skipped several beats, and she clutched her bouquet tight as she began her walk toward her future. Her father met her at the top of the stairs, wearing his military uniform. He kissed her forehead, and the smile on his lips made his eyes sparkle with happy tears.

"My darling warrior," he murmured. "I couldn't part with you to a man more deserving of you." He swallowed hard, and Hetty desperately blinked away her own tears.

"Thank you, Father."

"Let's get you to that man of yours." He winked at her.

Charles was downstairs in the grand hall, waiting for her. It shouldn't be possible to be married in a house, but Lord Lonsdale must have offered the local parish something very valuable in order to bend the rules a bit. Flowers covered the railings and hung from sconces, and petals littered the carpeted stairs.

The guests on either side of the hall faded away until all she saw was the man who was waiting for her. Who had *always* been waiting for her. He wore a black suit, and a white calla lily peeked out of the buttonhole on his coat. The lilies held so much more significance now that she knew of Lily's history in the Humphrey family. They were part of the Lonsdale title's romantic past.

She smiled as she let go of her father's arm and stepped up beside Charles and they faced the minister together. As the ceremony began, Hetty barely heard the man's words. She was caught in her memories of Charles. How he had looked at her that day she'd come into his office to discuss the Marriage Bureau. How he'd brought food in picnic baskets and furniture almost daily while they'd prepared their office, how he'd rolled up his sleeves and fixed furniture and helped install better lighting. He'd given his time for her repeatedly, with no expectations. He had always helped her, even after she'd tried to push him away that night at the Astoria because he loved her.

He'd had such faith in her that they had gone to Dunkirk together. He had put his faith in her time and again. Now it was her turn to have faith in him. She had to trust that he would come back to her, that he would not let the war take him from her. It was unreasonable to think he'd come back for certain, she knew that. War was indiscriminate in who it took away. And yet she had to believe he'd come back, because the alternative was too terrible to contemplate.

She remembered that morning in the little cottage adjacent to the sea where they had first made love and she'd fallen asleep in his arms. Nightmares had chased her close to dawn, and she had woken up, trembling, her hands feeling as if they were covered in the blood of men she had failed to save.

Charles had woken to her struggles and wrapped himself

around her, holding her tight so that he absorbed her trembling into himself until she finally calmed. He hadn't asked her what she dreamed of. He knew what had frightened her, and he had comforted her without a second thought.

"You saved them, you saved so many," he had said and kissed her temple. "And you saved me."

That alone had given her peace. That voice that cried out for her to run away, to never stop, never grow roots or feel trapped in one place had finally faded. A new voice had taken its place. A voice that said her life was *here*, growing old with this man. It would be a life full of joys and tempered by sorrows, but it would be the life that she'd yearned for.

"Do you, Charles Humphrey, take Henrietta Mary Louise Byron to be your lawfully wedded wife?" the minister asked.

"I do," Charles replied, his gray eyes holding Hetty's.

"You may give her the ring," the minister prompted. Charles held up a diamond ring and slid it onto her finger. It fit perfectly, and by its elegant design she knew it was a family heirloom.

"And do you, Henrietta Byron, take Charles Graham Alexander Humphrey to be your lawfully wedded husband?"

"I do." She removed the gold band from her bouquet when prompted and slid it onto Charles's finger. It was becoming a popular tradition for men to have wedding bands, and many men facing time in the service wanted that tangible reminder of home, the reminder that someone was waiting for them.

When the minister pronounced them man and wife, Charles pulled her into his arms and captured her lips with a searing kiss. She nearly dropped her bouquet as she wrapped her arms around his neck.

Someone whistled amid the clapping, no doubt one of Charles's friends. He had so damned many of them. She *loved* that, knowing that others felt as drawn to him as she did. The man was his own planet, with the force of gravity to draw almost anyone into his orbit.

When they broke apart, there were cheers from the crowded grand hall, and hundreds of flower petals snowed down on them from the upper-story corridor that overlooked the grand hall. Shielding her eyes, Hetty looked up to see several maids grinning impishly as they tossed handfuls of small petals down upon them.

"Come on," Charles laughed as he tucked her arm in his, and they walked down the aisle between their friends and family. The guests converged on them, and smiles were everywhere. For a brief while, Hetty forgot the war, forgot the beaches, forgot everything as she and Charles basked in their newfound happiness.

"Congratulations, Mr. Humphrey," a familiar voice greeted, and she almost startled as she came face-to-face with Damien Russell and his wife, Penelope.

"Mr. Russell!"

"Damien, please. We're friends now." He winked at Charles.

"I had forgotten you two know each other," she admitted.

Damien pretended to be offended. "What? Charles doesn't fill your days with tales of my glories?"

"Now listen here, old boy," Charles started, and the two began playfully arguing about a dozen things going all the way back to their school years.

Penelope laughed and hugged Hetty. "I wouldn't be surprised if Damien tried to tag along on your honeymoon just to see Charles. Even though he's been home from India for a year now, he missed Charles dearly while he was away."

"I had no idea. I've been so busy with the bureau the last

year that I haven't had much time to talk to Charles about anything but the war and the Marriage Bureau or his legal cases."

"Well, you'll have your honeymoon to spend time on that . . . and other things." Penelope lightly nudged Hetty with a wink. "Where are you two going?"

"I don't know. He was in charge of planning it." She had a feeling that wherever they went would be wonderful. "How are you and Damien? And the children?"

"Wonderfully well. Since Christmas, things have only gotten better. Cliff and Nella are growing up so fast. I can scarcely believe we've had them less than a year. It feels like they've been with us forever."

"That's so wonderful to hear." Hetty meant it. She loved the challenge of running the Marriage Bureau, the day-to-day meetings and strategies of pairings, but like Elizabeth, she felt that the best part was this. Hearing that they had made a match that worked and the two people were happy. This was what it was all for. And now that she'd had a taste of her own bliss, she was that much more driven to work for her clients. Everyone deserved this joy and love.

"I'll let you greet your other guests and pry my husband off yours." Penelope laughed as she went to pull Charles and Damien apart. Hetty thanked a dozen other guests before her parents found her.

"Hetty." Her mother was openly crying, but she was beaming through her tears. "I'm just so happy."

"Mama, *really*," she sighed and hugged her mother. "You mustn't cry." Then she looked up to her father, and her own lip trembled as she saw his face. She let go of her mother to embrace him. He held her close, his arms wrapped around her.

"My fierce lioness," he whispered. "I'm so very *proud* of you."

"For getting married?" she asked with a watery chuckle.

"No, for finding yourself and your own happiness. It's what every good father wants for his daughter, that she discovers herself and finds *joy* at the discovery."

Hetty hugged him again. She was a lucky woman. She had a man who loved her, even the darkest parts of her, and she had parents who loved and valued her. She saw Elizabeth out of the corner of her eye, watching everything with a wistfulness that tugged at Hetty's heart.

Elizabeth had nothing like that in her life except her brother, who was somewhere in the Atlantic, and her aunt Isabelle, who had worries and concerns of her own.

You have me, Lizzie. You have me.

⁂

WEDDINGS WERE *WONDERFUL* THINGS. ELIZABETH HELD HER hand up to catch the snowfall of flower petals as they rained down in the great hall. Hetty walked past her on Charles's arm, the white satin of her dress shimmering in the light, and Elizabeth couldn't stop smiling. Hetty had been brave enough to let Charles into her heart, and at long last she looked truly happy. It was funny to think she and Hetty had only known each other for a a little over a year, when it felt like they'd been in each other's lives a lifetime.

The wedding party moved out onto the gravel walk in front of the house, where Hetty's Morris Eight was packed and waiting. Elizabeth tossed rice along with the other guests as Hetty and Charles started for the car.

Charles opened the door for Hetty, and after a wave at the crowd watching them, they drove off toward their honeymoon.

A wall of sound rolled across the sunny countryside, and the sky was split by the shadows of three Spitfires racing low over the landscape.

The deafening growl of the aircraft should have been a comfort, but all she could see was *death* in the skies. Death and pilots crashing to the earth in flames. She shuddered, suddenly very cold, as though someone had walked over her grave. She watched the planes continue to cut across the sky until they vanished on the horizon.

Eva joined her at the top of the steps. Neither of them said anything. Remnants of the white flower petals drifted down and fluttered along the road in the direction Hetty and Charles had gone. Elizabeth stared at the petals and had a sudden and terrible foreboding that something much worse was yet to come.

Eva held up a letter. "Charles gave me this earlier. He said that this was all they could find about my parents. I could tell by the look on his face that it must be bad news."

Elizabeth turned to see that the letter Eva held hadn't been opened yet.

"I'm too afraid to read it," she confessed.

Elizabeth put an arm around Eva's shoulders. "Whatever it says, I'm here for you and Marcus."

Eva bit her lip, broke the envelope open, and removed the single sheet of paper from inside. It bore the seal of the British Foreign Office, with a lion and a unicorn on either side of the crown. The French phrase *Dieu et mon droit* was beneath it. *God and my right*, the motto of the British monarchy.

Beneath it were a few short, typed sentences. Eva sucked in a gasp and covered her mouth. Her other hand clenched the letter so hard that it crumpled. Elizabeth had but a moment to glimpse a few of the words: *executed for resistance . . . buried in a mass grave.*

Eva crumpled to her knees, and Elizabeth sank down beside her, wrapping her arms around her friend and holding her tight.

"It's all right. It's going to be all right," she whispered, trying to soothe Eva as she wept.

But it wasn't, and it never would be.

For the first time in her life, Elizabeth hungered for justice. No, not justice—vengeance. Something inside her that had remained untouched by the black heart of war was now consumed by it.

Elizabeth raised her tearstained face to the skies as another pair of Spitfires roared past. She prayed those pilots would taste victory today. Prayed that the people who had done these terrible things, wherever they were, would *burn*.

Hundreds of white petals escaped the doorway of the house and tumbled across the road to be caught upon the winds, taking flight to the west.

CHAPTER 26

 ugust 1940

"I TALKED DONALD BUTLER OUT OF HIS BUTTER RATION THIS morning," Mrs. Harrow announced, beaming with pride.

"His butter? Good God, woman, you are heartless," Colonel Cunningham replied as he spread liberal amounts of said bartered butter onto his muffin. "And what did that cost us?"

Elizabeth glanced up from her work at the kitchen table. She was back at Cunningham House for a few weeks to rest and see her friends in the country.

The housekeeper had taken well to the illegal but frequently orchestrated exchanges of rations and coupons with other villagers. It never ceased to amaze Elizabeth how Mrs. Harrow adapted to the ever-tightening restrictions of food, soap, and other supplies as though it were commonplace. But when she thought no one was watching, there would be a weariness to her face that made Elizabeth's heart ache.

Elizabeth watched the verbal sparring of the colonel and the housekeeper while she and Eva worked on answering letters at the kitchen table.

"Oh, nothing we'd miss," Mrs. Harrow said with glee just as the colonel bit into his muffin. He coughed and spit it out. "This tastes like dirt. There's no—"

"Sugar?" Mrs. Harrow cut in with a wicked smile. "I figured the one thing we could do with less of in this house is sugar. *Some* of us are putting on a pound or two." Her pointed gaze fixed on the colonel's belly, which was still trim for a man his age.

"What?" the colonel blustered as he got to his feet. "I'll have you know I'm as fit as any man still in uniform."

Eva stifled a giggle, and Mrs. Harrow shot them a wink when the colonel wasn't looking. It was a wonderful thing to hear Eva's laugh and see her smile. The last two months since they'd heard the news of her parents' death had left her a shell of her former self. If Mrs. Harrow and the colonel's good-natured bickering could restore some life to Eva, Elizabeth welcomed it.

"Now, see here, madam—" He'd started to wave a finger at Mrs. Harrow when a strange sound came from outside. It was a distant *rat-tat-tat* like pebbles hitting a window. But the sound grew louder, and soon the entire house vibrated with the roar of engines.

"What is that?" Mrs. Harrow screeched as she retrieved the pot of tea from the table's edge before it would have crashed to the floor.

The colonel was very still, his face hard as he held up his

hands.

"Everyone quiet," he hissed.

Eva and Elizabeth stared at him. Elizabeth could feel the very air around them becoming charged with deadly energy. The colonel moved to the nearest window in the kitchen.

"It's aircraft! There's a dogfight in the sky." He rushed toward the door that led from the kitchens out into the back garden. Elizabeth rushed after him, and they both skidded to a stop on the gravel walkway beneath the sky covered with vapor trails and zigzagging planes.

"Colonel?" Marcus rounded the corner of the manor house, pointing at the sky with excitement.

"I see them, lad." The colonel was breathing hard, his gray mustache twitching as he narrowed his eyes on the fighters.

"Spitfire . . . that's the silver one," he pointed out. "The other . . ." He lifted one hand to shield his eyes against the sun. "A Messerschmitt . . ."

Elizabeth tracked the planes, her breath trapped somewhere between her lungs and her lips. They had heard of dogfights happening in the countryside, but they hadn't seen one until now. Biggin Hill, the air force base south of London, was only an hour away, and the base had been the target of frequent bomber attacks over the summer.

Elizabeth's focus shot to Marcus. He was too young to be near such violence, especially if there was real danger.

"Should we take cover, Colonel?"

"They are a ways off. We should be safe right now."

The Messerschmitt suddenly arced up over the Spitfire, but the Spitfire was waiting like an agile shark in the shallows. It opened fire on the other plane. The German aircraft exploded at the tail and began to spiral toward the ground.

Elizabeth gasped and covered her mouth with her hands. "Oh my God . . ."

Somehow, the Messerschmitt managed to pull out of its death spiral, and while still trailing smoke, it coasted toward the ground in their direction. It landed somewhere nearby, and they felt the crash rumble through the earth, but they could not see it through the forest ahead of them. Smoke billowed up half a mile away. Marcus was already sprinting toward his bike, which lay propped against the stone wall of the house.

"Where are you going?" Elizabeth shouted at the boy as he pedaled off toward the plane, but she knew. Every boy for miles around was intent on retrieving bits of downed planes or parachutes, even ammunition. But it was dangerous to do so. Some had even been killed when they'd found a bomb that hadn't exploded right away. The last thing any of them wanted was for Marcus to be killed by his own curiosity.

"Colonel?" Elizabeth turned to him, but he was already running back into the house.

"What is it? What's happened?" Mrs. Harrow demanded.

"Downed plane. A German one. Bloody hell, the lad's gone after it." That was all the colonel said before he vanished down the corridor.

"Marcus did what?" Eva asked Elizabeth as they both rushed after the colonel. When they found him, he was loading two pistols.

"Can one of you handle a gun?"

"I can, but I'm not the best shot," Elizabeth admitted.

"I can," Eva said, and the colonel passed her one of the guns.

"We've got to go. The pilot and the gunner may still be alive, and they might hurt Marcus if they spot him. Every pilot is armed with a service weapon."

Elizabeth swallowed down a lump of fear. They couldn't let anything happen to Marcus.

They left out the back gate, leaving Mrs. Harrow calling after them. The smoke was black as it plumed up beyond the thicket of trees. They stayed behind the colonel as he slowed when he saw the wrecked plane.

It was a grayish-green except for the nose and the front of the engines on the wings, which were a bright yellow. A shark's mouth of open teeth had been painted along the front of the fuselage, which made it all the more menacing. The windows of the cockpit canopy were cracked, and Elizabeth ducked down as the canopy was thrown open.

A man climbed out of the front pilot seat of the smoking wreckage, coughing violently and stumbling several feet away. His black leather flight jacket was torn in places, and his face was covered in grimy smoke exhaust. He ripped his black leather helmet off, and it fell to the ground.

"Bernhard!" The man staggered back to the cockpit, where a second man sat unmoving in the gunner's seat.

Colonel Cunningham scanned the area around them. "Where's the boy?"

Elizabeth spotted Marcus, who was slightly closer than them to the plane. "There!"

The boy was crouched low, his lips parted in awe as he watched the pilot in the clearing. Eva tensed, her body shifting to move toward her brother, but Elizabeth curled her fingers around the other woman's shoulder, holding her still.

"Stay here," the colonel cautioned. "I'll fetch the boy. You keep your eyes on those men. Shoot if they look like they see us and go for their pistols."

Eva nodded, and the colonel moved stealthily through the underbrush toward Marcus.

"You watch the pilot, I'll watch the colonel and Marcus," Elizabeth whispered. Eva's hand on the pistol trembled slightly, but her gaze didn't waver as she stayed focused on her task.

An agonizing minute ticked by as the colonel reached Marcus and the pair of them began to make their way back. Every time one of them put their foot down, she feared they'd snap a twig or draw attention from the pilot. When they reached Elizabeth and Eva, Marcus hugged his sister and she scolded him in a harsh whisper.

"We can't leave," the colonel said softly. "That man is an enemy combatant. We have to capture him."

Eva gasped. "What?"

"Take your brother back to the house. Fetch a stout rope and put a sturdy chair in the drawing room. I will handle him." The colonel's eyes were bright with the prospect of battle. "Give your pistol to Elizabeth." Eva passed Elizabeth the gun, who held it awkwardly.

"Use two hands," Eva whispered. She mimed showing how to hold it. Elizabeth nodded in silent thanks before she motioned for Eva and Marcus to run home.

Colonel Cunningham moved into a crouch beside her. "Are you ready, Miss Mowbray?" She imagined this was the colonel in his true element. She mimicked him as they crept toward the plane.

The pilot was struggling to pull the gunner free, but he couldn't get the rear glass canopy of the rear gunner seat open. The man was gasping as he shouted the same name over and over.

"Bernhard! Bernhard!"

"*Nehmen Sie die Hände hoch!*" the colonel bellowed into the smoke-filled air. He stepped out from the bushes, his pistol raised at the pilot. The German whirled around, eyes wide and lips parted. He threw his hands in the air immediately.

The colonel continued to speak in German to the pilot. "*Entfernen Sie sich vom Flugzeug.*"

Elizabeth didn't know what he was saying, but the pilot's gaze shot to the cockpit as he spoke frantically to the colonel. Smoke darkened the man's face so that only two pale rings around his eyes remained untouched by the soot.

"*Mein Bruder ist darin gefangen!*" He pointed at the man in the gunner's seat. Elizabeth was now close enough that she saw tears in his eyes. She knew almost no German, but she did know what *mein Bruder* meant. *My brother.*

Her throat tightened as she saw how young the pilot was. He must be barely twenty years old. "Colonel . . ."

"I heard him," the colonel replied calmly before he moved his gun, waving it to make the German man step farther away from the plane.

"Keep your weapon trained on him, Miss Mowbray. I'll check on the gunner."

Elizabeth gripped the pistol in her hands, but sweat from fear slickened her grip. The wind changed, and smoke floated between her and the pilot. He kept his gloved hands in the air as he watched her and the colonel. Tears streamed down his cheeks and etched grooves in the soot on his face.

"Bernhard . . ." The young man breathed the name brokenly. Behind her, the colonel wrenched the rear gunner seat canopy open again.

"Keep it on him," the colonel grunted, and Elizabeth dared not look back at him while he tried to free the man's brother from the plane. The colonel moved into view as he dragged the body of the gunner away from the smoking plane. Flames now licked the tail of the plane and were steadily moving upward.

"We need to get away from this engine. We don't want to be near when the fuel tank ignites."

"Bernhard?" The pilot spoke the name again as the colonel hauled the body another thirty feet away into an open field. Elizabeth waved her pistol the way the colonel had earlier to indicate to the pilot that he should follow the colonel.

Colonel Cunningham was on one knee, touching the neck of the gunner with two fingers. Then he moved his hands over the man's leather jacket.

The pilot looked at the still body on the ground. *"Bitte . . ."*

"He's gone," Colonel Cunningham said to Elizabeth. Then he turned to the pilot and shook his head. *"Er ist tot."*

"Nein . . ." The pilot's legs gave out, and he fell beside his brother on the grassy meadow. Colonel Cunningham moved a safe distance away with Elizabeth.

"The poor fellow was shot in several places. He was the rear gunner, and when the Spitfire hit him, he must have taken some of the machine-gun fire at the same time their tail was hit."

"What are we going to do?"

"Give him a minute to mourn his brother. Then we will take him back to the house. I'll call Biggin Hill. It's forty miles away, but the officers there will know what to do with him and the body of the other man."

The pilot was on his knees, his hand on his brother's chest as he spoke softly in German. Then he wiped one gloved hand across his face, smearing tears and ash.

"Sie warden jetzt mit uns Zurückkommen," the colonel said.

The pilot let out a heavy sigh and slowly stood. He reached for his service revolver.

"Easy . . . ," the colonel warned him.

The young man slowly removed his gun and held it out, handle first, toward the colonel. Elizabeth's hands shook as she kept her own pistol up and ready, but from the look on the other man's face, he was devastated. Losing his brother had taken whatever fight he had left in him.

"What will happen to his body?" the German pilot asked them in English.

"We will come back for it. We won't leave him out here," the colonel promised.

The pilot's shoulders sagged. "*Danke.*"

The three of them walked side by side, their weapons trained on the pilot, but the closer they got to Cunningham House, the less Elizabeth feared the pilot. He was terribly young, with gray eyes and dark hair. She'd never given a thought to the enemy as individual men, but seeing this frightened young man made her wonder how many soldiers in the war were involved against their will. He certainly didn't have the look of a man who hated England and wanted to destroy it.

But Elizabeth checked herself. It wouldn't be wise to let her guard down for even a moment. So many people were dying, like all the boys on the beaches of Dunkirk. She couldn't forget those deaths, or who was causing them.

When they appeared in the back garden, Eva rushed out to meet them.

"Are you ready for us, Miss Wolman?" the colonel asked.

"We are," she said.

"Understood. You, this way." The colonel guided the pilot inside the house. They passed by Marcus and Mrs. Harrow in the kitchen. She clutched a carving knife and kept trying to push Marcus behind her, but he was taller and stronger than the housekeeper, so he kept putting himself between her and the danger.

A chair sat in the center of the drawing room, and a long coil of rope lay on the settee nearby.

"Sit," the colonel instructed.

The pilot sat in the chair, and Eva reached for the rope.

The pilot spoke again in his heavy accent. "That is not . . . necessary. I surrender." He nodded at his service pistol in the colonel's other hand.

"I need to call Biggin Hill. Eva, please keep him at gunpoint until I return." He passed his pistol to Eva. Elizabeth was glad she wasn't the only one still carrying a gun. She doubted she'd be able to hit anything.

Eva stared at the pilot silently, her eyes dark and her face clouded with rage. Elizabeth understood her reaction. Ever since Eva had learned of her parents' fate, she had been withdrawn and in such pain that it had still haunted her. Marcus had cried for a week, but after that, he'd seemed to accept their deaths. He was stronger than Elizabeth imagined she would be in the same situation. If Alan or Isabelle, or even her parents, had been mercilessly shot in the streets, she would be blind with rage. It would have destroyed her. It was a mercy she had been lucky so far, but Eva . . . Eva was still suffering, and Elizabeth didn't know how to help the woman who had become such a dear friend in the last year.

Eva kept the weapon raised, and her finger twitched on the trigger as she said something in Polish to the pilot. The last vestiges of hope died in the young man's eyes.

"I am sorry," he whispered in English to Eva. "I am sorry."

And the words carried such a weight that even Elizabeth believed him when he said it.

Eva's eyes narrowed, and she started to curl her finger around the trigger.

"Eva . . . no," Elizabeth said softly, her heart pounding as she realized what her friend meant to do.

"My family is dead," Eva whispered hoarsely. "Dead for what? For nothing."

Elizabeth let out a slow breath as she took a step toward Eva.

"Not all your family is dead. Marcus is here. Hetty, the colonel, Mrs. Harrow, and I are still here. We are your family too, Eva. You don't want to take this man's life. It won't bring anyone back."

"If I kill him, he cannot kill anyone else."

That was true, Elizabeth couldn't deny it.

"Not all soldiers want to fight, Eva. Some are called to do their duty, even if it's wrong. You cannot know what lies in his heart. Maybe he is glad today to be a prisoner and fly no more. He lost his brother today. He too is hurting." Elizabeth licked her lips anxiously. "Teach him compassion. Teach him why your parents resisted the spread of evil. Teach him what it means to show mercy."

Eva's hand trembled, and then slowly she pulled her finger away from the trigger, and Elizabeth let out another breath, this one far shakier than before.

The colonel returned a short while later. "Some officers from Biggin Hill will be here in an hour. They'll take custody of him. They will also see that his brother's body is retrieved and the plane wreckage collected."

The pilot's head dropped, his hair falling into his eyes. He was defeated, and he accepted it. The fight in him was completely gone.

"Colonel, I don't know if the guns are entirely necessary anymore," she said softly.

The colonel raised a brow at her.

"He lost his brother, Colonel Cunningham." Elizabeth lowered her gun. "Please. We believe in compassion, don't we? Even in times of war?"

The colonel stared at the German pilot for a long moment.

"We will lower our guns if you promise to act respectfully. I take it you understand?"

The pilot nodded. "I understand. I do not deserve it, but I am thankful." He wiped at his eyes and cleared his throat. "I will wait for your men to come."

"Well," Mrs. Harrow said, her voice calm though her hands were still shaking from the entire incident. "Why don't we all have a spot of tea and wait for the officers to arrive?"

Eva lingered in the hall, and Elizabeth kept her company while Marcus and the colonel stayed with the pilot in the drawing room.

"Eva." Elizabeth put her hand on the other woman's shoulder.

"Oh, Lizzie." Eva sucked in a sob. She fought so hard not to cry that the sight made Elizabeth's lips tremble. "I hate him so much. I don't even know him, and I *hate* him."

"I know. Listen, why don't we answer some letters from our clients? We could distract ourselves a bit."

About an hour later, the bell at the front of the house rang, and Mrs. Harrow rushed past them to answer it. Two men in blue uniforms entered the house. Eva wiped her eyes, and Elizabeth put her arm around her shoulders as the men approached.

"This here's Lieutenant Edward Gilbert." Mrs. Harrow nodded at the dark-haired man and then to the other man with light-brown hair. "And this is Lieutenant Gavula. They've come to see to our pilot."

Elizabeth guessed they were both in their early thirties, but they had the look of seasoned fighters. There was an ancient weariness to them that broke Elizabeth's heart. So many of the pilots who'd come through the bureau doors lately were barely twenty or twenty-one. These men had probably been in the RAF for more than a few years. Too young to fly in the last war, but wise enough to know the dangers they faced in the skies now.

"Please come in and follow me," Mrs. Harrow said.

"Thank you, ma'am," they said politely. Mrs. Harrow opened the drawing room door, and the RAF officers stepped inside.

"Gentlemen," the colonel greeted, his tone solemn. "This is Franz Hoffman. He has agreed to come with you peacefully. I informed him that our prisoners in England are treated respectfully."

"Yes," Lieutenant Gilbert said. "Mr. Hoffman, you will be assigned to a prisoner camp, and a transport ship will send you to Canada."

Franz's eyes widened. "That is very far away," he said quietly.

"Yes, well, we don't want anyone getting back to Germany too easily," Lieutenant Gilbert said. "Colonel Cunningham mentioned a gunner?"

"Yes," Franz said. "Our plane was an Me 110. It requires two men."

"And this other man, what was his name?"

Franz looked away. "Bernhard Hoffman."

"His brother," the colonel explained when the two RAF officers shared a look at the same surname. "We need to recover his body and provide a proper service. I can show you where the plane and the body are."

"Thank you, Colonel," Lieutenant Gavula said. "We'll see Mr. Hoffman safely to Biggin Hill and will handle the recovery of the body and the plane."

Franz began to follow the RAF men out of the room, and the colonel put a hand on his shoulder.

"I wish you luck and a better life."

Franz offered a sad smile. "*Danke.*"

Elizabeth followed them to watch the German pilot leave Cunningham House. When he and the RAF officers were gone and the house was quiet, it was as if Franz's presence had left a specter of fresh grief within these walls.

"You both performed admirably," the colonel told Elizabeth and Eva, his voice a little hoarse.

"I never wished for any of us to face this sort of thing," Elizabeth said. "This was supposed to be a safe, quiet place in the country."

"There's no such thing as a safe, quiet place when we're at war," the colonel told her. Then he turned to Eva. "To see one's enemy, to face him and handle it with grace when all you feel is pain inside . . . that is something not everyone can manage, Miss Wolman."

"I wanted to shoot him," Eva confessed, her hands twisting into knots.

"I know you did, my dear. But you didn't. And Franz won't forget that. Compassion leaves a mark. Whatever happens, he will *never* forget the hour he spent here with us."

Marcus had been quiet the entire time, but now he spoke up.

"Why do they do it? Why do they follow a madman like Hitler?"

The colonel let out a heavy sigh. "Hitler has spent the better part of a decade convincing his people that they have been victims, that they could return to a former glorious age that exists only in their imagination. And the people there had felt so little hope for so long that they believed him. Why do they believe him? That's one of life's mysteries. Why do good, decent men find themselves being used as the instruments of evil? There is no easy answer to that. Some men want to support their country, others need food and employment. Some simply do as others tell them to and do not question it. You cannot control what another man does, but you can control *yourself*. Are you the sort of man who wants to set fire to the world, or are you the man who stands between the world and the man with the torch? Today, this household stood up to defend not just England but the world. It's a choice we must make daily."

The colonel left them with that speech hanging in the air and locked himself in his bedroom for several hours. Elizabeth was worried about him, but perhaps he, like everyone, needed a few hours alone to process the events of the day. She finally sat back down at her desk, staring at the pile of letters from hopeful clients, trying to focus on work, but the colonel's words echoed in her mind over and over.

Am I the type of person to stand between the world and the man with the torch?

She'd never thought herself brave, but today she knew that she had to be part of the group who fought tyranny to the very end, no matter how bitter the battle. It wasn't just England at stake, but the world, and she would not cower. She would stand and fight with everything she had.

CHAPTER 27

L ate August 1940

"I HATE THIS," HETTY MURMURED AS SHE STARED AT THE hundreds of troops filling the station. She'd been here too often of late to say goodbye.

"I know, my darling." Charles pulled her into his arms and held her in a way that left her floating in safety and comfort. He was the *only* person who had ever been entirely hers, and she didn't want to let him go. She rubbed her cheek against his uniform.

"Are you certain you want to do this?" she asked. "Churchill offered you a place in the Foreign Office overseas. Intelligence work would be far safer."

Charles lifted her chin, his rueful smile twisting her heart until it ached unbearably.

"Since when have I been the man who takes the easy road? I am qualified for this, and they need men like me."

They had learned last month that he could join the Special Service Brigade which they were calling the Commandos now after his friend Will St. Laurent had returned from France during the Dunkirk evacuation. Will had been tasked with recruiting men who were incredibly fit and excellent marksmen. Charles spoke fluent French and German, and he'd always been an excellent shot. Will had visited them for dinner upon returning to London, and Charles had accepted immediately when Will invited him to join the Commandos.

Hetty had held back her own words. She had once stopped him from doing what was right. She wouldn't do that again. Will was Charles's closest friend, and he was a fierce man, one who would protect Charles with all he had. That was her only consolation in letting him go.

"You will write to me," Charles reminded her. "Tell me all of your latest matchmaking stories. You know how I love them." He stroked the tip of his finger down the bridge of her nose, and she closed her eyes, trying to burn this moment into her memory.

She wanted to stay here with him, the heat of the train steam and the August sunlight pouring into the station windows warming her. She could almost pretend they were in a hothouse among blooming flowers while he stole kisses from her.

A sharp train whistle forced her eyes open.

"That would be my train," Charles sighed, his arm around her waist tightening ever so slightly.

It took everything inside of Hetty to let go of him, to pry her hands from his uniform coat.

He retrieved his duffel bag and slung it over his shoulder as they headed for the train that began to fill with men. Dozens of women were crying and holding on to their husbands, brothers, sons, and sweethearts. Here were others who shared in her fear and grief, yet she felt like she stood alone upon a precipice of a vast abyss. One stiff wind would send her plummeting into darkness and despair.

"I don't know what I'll do without you," she said, her hands shaking as Charles paused near the edge of the platform.

He gave her that devil-may-care grin. "You'll do whatever you wish to do, just as you always have. You'll be fine. You were fine without me before, and you'll be fine now. The Hetty I love can handle a few months without me." He was teasing her, but she wanted to hold him and never let him get on that train. It was as though he'd cut a piece of her away and was carrying it farther and farther away with each step, making it harder for her to breathe.

She hadn't been fine before him and wouldn't be now, but she didn't dare tell him that. Loving a man like Charles was something that changed a person from the inside out. She could never go back to being the woman she was before. Their love was as deep as tectonic plates shifting in the earth. She had formed something new inside of herself by opening herself up to loving him. It could never be undone, this change. It was too vast, too seismic, too eternal.

"I love you," she whispered instead.

"You had better." He leaned in to steal one more kiss that began soft, but soon the tenderness vanished as desperation took control of him. His mouth ravished hers, almost bruising.

When he let her go, she touched her lips with the backs of her fingertips, trying to hold on to that physical sensation of his kiss as long as she could. He leapt onto the train and held on to the railing as the locomotive began to roll out of the station.

"Don't forget your promise to me!" she shouted, suddenly terrified that he would forget. His smile faded as she ran after him, dodging people in the station so she wouldn't lose a glimpse of him.

"Promise me!" she cried again as she reached the end of the platform.

"Lonsdales never die!" His words echoed off the steel and glass of the station. Such a sharp contrast of strength and fragility. She could only pray Charles would be steel if she broke like glass. Her last glimpse of her husband was him disappearing into steam and sunlight.

It took her a long while to walk back to the bureau office, but her mind and heart were still miles away.

"Hetty? How did it go?" Elizabeth asked as Hetty stepped into the upstairs interview room.

She set her handbag down on her desk and sighed heavily. "I'm so tired of train station goodbyes. I want no more of them."

"I know Charles. He'll be fine. He wouldn't dare do anything to upset you."

Hetty managed a chuckle, but the sound was hoarse. "Tell me you have good news."

"Well, actually . . ." Elizabeth giggled. "Mr. *Calcutta* is coming in any minute now."

"That's the *opposite* of good news. In fact, that's the most dreadful—"

Elizabeth bolted up. "Mr. Malcolm! Do come in."

Hetty rolled her eyes and grimaced before she faked a smile and turned around to face one of their least favorite clients.

"Ladies." He smiled at them, a far warmer smile than either of them expected. Standing beside him was another client of theirs, Madge Wilson. They'd introduced the pair some time ago and hadn't heard any news on how that meeting had gone. But it was clear the introduction had gone very well, if one judged by the socialite's beaming face.

"We are here to pay our after-marriage fee," Mr. Malcom said, and shared an intimate smile with Madge. Hetty couldn't believe that any woman would look at Frank Malcolm like that, like a woman madly in love, or that he would lose his natural condescension and show affection.

"Oh, wonderful! Let me fetch your paperwork." Elizabeth retrieved their information and set their fee paperwork on the desk for them to review.

"When did it happen?" Hetty asked the couple, still not quite believing what she was seeing.

"Last week." Madge retrieved a rolled-up magazine from her handbag and passed it to Hetty. There was a page dogeared, and she flipped to it to see a picture of Madge in a wedding gown and Frank beside her in a suit.

"It's all everyone's been talking about," Frank proclaimed with no small amount of smug pride.

"Papa was thrilled," Madge added. "He and Frank get along so well."

"That's wonderful." Elizabeth was glowing, as she always did when a match they had made ended up in marriage. Even with Frank, Lizzie was thrilled. Hetty secretly admitted she had her own bit of pleasure in matching someone as difficult as Frank.

There was nothing quite like the thrill that came with accomplishing something you once thought was impossible.

While Frank settled their fee, Hetty pulled Madge aside to inquire what their plans were.

"We're bound for New York. Frank has a new job in America with the Foreign Office. It's a temporary posting. We'll return to Frank's home in Calcutta within a year." Madge spoke with affection, and Hetty couldn't resist asking her the most burning question she'd had since they had walked into the office.

"Madge, you love him? Truly? I want to make sure, because . . ." Hetty's voice trailed off.

A secretive smile curved Madge's lips. "He adores his name and face in the papers, I know that. But he works so hard, you see, and he just wants someone to notice. If my name gets him noticed, I don't mind. He's really wonderful, if you don't mind him obsessing over the *Tatler*. Of course, I obsess over it too, so that makes us perfect for each other." The depth of her affection for him was undeniable.

"I'm glad." Hetty meant it. To hear that even Frank Malcolm was lovable gave her hope. If she could marry off a man like Frank, she could do anything. Like survive the war without Charles at her side.

"I hear that congratulations are in order for you as well, Mrs. Humphrey. Quite a lovely pair you make." Madge winked at Hetty. "Frank was most pleased to tell everyone at his club that he knew you. He even told his club friends to pop over, pay you a visit, and register as clients. Nothing like being matched by a future countess, he said."

Hetty almost laughed. "That is high praise indeed." Of course, their fame-obsessed client would adore telling everyone he knew a future countess.

"Well, we had better be off," Frank announced. "We've many more rounds to make to bid all of our friends goodbye before we leave."

"Be careful on the crossing over," Elizabeth said to them.

"And good luck," Hetty added with a chuckle.

When they were both alone, they sank into their chairs at the interview desk and dissolved into unladylike laughter. Hetty wiped tears from her eyes, and she couldn't stop laughing. She laughed so hard that she began to suddenly cry, and when she started . . . it became impossible to stop.

Arms wrapped around her, and Elizabeth's voice soothed her like a mother would a child.

"It can't be as bad as all that," Elizabeth murmured. "He'll be fine, as will you."

Hetty gasped as she tried to calm herself. "How . . . how can you know?"

Elizabeth scooted her chair closer to Hetty's, her blue eyes bright and glowing.

"I have faith in him. And I sense it, deep in my bones. He will come back to you, alive and whole." Elizabeth spoke with such an earnest intensity that Hetty felt she was back on that balcony the night they'd first met, hearing Elizabeth tell of her uncle's mad idea to start the Marriage Bureau. She'd felt it then too, that whisper of destiny, and she'd reached out to grasp the thread of the tapestry the Fates had woven for her. Now she felt that same sense that Elizabeth's belief in an outcome would make it come true. Fate had bound them together this far, why not further?

"You're right. He wouldn't dare disappoint me," Hetty said, her tone less shaky than before.

"Good. You'll feel better now that you've had a good cry. I

know men roll their eyes at a weepy woman, but I swear a good cry cleanses the soul." Elizabeth chuckled. "How about a cup of tea? As Mrs. Harrow says, everything is always better with a spot of tea."

Hetty chuckled and wiped at her eyes. While Elizabeth fetched tea, Hetty picked up the banknote Mr. Malcolm had left. Perhaps Charles was right. They were good at this, *she* was good at this, and she had plenty of work to focus on rather than letting herself drown in worries.

But her heart still felt like it was on a train, racing farther and farther away from her.

CHAPTER 28

Hetty and Elizabeth were discussing the air-raid drill that had happened the night before and how they'd heard train tracks had been bombed. The news had upset Hetty, and Elizabeth had only just managed to calm her down. They both turned at the knock upon their open door.

"I'm so sorry, am I interrupting?" asked the tall man who stood in the doorway. It was Marvin Asquith, a banker in his late forties whose two teenage daughters had come to the bureau on his behalf two months ago. They had wanted to see him remarry and be happy after losing their mother seven years before.

Hetty wiped at her cheeks hastily. "Mr. Asquith, do come in. You aren't interrupting anything." He had no doubt seen her crying, but he was too gentlemanly to inquire why. He smiled and removed his hat and coat before nervously stroking his mustache.

"How was your latest introduction?" Elizabeth asked.

"Well, that's just it. I'm rather baffled and quite angry." He cleared his throat awkwardly and touched his waistcoat.

Hetty could sense the man was upset, but not necessarily with them.

"What? Good gracious, what happened?" Elizabeth sat back at her desk and opened their introduction ledger. "You were to meet with Minerva Waterston, weren't you?"

"Was Miss Waterston unsatisfactory?" Hetty asked.

Mr. Asquith shook his head. "That's the thing—I'm not entirely sure it *was* Miss Waterston that I met for dinner." He slipped a finger in the collar of his shirt and tugged as though trying to loosen it. "You see, we exchanged photographs— nothing salacious, mind you, just simple photographs of our faces. We wanted to get a sense of each other, and it would help if we decided to meet in person."

"That's nothing to be ashamed of. We do encourage that when the time is right for our clients."

"Well, I received Miss Waterston's photo and was very pleased by her appearance. I wrote her a reply, enclosed my own photo, and sent it to her via your office, saying we should arrange a meeting if she was interested. She replied that she was, and we arranged to meet last evening for dinner."

"And you met her?"

"I met *someone*," Mr. Asquith said. "I do not believe it was actually Miss Waterston. She looked similar, but not quite the same."

"So you're saying . . . ?"

"I am concerned that the woman I met for dinner was an imposter."

"An *imposter*?" Hetty uttered the word with suspicion. "But how . . . ?"

"Damned if I know. She seemed familiar with Miss Waterston's life, but it didn't feel like her. I understand people can behave differently in person, but this was too different. Her makeup was overdone, her hair far too red, based on Miss Waterston's description of herself, and she . . ." Mr. Asquith's face reddened. "She made a very forward advance quite unexpectedly after dinner. I am a gentleman, and I certainly wasn't ready to . . . do anything more than dinner last evening."

As he spoke, the door of the office opened behind him, and Miss Plumley came in and set her handbag down on the side table by the door. She halted abruptly when she spotted them, and her face drained of all color. Hetty sharpened her focus on the secretary, like a hawk sighting prey.

Mr. Asquith turned around in his chair. "By God, that's *her*!" He pointed accusingly at Miss Plumley.

Elizabeth gasped. "What? Our Miss Plumley?"

The secretary backed up, her hand flailing behind her to find the doorknob.

"Is this true?" Hetty shot out of her chair. "Did you pretend to be one of our clients, Minerva Waterston?"

Miss Plumley's eyes filled with tears. "I . . . er . . . yes . . ."

"Mr. Asquith, would you mind giving us a moment to handle this?" Hetty asked as she escorted Miss Plumley into the hall. Elizabeth soon joined them.

"Oh, Miss Plumley, why did you do it?"

The secretary's hands shook as she adjusted her spectacles. "I was checking the letters, as you instructed me to do, and I saw that Minerva Waterston had politely returned his photo and his letters. It seemed she'd found someone else and was newly engaged. It broke my heart to think of how Mr. Asquith might take the news and . . . well . . . I liked the look of Mr. Asquith very much. I thought, why not me? Why couldn't *I* be the one for him? I thought he might not notice a difference, since I do look a little like Miss Waterston."

Hetty closed her eyes and pinched the bridge of her nose. This was a terrible mess.

"What you did was not only unprofessional but it will tarnish our company's reputation. Mr. Asquith trusted us, *all of us*, with his privacy, and you broke that trust."

Elizabeth nudged her in the ribs and then sent the secretary a pitying look.

"You can be *the one* for someone, Miss Plumley, but we need to register you properly. There's no need for deception. Wouldn't you like a man to meet you as you are?" Elizabeth looked so sweet and trusting that Hetty nearly groaned in frustration.

"Yes, I would," Miss Plumley sniffed. "Am . . . am I being let go?"

"Yes," Hetty snapped. "Immediately."

"No." Elizabeth's tone hardened as she shot Hetty a quelling look.

"*Yes.*"

"*No.*" Elizabeth's blue eyes were full of sparks, which stunned Hetty. "No, you are not being let go. We believe in people at the Marriage Bureau. But we will need you to apologize to Mr. Asquith. Then we must really talk about your hair and clothes."

The secretary glanced down at herself, tears streaming down her cheeks. "Do I look awful?"

"No, not at all, but you do look a little desperate. Remember, you are a wonderful, kind woman. You have no need to be desperate for anyone to love you. You need only to find the right man the right way," Elizabeth counseled. "Besides, these dark colors wash you out. You need soft pastels. Now, we will give you a minute to speak with Mr. Asquith."

Miss Plumley stepped into the office and closed the door.

"Lizzie . . . ," Hetty said softly. They had never fought about anything, but today they had come close. "She defrauded a client."

"I know." Elizabeth rubbed her closed eyes and sighed. "This is one exception I want to make. Miss Plumley has been excellent in her position, and I just believe a second chance would be good for her."

"Only her. We can't take any more situations like this. Someone could take us to court, and we'd lose the bureau."

Hetty knew Elizabeth wasn't a fool. She knew all the legal ramifications. Charles had counseled them well. But it didn't stop her from wanting to help their secretary. With anyone else, Hetty would have been furious, but she knew how much Lizzie truly cared about people.

"Agreed. She will be the one exception, assuming Mr. Asquith accepts her apology."

When the door opened, Miss Plumley's eyes were overbright, but she smiled and whispered a quick thank you to them before rushing downstairs to her desk in the reception.

Mr. Asquith stood and collected his hat, holding it between his hands as he eyed them uncertainly.

"She's not to be terminated, I hope? I know I was rather angry when I first came in here, but now . . . Well, I realize that everyone who comes in these days just wants something, don't they? We all want love. I should hate that I cost her employment when she only wants the same thing I do, to find the right person to be with."

"We were hoping you would say that. We will keep her

employed, if that's all right with you, and I will make sure to match her to someone immediately and supervise her, of course."

"Excellent." Mr. Asquith smiled. "Would you mind asking Miss Plumley if she would write to me directly at my address? I rather enjoyed our dinner, until she tried to kiss me." He rubbed the brim of his hat in embarrassment. "I liked the kiss very much, but she startled me, that's all. I'd like to at least give myself the chance to know the real Miss Plumley, just to see . . . well . . . if something is there."

"Oh?" Elizabeth beamed at him. "Yes, yes, of course, if she agrees. I'll give her your address."

"Thank you." He chuckled. "My daughters will be delighted if I make a match. I am eager to be a husband again." His face was a little ruddy as he admitted this. "Have a good day, ladies."

Once they were alone in the office, Hetty laughed and shook her head. "What if he had wanted her fired?"

"I would have sent her to work in the country and asked Eva if she wanted to work in London more often."

Lord, she loved Lizzie, but the woman believed the best of everyone, and reality had taught Hetty a far different lesson. "You are determined to save everyone, aren't you?"

"Yes, of course," Elizabeth replied with her customary cheek, as if that was obvious, and headed off to make the index cards.

Hetty shook her head. If anyone could save the world, she supposed it would be Elizabeth.

A moment later, air-raid sirens pierced the air.

Hetty grabbed their gas masks from their handbags. "Lizzie! We have to go, now!" It was the third time this week that the sirens had gone off. Some of the outskirts of the city had taken bombing hits, but the news of it had been kept fairly quiet. With each passing day, Hetty was convinced something worse was yet to come, the thing they all feared. She tried not to think of Charles still on a train crossing the English countryside. She could only pray that the bombers would not aim for trains today.

Elizabeth came flying back into the room.

"Down to the shelter." Hetty marshaled her friend downstairs. They met Miss Plumley in the reception, and the three of them bustled out the back door to the small bit of garden behind their business where they could squeeze in an Anderson shelter.

They descended the steps into the underground shelter, and each sat on one of the bunk beds inside.

"Oh, I do hate these drills," Miss Plumley whispered, her eyes wide with fear.

"We all do," Hetty said. She didn't bother to tell Miss Plumley that it might not be a drill. Somehow, the word *drill* made everything feel safer. To acknowledge it might not be a drill would have been more frightening.

"Well, why not distract ourselves with some work?" Elizabeth tossed her mask onto her bunk and held up nearly thirty index cards that she'd pulled from a pocket in her dress. "We can match clients while we wait."

Hetty smiled. "Only you, Lizzie, only you." But she was thankful for the distraction. It was going to be a long wait until they heard the all-clear sound on the streets. "Fine, let the matching begin." Hetty reached for the nearest set of client cards and did her best to put the sirens in the back of her mind.

PART III

CHAPTER 29

S *eptember 7, 1940*

IT WAS CLOSE TO FIVE O'CLOCK WHEN HETTY AND EVA finished the last interview of the day and were finally able to take a moment of rest upstairs in the warm sunlight that reached the roof. It was a brief respite for them after the last few months, as the odds of an air-raid drill during the day had been steadily increasing. Business was growing, and since the RAF had been keeping most of the bombers at bay, Eva was now sharing duties with Miss Plumley at the Bond Street office every other week. The rotations between the country and London seemed to give Hetty, Eva and Elizabeth something to look forward to. Being busy, working and going back and forth between the city and the country was a welcome distraction from concerns about air-raids.

"How is Marcus doing?" Hetty slipped off her shoes and stretched her bare feet out in the sun. It was a gloriously perfect day.

Eva leaned back in her chair and sighed, her face softening in a way it hadn't in months. "Better. Far better than me. He adores the colonel. Last weekend, they built the Anderson shelter in the garden. I heard the colonel tell Marcus stories about a safari in Africa while they worked." Eva paused, her voice suddenly a little husky with emotion. "The colonel is as close to a father as Marcus has now that . . ."

Hetty's heart stung as she reached out and put her fingertips on the other woman's arm.

"You and Marcus will stay here, won't you? Once the war is over?"

Eva sighed. "I honestly hadn't thought about it, about how our parents, even our country, is *gone*."

"You have a home here, a family, with all of us. Please don't forget that." She squeezed Eva's arm before letting go.

"I never used to be afraid of anything," Eva said. "But now I wake up every morning feeling so afraid of *everything*. Every birthday Marcus has makes me more and more terrified. What if we are still fighting in three years? He'll be eighteen. He could enlist, and if he leaves me too, well, then I'm done, aren't I?"

"Even if you were alone, you would still be yourself, and you wouldn't be gone," Hetty said. "You're stronger than you realize."

At this, Eva gave a watery chuckle. "I'm not as brave as you. I'm not as compassionate as Elizabeth. I wanted to shoot that pilot who crashed near Cunningham House."

Hetty's heart throbbed in sympathy. She knew that feeling all too well, that blind fury that could take over a person. She'd felt that way the moment that young soldier had died in her arms on Charles's ship and she'd rushed up to fire at the German fighter as it bore down on the beaches of Dunkirk. It was hard to let go of the guilt that came after experiencing fury like that.

But she'd also had time to make her peace with it. She had not grown up like Elizabeth. As a brigadier's daughter, she knew that one had to fight back to stop evil before it spread.

"If there is one thing my father taught me, compassion toward the enemy is often misplaced. Another pilot might have tried to shoot you and escape. When you are at war, you have to remember that kind words and no weapons will often seal your doom. Evil is not moved by compassion or love. In fact, it's driven all the harder to destroy anyone who shows such qualities. It's better to be the person who is able to take the shot and save everyone than to become a martyr trying to surrender and be killed. I know we are told to believe in peace, but there will always be someone out there with a gun ready to take everything you hold dear, because they can. Rose-colored glasses will not create peace between warring nations. A bully is a bully, and there's only one way to stop them. That is the reality we're living in."

Eva looked away, her eyes sweeping the skyline of London. A low hum swept over the city.

"What's that? Is it—?" Eva's words halted suddenly as a swarm of planes appeared on the horizon. An airborne armada was sailing straight for them across the clear skies. The air-raid sirens blared to life, the haunting sound filling the air as the hum of the planes turned to a growl.

"Oh my God." Hetty stumbled out of her chair, throwing her shoes on, and then she and Eva were running down the stairs.

"What about Elizabeth?" Eva gasped as they burst into the back garden and headed for the shelter a few feet away.

"She's out shopping, but I'm sure she'll be fine." Hetty's hands shook as she slammed the shelter door closed. Lizzie was out there alone, with bombers flooding the skies.

The distant sound of thunder rumbled the earth, making the metal walls around them rattle. Hetty's legs gave out and she collapsed. Eva caught her, and they both sat on the nearest bed, their hands clasped so tight their knuckles were white.

Above them, hell rained down from the skies. For once, Hetty was glad Charles wasn't here. She knew she wouldn't hear from him for perhaps a very long time. Will had warned her of that. The Commandos would be taking on some of the most dangerous missions across the world. It was where Charles belonged, just as she belonged here, fighting for her country in her own way, fighting to give people hope by helping people find love.

"You were fine without me before, and you'll be fine now . . ." Charles's words wrapped around her heart as she closed her eyes, clinging to them.

"We'll be fine," she whispered to Eva. "We'll be fine." She hadn't understood until that moment that Charles's words had been seeking a promise from her in return. She would be fine. She would survive this so she would be here when he came home. She wasn't about to disappoint the man who held her heart. There was no amount of bombing that could make her break that promise.

"Our boys will beat the bastards back, you'll see." Hetty closed her eyes as the thunder of bombs continued to storm above them, and they held fast to each other.

IT HAD BEEN AN HOUR SINCE THE BOMBING STARTED, SINCE Elizabeth had taken shelter in the basement of a little shop with a group of strangers, including a scared little boy who had finally fallen asleep on his mother's lap as she stroked his hair idly with her fingers.

The others, however, had hung on her every word. Her time in India, meeting Hetty, the Marriage Bureau. They had been particularly interested in some of the more colorful matches they'd made, even more than Hetty's adventures in Dunkirk or the pilot Elizabeth had helped capture. They needed the normalcy of finding love more than daring deeds at the moment, she supposed.

"And that is how I ended up here," Elizabeth said, finishing her story, and everyone in the basement of the shop was quiet.

"That might be the single most brilliant thing I've ever heard," Nathan Sheridan said as he rolled his cane over his thighs. "Quite spectacular, Miss Mowbray." His brown eyes twinkled with a playful charm.

Elizabeth looked at the pilot, Philip, the blond RAF pilot who sat beside him. The man was quiet, his gaze strangely intense as he looked at her. His blue eyes burned beneath the lamps.

"You made even me forget our troubles for a time," he said softly. His eyes then lifted up to the ceiling. Everyone followed his focused stare.

"It's quiet," Nathan observed.

"Good quiet, or bad?" a man sitting next to Elizabeth asked.

"I don't believe we'll ever define *quiet* as a good thing in quite the same way again," Philip said. "If we don't hear bombs or feel them, it must be good enough for someone to try to go to the surface. Nathan, are you with me?" Philip stood and held out a hand to his friend to lift him to his feet. Elizabeth got up as well, brushing dust off her dress.

"Everyone, stay here. We'll see if it's clear," Philip instructed before he and Nathan climbed the basement stairs. The two men pushed the door above them open, and Elizabeth listened to their footsteps overhead as they crossed the ground floor of the shop. More dust drifted down through the slats of wood, and Elizabeth shielded her eyes. A different siren wailed above them as a long, even, continuous note.

"All clear," one man whispered to himself.

"It's safe to come up," Philip called down to everyone in the basement.

"Let me help you." Elizabeth opened her arms to the mother, who gratefully passed Elizabeth her sleeping boy so she could collect herself and stand.

"Thank you for the food," the woman said as she took her child back. "This is the first time he's really slept since his father left for the Continent last month."

"I'm glad I could help." Elizabeth offered her a smile before she collected her bags of groceries and climbed the stairs. The world around them was indeed quiet, but the air was acrid, with a sharp scent that made Elizabeth think of burnt wax and paint. It made her uneasy.

"What is that smell?" the shopkeeper asked.

Philip stood in the open doorway, staring out at a wall of fire and smoke in the distance. "Paint and paint thinner, I think. Rubber, tar . . ."

The noxious cocktail of scents only grew stronger as the breeze blew smoke in their direction. They could see the fire in the distance looming over the skyline. Elizabeth had never seen so much smoke in her life. It was quickly swallowing the city.

"What did they hit?" Nathan asked. "Was it the docks?"

"Seems to be. Christ, a full hour of bombs . . . ," Philip muttered. "It's a miracle there's anything left."

The roar of the fire took the place of the hum of aircraft. They could hear the blaze even at that distance. A fire truck suddenly raced past, its bell clanging, and several men in Auxiliary Fire Service uniforms were huddled inside the truck as it made a sharp turn at the end of the street. Smoke billowed up from the docks, thickening the sky and blocking out the very sun itself.

Elizabeth's knees shook as she joined Philip in the doorway of the little shop. His gaze caught and held hers, his eyes fathomless. "You did well in there."

Elizabeth found herself lost in the man's eyes. "What did you say?"

"Your story. That was well done." This stranger's praise of her sent an odd flutter through her lower belly. "You have no idea how much those people needed a distraction."

"Even you?" she asked.

Lord, his dark-gold lashes were long, and his lips were so pleasant to look at. He really was a singularly attractive man. It struck her that her ability to focus on his looks was rather a marvel given that the rest of her was still in a state of deep shock about everything they had gone through.

Perhaps that was why he stood out to her in this moment so clearly. He was a detail that wasn't frightening, something that was beautiful and inspiring rather than terrifying. His blue uniform was covered in a layer of dust, yet his buttons shone defiantly through the smoke and haze. She had the strangest urge to reach up and touch one of those buttons, to cement herself in the moment so she didn't have to face what was ahead of her.

"I daresay I needed it the most. To not be there, to not be in the sky fighting for our country . . ." His lips curved in a wry grin that held just a hint of mischief mixed with melancholy. "It's a pity I won't likely see you again."

The thought of never seeing Philip again drove a spike of panic through her. "You could drop by the Marriage Bureau."

His solemn eyes twinkled with a hint of warmth. "To listen to more of your wild stories?"

"To register, of course. All the men in the sky need sweethearts. Don't you?"

Philip's lips kicked up into a wider grin. Her heart stuttered a beat as he leaned down toward her.

"I don't believe a matchmaker can truly make people fall in love, but I enjoyed listening to *you* talk all the same." He kissed her softly upon her lips and left her standing in the doorway, completely stunned. Her mouth tingled in the most delicious way, and her body was electric with it, as though that single kiss had sent a bolt of lightning through her, awakening something inside of her that she hadn't realized had been asleep.

"Sorry about him," Nathan murmured as he passed by her. "Please expect me to call upon you tomorrow at the office, assuming we're all still alive come morning. I think I would like to register." He winked at her and then hastily rushed after Philip, who seemed to be headed straight toward the distant fires. Toward danger. She knew what sort of man he was, the kind who would go forth into the fires of perdition itself to save lives.

Another fire truck went past. Nathan put his fingers to his

lips and whistled sharply. The fire truck slowed long enough for Nathan and Philip to hop on board, and then it sped off into the haze of the spreading smoke. Just like that, the two men were gone.

"Everyone had better get home quickly," the old shopkeeper urged the remaining survivors of the basement. He stood there wiping dust off his spectacles with a handkerchief, seemingly calm, yet Elizabeth witnessed the tiniest tremors in the man's hands. "We don't know what we'll be facing tonight. Those fires are a beacon to any bombers that may follow the first. The blackout won't matter if they come back tonight."

The rest of the men and women emerged from the shelter of the man's basement to stand dazed in the street. It was one thing to prepare oneself for a bombing, to know what to do in theory, to put tape across one's windows to keep glass from shattering in dangerous ways, to operate the hand pumps in case an incendiary device started a fire. But to see a conflagration consume the city one lived in and loved. To feel the very ground shudder like a poor beast of burden being whipped each time the bombs struck it.

To know that nothing truly protected you from death.

The realization sent Elizabeth reeling for a moment, but she forced her mind back on Philip, the way his lips had looked as he smiled, how he'd teased her about matchmaking, how he'd said she'd done well today. Those things could never be turned to ash.

The young mother came up beside Elizabeth on the pavement.

"Will you be all right getting yourself home?" Elizabeth asked.

"Yes, I think so." The child had woken, and she set him down on his feet for a moment. He curled his fingers into her skirts and stared at the smoke now filling the street.

Another of the men from the basement stepped up. "I can escort you home, ma'am."

"Oh, I couldn't ask you to—" the woman began.

The middle-aged man's smile was kind and a little sad. "Please, ma'am. I have no one at home to worry over. My son perished at Dunkirk, and I lost my wife three years before. It's just me now. Seeing you home would give an old man like me some purpose."

The young mother's shoulders sagged in relief. "Thank you. I would appreciate that."

As the woman and her child walked away with the older man, she heard the woman speak. "Would you tell me about your son? I should very much like to hear about him."

Clutching her bag of groceries, Elizabeth stood in the street for a long moment as the shock of the last hour slowly wore off. It had finally happened—they had been bombed, and she had survived.

As soon as that thought passed across her mind, it was followed by another. What about Isabelle? What about Hetty and Eva? Had they been at the Bond Street office or had they gone to Charles's Townhouse early for the night? Her inability to move immediately ceased as she broke into a frantic run. People were emerging from shelters all around her and pausing in the street to stare just as she had at the smoke-filled horizon.

It took her almost half an hour to reach Isabelle's townhouse. It was a relief to see it still untouched after what she'd heard while she was trapped in that basement. She fumbled to find her key in the pocket of her dress before she burst into the townhouse.

"Isabelle?" she called out before setting the shopping bag on the table.

Silence filled the empty house with an uneasiness that she didn't like. Elizabeth set her handbag and gas mask down on the sofa before she picked up the telephone and dialed the upstairs office number for the bureau. Hetty and Eva had planned to stay late to review the latest batch of letters from the postman. He had started treating the Marriage Bureau correspondence with extra care, ever since they had successfully matched him to a nice woman whose husband had died a few years before. The two had gotten along famously.

Elizabeth's heart pounded as she waited for someone to answer. The receiver clicked, and someone breathed sharply on the other end of the line.

"Hel-hello? Marriage Bureau," Hetty said unsteadily.

Elizabeth lost her ability to hold in her sense of relief. "Hetty, thank heavens."

"Lizzie, you're all right, I hope?" Hetty sounded just as shaken.

"Yes, I'm afraid I was a little too close to the bombing. I should like to avoid that in the future." She tried to laugh, but the sound was strangled by a little gasp as she fought off a sob.

"Take a deep breath," Hetty soothed. "You're experiencing a rush of emotions and energy. It's common among soldiers. You must sit still and breathe and it will pass."

"Is Eva all right?"

"She is. She's safe with me. We were taking a moment to rest on the roof when we saw the bombers come in. Thank heavens, we'd sent Miss Plumley home an hour ago. Eva and I raced down to the shelter. It was . . ."

But she didn't finish. There would never be words to describe seeing those harbingers of doom on the horizon.

"I can't find Isabelle. She isn't here," Elizabeth said.

"She's probably still at her office. She works late, doesn't she?"

"Oh heavens, you're right. I was just so worried. I can't seem to think clearly."

"It's the stress of the moment. Like I said, the best thing you can do is sit and breathe deep. Eva and I are going to go to Charles's townhouse tonight. Call us when Isabelle comes home." Hetty had sold her own townhouse after the wedding and Charles had insisted that two extra rooms be prepared for Eva and Marcus whenever they came to London, which Eva did frequently to work at the Bond Street office.

"I'll call when I find her." Elizabeth dialed Isabelle's office after that. When no one answered, she set the phone back in the cradle. *Please come home safe, Isabelle. Please.*

She spent the next half hour trying to cobble together a decent dinner of sandwiches and salad with lettuce from the garden. A few of the tomatoes they'd planted were ripe, and she'd picked those as well, happy to have something to do. When she heard the door open, she rushed from the kitchen to see Isabelle standing there, face ashen, her once-immaculate clothes covered in dust.

"Lizzie . . ." Her aunt rushed over and flung her arms around her.

"Isabelle, you're all right! Were you at your office? I tried to call, but no one answered."

"No, I was near the Liverpool Street station when the sirens started. I rushed down there with a few hundred people. We were all huddled up, waiting it out. Every time a bomb struck, the lights flickered and people screamed. I kept thinking we might not make it, or that we'd be trapped in darkness and never find our way out . . ." She shuddered, and a tiny cloud of dust drifted off her clothes and hair. The sight of her aunt in such a fragile state made Elizabeth's own fears recede.

"Let's get you out of those clothes. I've made dinner."

At this, her aunt smiled a little. "It really is the end of the world if you're making dinner."

Elizabeth laughed. The sound loosened something between them, and Isabelle laughed too.

After a hasty call to Hetty at Charles's townhouse to reassure her that Isabelle was safe, she and Isabelle had dinner and were in the middle of washing the dishes when the air-raid siren wailed again. Elizabeth glanced at the clock. It had only been two hours since the last attack ended. How could they stand this?

"Fetch the torches. I'll get the masks," Isabelle said. They rushed through the house, collecting house coats, blankets, and other things they thought they might need before they stumbled into the dark garden.

Isabelle screeched and tumbled to the ground halfway to the shelter. Above them the moon was bright, and the still-burning docks in London acted like a beacon. Elizabeth grasped her aunt by the arms and helped her up.

"Are you hurt?"

"My ankle. I've turned it. Tripped over that bloody watering can." The metal can gleamed beneath the moonlight, such a silly thing, yet Elizabeth cursed its very existence. They hobbled to the Anderson shelter and descended inside.

"Sit and rest your ankle," Elizabeth counseled as she went to close the door. The distant droning sound, almost like a swarm of bees, grew louder and louder. Elizabeth slammed the door shut against it, slightly muffling the sound. The walls of the shelter rattled, and a thin stream of water trickled down from last week's rain to pool on the floor. Isabelle turned on one of the torches and swung her beam over the dark shelter.

"Should we light a candle?" Elizabeth asked. They had brought several candles down the week before when they'd prepared the shelter. She was very thankful they had done that.

"Yes, let's." Isabelle retrieved one of the candles and a pack of matches. Elizabeth lit the candle and set it in the candle-holder before she unfolded the blankets on the two cots nearest each other. She urged Isabelle to lie back and then tucked her in beneath the blanket.

Thunder rumbled in the distance, a storm that charged the air around them. But these sounds were bombs, not rain. She wished she was back inside Isabelle's townhouse, warming herself by a coal fire and not here in this inky, eerie darkness, broken only by the fluttering light of a slender candle.

"Tomorrow is our night," Isabelle said quietly as she sat up in the bed suddenly.

Elizabeth had been lost in her own thoughts. "What's tomorrow?"

"The AFS. We're on duty tomorrow night. What if the bombers come back? What if . . . ?" The note of fear in Isabelle's voice was so uncharacteristic of her that Elizabeth joined her on the bed and put an arm around her, squeezing her gently as she tried to comfort her.

"If they come tomorrow, we'll handle it," Elizabeth said. How could they not? They were required to serve in some capacity if they were between the ages of twenty and thirty-nine years old and unmarried. Both she and Isabelle had chosen the Auxiliary

Fire Service, since it needed the most volunteers. It also meant she'd spent less time in the country, which meant she missed seeing Mrs. Harrow and the Colonel as often as she'd liked to.

In the last year, they'd had a fairly easy time of patrolling the streets at night. They had one primary duty, which they hadn't been called to do yet, which was to drive the men to any fire outbreaks in the fire trucks. Their second duty was to take over in all aspects of the fire service if enough men went into military service and the AFS at home became dangerously understaffed. They both prayed that neither of those things would be needed. But now they feared it might be.

Something nearby exploded, and the impact rolled through the earth so hard that Elizabeth saw the corrugated walls ripple with the impact. Elizabeth hugged her aunt tight, shutting her eyes as dirt rained down from the ceiling.

Throughout the night, the sound of planes overhead came and went. Elizabeth felt like a cornered fox, hiding in a bush while hounds howled and circled her, homing in on her scent.

Somewhere close to four in the morning, she crashed into her bunk and burrowed beneath the thin woolen blankets. She clenched her fists each time a bomb dropped, but exhaustion dragged itself over her, finally pulling her down enough that she could sleep if she but dared to close her eyes.

All she could think of was what the world above her would look like when the German bombers finally flew back to their roosts. Would anything she loved in the city be left? Would the people she loved still be alive?

CHAPTER 30

"They're coming," a voice hissed urgently in the dark.

"Who?" Elizabeth tried in vain to make sense of the darkness enveloping her. Moonlight slowly spread out around her, and she saw the eerie shapes of people walking along the street. Their steps dragged, their arms swung too slow, as though trapped in molasses. All the shops around them were shuttered; no life stirred within the boarded-up windows, nor did any light escape from beneath the thick black curtains. Colors blurred together into a range of blue and gray shadows until it hurt her eyes to try to see anything around her.

"They're coming," that voice said again.

Elizabeth rushed toward the nearest person she could find on the street. It was a man. She grasped his arm, pulling him to a stop. His feet ceased their restless shuffling. When he turned toward her, the skin of his face was ashen and bare of any features. A pale mask of *nothing*. A slit opened and a black hole appeared where his mouth should have been, as though he was silently screaming.

Fear slashed Elizabeth from the inside and she couldn't move. It was like a nightmare she'd had as a child over and over, when she'd been afraid of being left alone among strangers. But these strangers had no faces.

"Beware the bomber's moon," that voice whispered again. She drowned beneath the drone of bombers overhead. They blacked out the silvery moon, and their arrival shook the earth beneath her feet.

Finding her feet again, Elizabeth started to run, but she slipped on shattered glass next to a darkened bookstore and fell. Pain exploded through her, and she shrieked.

"Lizzie!"

Elizabeth bolted up, gasping as her heart battered against her ribs. She looked desperately about to find her bearings. Sunlight poured in through the small door to the Anderson shelter. Her aunt leaned over her, her face strained.

"What . . . what time is it?" Elizabeth asked.

"Eight o'clock. You slept in. I imagine most of London did."

A heavy weight settled over Elizabeth. Last night hadn't been a dream. They had been bombed. She dragged herself wearily out of the little cot she'd slept on. "Dear God. Have you been outside on the street? Did anyone . . . ?" She couldn't bring herself to finish that dreaded question.

Isabelle moved to help Elizabeth stand up. "I think the East End took most of the hits. Mr. Cox said he saw fires raging all through the night on the horizon." Mr. Cox was their neighbor across the street. "I don't believe the poor man slept a wink."

Elizabeth stood and ignored her body's protest of aches and pains from the tense night. "How is your ankle?"

"Stiff, but I'll manage. The phones are still up. I've called my office, and they said I don't have to come in today. How about you? I spoke to Hetty earlier on the phone and she thinks she'll go into the office."

Elizabeth stared at the interior of the shelter and shuddered. "I think I'll go in to the office as well. I need a distraction."

They climbed out of the shelter and walked across the garden. Elizabeth paused by the overturned watering can that Isabelle had tripped on the night before and lifted it up to set it on top of an unused flower bed.

"Are you hungry?" Isabelle asked.

"I am a bit peckish," Elizabeth admitted.

"We have some bread. There's treacle and a bit of marmalade. We have plenty left over from our monthly allowance. There are also some fresh eggs."

"Not powdered ones?" Elizabeth's somewhat waning appetite resurfaced at the thought of a real egg with a bit of toast and marmalade.

"Mr. Cox's chickens were quite busy. When I went over to see him this morning, he gave me two eggs and called me a dear." Isabelle blushed.

William Cox was an older man in his early seventies, but he still moved with this spryness of a man thirty years younger. His wife, Dolores, had passed a few years before, and the twinkle in Mr. Cox's eyes had dimmed a little since then, but he seemed resolute not to surrender to despair, let alone the Germans.

Elizabeth helped Isabelle in the kitchen, finding relief in everyday things—the way cold water from the tap felt on her fingers as she washed her hands, or the sizzle of the eggs cooking on the stove. The taste of that pinch of salt they were allowed on their breakfast and how it teased her tongue. Her mind and body seemed to catalog every small detail, even the Royal Copenhagen floral patterns on the china plate she was cleaning in the sink at this moment. She traced the delicate floral pattern on the center before she dried it with a dishrag.

"These dishes were a personal gift from Mr. Hartnell," Isabelle said fondly. Her eyes softened as she looked at the plate. "He loved my designs two years ago, which were such a success at his fashion show, and he gave me these. They cost a fortune, you know."

Elizabeth carefully set the one plate she held on the counter, afraid to break it. "We shouldn't use them, then."

Isabelle set her dishrag beside it. "Before yesterday I would've agreed, but now I think we should. I mean, if we are to be bombed here in London . . . any moment might be . . ." She swallowed hard. "I rather think we ought to enjoy everything while we can, don't you?"

"I don't wish to argue with that." Elizabeth finished cleaning the last two dishes, then went to change into a sensible green dress and her most comfortable walking shoes.

"Well, I'm off to the bureau. I'll leave a note on the door and be back as soon as I can."

"Be safe," her aunt called after her as she stepped out of the townhouse and onto the street.

Mr. Cox stood in the doorway of his home, holding a plump brown hen in one arm. He waved at her, and she waved back.

"Thank you for the eggs!" she called out.

Mr. Cox grinned. "I hope to have more tomorrow. Lucy and the other hens had laid a few eggs last night in the thick of the bombing. She'll not let those planes stop her from doing her duty." The man cooed and patted the chicken's head with affection. Lucy bobbed her head a little and let out a self-satisfied series of clucks.

Elizabeth made her way to Bond Street, eyes fixed on the skies. Smoke still left a haze over the city, but the sun valiantly struggled to break through. She rounded the corner in the direction of the bureau office and barreled straight into a man who was standing still on the pavement.

"Oh, I'm so sorry," she apologized. "That was rather clumsy of me."

He tipped his hat at her. "Not at all, miss."

As she walked around him and started back down the street, she halted abruptly. There was a queue of people filling the pavement. The man she'd bumped into had been at the very end of the line.

She questioned a woman nearest her, who held the hand of a young girl who looked to be about six years old. "Excuse me, do you mind if I ask what you are waiting for?" The mother and daughter were fashionably dressed and wearing almost identical clothing.

"We're in line to meet the *matchmakers*," the woman said.

"The match . . . You mean the Marriage Bureau? All of you?"

The woman nodded and gave Elizabeth a puzzled look. "The end of the queue is that way."

"Yes, I can see that, thank you," Elizabeth replied.

In a daze, she reached the bureau's distant door, passing so many people that she lost count somewhere after sixty. She found the reception door was open. Miss Plumley and Eva were directing people to fill out questionnaires and setting appointments

"We'll see as many as we can, but if we can't see you today, we will schedule you later," Eva announced to the cluster of men and women clamoring at the front desk.

Miss Plumley frantically waved her arms. "Miss Mowbray! Thank God you're here."

"What happened? I thought for sure no one would be out after last night."

"As did I," Miss Plumley said. "But when I came to open up the bureau, I saw the line had formed and I rushed inside and called Mrs. Humphrey immediately."

"Hetty's upstairs?"

"Yes, she's conducting an interview with a new client. She didn't want to rush you this morning. Your aunt called a little while after Mrs. Humphrey arrived and said you were safe but still sleeping."

Elizabeth removed her hat and coat and dropped her handbag and gas mask bag behind Miss Plumley's desk before she hurried upstairs. Hetty was at the interview desk speaking with a man. She had just finished up, and the man shook Hetty's hand before leaving.

"How long have you been here?" Elizabeth asked.

Hetty checked her wristwatch. "Seven thirty?"

"Why didn't you call me? I only came to put a notice on the door that we were closed. I didn't think anyone . . ."

"No time! When Miss Plumley said we had a line of people, I thought she was exaggerating. I meant to call you, but once we got here, well, we all dug in and have been far too busy. Then Isabelle called. She was worried about you. She said you barely slept last night."

"*No one* in London slept last night." Elizabeth didn't want to be upset with Hetty, but she was a little. It was important to be here, to do this work today of all days.

"I'll call you next time, no matter what," Hetty promised.

"Thank you. Now, where are we with the interviews?"

"Eva and Miss Plumley are handing out questionnaires. You and I can do two interviews at one time. I can handle a client in the back office and you can handle a client out front, if that's acceptable?"

"Yes, I believe that should work." They had both gotten so experienced at interviewing that they no longer had to do it together, if time didn't allow for it.

"Let me fetch my pad and pen, then I'll be ready." Elizabeth dug around in the drawer of her interview desk, while Hetty called in the next two clients.

The first man was István Németh, a widower from Hungary who had been working in banking in London for the last ten years.

"I'll see you in my office, Mr. Németh. This way, please." Hetty gestured to the handsome salt-and-pepper-haired gentleman.

Elizabeth waved for the next man in the hall to follow her in.

"I filled out the questionnaire," the man said as he handed her his forms. His Scottish accent was faint, but strong enough for her to notice.

"Mr. William Naphys?" She read the name from his form.

The man grinned. "That's me." He was in his late twenties, with reddish-brown hair and soft brown eyes.

"You're Scottish?"

"Yes, ma'am. I live on an estate near Glasgow. My uncle died six months ago, and he had no heirs except me. I took over the property after he passed."

"Please sit down, Mr. Naphys. How did you hear about us?"

"My sister. She married an Englishman, and I came to visit them last week. She said she'd come to see you."

"Oh? What's her name?"

"Jenny Naphys. You matched her to her new husband, Jason Garlough. He's a tall redheaded fellow, quite lanky."

"Oh, Jay Garlough!" She remembered Jay was Jason's nickname. His match to Jenny had been quite easy. The pair had only met three times before running off to marry.

"Anyway, Jenny recommended I come see you. And after last night, well, it put a sense of urgency in me." He glanced down at his hands clasped in his lap. "After seeing the line that formed this morning, it was a relief to see I wasn't alone."

"Well, Mr. Naphys, I can certainly help. Tell me what you're looking for in an ideal woman."

"I suppose I would want a lass who doesn't mind the cold, but can enjoy warm summers in the Highlands of Scotland. Country life is a part of that world. She would need to be comfortable with that. I dinna want to marry a woman who willna be ready for a life of at least *some* work. My uncle's land is beautiful, but it needs a steward and a mistress. Someone who lives in a place like that must fight for it, must *love* it."

Elizabeth made several notes on her sheet about potential matches.

"I dinna have a large income to sustain the estate. I'm not asking ye to find me a rich wife, but either one with a little money who might spend it on the land or a woman who can live frugally if we need to."

Elizabeth ran Mr. Naphys through the additional questions they asked all the clients and then set him on his way so she could continue with further interviews.

Several clients later, she welcomed a young woman named

Gladys Wille. The woman wore a beautiful pale-pink dress and a coat made of silver fox fur. When Elizabeth raised a brow slightly at her attire, Gladys blushed.

"It's warm outside, I know, but after last night, I can't bear to leave this at home. If I am to die, I wish to die in my best clothes."

"Well, that's not insensible," Elizabeth said. "Please sit." As Gladys took her seat, Elizabeth looked over the woman's questionnaire.

"You're widowed? So young?" The woman couldn't have been more than twenty-four or twenty-five. "How recently, if you don't mind me asking?"

"Two years. My husband was a little older. It was a society match arranged by my parents. But now that I'm alone, I would like to choose who I spend the rest of my life with."

"Do you have any living requirements, such as preferring the town or enjoying the country?"

At this, Gladys's eyes brightened with an adventurous spark. "I've always lived in the city, but frankly, after last night, I'm rather done with it. I think somewhere in the country would be grand."

"And what of your income? Are you opposed to marrying a man who may have less money than you?"

"Robert, my departed husband, was wonderful, quite wonderful, and left me abundantly well-off. I don't wish you to think me callous. I loved him. We were dear friends by the end. But he was forty-four and I was only twenty when we married, and there is still so much life ahead of me left to live."

A little flair of excitement rippled through Elizabeth, the sort she always felt when she was sure two people would suit each other.

"How do you feel about Scotland?" she asked.

"I've never been, but I hear it's marvelous," Gladys said without hesitation.

"Excellent, then I think I might know who to introduce you to first. Give me a few days to reach out and connect you both."

"Just promise me that he is dashing."

"Quite dashing," Elizabeth promised. She could already imagine Mrs. Wille and Mr. Naphys standing on his property, facing a beautiful estate with a Highland wind ruffling the fur of Gladys's beloved silver fox fur coat, which would keep her warm in the harsh winters.

"Would you like my advice, Gladys?" Elizabeth said as they concluded the interview.

"I would welcome it."

"The best marriages are based in liking rather than romantic love. Romance can wither and wash away, but liking someone, having a *true affection* for who they are day to day, lasts forever."

"Robert was like that," Gladys said. "If he had been but twenty years younger, we would've had the romantic affection to accompany our liking. But I still loved him and liked him, and that was more than enough. I just hope this time I might have both affection and passion."

"We'll do our best to find you both romance and affection." Elizabeth gave her hand a squeeze before Gladys left the office.

Eva popped upstairs. "We still have quite a line, but more than half of the potential clients have scheduled appointments through next week and have gone home."

"How many more are waiting for interviews today?" Hetty had opened the door at that moment while she let a gentleman move past her. He nodded at all the ladies in the room before he proceeded downstairs.

Eva bit her lip. "At least twenty?"

"Well, send us whoever is next," Hetty said, and shared a weary smile with Elizabeth.

"That would be us." A familiar voice came from behind Eva. Eva turned and stumbled back awkwardly into the interview room. "Wait a moment, I *know* you." The man stepped into view, and Elizabeth recognized him at once.

"Mr. Sheridan, you came!" Elizabeth cried.

"Miss Mowbray, a delight as always." Nathan smiled and turned back to Eva. "Do you remember meeting me last year Miss. . . ?"

Eva's face reddened slightly. "Miss Wolman, Eva Wolman."

"Oh goodness, Mr. Sheridan!" Hetty laughed as she stepped farther out of the back office. "I hadn't heard from you. I sent you a letter that night we met."

"You wrote to me? I must've missed it. I've been living at the Royal Air Force base in Biggin Hill most of the year, and my butler back at my estate only informs me of any urgent matters that arrive in the post."

"Wait, Hetty, how do you and Eva know Mr. Sheridan?" Elizabeth asked.

"He's the one who saved Marcus and me that night we first arrived in London."

"I helped," Hetty interjected with an amused chuckle as she crossed her arms and leaned on the doorjamb to the inner office.

"You did, and I'll never be able to repay either of you that debt."

"Nonsense," Nathan said. "It was an honor to render any service to you." Nathan's tone was so full of sincerity that Elizabeth didn't doubt him. He was the sort of man one liked and trusted instantly.

"Lizzie, how do you know Mr. Sheridan?" Hetty asked.

Nathan chuckled. "I had the honor of spending time in a basement with her last evening, along with a dozen others. She told us all about the Marriage Bureau, didn't she, Philip? I didn't get a chance to tell Miss Mowbray when she mentioned you, Mrs. Humphrey, that I'd had a chance to meet you." Nathan stepped aside to let the dashing RAF pilot who'd kissed her last night walk into the room. Elizabeth's smile faltered as she saw the man's left arm was in a cast.

"What happened?" Without thinking, she walked straight to him, reaching out to examine his cast with gentle fingers. Then her eyes lifted to meet his, and she realized, foolishly, how close she was to him. His full lips parted as he stared back at her in that intense way of his.

"Philip played the hero during the next bombing and broke his arm lifting rubble off some people trapped in a building," Nathan answered for his friend.

Philip used his uninjured hand to remove his cap. "I wouldn't put it quite like that, but yes, I was aiding in a rescue."

Elizabeth stepped back from him, putting some much-needed distance between them. The pilot had a way of muddling her head and making her act silly.

"Well, Hetty could interview Philip—"

"No need. I'm only here to observe," Philip said, his lips twitching up ever so slightly.

"Observe who? Me?" Elizabeth wasn't sure she understood what he meant.

"Yes, just imagine me as Charles Darwin voyaging on the HMS *Beagle*, and I'm here to document this fascinating matchmaking process for posterity." Philip was teasing her now, and she didn't like it. Part of her wanted to tease him back, but another part wanted to curl her fists in frustration. He didn't believe in what she and Hetty could do, that was obvious, but then why was he even here? Surely he wasn't bored enough to come watch his friend be interviewed.

Nathan elbowed his companion. "Oh, don't tease her."

"Very well. I shall be as silent as a church mouse and just as well behaved." Philip pushed back his shoulders and straightened to attention, his stare focused directly ahead. Elizabeth very much doubted Philip would accomplish being silent *or* well behaved.

"I'll fetch you another client, Hetty," Eva said, and practically fled the room. Elizabeth almost chased after her, but they didn't have time to talk, not with all the clients still waiting to see them.

Hetty greeted the next client and escorted him to the back office.

Once they were alone, Elizabeth did her best to ignore Philip's observant stare. He'd abandoned his mock military stance and had taken a seat next to Nathan.

"Just ignore him." Nathan smiled in a relaxed sort of way. "I do."

"You don't mind him sitting in on such a personal interview?" Elizabeth asked.

Nathan laughed, the sound warm and rich. "No, not at all. Philip may even know me better than I know myself. Besides, with him out of commission for about six weeks while his arm heals, our squadron leader begged me to keep him away from Biggin Hill. I believe this matchmaking business will keep him sufficiently intrigued."

Philip's blue eyes pinned Elizabeth to her chair, and an unexpected hot flash rippled across her skin. She pulled at the collar of her dress and shifted restlessly in her seat.

"Well, let's begin, shall we?" She studied the questionnaire Nathan had filled out and began asking questions, but even as she focused on him, not a moment went by where she wasn't aware of Philip's gaze. It'd been a long time since anyone had looked at her like that. Algernon certainly hadn't. It was as if Philip's sole focus was on her, and nothing in the world could pull him away.

She cleared her throat. "Well, that's it for now. I'll be in touch soon with someone to introduce you to."

Nathan shook her hand. "Wonderful." Then he glanced at Philip. "I heard from the secretary downstairs that the bureau has a country house with rooms to let. Do you know if any of those are still available?"

"Cunningham House? Yes, yes, of course. Have Miss Plumley provide you with the address and lease information." Elizabeth shot a glance at Philip, who was still smiling at her. His bemused expression rankled her. "Are you both in need of a place to stay?" she asked Nathan and continued to pretend Philip wasn't there.

"For a few weeks. Philip needs to cool his heels, and I've been all but ordered to keep him far away from the base until his arm is better. He kept trying to get back in the bloody cockpit, and the other pilots were tired of dragging him out of it."

"Sad but true," Philip admitted. "Damned nuisance. I told them I could still fly—"

"With one arm?" Elizabeth challenged. "Don't be daft."

Nathan choked down a laugh, but Philip's eyes narrowed on her. "I'll have you know—"

Nathan interrupted. "*Thank you*, Miss Mowbray." Then, when he realized Philip hadn't stood with him, he tapped his friend's knee with his cane. The pair quickly departed, and Elizabeth sank into her chair, frowning. Pilots were always trouble, weren't they? Very attractive and utterly irritating trouble.

By six o'clock, Elizabeth had managed to forget that London had been bombed. Work had successfully consumed her entire day. But now that work was over, the fear and worries came back, gnawing away at her composure like rats.

Hetty sighed and collapsed into a chair beside her. "Well, we survived." They'd just sent Miss Plumley home, and Eva was busy putting away the files for their new clients in the inner office.

"Honestly, I never could've imagined so many people would come to us like that," Elizabeth said. She massaged her hand. Her fingers ached from the hours of endless note-taking.

"When someone faces death, it has a way of making them want to reaffirm their life," Hetty said. By the soft tone of her voice, Elizabeth knew her friend was thinking of Dunkirk. What she'd faced that week had sent her into Charles's arms without ever looking back.

A sharp longing reverberated deep inside Elizabeth. She had chased that elusive joy in the hills of India and had nearly made a terrible mistake in the process.

"Don't give up, Lizzie," said Hetty. "There's a perfect man out there for you somewhere."

Elizabeth laughed, but the ache in her chest didn't diminish. "How do you always know what I'm thinking?"

Hetty's eyes carried wisdom beyond her years. "You wear your heart on your sleeve, and in your eyes."

It wasn't the first time she'd heard that. But she remembered, too, that she'd been warned that those who wore their hearts on their sleeve were often hurt the most. Algernon had hurt her easily. Could she trust anyone like that again? She told her clients love was a leap of faith, yet right now she was too afraid to jump herself. To realize that she was a coward when she asked her clients to be courageous was a sobering thought.

"Perhaps Eva and I should match you. Some lovely quiet accountant, perhaps, who doesn't like adventures. Or an elderly banker who has an annoying little dog that barks at strangers. Or that man who called who wanted a woman who enjoyed stamp collecting . . ."

The tightness in Elizabeth's chest eased as she burst into laughter. Who needed romance when she had friends such as these?

CHAPTER 31

Every night the planes came, and every night London burned. Elizabeth was beginning to fear dusk each time it settled over the city. Her dreams were filled with the shrill screams of sirens, bombs falling to the earth, and the rattling cough of antiaircraft guns firing desperately into the night sky.

She and Isabelle shared Auxiliary Fire Service duties two or three nights a week, and the stress of hauling water hoses and driving firemen to burning homes was leaving a black mark upon Elizabeth's soul. During the day, Elizabeth buried herself in work, but after a week of constant bombardment and nights spent shivering in her shelter, she was struggling. She felt herself withdrawing from life, her face turning pale and her appetite waning.

Hetty pulled Elizabeth aside one morning and gently but firmly ordered her to stay at Cunningham House for a spell. After reluctantly agreeing, Elizabeth and Eva took Hetty's car and waited outside the bureau to meet two new lodgers whom Hetty had leased two bedrooms at the country house to. Hetty had assured her it was safe to travel with whoever was coming and that they were friends of Charles's.

"Do you know who we are meeting?" Elizabeth asked. "If they were friends of Charles's we might have met them at the wedding."

"I asked Hetty that very question, she said they'd both been on active duty and couldn't come. She noticed how worried I was and told me that we knew them and would be glad to have them join us at Cunningham House" Eva straightened as two men came into view at the end of the street. One had a slight limp. The other had a swagger to his steps. Both were men she recognized. It never amazed her how small the world could be sometimes. Two friends that knew Charles but had missed his wedding while serving for the RAF...of course it would be these two men.

"Bloody hell," Elizabeth said a little sourly.

Nathan Sheridan greeted her warmly as he reached them. "Miss Mowbray."

"Mr. Sheridan." She didn't mind Nathan at all, but his companion was another matter. "Mr. Lennox," she said with a curt nod. They both greeted Eva, who glanced away shyly.

The pilot gave Elizabeth a cocky grin that made her curl her fingers into fists.

"Play nice, children," Nathan said, reading the tension between them correctly.

Elizabeth looked at Philip's cast. "How is your arm?"

"Five more weeks, then I'm back in the sky." She could tell he was counting the days down to that moment.

"So, you two are moving into Cunningham House, then?" Elizabeth asked Nathan.

"Yes, for a few weeks. I imagine we'll visit London frequently, though. Are you both bound for the house for a while as well?"

"Only for a week or two," Elizabeth said. She wasn't about to admit the mortifying truth that Hetty had banished her to the country to rally her spirits. It felt like she had failed somehow. Whereas Eva and Hetty managed to soldier on, she had faltered.

"Well, that's good news. I was worried we'd have no company out in the country," Nathan said in his own good-natured way, and his gaze turned to Eva briefly.

"This will give me a chance to narrow down the female clients for you, Mr. Sheridan. I have copies of our records in the country that should be a close match to our London office records, thanks to Eva's hard work. We can look over a few options for introductions."

"Is that so? Splendid." Nathan reached for Eva's travel case. "Allow me to put that in the car for you, Miss Wolman."

Even though he had a slight limp, Nathan was quite capable, and Eva's eyes widened as he handled her case with ease. Elizabeth wondered if Eva had had a beau back in Warsaw, or if she'd never had the chance to fall in love before she and Marcus had fled. Perhaps Lizzie ought to arrange an introduction or two for Eva if Eva wanted her to. Perhaps even arrange for Nathan to take her to lunch, assuming Eva didn't run away at the sight of the tall pilot.

Nathan loaded the rest of the luggage with Philip's help, and then Eva and Nathan got into the back of the car. When Elizabeth went to the driver's side, she and Philip both reached for the handle at the same time.

"What are you doing?" Elizabeth demanded. "You can't possibly drive with your arm—"

"A gentleman, even one with a bad arm, can still open a door for a lady," he cut in with a superior tone.

The pair of them stood toe to toe. His breath fanned her face, and his body stiffened as he leaned in ever the slightest toward her. Elizabeth parted her lips, not sure what she was about to say, only to feel a storm of mad butterflies swirling about in her insides. Their silent war of gazes abruptly ended as Philip rolled his eyes and sighed dramatically as he opened the car door.

"Oh, right . . ." Elizabeth felt like a fool for thinking he'd insist on driving, and her skin now flamed with embarrassment. She clamped her lips together and slid into the driver's seat. Philip closed the door behind her. Nathan and Eva grew quiet in the back seat. As Elizabeth adjusted the rearview mirror, she saw Eva bite her lip trying to hide a little laugh. *Wonderful.*

The journey from the city to the countryside was strangely soothing, despite the company she was keeping. Elizabeth felt the heat of the sun on her face, and the sky above was unmarred by German aircraft. She could almost forget the war, almost forget the dangers all around them.

Nathan guided the conversation much of the time, and he was now asking if anyone had seen any motion pictures of late.

"There's this one, a rather smashing one, actually, *Gone with the Wind.* It's an American film and has that Clark Gable fellow. Bloody brilliant. You must have heard of it."

Elizabeth hadn't been to a motion picture in months, but she had heard about *Gone with the Wind.* The audiences grew rather raucous at times, and she found it stressful. Before each picture, they always ran newsreels that depicted British victories in battle, and such reels were usually rewarded with wild applause and thunderous stomping of feet.

But if newsreels showed Hitler or German troops, people booed and sometimes threw things at the screen. Elizabeth remembered one reel that had showed Hitler giving a heated speech. His sour, pinched, ugly little face held such menace in it that it had turned Elizabeth's stomach and she'd been ill.

The sight of German troops marching in unison, their arms raised in a salute to their leader, to the cause of destroying all that England held dear, had sent a chill so deep through her that she had felt icy for days afterward.

Even the brilliant fantasy world of *The Wizard of Oz* motion picture that had followed hadn't been able to erase that image from her mind. She was thankful now that Nathan had a talent for distracting conversation.

Philip stayed silent for much of the drive, and yet she felt he was listening to every word she said. She couldn't help but wonder why the man seemed so interested in her. No doubt he was waiting for a chance to mock her matchmaking efforts again. He did seem to enjoy that.

At long last, Elizabeth parked the car in front of Cunningham House.

"So, is it true some old colonel runs this house?" Philip asked.

"Yes, Colonel William Cunningham."

At this, Nathan and Philip both stared at her. "Pardon?" they said in unison.

"Not *the* William Cunningham?" Philip asked. "The hero of Passchendaele?"

"Passchendaele?" Elizabeth mouthed the word. It felt familiar, but she couldn't place it.

"It was also called the Battle of Ypres," Philip added, his tone full of sorrow and awe. It was a battle from the Great War, with terrible casualties. The city and the area around it had turned to mud from the shelling and the torrential rains. Many men and even horses had drowned in it. "My God . . . I can't imagine what that fight must have been like for him."

Nathan let out a soft breath. "The Great War was horrible beyond our imagining. A few battles were far worse than the rest. Ypres was one of those."

Elizabeth shivered. There were many times she had seen a faraway look in the colonel's eyes, and she had known he'd endured terrible things, but she'd never dared to ask him about it. It seemed wrong to drag his grief out into the light, yet she wondered now if she'd failed him as a friend by not providing an ear to listen.

"Why don't we go inside and find Mrs. Harrow? I think we all need a cup of tea," Eva suggested.

"Tea sounds lovely," Elizabeth agreed. She needed a moment to collect herself. This revelation had left a hollow feeling in her chest she didn't like.

Philip and Nathan collected the luggage and carried it up the steps and into the foyer.

"Feels like home, eh, Philip?" Nathan teased.

"Home?" Elizabeth echoed in confusion. Philip's face flushed a little, as though embarrassed.

"Oh . . ." Nathan also colored a little. "It's just that, well, we've grown up in manors such as these. My father is a viscount, and Philip's is a baron."

That stunned Elizabeth. She was a simple country girl. It had taken her some practice to get used to being around the aristocratic men who'd joined the bureau as clients, but to know that *these* two men whom she'd spent an hour with facing death in a basement were the sons of English peers was a bit daunting.

"Lizzie? Eva? Is that you?" Mrs. Harrow's welcoming voice echoed from the kitchen. Down the opposite hall in one of the sitting rooms, a hint of cigar smoke lingered in the air. No doubt the colonel was relaxing with his usual afternoon smoke. It reminded her of Uncle George, and a wave of longing for Assam and her life back in India made her heart clench and her eyes burn.

Elizabeth cleared her throat. "Yes, it's us. We've brought two guests." She was used to seeing them in their uniforms, and to be around them now in civilian clothes was a bit startling. Both Nathan and Philip wore fashionable trousers and coats and were just as attractive now as they had been in their uniforms.

"Welcome, dears." Mrs. Harrow bustled into the foyer and hastily touched her hair to make sure nothing was out of place before she greeted the two men. Elizabeth made introductions, and Mrs. Harrow told her which rooms would be made ready for "these darling RAF boys" to stay in.

"Follow me." She led them up the stairs. Nathan took the first room at the top of the stairs in the east wing, and Elizabeth left him to settle in. She walked down the hall and showed Philip his room. It overlooked the gardens in the back of the house. He followed her inside the room.

"It's so quiet," Philip noted as he set his duffel bag down and stood behind her at the window. Elizabeth's heart sped up as she felt his body so close to hers.

"We're quite a bit away from the city, but its not without danger."

"This is where the German pilot crashed, correct? The one you told us about in the shelter?" Philip came a step closer, until she felt his chest touch her back. A thrill shot through her at his nearness, but she pushed it away. She pointed to a spot in the distance.

"Yes, through those woods over there."

"I was there when they brought that man to Biggin Hill. I had just come back after a nasty dogfight and saw him being escorted to our commanding officer on the base."

Elizabeth stared at the trees, but everything in her was focused on the man who stood so close behind her.

"When your arm heals, you'll really be flying again?" she asked in a whisper, even though she wasn't sure why she was speaking so quietly. It was as though she was afraid the universe was listening and might decide to take everything away from her again, even this frustrating pilot.

"If they let me. It was a clean break. The surgeon thinks it will heal well and I'll be back to my old self in no time."

"Back to being a terror of the skies?" she tried to joke, but the thought of him flying again frightened her. So many planes were shot down. So many.

"*Absolutely*. My father was a flying ace in the Great War. I suppose it's tradition now." He chuckled, but Elizabeth saw no humor in it.

"Well, try not to get yourself killed," she snapped and stepped around him. He caught her arm, turning her toward him. It amazed her that he could so easily take hold of her with just one good arm.

"You are delightfully *prickly*, darling, and I admit you fascinate me," he said.

"I'm not prickly. And even if I am, it's none of your—"

Her protest was silenced as he pulled her into his arms and kissed her. The man had the most infuriating habit of kissing her when she was about to tell him off. And then after, she always had the worst time remembering why she was angry at him.

"I don't know whether to slap you or kiss you."

He grinned. "I think you can guess which I'd prefer." Then he pulled her in for another kiss, this one longer, sweeter. Elizabeth clutched the collar of his coat as his mouth moved over hers, exploring her and savoring her taste. Philip was an excellent kisser, perhaps too excellent. He made it hard to remember what Algernon's kisses felt like. It had never felt like this with anyone else, like this kiss would carve itself into the mountains and rivers of her soul. It was a kiss built upon promises of a lifetime, more to come. She feared and craved Philip's kisses.

When their mouths broke apart, he smiled down at her, but it wasn't that cocky grin she was used to. His expression was softer, and her heart quivered with dangerous longing. His look made a woman feel happy. It was a look that promised she was cared about, even loved. But how could he feel that for her? They barely knew each other.

"I . . . need to see Mrs. Harrow about . . ."

"The tea?" he suggested, his voice just as soft as hers.

"Right, yes, the tea." She extricated herself from his hold, and he let her escape.

She rushed into the corridor and placed her hands against her flaming cheeks. She couldn't believe she was to spend two weeks here with this man. But she had to, so she could get herself together and return to London. The sooner the better, so she could put distance between herself and Philip.

As she descended the stairs, she saw the colonel emerge from whatever room he'd tucked himself away in for his private smoke.

"Did I hear *we* have guests?" he asked in a disapproving tone.

He still hadn't accepted the fact that he no longer owned Cunningham House.

"Yes, two RAF pilots."

"Pilots? Out here? Why are they not staying at Biggin Hill?"

"One has a permanent injury and is now a flight instructor, and the other is recovering from a broken arm. As I understand it, the one pilot was disobeying orders, trying to fly again, which was causing problems at the base."

At this, the colonel's brooding vanished and he chuckled. "Now *those* are the sort of men who are welcome in my house."

"That's a good thing to hear." Philip's voice carried down from the top of the stairs. Elizabeth didn't dare look back at him. She was convinced her face was still very red.

She made the introductions without looking over her shoulder. "Colonel Cunningham, this is Captain Philip Lennox."

"It's an honor, sir." Philip came down the stairs and held out his hand to the colonel, who shook it.

"You must be the chap still trying to fly?" The colonel's gaze swept over Philip, taking his measure.

"Yes, I am, Colonel. I was forcibly removed from Biggin Hill by my friend, Nathan Sheridan. He's the other guest who will be staying here for a time. It's a privilege to stay in your home. I hope we meet with your approval." Philip spoke with such respect that the colonel nodded affably.

"Yes, of course you are welcome. I hear *that woman* in the kitchen is making tea. This way." He marched on ahead toward the kitchens.

"*That woman?*" Philip asked quietly as he fell in step beside her.

"Mrs. Harrow, the housekeeper," she whispered as he leaned

in close. "She and the colonel are a bit cantankerous around each other. They have these little battles for control."

"I don't know if I'd want to stand up to the colonel," Philip said sagely.

Elizabeth grinned. "You haven't seen Mrs. Harrow yet."

❧

LATER THAT AFTERNOON, ELIZABETH, EXHAUSTED FROM spending the day looking over the latest stack of letters from clients with Eva, decided to walk down the lane for a bit of fresh air.

"Will you watch for Marcus?" Eva asked as she tidied up their desk. "He should be coming back from school soon." She began filing new client forms into the many boxes stacked about the study.

"I'll go and meet him," Elizabeth promised. She stepped outside the front door and drew the clean country air into her lungs.

"Mind if I join you?" a voice said from behind her. Philip stood in the open doorway of the house. He removed his coat and rolled up the sleeves of his shirt past his elbows, revealing tanned, muscled forearms. Even though he still had one arm in a cast, he gave off a masculine sense of power that made Elizabeth all too aware of his strength. Her stomach gave a traitorous flip of excitement. Why on earth did a man's bare arms elicit excitement in her?

"I'm beginning to wonder if you're following me," she said. The man seemed to show up whenever she least expected him to.

He laughed at her disgruntled expression. "I promise I'm

not. I just can't stand to stay inside that long. I need to keep moving."

"Very well, come along then." She started down the gravel lane, and he soon caught up with her.

"So . . . you're from Cambridge, eh?" he asked.

Elizabeth quickened her pace. "Yes." The thought of small talk with Philip sounded, well . . . odd. After sharing a basement with the man and then being kissed by him three times, this was yet one more reminder that they were strangers who had a strange bond, one that she wasn't sure she liked. It left her vulnerable in a way she didn't want to analyze too closely.

"You know far more about me than most people," she said, yet she wasn't sure why she felt a need to point that out.

Philip slid the hand of his uninjured arm into his trouser pocket as he walked by her side.

"Do I?" He seemed intrigued by the idea.

"Yes, I don't . . . I don't share so much about myself. It's not . . . ," she faltered.

"You made a poor choice in men in India, and now you doubt the whole lot of us, is that it?"

Elizabeth halted at the end of the private road that led back to the house. Beyond them, the blue skies and golden fields rolled toward the nearby village.

"A *poor choice* in men?" she replied, her tone sharpening like a dagger. "You can't summarize my life into one moment, not like that. I trust men. I simply don't trust *you*."

Philip's blue eyes grew full of fire, but he didn't seem angry. "Am I like that other fellow? The one you broke it off with?"

At that, she almost laughed. "You're nothing like him." She turned and started walking again toward the village.

He caught up with her. "I hope that's a compliment and not an insult."

"It is certainly not an insult." She didn't say more, but she could sense him grinning even though she dared not look his way.

"I attended Cambridge, by the way," Philip volunteered. "It's a tradition for my family and the families of my friends."

"Oh?" For some reason that intrigued her more than she wished it did.

"Nathan and I, as well as Will St. Laurent and—"

"You know Mr. St. Laurent? He's a friend of Hetty's husband."

"Charles Humphrey?" he added.

"Yes. You know Charles then too?"

"I know him very well."

"Why didn't you say something that night in the basement when I was telling everyone my story?"

"I would have, but I admit I was a little preoccupied thinking about the bombing."

"Oh, yes." She wanted to smack herself. Of course he'd been focused on that.

"Besides, such name-dropping would have distracted the others from your . . . er . . . distraction."

That made her chuckle, despite herself.

"Look—Lizzie—" he began, but they both halted at the sounds of distant shouting.

"What the devil is that all about?" He pointed to a band of loud boys farther down the road who were clearly in the midst of a bout of fisticuffs. As they drew closer, she recognized Marcus as the focus of the group, his fists raised as he deflected blow after blow aimed at him by the others.

She gasped. "Oh, Philip, we must stop them!"

"Gladly," the pilot growled and dove into the crowd of boys, sending most of the young men sprawling on their backsides.

"That's enough!" Philip bellowed. The boys who'd fallen scrambled to their feet, keeping their distance from him.

"Marcus? Are you all right?" Elizabeth rushed over to him as the boy wiped his mouth with the back of his hand. It came away bloody, though he didn't seem overly injured.

"I'm fine," he muttered, but he didn't meet her eyes. Fury rose inside her, and she whirled on the boys, who were now trying to slink away.

"Why were you fighting?" she demanded. No one said a word. "*Why?*" she repeated to Marcus this time.

"They think I caused this war. They said I'm a Nazi. They—"

Elizabeth didn't let him finish. She stared down the boys facing her and spoke with deadly calm. "This boy's parents were *murdered* by the Nazis. How very small and cruel you boys are to attack him when he is no different than you. We are *all* fighting the Nazis."

"But he's a Jew. My dad said it's all their fault . . . ," one boy said.

Philip scowled. "A moment ago, he was a Nazi. Sounds to me you're just eager to find a target."

"By your logic, it's *your* fault that Hitler bombed England," Elizabeth said. "That is what you're saying. That people who are undeserving of such attacks are to be blamed for those attacks?"

"No, I didn't . . ."

The boy looked confused by Elizabeth's words, but she didn't stop.

"If anything, Marcus is braver than the rest of you. He captured a German pilot, an airman who crashed near here.

Marcus helped bring him in and turn him over to the authorities."

"That isn't true!" one boy said.

"It certainly is," Philip said. "I saw the German pilot myself."

"Oh yeah? And who the hell are you?"

Philip seemed somehow taller and more intimidating than before as he stared down the boy who'd spoken to him. "I am Group Captain Philip Lennox of His Majesty's Royal Air Force."

The boys all exchanged uncertain glances.

"The next time you want to act brave, do something that *helps* people. By attacking this lad, you've proven you're just like Hitler. He's a bully. Now *you* are bullies. Do you want to be like the man who is attempting to destroy our country?" Philip asked them.

The collective mutters of the boys earned a nod from Philip.

"Right, then. Off you go. Stay out of trouble."

The lads all ran down the road, and when they were gone, Marcus faced Philip.

"Thank you for that, sir." He wiped at his bloody nose, and his brown eyes were full of shame.

Elizabeth bit her lip. She wanted to hug the boy, but he wasn't quite a boy anymore. He was a young man, and right then she was glad Philip had been there to set an example for him.

"You fought well, lad, even outnumbered. No shame in that." Philip held up his broken arm. "We can all get hurt when doing the right thing. The best you can do is hold your head high and continue to fight." Philip clapped a hand on Marcus's shoulder and smiled.

"Are you staying at the house with us?" Marcus asked as he and Philip started the walk back.

"I am. Is that all right with you?" Philip asked him seriously.

"Yes," Marcus exclaimed. "Did you fight in the Battle of Britain last summer?"

Philip chuckled. "Is that what they're calling it?"

The lad nodded. "Churchill said never was so much owed by so many to so few. He meant you, the airmen."

"Did he, now?" Philip looked over his shoulder at Elizabeth as she followed behind them. His bemusement and gentle smile warmed her heart in a way like nothing else ever had. That feeling of being lost, of being alone, was beginning to fade. If Philip could get into the cockpit and face death in the sky, she could stay in London and face the dangers of whatever was on the horizon.

CHAPTER 32

lizabeth spent fourteen nights watching bombers pass over Cunningham House as they headed for London. She found herself waking each night with the rumble of the engines. She'd rush outside to stand in the garden and watch the shadows of the German planes stain the moon's pale glow. Most nights, Philip would find her and join her. He would stand in silence with her during her nightly vigils, his presence offering her a comfort she hadn't expected.

She hadn't wanted to be a coward and stay away from danger. She felt so helpless, seeing burned homes, the soot-covered faces of friends and strangers as they dug through the remains of their homes, searching for anything that could be saved—it was breaking her heart. The sight of bodies lining the streets, waiting to be taken to their graves. It was all breaking her soul. Whenever Elizabeth looked upon the destruction her city suffered, she was struck blind with a fury tinged with despair that overcame her so swiftly she had trouble breathing.

As she watched the pale lavender of a predawn sky creep across the horizon, she straightened on the bench she'd been sitting on. She blinked in a daze as she remembered Philip was there beside her. At some point during the night, she had leaned her head against his shoulder, her body succumbing to exhaustion.

"Did you sleep at all?" he asked in a weary voice that rumbled out of his chest and into her.

"No . . . maybe. I don't honestly know. My sleep is full of nightmares. It's rather hard to know when I slipped between this hell and the one my mind conjures up."

Philip wound his good arm around her and pulled her close to him, tucking her against his body almost protectively. The comfort of his embrace made her nose sting, and tears threatened to form at the corner of her eyes.

"What is the worst thing you fear? Dying?" he asked her. He leaned in, and his lips brushed her left temple in a faint almost kiss. As infuriating as he could be when he teased her, these moments also spellbound her. They held her in a place of safety and security. She had never realized how much she needed someone to cling to like this. She wanted to push him away, to not need him, but the man had an irresistible quality that she couldn't fight. It was also easier to talk to him about grim matters like this, though she had no idea why. She'd thought she didn't like him, but now she realized she'd liked him too much from the very start. She'd surrendered to how she felt and wasn't fighting her feelings anymore. Letting him in made her feel safe rather than scared.

"Not me. I mean, no one wants to die, but it's the helplessness I can't stand. I get so angry about how powerless I am that I can't think straight. I wish I was able to get in one of your planes and chase them away from London. They wouldn't want to come back after facing me in a dogfight."

At this, he chuckled and kissed her temple. "You are rather bloodthirsty, in the most adorable way. God forbid anyone cross you, but you mustn't fear your fierceness. That comes from your empathy. You *care* more about people being hurt than anyone I've ever met. You don't just see the injustices being done to them—you take them on as your own."

Hetty had often warned her that she cared far too much about everything and everyone, but Elizabeth couldn't change that about herself.

"When you go back to London and find you have moments when you are terrified or overwhelmed, I will teach you a trick." He offered this with a grin.

"A trick?" She wasn't sure she liked the sound of that.

"Yes, Miss Skeptical. Now, close your eyes."

Elizabeth closed her eyes, then opened one again to squint at him suspiciously. He fought to hide a grin. The blue of his eyes was so soft in the morning, rather than burning with their usual intensity.

"No peeking," he said in a more commanding tone. "I'm not about to steal a kiss from you, if that's what you're thinking." She sighed and closed her eyes as he continued. "Now, think of the most important place in your life. A memorable place. Something that fills you with love whenever you think about it. It has to be powerful, something that obliterates the dark with its light."

Elizabeth searched her memory, pausing at places like Isabelle's garden or the bureau office on Bond Street, but in truth there was only one real place that had ever brought her such joy. Even thinking about it now made her skin break out with goosebumps, wishing she could return to it.

"Did you find it?" Philip asked.

"Yes."

"Good. Now, tell me about it. Don't tell me where you are, but describe every detail you can remember."

"I'm in a courtyard with a fountain. It's just before dawn, and the sound of the water echoing off the stones is so wonderful."

"What do you smell?"

"Lavender, jasmine, and saffron." The smell of Aabha's cooking scented the air in her memories.

"Sounds wonderful, but let's move somewhere else. Let your feet guide you."

In her mind, she was walking up the stairs of Uncle George's home in India, her fingertips trailing along the banister. Above her, orchids overflowed from the baskets in waterfalls of color and explosions of floral scents.

"What do you see now?"

"Veils of every color hanging as curtains in open doorways, gold glittering from the china on the table, gleaming silver, cigar smoke coiling up in the air."

She could see Uncle George at the dining room table, his newspaper spread out, as he drank his coffee and puffed away at his cigar. But he wasn't there, not really.

"I miss him," Elizabeth murmured and shivered.

"Who?" Philip asked.

The spell was broken. She opened her eyes and stared into Philip's searching face.

"My uncle." She pictured his face, his gentle smile, the way he hugged her and always insisted she stay up late to talk with him about everything in her life.

"Tell me about him."

"He's like a father to me, more than my real father." The words hurt as they slipped out, and she pushed away the bitter pain of her father's disinterest in her life. "Uncle George is the one who suggested I do this . . . the matchmaking. I had a gift for it back in India, and when he knew I had to return to England, he suggested I make it my occupation." She smiled a little. "You would like him. He's such a dear, and very brave. He fought in the Great War, like Hetty's father. Now he wants only a peaceful life in the hills of India. He and Aabha."

Philip pulled Elizabeth close again and wrapped his good arm around her shoulders. "Who is Aabha?"

"She's his housekeeper, but also the woman who holds his heart." For a long moment, they stared at the skies in silence as dawn conquered the night.

"I want you to hold on to that place and those people when you feel the darkness closing in. That memory will keep you focused."

"What about you? What's your place?"

Philip smiled as a touch of joy spread to his voice. "Nathan and I attended Cambridge with our friends. We were members of Magdalene College. Have you ever visited that area?"

"Yes, it's so beautiful." It was one of the smaller colleges within Cambridge. There was a nice peacefulness to the grounds.

"I don't know if you remember, but there's that river that flows through part of the colleges, like Magdalene. Nathan and I used to sit on the river banks with Will, Damien and Charles, and we would watch the dark-green currents reflect the grass and the sky as the water flowed past." He paused and his voice softened. "Do you know what ley lines are?"

"Ley lines? What do you mean, like magic?"

He chuckled. "Of a sort. A ley line is an old path, one traveled by many people over thousands of years. Ancient paths that are far older than the men who travel them. There is a ley line that passes right through Magdalene College. It's true that some say that these pathways hold power. What kind of power, men cannot say, but there is an odd feeling there when you stand alone on the path. The world falls away, and it is only you and the feeling that you belong there. That you have found home after traveling for such a long time. My friends and I heard all sorts of romantic and gothic stories about these ley lines, and one night, we decided to get rather tossed and try to summon spirits to us on the banks of the river."

Elizabeth couldn't deny her fascination with Philip's story. "What did you do?"

"We waited for a full moon night and snuck out of our dormitory. Then, after we were properly drunk, we stood on the banks and whispered, 'Knight to knight. Come to me.' We believed that an ancient warrior would appear on horseback and chase us or something rather dramatic . . . but something entirely unexpected happened instead."

"What?"

"The fog rolled in from downriver, and it became hard to see. Then we heard voices, men shouting to each other in the growing gloom as the moon above was cloaked in clouds, and I swore I saw . . ."

"What did you see?" Elizabeth pressed, her heart pounding.

"I saw myself—or rather, a man who had my face—as he rushed past me and into the river. He kept calling out a name, and he dove under the surface, but I heard no splashes, and the other voices faded and the mist rolled away."

"A man who had your face?"

"Yes. Me, but not me. I don't know how to explain it, exactly. The others said they saw something similar, men who looked like them but weren't. It was all rather surreal, but that night I felt bound to that riverbank and bound to my friends more than I ever had before. Our families go way back, you see, at least by two centuries. Part of me feels . . . It's silly, I know, but . . ."

"You feel as if everything is connected?"

He nodded. "When I need to feel peace, to feel joy, I am back at that river, my friends beside me and the ancient magic of the ley lines pulsing like a heartbeat that will never die."

Elizabeth sat up a little. Something was niggling at her memory. "Hetty always says that Lonsdales never die. Perhaps the same is true of Lennoxes?"

"We all die," Philip said. "Everything in life is a cycle of living and dying. That's rather the point, isn't it?"

"But you know what I mean. That in some way . . . sometimes a person can find a way to go on, even when they think they don't want to." She wasn't sure how to say what she meant.

"You become so philosophical with so little sleep."

"I'm not trying to be—"

Just then, Mrs. Harrow called out to them in shrill alarm. "What in the blazes are you two doing out here?" She stood in the doorway that led from the back gardens to the kitchen. "Come in before you both catch a chill. I'll put a kettle on."

Her housecoat was securely tied about her waist, and her hair was bound in little knots of cloth that set her curls. She looked like a grumpy, but still loveable, Medusa as she turned and went back into the kitchen.

"Oh heavens." Elizabeth pulled free of Philip's arms and hastily hopped off the stone bench, though Mrs. Harrow was no longer around to bear witness. Philip was slower to stand, clearly not as upset as her at being discovered in such a state. Not that they had been doing anything truly indecent, but still . . .

Elizabeth ignored Philip's laughter as she hurried inside. Mrs. Harrow busied herself with tea and breakfast preparations, and thankfully said nothing about what Elizabeth had been doing out there, which gave her a chance to hurry upstairs and get dressed for the day.

Despite her lack of sleep, she felt strangely renewed with the need to face London again. When everyone was assembled in the dining room for breakfast, Elizabeth cleared her throat.

"I . . . er . . . was thinking I might go back to London. Today."

Mrs. Harrow made a soft sound of protest, but the colonel folded the newspaper he'd been engrossed in and pointedly cleared his throat, silencing Mrs. Harrow, and then focused on Elizabeth.

"Well, if you are ready, then you should go. The more men who enlist means that every woman counts twice as much in keeping this country together." Colonel Cunningham's approval bolstered her resolve to go back.

Nathan glanced at Eva with clear disappointment. "So soon?"

"Oh . . . no, just me. Eva should stay; she has Marcus to look after."

Marcus gave Elizabeth a rebellious look. "I don't need looking after."

"Your black eye and bloody lip from last week would say otherwise," his sister reminded him.

"I'll return to London with you," Philip said.

"You, sir, are supposed to stay here," Nathan reminded him. "The whole point of this exercise is to keep you out of trouble."

Philip grinned as he looked at Elizabeth rather than Nathan as he replied, "Ah, but then who keeps our dear Lizzie here out of trouble?"

Elizabeth's temper flared. "I do not need—"

"Well, if it keeps him out of trouble, then let the lad go with you," the colonel declared, as if that was the end of things, and lifted his paper once more.

But Elizabeth wasn't truly upset. These people, the old colonel, the ever-fussing housekeeper, the two Polish refugees, the dashing RAF pilots . . . they were her family in a way her own had never been, save her uncle. Though they were all seated around her in that moment, she feared that they might never be like this, here, *together* again.

A powerful melancholy caught her off guard, so much so that she wilted back into her chair, her mind desperately trying to imprint everything about this moment. The sound of Mrs. Harrow's tittering and Eva's fretting, Nathan's rich laugh and the colonel's fatherly gaze, Marcus's boyish enthusiasm, and the way Philip's eyes never left her all through the meal. It became as powerful a moment of joy for her as India had been.

She knew she had to return to London but suddenly feared what would happen if she left. *What if . . . ?* Those two terrible words held a note of doom in them. Perhaps she was being foolish, but if she had learned anything, it was that every second of life was precious, that the people she cared about were all that really mattered. Love was the only thing worth fighting for in this life. Love of family and friends, love for her neighbors and strangers, love in all its forms. That was the only thing she had to fight the coming darkness from across the Channel.

The bureau. She had to get back there and work harder than ever.

As everyone cleared the plates away, she went to pack her bag. By the time she'd readied herself to leave, Philip was already waiting for her at the foot of the stairs. Mrs. Harrow hugged and kissed her, wiping tears from her face before rushing back to the kitchen, mumbling about having some washing up to do. Marcus and Eva shared a quick hug with Elizabeth before they stepped away, Marcus to finish his schoolwork and Eva to finish her paperwork for the bureau in the study.

"Nathan, you will watch over them, won't you?" She had grown to trust the captain more than she'd imagined. He was strong, both of body and spirit, yet full of compassion and endless gentleness. He made her think of that story Philip had told of them trying to summon an ancient knight of old on the magical ley lines. Perhaps the spirit of the knight had come after all and embedded itself in the spirits of those young men on the bank of the river. Charles had joined Will St. Laurent in a dangerous elite fighting force, and Philip took to the skies as Nathan had before he was injured in the Battle of Britain. They were all fighting, all noble to the bloody end, like knights of a new age.

"I'll stay with them," Nathan promised.

"Thank you. Knowing you are here . . ."

The colonel harrumphed beside the younger man. "And *I'm* here," he reminded her.

Elizabeth stood on her tiptoes and kissed the colonel's cheek. "You'll keep Mr. Sheridan safe, won't you?"

"Until your return, my lady," the colonel said with a solemn nod.

Nathan smiled almost bashfully at Elizabeth as he understood her words, that even he mattered, and the colonel would keep watch over everyone who slept under Cunningham House's roof. It was a funny thing, she realized. They'd all called it Knight House when they'd first toured it before they knew it was Colonel Cunningham's house, because of the suits of armor, but now it had the protection of real flesh-and-blood knights.

"Take care of her, lad," Colonel Cunningham said to Philip with grave seriousness. "There's no one like her in the world."

Philip nodded in agreement as he escorted Elizabeth to Hetty's car parked out front. She opened the car door and paused and looked back once more at the place she'd come to see as home.

"You'll see it again—you'll see *them* again too," Philip said.

She looked across the roof of the car at him. "How can you be sure?"

His mouth twitched up in a rakish grin. "Because I know you, and you will survive whatever comes."

Heat flooded her face at his words. Did he really think that?

"You had better make it back too," she said. "Nathan would be terribly upset if you injure yourself further."

"I'm sure he would be." Philip was still smiling, but somehow, she knew he understood what she'd been too afraid to say—that *she* needed him to be safe.

"We had better go." She hastily got inside the Morris Eight and started the engine. As they headed down the road, a cloud of dust picked up by the wind obscured Cunningham House from view.

CHAPTER 33

O ctober 1940

HETTY STIRRED THE SPOON IN HER TEACUP AND WATCHED THE steam rise up in inviting curls. She lifted the cup up to her nose and took in the aroma, but as the scent hit her senses her stomach suddenly turned. She rushed to the sink and poured the tea out but was a second too late. Her stomach purged itself of the toast she'd eaten half an hour before she had left for the bureau.

Elizabeth was at her side at once, rubbing her hand up and down her back as she gagged and coughed. Her body seized in wrenching cramps. She frantically pushed her hair back from her face as she threw up again.

"Let me." Elizabeth gently gathered her hair back for her.

Hetty braced her hands on either side of the small sink and coughed as she fought to breathe and relax. Her body kept tensing and fighting to lose control again, but after several breaths she finally calmed down.

Elizabeth encouraged her soothingly, "That's it. Slow breaths."

"Christ," Hetty whimpered as her body shook violently, but the spasms that had bent her double eased after a few moments.

"You should lie down on the sofa in the other room. Lying flat always helps me when I feel unwell."

"Good idea." Hetty allowed herself to be led like a child to the sofa and eased herself onto her back.

She closed her eyes and breathed for a while before she opened them and found Elizabeth staring at her. Her friend's eyes were wide with worry.

"How far along are you?" she asked in a soft voice.

"Two months," Hetty admitted. It had been toward the end of August when she and Charles had shared their last night together. She'd always been *careful*, even when she had been married to Roger, but that last night, she had broken her own rules and refused to use any sort of contraceptive.

Charles didn't know yet, he'd left long before she'd found out she was carrying their child. Some part of her, some small feminine part of her, wanted to hold on to the secret, the secret that meant *everything* to her now. But she wouldn't lie to her friend. They were and had always been in this fight together.

"Are you all right?" Elizabeth knelt by the sofa and clasped Hetty's hand in hers.

Hetty chuckled, though it made her stomach clench in warning.

"I'm *terrified*, Lizzie. When Charles left, I had this mad

notion that I needed a piece of him if he didn't come back. But now . . . now I fear that I made a mistake. What was I thinking of? Bringing a child into the middle of this? We've been bombed every night for over a month. What if I have a miscarriage?" Perhaps she ought to have listened to her parents when they'd suggested leaving London, but she'd felt she needed to stay here and do what she could to help the city she loved.

Elizabeth sat down on the floor beside the sofa, still holding Hetty's hand in her own. "Right now we all feel lost in the dark, but oh, Hetty, this is a *brilliant* spark within that darkness. A spark that will catch fire, and we won't let it burn out."

Hetty stared up at the ceiling, the one she and Elizabeth had so painstakingly painted before the war started, to cover old water stains and peeling gray paint. They had chosen a robin's-egg blue to look like summer skies. Somehow, the ceiling had managed to avoid taking on a hue of gray from smoke and dust from the continual bombings.

"Well, it's safe to say your avoidance of onions paid off," Elizabeth said with a giggle.

Hetty blinked and stared at her friend. "Pardon?"

"No onions. The fortune-teller said you'd want to avoid them if you wanted a child."

Hetty suddenly burst out laughing. She'd forgotten all about that nutty woman and her "sea-adjacent" cottage.

Miss Plumley stepped into the office and saw the pair of them at the sofa. "Is everyone all right?"

"Oh yes." Hetty sat up and, after a quick glance at Elizabeth, made her announcement.

"I'm pregnant."

The secretary's eyes lit up. "Oh, Mrs. Humphrey, what

wonderful news!" Miss Plumley set her handbag down on her desk before coming over to embrace her.

There were more tears of joy and a lengthy discussion of nurseries before a knock at the door interrupted them. Miss Plumley opened it to find one of their clients, Miss Liza Mason, her face red and eyes watery as she clutched her handbag to her chest like a protective vest. Liza was a young city typist and had been matched to an attractive bank clerk named Glen Robinson a month ago. The two had been writing letters to each other through the bureau offices.

"May I speak to Miss Mowbray or Mrs. Humphrey?"

Hetty got up off the sofa. "Please let her in."

The client sniffled and thanked the secretary, who returned to the reception downstairs.

"What's the matter, Miss Mason?" Elizabeth gestured for the woman to sit, but Liza only paced about the room, fitfully twisting a pair of worn gloves between her fingers.

"I had an engagement to meet Mr. Robinson for lunch. We met under the clock at Waterloo station and agreed to go to a nearby café for tea. I collected a tray, grabbed a few sandwiches and other treats for our meal. Mr. Robinson went to secure a table and left me with the food. He was supposed to come back and pay for the meal . . . I had selected the best delicacies, plenty for two, and I waited . . ." She paused, her voice hitching. "I waited in the queue, and I had the tray in front of the counter, ready to pay . . . but he never came back."

Hetty and Elizabeth shared a look at that.

"I waited a quarter of an hour, and all those waitresses gave me the most pitying looks. When I couldn't take it anymore, I paid for the food and had it wrapped up so I could eat it at the office." She drew in a deep breath and faced Hetty and Elizabeth. "I was so excited to meet him after all those letters we had written to each other. But it seems like he took one look at me and ran off. Is this the kind of clientele you are introducing to women?"

"Of course not," Hetty said at once, affronted at the very idea, but sympathetic to her pain. "We will get to the bottom of this, Miss Mason. We vet all the men who set foot into this office, and we are well qualified to recognize the sort of man who would run off like that. Rest assured, we will discuss *why* he left you like that and handle the matter accordingly."

At this, Miss Mason's shoulders slumped. "Oh, do forgive me. I don't mean to be so cross. It's just . . . with all these bombings every night, I can't seem to manage my irritation. The littlest things upset me now. I spilled a glass of milk yesterday and actually wept. Milk, the very thing they say *not* to cry over."

"We are all feeling that way," Elizabeth said. "All of us. I found myself upset over the roses in my garden when they were destroyed to make room for our shelter."

Liza wiped her eyes. "Well, I'd best get back to work. I am sorry to have troubled you."

"We will call you when we find out what happened with Mr. Robinson," Hetty promised.

"Thank you." Miss Mason saw herself out and once they were alone, Hetty and Elizabeth put their heads together.

"We had better get to the bottom of this," said Hetty. "I remember Mr. Robinson. He didn't seem the type to leave her like that. Something must have happened."

Elizabeth retrieved Glen Robinson's file and looked up his contact information. "We could try calling him. It says he works at his home two days a week, and today is one of those days when he should be home."

"Ring him." Hetty waited as Elizabeth telephoned him. When the line connected for his residence, a man answered.

"Mr. Robinson?"

"This is John Armstrong, his roommate."

"Oh, is Mr. Robinson available? This is Miss Mowbray from the Marriage Bureau. It's quite urgent that we speak to him."

The man sighed. "You haven't heard the news, then?"

"Heard what?" Hetty demanded. She'd been leaning in to overhear the conversation.

"No, we haven't heard. Please tell us," Elizabeth added.

"Glen was hit by a car. He's in the hospital. He'll be all right, but he'll be there for a while to heal up."

"Oh, good heavens! Which hospital?" Elizabeth asked.

"Guy's Hospital in Southwark," John said.

"Thank you so much, Mr. Armstrong." Elizabeth was about to hang up, but the man stopped her.

"What's this Marriage Bureau you mentioned?" he asked.

"Oh. We match men and women up . . . romantically. Are you in the market for a wife, Mr. Armstrong?"

"I might be. Lord, I suppose everyone needs someone to look after and be looked after by in these dark days, eh?" John chuckled. "How does this business of yours work?"

"I'll give you our address. Feel free to drop by anytime, and we'll start your paperwork and conduct an interview." Elizabeth provided him with the office address and hung up.

She shook her head in disbelief. "Hit by a car! Poor Mr. Robinson."

Hetty seemed skeptical. "How does one get hit by a car when one is supposed to be at lunch with Liza Mason?"

"Should we go ask him? We have no meetings scheduled this afternoon."

"Very well, I don't mind playing detective," Hetty said.

"Has your stomach settled down?" Elizabeth asked her.

"Yes. Much more than half an hour ago. It seems a good *intrigue* does the trick to make me forget."

"Then a little outing should be good for you," Elizabeth said with a smile as they fetched their coats.

Hetty placed a trembling hand on her abdomen after she buttoned her coat. Elizabeth was right. This child inside her was a spark that she would guard with her life until it was a beacon burning bright enough to show Charles the path home through the fog of war.

GUY'S HOSPITAL WAS PACKED, AND IT TOOK ELIZABETH AND Hetty a quarter of an hour to locate a night ward adjoining the surgery area where less injured patients requiring observation were allowed to spend the night with medical care. An almoner poured tea for a few men and women, while nurses in white caps made the rounds to those sitting in chairs or lying on beds.

In the far corner, a bed was tucked up against the wall, and a man lay fully on his back, asleep, one of his legs in traction and his arm in a cast. He was by far the worst of the lot in the room. Elizabeth's heart went out to the man. With the Blitz, so many people were getting hurt or killed. She didn't even want to imagine what had happened to put that fellow into so many casts.

Elizabeth stopped a passing nurse. "Excuse me, I was told I could find Mr. Robinson here?"

"Yes, ma'am, in the corner there." The woman in the white nurse's cap nodded at the man with a broken arm and leg.

"Oh dear." Elizabeth's heart clenched as she and Hetty made their way to the bed in the corner.

She believed him to be asleep, but as she got closer, she saw his eyes were open. He was gazing listlessly at the ceiling.

"Mr. . . . . Mr. Robinson?"

The injured man blinked and lifted his bandaged head. Elizabeth recognized his eyes at once, a bright, clear, solemn gray. Angry red scrapes marred his cheeks.

Glen's lips parted in shock as he struggled to sit up. "Miss Mowbray?"

"Here, let me." Elizabeth helped him up, and Hetty propped a few pillows under his back and neck.

"Not that I'm not delighted to have visitors, but how did you even know I was here?" he asked.

Elizabeth shared a look with Hetty. "Well, we called your home, and your roommate said we would find you here."

"The reason we are looking for you is because a very mortified Miss Mason came to our office after she believed you abandoned her at the café."

"Oh God, Miss Mason," Glen gasped and then winced in pain. "I meant to contact her, but I didn't have her address. We'd been writing letters to each other through your office, you see. Christ, I never meant to leave her like that."

"What happened, Mr. Robinson? She waited a very long while for you to come back."

Glen's eyes filled with sorrow. "I never meant to leave. I had just secured a table for the two of us when I saw a childhood friend of mine, Kenneth Ball. He was in an army uniform, walking along with other soldiers toward Waterloo station." Glen paused as his voice broke. "I had this terrible sense of dread overcome me, that I might never see him again, so I crossed the street to go speak to him. But just before I reached the curb, a bloody cab hit me. Someone said I flew half a dozen feet, though I don't remember that, of course. I only remember waking up here in pain, and Kenneth was long gone. I never got to say goodbye . . . or good luck." A tear ran down Glen's cheek, and he wiped it away with his uninjured hand.

Elizabeth's lips trembled as she fought the urge to cry herself.

"And poor Miss Mason. I must have terribly upset her. No doubt she thinks me a cad." Glen's sigh carried such a weight to it that it made Elizabeth's heart feel heavy as well.

"She was upset, but only because she didn't know why you'd left. May we tell her what happened?"

"Yes, of course," Glen said. "I hope she can forgive me. I really rather like her. She was my favorite of all the women you suggested I begin a correspondence with. When I saw her beneath the clock at Waterloo station, it was like seeing the sunlight after many months of troubled skies. When she noticed me and smiled, I fairly forgot to breathe."

Hetty patted his hand. "We will tell her, Mr. Robinson. And perhaps if you feel up to visitors, she could come and see you?"

"I would very much like that. I'll be here another three days before I am allowed to convalesce at home."

"Wonderful. We'll see if she'll come round and visit you." Hetty gave Glen's shoulder a gentle pat.

They left Glen to rest. On the way back to the office, Elizabeth and Hetty talked about all the boys they had grown up with who were all far away now, fighting for their lives and the lives of everyone in the free world.

"I've felt so static these last few months," Elizabeth confessed. "As if keeping the same rhythm would help me go forward with a smile and a laugh. But laughter doesn't come easy anymore, does it? I think of all those boys in the darkness and the mud and the cratered holes as they battle in the crumbling shells of once-great cities, and I think there can be no laughter there. Perhaps it's too dark to hold on to those memories that are full of light."

She and Hetty reached the front door of the bureau just as a cold October wind came in across the pavement and grass toward them. Slithering like an invisible serpent, it twined and twisted itself about their bodies until both women curled inward from the cold.

"I know how you feel," Hetty said. "I think of Charles and how he cannot even receive my letters because of the nature of his missions. I think of him dying somewhere and his body being rolled into a cold grave, with hard earth tossed hastily over him. The realization that every horror one could imagine, and even the ones I cannot, could come to pass . . . It sweeps over me, and I want to *scream*. Scream until my body explodes and there's nothing left of me to hurt or to ache with the fear."

Hetty drew in a deep breath. "And that is why we must fight here. We must give those boys our laughter, our smiles, every last bit of our strength, because if we are strong, it keeps *them* strong enough to make it home."

Elizabeth closed her eyes, thinking of a woman they had passed on the street who worked at a grocer's around the corner. A polished and beautiful woman who had so often bragged with motherly pride about her young lad who had passed his flight exams with flying colors and how today he'd been allowed to fly for the first time. But as she had spoken of her son, Elizabeth had noticed her eyes were a little too bright and her nails were bitten down to the quick.

A flame fueled by sorrowful pride had lit within Elizabeth in that moment, and now she protected that flame as if it were the only thing that could help the world from being swallowed by darkness. They had to be proud of everyone who continued to fight on, even if they couldn't fight themselves.

THUNDER SHOOK THE HOUSE CLOSE TO ONE O'CLOCK IN THE morning, and Elizabeth bolted upright in bed, her heart pounding wildly.

"It's only a storm," she told herself. "Just a storm . . ." Lightning flashed across the heavily curtained windows, but there was no sound of rain upon the windowpanes. Only the rapid *tat-tat-tat* of distant antiaircraft guns firing into the night. The air-raid siren roared to life, howling, fading, then growling like a wolf on a moor baying at the betrayal of the bright bomber's moon.

"Izzy!" Elizabeth yelled as she finally got her body to move. She grabbed her housecoat and slippers and rushed into the corridor. Her aunt exited her bedchamber at the same moment.

"To the shelter," Isabelle urged.

They rushed down the back steps into the garden. The night was still. Only a few fallen leaves scuttled along the ground as the wind tugged at them. Distant fires burned to the north, and the orange haze on the horizon sent shivers through Elizabeth. Searchlights filled the sky, their beams seeking enemy planes hiding within the starry skies. Whistles of falling death were barely shut out when Elizabeth and Isabelle slammed the shelter door closed.

Bombers growled like hungry beasts against a chorus of rumbling, distant explosions. Neither Elizabeth nor Isabelle spoke as the bombing drew nearer. They sat together on one of the beds, arms wrapped around each other. The walls of the shelter creaked and groaned in protest. The sounds were so loud —so loud that Elizabeth couldn't think, couldn't even breathe. It felt as though bombs were dropping close to the shelter. Dirt rained down on them, and the cacophony of explosions deafened them over and over while their bodies rattled with the earth's violent quaking. One particular bomb hit so close that Isabelle and Elizabeth were knocked clear out of their bunk beds and onto the floor.

It went on for three hours before the all-clear siren sang through the night, giving them blessed relief.

Elizabeth emerged from the shelter first. Her legs gave out at the sight before her. Isabelle's lovely townhouse was *gone*—or rather, half of it was completely destroyed, like someone had sliced down the middle of it and cut away the house like a slice of cake. She could see every floor and everything inside as though it were a giant dollhouse.

Dust covered the yard in a damp cloud of gray. A sofa from the upstairs drawing room dangled halfway off the severed edge of one floor. Chairs and tables and other furniture teetered at odd angles. A trio of houses across the street had completely disappeared. Nothing was left but piles of smoldering rubble. Their elderly neighbor Mr. Cox held two chickens under his arm, still wearing his housecoat as he stared at the place where his home had been.

Elizabeth gaped at the smoking ruins. Something old within her told her that the destruction of great cities was an ancient story, a tale from another age where barbaric men burned down what they couldn't have. It wasn't what civilized people did.

But to see these not-so-distant fires, to taste the ash and

plaster dust upon a scorching wind like the fetid breath of a god of war . . . she finally witnessed a new depth to human suffering.

A frantic shout echoed across the street. "Over here! Help!" The words strung out somehow, as if the person screaming was moving too slowly. Elizabeth shook her head as the faint ringing in her ears subsided only slightly. Isabelle stood frozen beside her, her hands covering her mouth as she stared at her beautiful home, now in ruins.

"Help me!" Another shout broke through Elizabeth's mind, which had been so full of horrors as to be empty of any other thoughts. She ran across the garden, picking her way over the rubble of Isabelle's home to reach the house across the street, or what was left of it.

A woman wailed like a banshee set free by the curse of the falling bombs. She was frantically pointing at the house. It was one of their neighbors, Mrs. Wesley, covered in dust, and her dark hair was powdered white in the moonlight.

"Please . . ." She grasped Elizabeth's arm hard, and the bruising hold forced Elizabeth to bite back a cry of pain. "My daughter . . . my Mary . . . she's buried. She's *buried*." The woman repeated the words over and over.

Elizabeth stared in horror at the house. Where could a small child be within such destruction? "We'll find her," Elizabeth promised. A few fire wardens came rushing toward them, barely boys pretending to be men. Both were out of breath and their faces were streaked with ash. One of their uniforms was already singed. In the distance, more whistles sounded as other fires blossomed to life.

"Are you both all right here?" one of the young men asked.

"We've got incendiaries to put out all over the street," the other said.

"Can you handle this?" the first man asked Elizabeth, his gaze darting between her and Mrs. Wesley.

"Yes, I'll help her," she assured them, but a dark fear coiled inside her, one that warned her there wouldn't be any way to help Mrs. Wesley if they didn't find her daughter alive.

With grateful looks, the boys rushed toward the flames farther down the street.

"Mrs. Wesley, where was Mary when you last saw her?"

"Right behind me. We were just leaving the house, and then a bomb dropped on us and I was knocked out. I only just came round . . ." The woman's housecoat drifted open on the breeze. Blood streaked the nightgown the woman wore.

Elizabeth peered more closely at her. "Are you hurt?"

"What? I don't care about me—find Mary!" Mrs. Wesley nearly shrieked as she waded into the rubble, her eyes wild as she tugged in vain at heavy pieces of concrete.

Elizabeth helped her lift debris away from the front door. Her hands grew raw scraping across rough stone, and she yelped when the splinters of a support beam embedded themselves into her fingers and palms, but she didn't stop shifting rubble. The smoke from the fires tainted her lungs with invisible poison, making her cough, but she didn't dare stop.

A pale white hand emerged from beneath a nearby rock. Mrs. Wesley clutched at the hand, and the tiny fingers curled around her own.

"Mary!"

A faint reply came. "Mama!"

"Mary," Elizabeth called out. "Are you hurt? Can you move?"

"My arm is stuck . . . ," the little girl said, her voice sleepy.

Elizabeth crouched by the rubble covering the girl and, with all her might, shoved it away. The girl's tiny body had been tucked into a crevice between the heavy stone and wood. She looked unharmed, just covered in dust.

"Mary, thank God!" her mother cried.

"Wait. Let me fetch her." Elizabeth lifted the girl, who couldn't have been more than six years old, into her arms.

"Am . . . am I going to die?" The little girl's words barely carried upon the wind as Elizabeth shifted her higher in her arms.

"Of course not, darling," Elizabeth assured her.

The child's face smoothed, freed of worry, and she smiled faintly as she looked up at the night sky.

"Papa's come back."

She sighed and closed her eyes. The pulse of life faded, and Mrs. Wesley's breath stopped along with that of her child.

"No, no, no, no . . ." Mrs. Wesley took the girl, who was now gone from the world, from Elizabeth's arms. She crumpled to the ground, her daughter's body in her arms, and threw her head back, letting out a howl of an animal in deepest pain and unendurable agony.

Elizabeth had never heard a sound like that. It was a sound ripped from someone's very soul. A sound only a mother could make. Elizabeth had no children of her own, but she knew on some level, the way any woman would, what it felt like to lose a child. A child was something a woman gave of herself, putting it out vulnerable and beautiful into the universe. And now . . . this poor woman held that part of herself in her arms as she perished too soon. How could the mothers of the world bear this loss, night after night, their sons dying in foreign fields, their daughters buried beneath rubble and stone?

Elizabeth sank down next to Mrs. Wesley, curling an arm around the woman's shoulders as she rocked Mary's body as though she were a babe. The girl's body was unbroken, unmarred by the marks of war, but she left behind a gaping void that could fill the universe with its hollow pain.

Tears carved paths through the dust on Mrs. Wesley's face, which was devoid of hope, devoid of life. Bits of ash, still glowing like embers, danced around them like hellish fireflies.

"If this is life now . . . I want no more of it," she murmured in a daze. "First my Donald dies at Dunkirk, and now . . ."

She didn't finish. She simply rocked the body of her daughter as fires raged all around them and the last breaths of so many others were stolen by the winds of war.

CHAPTER 34

N*ovember 1940*

Isabelle sipped her tea and looked over a copy of the paper at breakfast. "Good Lord."

"What is it?" Elizabeth and Hetty asked at the same time. They were nestled in the cozy dining room at Charles Humphrey's townhouse, where Hetty had insisted they move after Isabelle's home had been lost in the bombing last month.

Isabelle spread the paper flat on the table. "They've cut rations again." Elizabeth leaned over her aunt's shoulder to see the article.

"Well, how bad is it this time?" Hetty asked as she spread a meager pat of butter on her toast.

"Sugar allowance is only eight ounces a week now," Elizabeth said. "Tea is two ounces, and margarine as well as cooking fats join butter on the ration books. They're stopping production on cups, cutlery, kettles, clocks, furniture, toys, and prams. We likely won't see any more pencils, gardening implements, or knitting needles either."

"Thank heavens I never did learn to knit," Hetty muttered.

"I can't survive much longer on a diet of salted cod." Elizabeth sighed. Her stomach rumbled at the thought of all the real food she dearly missed. "Thank God your neighbor gave us his chickens."

Their elderly neighbor, Mr. Cox, had given them his three hens the morning after their street was destroyed. He'd decided to move to Yorkshire to be near his son and daughter-in-law and didn't want to risk traveling with his poultry. So his three beloved plump red hens now lived in the back garden, roosting over porcelain eggs that Elizabeth had put in their nests to encourage them to brood more quickly, and it was working. They'd made good eggs for the last two weeks.

"Will there be anything left?" Isabelle asked in a softer voice. "We have no clothing for children, no food, no supplies, and the Germans have an endless number of bombs. It's . . . it's not right."

Hetty shuffled through the letters she had brought from the office the day before and tore into one. Elizabeth sank into the chair beside Hetty.

"Here." Hetty handed her the next letter in the stack. It had an unfamiliar address. Elizabeth opened it, and a folded sheet of cream-colored stationery fell out. She opened the expensive letter and read the words printed upon it. A smile stretched across her face, and her head was filled with songs and dancing.

"Hetty . . ."

"Hmm?" Hetty was still focused on whatever she held.

"We have an update."

"On what?"

"Miss Liza Mason and Mr. Glen Robinson."

"Oh?" Hetty put down the letter she'd been perusing and took the one Elizabeth held out now.

Hetty gasped as she read the note. "Married! They had a small ceremony yesterday." She smiled at Elizabeth.

"It says that she went to visit him and spent every day with him at lunch while he recovered, and—oh, it's wonderful, *simply wonderful.*"

"Perhaps we should start a service of hitting clients with cars whilst on dates," Hetty suggested. "They'll all be married a lot sooner."

Elizabeth tried not to laugh at the mischievous gleam in her friend's eye.

"Well, that's good news. We certainly need it."

"Indeed." Elizabeth snuck a glance at her aunt, who had become pale and thin since losing her home.

That night had changed *everything.* Elizabeth had worked herself to exhaustion digging through the neighbors' houses trying to find survivors. She'd even had to use the hand pump to put out two incendiary devices. They had waited in agonized silence as another neighbor's house had to be dealt with by the bomb-disposal group who were trained in disarming unexploded bombs.

Elizabeth and the other civilians had stood shivering in their housecoats and slippers while men carefully dug along the course of the bomb's entryway into the rubble until they were able to locate the device. Then they had to roll the bomb over to expose the fuse. The senior most experienced officer unscrewed the retaining ring and carefully removed the fuse. Once this was done, the men wedged the bomb up toward the surface until they were able to roll it out of the rubble.

Once that bomb had been handled, everyone on the street blew out a collective sigh of relief. She and Isabelle had slept a few more hours in the shelter before waking again and starting the hard day of retrieving whatever possessions they could from the house. She rang Hetty from a neighbor's home that had suffered less damage. When Hetty heard what had happened, she rushed over to help.

They had worked tirelessly, cleaning plaster off the few unbroken remains of Isabelle's beloved china and stuffing clothing into travel cases. Others swept the streets of plaster dust and glass. Each time a pile of debris was dumped into an ash bin, the glass tinkled, rather like the bells of a distant wind chime. Beneath that sound was the hard rapping of men nailing wooden boards over gaping windows of homes that were still habitable.

Elizabeth had watched the activity in the street from the doorway that no longer led to her home. For a long while she had no fear, no dread of the night, no regrets, just an awful numbness to everything, even the faint sunshine that tried to warm her cheeks. Their neighbors looked the same on the outside as she felt on the inside—weary-faced, beaten-down, dirt embedded into their skin and clothes like a second gray skin.

Once they'd salvaged what they could, they took a cab to Hetty and Charles's home.

"You'll move in, of course," Hetty had said matter-of-factly.

Isabelle had attempted to protest. "Oh, but we couldn't—"

"Nonsense. My husband is out fighting God knows where in

Europe, and I'm two months pregnant, terribly hormonal, and need looking after—don't I, Lizzie? You'll stay."

That was how the three of them ended up becoming residents of the Humphrey London townhouse. Charles's butler, Mr. Jarvis, seemed quite delighted to have more people to look after. He had casually remarked one morning a few weeks after the bombing as he brought tea in for them that looking after a young bachelor had been the height of boredom. He was glad to have more activity in the house.

The three of them were certainly active, since all three women worked and were constantly going in and out of the house. But they managed to settle into a routine after a time.

"Anyone fancy visiting the shops this afternoon?" Isabelle asked one day when the three were finishing up lunch.

As it was a weekend, Elizabeth and Hetty agreed an outing might be nice. Over the last two months, the residents of London had started to accept the nightly bombs and shells and all the fire that came with it. They had to adapt or die. No one became cold or callous, but a need to go out and pretend life was normal, even for a few hours, was an infectious attitude that swept across the city.

They took a cab to the corner of Oxford Street. Their first stop was Selfridges, which was still in business, but their windows had been replaced with wooden frames reinforced with sandbags. Broken glass and piles of debris recently swept out of the way on the pavement were evidence of last night's attack. Elizabeth followed her friend and aunt into the store, while Isabelle proudly showed off some of the utility clothing lines the government was starting to produce. Her boss, Norman Hartnell, and other designers were working in tandem with the government to create outfits that used far less material and were designed with a utility style. *Usefulness* was the word in the London fashion scene now, not glamor.

As they examined the meager offerings of the department store, Elizabeth noticed new signs for shelters hanging on the walls that led down to the basement below. She wondered how many people the store could fill the basement halls with when the bombs fell. The people in the city had to be ready to take cover, no matter where they were when the air-raid siren started.

By early evening, Elizabeth and the others returned to the house with only a few purchases. An excited Mr. Jarvis greeted them.

"Miss Mowbray, you have a visitor. I didn't think it proper to make him wait outside. He's in the drawing room."

Elizabeth removed her coat and set her handbag down, curious. She entered the drawing room a moment later and halted at the sight of a uniformed officer with his back to her. He had one hand braced on the mantel of the fireplace, and his other deftly wielded a poker, prodding the logs closer to the flames. The faint pop and crackle used to be a comfort to her, but now it only reminded her of the flames destroying her home and the city of her dreams. The man set the poker down and turned to face her.

"Philip?" she said in shock as she recognized him.

Since they had come back to London, she had seen him perhaps only once a week. He would drop by the bureau and tease her for a bit, sometimes bring her lunch, and then take off again to destinations unknown. But he had always been in his civilian clothes. Now he was back in his RAF uniform.

She had flashes of the night they had met—Philip dragging her into the safety of the shop cellar and stealing a kiss later as he rushed off with Nathan to join the fire brigade. Somehow, she'd managed to forget while they were in the countryside that he was eventually to be back in the skies. It stopped her heart to look at him now in that uniform he wore with quiet pride. The cast was missing from his arm, and she knew with a terrible dread what that meant.

"No . . . ," Elizabeth murmured.

Philip came to her slowly, his blue eyes deep and solemn, like a thousand heroes who'd come before him. He too knew what today meant for the both of them.

"It's time I returned to Biggin Hill. I report first thing tomorrow morning."

Her voice cracked. "So soon?"

"I can't wait another day, Lizzie. My men are fighting without me, *dying* without me. We have boys only a few years older than Marcus facing seasoned German pilots in their thirties. Our lads have a life expectancy of *only four weeks*. We have no advantage left to us except our reckless youth. It's my duty to bring as many of those lads back as I can."

He curled his fingers under her chin, lifting her face to him when she wanted to look away. She blinked back hot tears.

"That happy to see me leave?" He tried to smile, but the false amusement quickly faded. "Perhaps you ought to throw a parade in Trafalgar Square."

"Oh, stop!" she gasped and hit him hard in the chest. He winced but caught her wrist before she could strike him again.

"Let go of me!" Elizabeth demanded, her body fighting not him, but the reeling feel of suffocation that threatened to kill her.

"Shh." He pulled her into his arms, and she pressed her cheek to his chest. The steady thump of his heart reminded her of the grandfather clock in Isabelle's home, which even after being bombed had continued to tick away in sheer glorious, utterly English defiance.

Please . . . let his heart be as strong as that clock, she silently prayed.

"Does that mean you'll pine away for me while I'm gone?" Philip asked.

She lifted her head. "I'm not pining for a scoundrel like you."

His responding laugh rumbled out of him into her, sealing her heart with a stamp of his making.

"There's my girl. I wouldn't want you pining for me." He stroked her hair and kissed the top of her head. "I want you fighting, laughing, *living*. I want all of that for you, so when I'm up in the clouds I'll know you're all right. Understand?"

Elizabeth's hitched breathing eased a little. Algernon had never made her feel like this. Philip did not see her as a shadow. He saw her as an equal. He *believed* in her. In his adorably infuriating way, he was telling her something momentous, but neither of them dared to say those words, not when they could so easily be robbed of them.

She breathed in the smell of him and burned it into her memory. The hint of cologne and aftershave, she could even swear she smelled the wild northern wind upon his uniform. Had he already flown today? A simple test of his arm, perhaps? She didn't dare ask. She didn't want to think about it.

"Come out with me tonight. Dinner and dancing."

She looked up at him, their mouths almost touching as he leaned down. Between the softness of his mouth and the fire of life in his eyes, she was lost.

"All right . . . dinner and dancing. I need to change."

He pressed his lips to hers, a soft, feathery kiss before he let her go, and she ran upstairs to change into her best frock and shoes. If tonight was all she had left with him, she wasn't going to have any regrets.

Elizabeth came down the stairs wearing her favorite bright-red dress, which had small buttons down the center and the skirt rippled like flower petals when she twirled. Her black pumps were a little scuffed, but they were the most comfortable shoes she had for dancing.

Philip whistled in appreciation and tilted his officer's cap back on his head as she appeared. Hetty and Isabelle grinned at each other before hugging Elizabeth when she reached the bottom of the stairs.

"Are you two plotting?" she asked suspiciously.

"Us? *Never.*" But there was a twinkle in Isabelle's eye. It was good to see her aunt smile again.

"You bring her back safe and sound, flyboy," Hetty warned Philip.

"I will," he promised, and the look he gave Hetty was one of deadly seriousness. Then he turned his attention back to Elizabeth with a cocky grin that made her heart flutter. "Come on, Lizzie, let's tear up the town."

THE HEAVILY SANDBAGGED ENTRANCE OF THE RITZ STOOD defiant under a half-obscured moon. It was a little cloudy, but likely not enough to keep the bombers away. But Elizabeth was pulled along by a sense of reckless abandon as she and Philip reached the entrance. The blackout curtains and heavy drapes kept the light within hidden, but as she and Philip stepped inside the hallowed ground of the hotel, they were almost blinded by the glow. Every surface gleamed or sparkled with golden light, as if the war did not exist beyond the sandbag walls.

"The hotel is full of exiled aristocrats and foreign royals," Philip said as he tucked her arm in his and escorted her through the reception.

"Oh?" Elizabeth craned her neck to look at the crowd around them. Women in fine fur coats and jewels clucked like hens as they preened and gossiped. Men in dapper suits huddled around each other, glasses of scotch or brandy in hand as they whispered the latest news on the war fronts.

"See that man?" Philip nodded his head toward a dark-haired, mustached man who stood out among those around him. He wore a dark wool suit, and there was a serious air about him that called for one's attention. Around him were several women and a few young men, all speaking a language she didn't recognize.

"Yes, I see him."

"That's Ahmet Zogu, or King Zog I, of Albania."

Elizabeth stared in fascination. "The king of Albania is here?"

"The woman at his side is Queen Géraldine. He brought her, the crown prince Leka, the king's six sisters, two nieces, and three nephews with him. Rumor has it he brought the royal jewels and gold from their treasury to England. I bet they stashed them in a storeroom downstairs." Philip eyed the man with a kind of respect.

Elizabeth felt her heart go out to the exiled monarch and his family. "Can you imagine how far he is from home?" Many people fleeing Hitler had nothing but the clothes on their backs. Eva and Marcus had been among the lucky ones to reach London and make friends and find a home and employment before the bombing started.

"Everyone who can't fight must run," Philip said, and his tone held an edge to it. He was right, of course. Not everyone could stand in front of guns and tanks and fight.

The Ritz was a small pocket of comforting decadence in the midst of the bleak, bombed-out city. Elizabeth felt she had stepped into another world. The French château-style architecture and plush furnishings left her feeling as though she was in a palace.

"They fight the war with a cocktail in one hand here," Philip chuckled.

Elizabeth shook her head in amazement. "They certainly do, don't they?" Porters slipped among the guests, seeing to any needs they may have.

"Let's have dinner." Philip led her to the famous Ritz grill room. The white cloth-covered tables were almost entirely occupied, but when the head waiter saw Philip, he smiled broadly.

"Mr. Lennox! Welcome back, sir. And you've brought a guest —wonderful, just *wonderful*." The man waved for them to follow him.

"A favorite here, are you?" Elizabeth asked, trying and failing to hide a grin.

He smiled back. "Perhaps. Nathan and I and a few of our mutual friends used to come here all the time before the war."

"And have you brought other ladies here?" she asked, keeping her tone casual.

He tapped the tip of her nose with a finger. "Jealousy is a lovely color on you, Lizzie."

"I'm not jealous!" she protested.

He continued to smile as they reached their table and the waiter gave them the evening specials.

"I think I'll have the wild mushroom consommé and the veal," Philip said.

Elizabeth's mouth watered at the thought of such delicacies. The last meal she'd eaten had been rabbit . . . freshly caught from Hetty's garden and baked in a less-than-appetizing mince pie. "May I have the quail salad and Bresse duck?"

"Of course, madam."

When the waiter disappeared, Elizabeth sat back in her seat, her gaze roaming over the gilded room with its fine crown moldings and mirrors. Opulence was all around her.

"It's a lot, isn't it?" Philip's eyes lit up with amusement.

"Yes. I mean, Isabelle took me to the Savoy once, but this is, well . . . I can't quite believe I'm here. It's different from what I'm used to." She was all too aware again that she and Philip were from different classes in society. He must have lived in a world like this all the time before the war.

"I wish I could cook like this. But I'm simply dreadful, so I avoid it," she added as she glanced around at the fine dishes being served at other tables.

"Not a fan of cooking?" he asked.

There was no judgment in his voice. Algernon had made it clear that she was expected to be a talented cook. Elizabeth had hoped to learn, but it seemed she lacked all talent and that it was best to simply take orders from others.

"Well, no, actually. I just let Isabelle tell me what to do. Last night, we helped Jarvis and Hetty's cook in the kitchen—just for a bit of lessons, mind you."

"And what did you learn?" He leaned forward, apparently interested in something so silly and mundane.

"Well, we had a bony mutton left over from yesterday's luncheon, and we made a lovely casserole with it. We fried onions, celery, and carrots. Oh, and a turnip. Then it cooked for several hours before we added potatoes. Mrs. Kelly, the cook, made a big pan of suet pudding. She'd minced the suet from a cow kidney she'd bought. We boiled orange peels in honey and water until they were tender, and then she beat an egg in hot water and used a pot of sweetened bun flour and a tablespoon of sultanas. Don't ask me how she knew to do all that." Elizabeth sighed. "It was like magic. I'll never have the ability to cook like that."

"So it's wholemeal bread and jam for you?" he teased.

"Apparently." She nudged his shin under the table with her foot, and he laughed.

"But I am good at setting rabbit snares. I hate catching the little darlings, but meat is meat, you know?"

"I do," he agreed. "Barracks food isn't exactly fantastic on the base either."

The waiter returned with two glasses of wine, and Elizabeth took a long drink.

"Easy there," Philip warned. "We don't want to miss out on the dancing. I paid an extra two shillings and sixpence for each of us."

"They charge customers for dancing?" Elizabeth frowned and set her wineglass down.

"Oh yes. They also charge an additional six shillings above the fixed five-shilling restaurant meal price."

"What? Oh, Philip, that's too much." The government had set a fixed price of five shillings for all restaurants, but it seemed the hotels had found a way around that.

"Nonsense," he said. "I don't mind spending it. Besides, I want to enjoy tonight. I'll be back in the barracks and eating tinned meat in the morning, which is far less edible than anything Mrs. Harrow cooked for us while we stayed at Cunningham House."

Elizabeth's soul felt heavy at the thought of tomorrow. "The barracks . . ."

They stared at each other, and Elizabeth did her best not to let him see how much she feared his leaving. The last thing she wanted was to give him worries as he flew.

Philip sipped his wine, and then, seemingly knowing she needed a distraction, he changed the subject. "So, tell me about your latest matches." Thankfully, he always knew just how to distract her from her worries about tomorrow.

As they dined, Elizabeth lost herself in telling him the latest news from the bureau. He was particularly interested in the story of Mr. Robinson's cab accident.

"I don't blame him, wanting to say goodbye and good luck to a friend. I don't know how many times I've come back from a raid only to find another few men that I'd gotten to know hadn't come home."

He played with the stem of his wineglass for a time. "If there's one thing we have, something the Jerries don't, it's the defense of our land. This countryside, these cities—they are our *home*. Even the youngest pilots seem to get intensely focused in dogfights because they know what's at stake. Sometimes the German pilots fly like it's just another day at work. They aren't fighting to keep their families and homes. Hitler made a grave error calculating against the us. We defeated Napoleon, and we beat back the kaiser. Hitler is no different. We'll beat him back too."

Philip spoke with such confidence that Elizabeth's spirits rose higher. A niggling fear and dread still pulsed deep within her, but the more he spoke, the more it was smothered by hope.

"Are you ready to dance?" he asked as the waiter collected their empty plates.

"Yes." Elizabeth placed her hand in his, and they headed straight to the dance floor. The band played a popular tune, and Philip spun Elizabeth into his arms. At least a dozen other soldiers and RAF boys were twirling their girls amid the glamorous set of London's elite and Europe's exiled royalty.

Philip was a wonderful dancer. His hands held her close, and his body moved gracefully, even during the sillier, more energetic dance moves. They laughed as they danced a samba and a tango, and then they foxtrotted. He even knew the rumba, which was Elizabeth's favorite because it was so slow and seductive. Through the succession of dances, she fell deeper and deeper under Philip's spell, until all she saw were his eyes and all she felt was his body and hers moving perfectly in rhythm.

Every second she was with him, his calm control made her feel safe. Beneath the electric chandeliers and sconces lighting the room, the rhythm of the music set new heartbeats for the dancers.

Elizabeth felt a cosmic pull toward Philip. It was as though every moment, every choice of her life had tumbled her wildly downhill until she'd stopped right in front of him. Something settled into place, something that she thought had been long lost in the hills of Assam. When Algernon had shown his true colors, she had thought herself never capable of trusting herself to love again. But denying what she felt now was as impossible as denying her body its next breath.

"Don't think about tomorrow, Lizzie," Philip said. "There's only tonight."

But he was wrong—her life had been built upon the dreams of a thousand tomorrows, and that was what made tonight all the more dear to her. Tonight would give all of those tomorrows a shining light that would keep the darkness at bay.

Without warning, the air-raid sirens went off, and their lovely dance suddenly ended. She was jarred roughly in his arms by a few people stumbling nearby. Everyone stopped dancing, and the band abruptly set their instruments down as they listened to the sounds outside. After a moment, they started playing again. Elizabeth guessed they had gone through this many other nights and were supposed to keep the spirits of the guests up. It put her in mind of the musicians who'd played on the deck of the *Titanic* as it was slowly swallowed by the cold North Atlantic.

"Sleepers to the left, diners to the right, if you please," the hotel steward called out, giving everyone directions. There were two hallways to take shelter in. "You can stay and dance and eat if you wish, but for those taking shelter, we have plenty of space to offer."

"What do you want to do?" Philip asked her.

"I don't know . . . Shelter? I've had enough food and dancing for the night." She didn't like the idea of being so far away from her Anderson shelter and staying exposed. It would be better to take cover with the others.

"Shelter it is. This way, darling." He put an arm around her waist, and they followed the steward's directions toward safety through the dining room.

Bombs began to drop nearby a minute later, and the explosions made everyone dive to the floor as the Ritz quaked. The band fell off the rostrum, their instruments clattering to the ground. A moment later, the piano player got back up and sat down at his bench, his fingers striking up a tune. He sang out the words to "A Nightingale Sang in Berkeley Square," which calmed everyone as they got up from the floor. Philip pulled Elizabeth to her feet and wrapped an arm around her waist.

"To hell with the Blitz—I'm dancing at the Ritz," a young soldier cheered. He and his girl started doing a mad dance, whirling around the floor while other couples headed for the safety of the hallways.

Elizabeth shot a glance back at the dancers as they joined the evacuation. It was just too surreal. The chandeliers above the dancers tinkled with the shaking roof as bombs warred with the sounds of the antiaircraft guns. This was the spirit of England. Defiant in the face of death. It made her heart swell with pride.

"This way, darling." Philip ushered her toward the hall where the diners were to take shelter. Dozens of chaise longues lined the hotel corridor.

"Sleep when you can. We will wake everyone when the all-clear sounds," the steward announced to those who had filled up the hallway. The chaises were just wide enough to allow two people to lie together, assuming they didn't mind being close. A few maids passed out pillows and blankets. Philip collected a pair of pillows and blankets before they approached one of the empty chaises.

"You sleep there. I'll take the floor beside you." He dropped his pillow to the carpeted floor as another rumble of bombs overhead vibrated the walls.

Elizabeth grasped his hand and pulled him down beside her on the chaise. He arched a golden brow at her, silently questioning.

"There's room for two," she said. His gaze searched hers for a long moment, their hands linked together, the connection stronger than any weapon Germany might throw at them.

Philip sat down and removed his coat. She slipped off her

heels and tucked herself between Philip and the wall. Strangely, she'd never felt safer in her life, even as the lights flickered above them. He rolled onto his side to face her and wrapped his arm around her waist, tucking her into his body. They stared at each other a long while without speaking before he pressed a kiss to her forehead.

"Get some sleep. We'll be all right here tonight," he promised.

She tucked her head beneath his chin, nuzzling his throat. The bombs and the antiaircraft guns faded beneath the layers of exhaustion as she slept.

A few hours later she woke to find she was cradled in Philip's arms like a child as he carried her down a corridor.

"What's going on?" she asked drowsily.

"It's all clear. No more planes tonight. I paid for a room. I wanted you to spend the rest of the night in a real bed." He set her down as he reached a door and used a key to open it. An opulent suite was brightly lit by a lamp on a bedside table, and the bedsheets were already turned down. Even in the middle of a war, the Ritz held on to its standards.

She walked to the bed and stopped, turning to Philip as he closed the door. Their eyes met and held as something passed between them. She held a hand out to him, an invitation so instinctive that he could not resist. He came to her and wrapped her in his arms, claiming her mouth with his. Elizabeth burned with a need that she'd never experienced before. There was a wildness that ran like quicksilver in her veins. She pulled at his uniform and waged war upon the buttons until she removed his coat.

Then she tugged his shirt up and over his head until she was able to press her hands against his bare chest. All the while, her dashing pilot stole gentle kisses. When she turned her back to him to have him undo the buttons of her dress that ran down her spine, he pushed her hair back from her neck and pressed his mouth to her skin in a way that made her dizzy with delight. Then he slipped the buttons through the slits to free her of her dress.

"Lizzie, are you sure about this? I didn't plan for us—"

"Hush and kiss me, Philip." She let the dress slip to the floor and stepped out of it before returning to his arms. He carried her to the bed and laid her down with such tenderness that her heart clenched in sweet misery.

Philip lay beside her, his mouth exploring her collarbone before moving back up to her mouth. Their lips met again and again as their breaths mingled in the quiet room. Somewhere, the distant sound of music flowed up as someone played a piano one floor below.

Everything that followed was a wonderful dream, and for an instant toward the end, she soared through the clouds with Philip and knew what it meant to *fly*.

ELIZABETH WOKE THE NEXT MORNING, STARTLED FOR A moment to find herself in a hotel room, until she remembered how she had ended up there. She rolled over, reaching for Philip, but the bed was empty beside her. A hint of his warmth still lingered on the sheets, but she knew by the stillness in the room that he was gone.

A piece of hotel stationery lay on the pillow where his head had been, and on top of that was an RAF sweetheart pin. The silver wings were bright in the sunlight that now came through the windows. Philip must have opened the blackout curtains to let the morning light in before he left.

She picked up the pin and the letter he'd written.

LIZZIE,

I am sorry I wasn't here to see you wake, but I had to report to Biggin Hill early this morning. Last night was everything. I wish I could've said a thousand romantic things to you, but I'm no poet. So I will say only this: you will be with me, today and every day, and with every breath and every flight I take to the skies. A man couldn't be more honored than to fight for someone like you. Wear this pin for me, and it will be a talisman to bring me home to you.

Yours,

The scoundrel you shouldn't pine for

SHE LAUGHED, EVEN AS TEARS BLINDED HER EYES. SHE clutched the pin tight and pressed it to her heart.

"Keep your promise," she whispered to the air. "Come back to me."

CHAPTER 35

M*ay 1941*
After sustaining six months of almost nightly bombings, London had become a shell of its former self. On December 29, 1940, a fierce night of bombings resulted in a conflagration so widespread that *all* of London seemed to burn. It was a night everyone wanted to forget like some awful nightmare, too savage and devastating to believe to be real. The fires had been so great they'd lit up the night sky as though it were day, but day on a hellish planet somewhere alien that no one recognized. Screams, sirens, calls for help, and the sounds of emergency vehicles blurred into the roar of flames until one could barely hear anything but the suffering of London and its people.

Yet despite it all, London hadn't fallen. It had become a gaunt, haunted figure of its former self, but it was *still* London, one of the greatest cities in the world. When it had entered a staring contest with the devil, it hadn't blinked. And because of that strength, fate had intervened. Poor weather conditions in the early spring of 1941 left the city free of frequent bombings. But the memory of the fires of that late December had left many people full of terror for what good weather would eventually bring.

Elizabeth had been on duty with the Auxiliary Fire Service that December night, standing smartly in her uniform on a street corner near Hetty's house when the sirens went off. She and many of the men and women who had fought fires before had seen the true face of hell that night. Fiery columns of smoke rose above them as the flames blazed. Row after row of houses and businesses burned and fell as she and the other members of the AFS could do little more than stand and watch. Heavy canvas water hoses ran dry or became trapped between sheets of flame. The bombing had damaged the water mains, and the Thames was at low tide. All that could be done was to rescue pets and valuables before the fire crept farther down the untouched streets.

Staying up all night, Elizabeth had done her best to aid in controlling the inferno as blazing timbers crashed down and burning rubber belched out black smoke. The sickly stench of burning tea and sugar in dockside warehouses carried upon the wind. Boiling paint misted in the air, coating water hoses and nozzles with a sticky varnish. Buildings collapsed and the heat grew so intense that the painted sides of boats on the Thames blistered. The air was so full of burning things that it became impossible to breathe without pain.

But Elizabeth had survived, just as her city had. Philip's sweetheart pin had been fastened to the thin shirt she wore under her AFS uniform. It was silly, but as long as she had that pin with her, she felt protected, and she felt Philip was still with her, at least in her heart.

His missions were becoming more and more dangerous as they sent him farther out across the Channel. As a group captain, he apparently had decent phone privileges, because each time he returned home, he always called Hetty's home and spoke to Elizabeth. He could never talk long, so she also sent letters to Biggin Hill to tell him all about her adventures in the world of matchmaking. She didn't tell him about the fires, or the incendiary bomb she'd put out with a hand pump in Hetty's garden, or a dozen other nights full of danger. Still, he seemed to know what she faced, no matter how she tried to hide it from him, because after a terrible night of bombs, Nathan would come and check on the residents under Hetty's roof to make sure all was well. He'd leave Philip's latest letters behind for Elizabeth to read about the men he flew with, his home, his parents, the flights and battles he faced. He signed every letter with the closing line: *Until then, I dream of you in the clouds.*

Hetty teased her constantly about her *fly boy*, but then one day in late March they learned Philip had earned a new nickname at the base. *Ace.* He had received enough recognitions for downed enemy combatants that he joined the ranks of his father, Andrew Lennox, as a flying ace. Hetty had stopped teasing her and simply hugged her tight whenever a new letter arrived. She understood that Philip's missions were becoming more deadly, and the risks of him never coming home continued to grow.

Then, in early May, Elizabeth and Hetty took a lunchtime walk through Regent's Park. They were both eager to feel a little sunlight on their faces, even though the clear skies meant bombers were likely to appear at any moment. They wandered down one of the quiet side gardens. The park itself was full of people. Only a few men were in uniform; the rest were with wives and children or sweethearts. These mild sunny spells often took turns with slightly chilly winds, which brought seagulls screaming overhead as they arced toward the Thames. Other birds, songbirds and the like, chirped gladly. Clumps of golden crocuses gave evidence of a winter finally having passed. The city seemed to be taking a collective breath.

"I used to love the spring," Hetty said. Her palm lay protectively over the swell of her belly, where her child grew every day. She was nine months pregnant and could have the baby at any moment. Elizabeth frequently found herself hovering at Hetty's side like a mother hen. Hetty was so large about the middle now she couldn't move that quickly, and Elizabeth worried about getting Hetty to a shelter when the sirens went off.

"You don't love it anymore?" Elizabeth asked as she helped Hetty down onto a bench.

"I just have this terrible feeling that once summer is here, Hitler will lift the lid off hell and start the bombings again every night. And . . . I worry that the letters Charles sends will stop coming. He doesn't even know I'm pregnant. I think I'd go mad if I didn't have his parents and my own constantly watching over me, along with my grandmother of course. They're all so thrilled about the baby, but I want Charles to come home, I want this all to be over...I want life to go on without all this darkness."

Elizabeth put an arm around her friend. "Do you remember that day we went to see that stodgy old solicitor about starting the bureau?"

The shadows in Hetty's eyes vanished as she chuckled. "Lord, what was I thinking to take us there? He was terrible. Good thing we matched his secretary up with that handsome engineer. What was the engineer's name again?"

"Arnold. Arnold Fredlund."

"Last I heard, they had honeymooned in Scotland. I believe they're working together now, helping rebuild the bombed areas in London."

"It's wonderful, isn't it?" Elizabeth said. "The lives you change."

Hetty took Elizabeth's hand and squeezed it. "The lives *we've* changed. From the beginning, we've been together in this. You won't leave me now, Lizzie, will you?" Hetty so rarely showed her softer side, but now, as she held Elizabeth's hand, Elizabeth saw that her strong, beautiful friend was terribly afraid.

"I'll never leave you, Hetty. You're my best friend. Besides, someone must keep you from running off to fight on the Continent."

Hetty smiled again. "And someone has to remind you to marry that ace of yours when this war is all over. I won't let you run away from him. He isn't Algernon, and this isn't India. You've nothing to blind you to who he is and who *you* are."

Hetty was right, of course. They sat in quiet silence for a time in that solitary garden, the scent of summer on the breeze.

"Well . . . we had better get back to the bureau. John Kirby, you remember, the handsome veterinarian? He's coming in today." Hetty had tried to call him Dr. Kirby, but the formal title had made him laugh and he'd then insisted on being called John or Mr. Kirby if they'd preferred.

They rose and walked back to the office. For the moment it was forgotten that Hitler now controlled most of Europe and was turning his eyes east toward Russia.

MISS PLUMLEY STEPPED INTO THE INNER OFFICE WHERE
Hetty and Elizabeth were sorting client index cards on a desk. It
was far too difficult for Hetty to bend over now and sit upon the
floor as they used to do when they matched people.

"Is that Mr. Kirby for us?" Elizabeth asked.

"Er . . . no, Miss Mowbray. It's a young woman. She says she
doesn't have an appointment, but I think the poor creature *needs*
to talk to someone."

Elizabeth and Hetty shared a worried look before they told
the secretary to send the woman in.

They went into the outer office and waited for the girl to
come up from the downstairs reception. A young woman with
large doe eyes framed by thick dark lashes stepped inside the
office. A slight frown creased her forehead. She wore a sensible
dark-green dress and clutched a handbag in a white-knuckled
grip. She was lovely, but her looks were dampened by the way
she was rigid with fear.

"Are you . . . the matchmakers?" The woman's voice quivered.
Her eyes were overbright, and she seemed to be on the verge of
tears.

"Yes, please sit, Miss . . ."

"Hazel Cochran." She inched toward the nearest chair, and
Elizabeth noticed that as she did so, one hand briefly rested on
her belly. It reminded Elizabeth of Hetty's actions of late. She
hated jumping to conclusions, but her instincts already had an
idea of where things were going.

"Now, how can we help you, Miss Cochran?"

Hazel bit her bottom lip, then drew in a deep breath. "I need
a husband . . . *quickly.*"

"How quickly?" Elizabeth asked carefully.

"Within the next month? I . . ." She halted on the next few words. "I am with child, and I will lose my job and be cast out of the boardinghouse I'm in once my landlady discovers my condition. But if I'm married, well, it would fix things."

Hetty shifted forward in her chair. "Miss Cochran, you are among friends now. Please tell us what happened, if you don't mind. We will keep everything you tell us confidential."

"It was four months ago now . . . I heard the sirens and ran for cover. But as I passed a bombed-out building, I thought I heard a child's cry. I feared a young child was trapped inside. I managed to get into the house, and the sound was coming from the cellar. I went down the steps, but . . ." The woman halted again, her throat working as she fought off tears. "*He* was waiting there for me."

"He? Who was it?"

Hazel swallowed before going on. "I never saw his face. He grabbed my legs and pulled me down the remaining stairs and threw me on the floor." She closed her eyes, her lips quivering for a moment before she continued. "He hit me across the face. I think I was screaming, and he hit me to shut me up. It hurt—he *hurt* me."

Elizabeth lay a hand on Hazel's knee, her heart in her throat as the woman stiffened at the touch. "I'm so sorry, Miss Cochran. No man has the right to hit a woman."

Slowly, Hazel met Elizabeth's eyes and took a shaky breath. "He *took* what he wanted then. I think the blow did something to my head. I couldn't move—there was pain, yes, but more than that, I just couldn't move." Her eyes shone with liquid, but her voice was strong, the voice of a woman who knew she had done nothing wrong but was still made to suffer for it. "I lay there, waiting. He finished and I still lay there. And then finally, after what seemed like hours, he got up and left."

Elizabeth's chest tightened with the horror she felt at the story, but words escaped her as Hazel went on.

"I saw the bombers overhead, through a gap in the ceiling. I lay there and watched them, and I wanted to scream at them to drop their bombs right there—on me. I just . . . I wanted to die," she admitted in a low voice, a tear escaping one eye to travel down the length of her cheek.

Elizabeth's stomach was lead, her heart swollen with Hazel's grief and a rage for this unknown man who could harm this woman so irrevocably.

"I finally picked myself up once the all-clear sounded." Hazel's voice was strained, and she didn't bother to wipe the tear from her cheek. "It was dark, but I walked home as fast as I could, and when I reached my room . . . I discovered I was bleeding. Quite badly." She gripped her handbag handle tightly in one hand.

Elizabeth watched as Hetty pressed a handkerchief into Hazel's other hand, her friend's eyes as wet as their guest's.

Hazel took the handkerchief but only held it, making no move to use it as she finished her story. "I tried to wash *him* off me in a tub of cold water, but . . . I still felt him. I felt him everywhere on me. I pass men on the street now, and I think . . . could one of them be him? It's enough to drive a woman to madness." She still clenched her handbag, but her fingers had loosened a little. "I'm sorry. I shouldn't have come to you. You couldn't possibly find anyone who'd . . . who'd want someone who . . ."

Her resolve crumbled, and she wept in silence, tears streaming down her face.

Before Elizabeth could act, Hetty was standing beside the weeping woman, an arm around her shoulders.

"Someone will want you, Hazel. Some wonderful man out there will want you as his wife, and you will be loved and cherished," Hetty said.

"But what man could accept a child that was born of *rape?*" Hazel whispered the last word as though she feared she would summon the devil himself.

"You are not defined by the tragedies that happen to you. Someone will love you and the child because that child is half of *you*. And we will find that man for you."

Elizabeth was stunned at her friend to make such a monumental promise, but it was exactly what she would have said in Hetty's place.

Hetty gave the girl a handkerchief. "Dry your eyes now. Then go downstairs and fill out a form for our secretary. Tell her the registration fee has been waived."

"Oh, but I can pay," Hazel insisted and started to open up her handbag.

"Nonsense," Elizabeth said. "This is a gift. We must stick up for each other, mustn't we, Hetty?"

"We must indeed. Especially us mothers." Hetty patted her stomach.

"Once you fill out your form, we will schedule an interview with you to go into more detail about what interests you in a man."

Hazel blinked and glanced between them. "You truly mean it?"

"Yes," Hetty and Elizabeth said in unison.

Hazel's shoulders fell, and the tension in her face eased. She even managed a little smile. "You're not matchmakers—you're angels."

After she left, Mr. Kirby strode in and firmly closed the door behind him.

"Mr. Kirby, I'm sorry we kept you waiting, but—"

"I want to meet her," he said abruptly. His face was deadly serious.

"Her?" Elizabeth asked as she retrieved his file from the desk. Mr. Kirby had been matched with twelve lovely ladies in the last several months and had been writing letters to all of them. Elizabeth was curious about which one had held his interest enough to ask for an in-person meeting.

"That woman who was just in here with you. The door was open enough that I heard what happened to her. I shouldn't admit to eavesdropping, but it happened, so I don't regret it. And I want to meet her."

Hetty took the file from Elizabeth and set it back down on the desk, fixing the veterinarian with a stern look.

"We will not send Miss Cochran out with men who will see her as an object of pity. Her situation is—"

"Mrs. Humphrey, there is a vast difference between pity and *compassion*," John Kirby said. "What I feel for Miss Cochran is the latter. I will not judge her for the evil actions of another, nor will the child she bears be treated any differently than one of my own making."

He spoke with such conviction, his face glowing with his passion to do the right thing, the good thing, that Elizabeth truly believed he could be the right man for Hazel. She'd had enough interactions with Mr. Kirby in the last year that she felt she truly knew when he was being sincere. Elizabeth and Hetty shared a look, and she was glad to see Hetty seemed to be with her in trusting him as a possible match for Hazel.

"Very well. We will call her this evening and recommend you once we have interviewed her properly and reviewed her file. If she likes the sound of you, we will have you write to each other," Elizabeth said.

"Thank you." He turned to leave, but Elizabeth halted him.

"Mr. Kirby, what about the other ladies we've introduced you to?"

He paused, hand resting on the doorjamb as he looked over his shoulder at them.

"They were all quite wonderful, and I'm sure you will find them all suitable husbands. But I respect a woman who has been through the fires of hell and come out stronger for it. Miss Cochran is such a woman. She makes me want to be better, to be worthy of her and her courage. Every man should want to marry a woman like that." He then exited the office, leaving them in stunned silence.

"He's like some knight of old, isn't he?" Hetty said as she opened his file to make a note about his introduction to Miss Cochran.

Elizabeth smiled. "He certainly is." But it was more than that. She knew Mr. Kirby would see Hazel as more than just a victim—he would see the person beyond that. That feeling of certainty she often got about people rippled through her like quicksilver. She had found a *hero* for Miss Cochran.

TWO WEEKS LATER

"Do you really not mind having dinner with my grandmother?" Hetty asked Elizabeth. She felt silly for asking, but she didn't want to go anywhere alone. She felt as though she was ready to pop with this baby. Being pregnant made her feel both powerful and vulnerable at the same time. To hold a life within her, to grow it on her own, yet knowing that the little life was so fragile, was terrifying. All she could think was that if something happened to Charles, she couldn't lose their baby.

She'd been spending every few days in the country at Charles's parents' estate or at Cunningham House, thinking it would be safer for her child, but at the same time, she had this desperate need to keep coming back to London, as though being brave enough to stay in her city would make Charles proud. It was silly, but she was dealing with the unpredictable emotions that came with her pregnancy and she'd tried to stop berating herself for decisions she made that might seem a bit foolish.

"Of course I don't mind. You know I adore your grandmother. She may be a bit of a battle-ax, but she is so delightful too." Elizabeth helped Hetty to her feet, and they grabbed their handbags, turned off the lights, and left the office.

Mr. Jarvis was waiting for them on the outside stairs when Elizabeth locked the bureau's front door. Hetty gratefully accepted the butler's hand as he helped her walk down the stairs.

"Hello, Jarvis."

"My lady," Jarvis said with a fatherly smile. Over the last two months, he had insisted on escorting Hetty to and from the office. He had explained that Charles would expect nothing less for the future Earl of Lonsdale's wife and child.

"Are we still bound for the Ritz?" Jarvis asked.

"Yes, my grandmother has a dinner reservation for us."

He waved toward the car he had parked a short way down the street. Where he found the petrol these days, Hetty had no idea, but she was grateful. Riding on a bus made her wildly nervous. Ever since she had seen a double-decker full of people hit by a bomb and get blown straight into the side of a building where no one had survived, the sight had permanently kept Hetty away from stepping onto that particular means of public transportation.

Hetty had been having dinner with her grandmother every few months ever since the bureau had opened. Lady Agnes wasn't afraid of the bombings. She claimed she was too old to let some bullies in aircrafts frighten her. Hetty was convinced that it was really because she wanted to stay close to Hetty in case she could help in some way. It was still a marvel to her that the woman who she had so often quarreled with about her future was now so proud of her and Elizabeth for the bureau's remarkable success.

When they arrived at the Ritz, Jarvis escorted them into the hotel and stayed in the reception, where he would wait for them to finish dinner before driving them home.

Hetty's grandmother, Lady Agnes Allerdale, was already seated waiting for them. She was frowning at her menu, but when Hetty and Elizabeth joined her, she was all smiles.

"My dears! Sit, sit. Oh Hetty darling, I can't believe it's been nearly nine months already?"

"Yes," Hetty laughed breathlessly as she let a waiter carefully assist her into her chair.

"I must say, I've never been terribly excited about babies," Agnes admitted, "but something about this one, my first great-grandchild—it's going to be special."

"I just want it out of me," Hetty muttered. She adored her baby madly, though they still hadn't met, but she was very much done with being the size of a German zeppelin.

"Everyone feels that way at nine months. I remember being both terrified and desperate," Agnes said.

"I am a little scared," Hetty admitted, her tone softer now. She didn't like admitting to weakness, but it was true. What if something went wrong, or the baby didn't survive after the birth? Or *she* didn't?

In the last few weeks, she had played every terrible scenario through her mind as she lay alone in bed. She would have given anything to have her husband home and safe, his arms around her, reminding her that Lonsdales never die, which meant that she and the baby as Lonsdales were within that magical protection.

"Why don't we order, and then we can discuss your nursery?" Agnes suggested.

As they ate, Hetty shared the latest developments with the baby's nursery and how Hetty had stayed up past midnight the previous night, putting the final touches on the room and getting blankets nestled in the cradle. Then the talk turned to the Marriage Bureau, and Hetty sat back, resting as Elizabeth took over the conversation.

It was just after dessert when something inside Hetty started to tighten. Like a fire was burning somewhere far south of her belly, and then the building pressure within her womb suddenly eased. Wetness coated her thighs, and the wetness simply kept coming and coming, until her shoes were wet. Shock and embarrassment had Hetty scrambling for her napkin. She'd been having the occasional false labor pain for the last few days and she hadn't thought today would be any different with the frequent pains.

"Hetty?" Elizabeth halted her talk as she and Agnes watched her.

"My . . . my water broke," she gasped in a frantic whisper.

"We had better get you—" The piercing wail of an air-raid siren cut Agnes off. "Bloody Germans!" Agnes snapped. "How dare they bomb us when you're ready to have your baby?"

"I don't think they particularly care," Hetty muttered as she stood. The leaking had changed to a steady dribble that she couldn't stop if she tried. All the other diners, to her relief, hadn't noticed the puddle she had left on the chair or floor. They were all exiting the dining room, occupied by their own worries.

Agnes snapped her fingers at a passing waiter. "You there!"

"Yes, ma'am?" the young man asked.

"We need a room immediately. A nice one, if you have any left. My granddaughter is about to have a baby. And fetch a midwife, while you're at it."

The waiter's eyes bulged as he noticed Hetty's round belly and the way she was slightly hunched over.

"Don't just stand there gawking!" Agnes bellowed at the young man. He tripped over a chair leg as he ran to do as the formidable older woman had commanded.

Hetty winced as a cramping pain made her bend over and clutch the back of the nearest chair. But thankfully the pain vanished just as quickly.

"Come on now, we have no time to waste." Agnes marshaled her and Elizabeth out of the dining room. Jarvis spotted them when they reached the reception and came straight toward them.

"Are you all right, my lady?" He took Hetty's arm, steadying her.

"It's the baby, Jarvis. *It's coming.*"

The butler paled and his mustache twitched, but his brown eyes were fixed with determination. "We need a room."

"We're waiting on one," Elizabeth assured him.

Soon, a very anxious hotel steward arrived. "Please, this way. We have a room you can use."

"It had better be a good one. This is Mrs. Henrietta Humphrey, future Countess of Lonsdale," Agnes declared.

The steward rushed to assure Agnes that the rooms were suitable. The air-raid sirens grew louder and then softer again, but Hetty didn't care. She had but one goal—to bring her and Charles's child into the world safe and healthy.

They were settled in a three-room suite with plenty of space and located on the ground floor. The young waiter from before bustled into the room.

"My lady, I couldn't find a midwife among our guests in the shelter."

"No midwife?" Agnes said sharply. "Unacceptable. You will have to leave the hotel and go find one."

The poor boy's face paled as the air-raid siren rose and fell again. "I'm very sorry, my lady, but—"

"My lady," Jarvis said as he took Hetty's hands in his own. "My mother was a midwife. If you wish, I can help you deliver the baby."

Hetty stared into the older man's eyes. Charles trusted him with his life, his home, and his wife. Why not their child?

"Yes."

"Oh, thank God," the waiter whispered in relief. But that only caught Agnes's attention.

"You there. Don't stand about. Fetch us some towels." The waiter fled to do her bidding.

"All right, what do we do?" Hetty asked, trying to stay calm even though her heart was pounding and her body ached between the contractions.

"You must remove everything but your underclothes and get beneath the blankets."

"I can help you," Elizabeth volunteered.

"As can I," Agnes said. "I've delivered a baby a time or two in my day."

"Good." Jarvis began issuing orders, but Hetty was focused on getting to the bed and stripping out of her clothes with Elizabeth's help. A fresh wave of cramps made her lose all modesty in front of the butler.

"Make her comfortable. Prop up some pillows behind her back so she'll have the strength to push when the time comes."

The waiter returned with the towels, and Jarvis instructed him next to bring him hot water, a pair of scissors, some needles, and thread.

Hetty let Elizabeth make her comfortable as she lay back and stared at the closed blackout curtains. The sound of the distant explosions filled her with a rage she'd never felt before. How dare those bloody bastards bomb her city just as her baby was coming into the world?

Jarvis and the others moved around in a flurry of orders and actions over the next several minutes. After that the time seemed to slow down as they waited for each contraction to come and go. Finally Hetty bent her legs and pushed when Jarvis told her to. Pain threatened to tear her in half as each contraction ripped through her. Then the pain would fade and she would fall back against the pillows, gasping for breath.

"Damn. The babe is stuck. Its shoulders are too big," Jarvis snarled in frustration. "We need something to pull the baby out."

Hetty lay back, her head tilting up to the ceiling as she closed her eyes, trying to stay conscious. It felt as though she was drifting away from her body . . . drifting away upon the wind.

A gray mist formed against the backs of her closed eyelids, where shadowy figures moved. She could make out the faces of men in British Army uniforms crouched behind a crumbled farmhouse. Melting snow dusted the ground, and yet buds bloomed on distant trees as though fighting against the lingering winter. They held their guns ready, hearts pounding. Dirt, smoke, and ash showered over them as something exploded nearby.

"Men to me!" a voice bellowed. Its sound was distant yet clear at the same time. The man who shouted bolted over the nearest wall, firing his weapon at the approaching enemy, and every man followed behind.

"Charles!" Hetty's scream broke her from the strange and awful dream. Her eyes flew open, and she wailed as another contraction knifed through her.

"Push now, Hetty. Push or we lose the baby!" Jarvis shouted.

Elizabeth was at Hetty's side, clutching one of her hands as she crouched on the bed. Their gazes met and held. Hetty squeezed her friend's hand as if it was the last life raft in a vast and terrible storm.

"Lizzie, I can't do this . . . *I can't*," she wept as tears blinded her.

"Hetty," Elizabeth said. "You are the daughter of a brigadier, a heroine of Dunkirk. You are the reason Charles will come home. You're stronger than anyone I've ever met. You can do this. *Now push and mean it!*"

Hetty's life flickered before her eyes, like the old moving pictures she'd seen as a child. Choppy frames, fleeting images . . . *Standing at the railing, watching Ceylon vanish on the horizon. The scent of cigarette smoke as she lingered on a shadowy balcony, only to be startled by a pixie who spoke of second chances at life and love. Charles holding her in the river, arms wrapped around each other as the currents drifted past. The boy who died in her arms at Dunkirk. Major Taylor taking her hand and coming home. Charles on the train platform, dissolving into steam . . .* The last was a sunny memory that would never leave her in a thousand years.

Lonsdales never die . . .

Hetty screamed, releasing her rage, her fear, her love out into the world all at once, and then something *moved*. The pressure that had made her feel trapped suddenly gave way.

"There we are!" Agnes shouted. She helped Mr. Jarvis take the baby when it finally emerged. Hetty collapsed, gasping for breath.

"You did it, Hetty, you did it!" Elizabeth was crying tears of joy. "It's a boy. A *darling* little boy."

Hetty tried to lift her head. She was so tired . . . so bloody tired. The clear, strong note of an all-clear siren sounded outside.

"They've stopped bombing so soon?" Hetty mumbled drowsily.

Elizabeth placed a fresh wet cloth over Hetty's forehead. "Hetty, it's past four in the morning. You've been in labor for more than eight hours."

Hetty's body still squeezed with a few contractions as she delivered the afterbirth and finally could truly rest. Every bone in her body seemed to have turned to liquid and she just wanted to see her child and then sleep for days.

Agnes came up to Hetty on the other side of the bed, a bundle of blankets in her arms.

"You did very well, my dear, so very well. Would you like to hold him?" Agnes bent over and offered the bundle to Hetty. A tiny wrinkled red face was tucked up beneath the blankets. One small fist was curled up by his little cheek.

"Hello there," Hetty said to the baby, feeling strangely shy. And yet as she gazed upon his face, she felt she knew this baby as well as she knew herself. He was a part of her that she had put out into the world, a part of Charles too, and it was then that she understood how Lonsdales could never die . . .

Nor can Byrons, she added silently.

She gently stroked his cheek. "Welcome to the world, Theodore Byron Humphrey."

She could have stared at him for hours, mesmerized by his tiny facial expressions and counting his fingers and toes. He wrinkled his nose and let out a soft little surprised gasp, then settled once more, falling back asleep. He did very little crying in those first few minutes. He was as calm and good-natured as his father, it seemed.

"We'll find a bassinet for him," her grandmother said. "You need to rest."

She reluctantly surrendered little Teddy to Elizabeth while Jarvis helped her up from the bed and into a chair nearby. He summoned a maid from outside to come change the sheets and remove the covering on the bed that Jarvis had the maids put down to protect the mattress beneath. Jarvis stood by Hetty's side, his hand on her shoulder.

"Thank you, Mr. Jarvis. You saved us. Both of us," Hetty said quietly. When she looked up, she saw tears in the man's eyes.

"Jarvis? What's the matter?"

The butler cleared his throat. "His lordship, Charles's father, saved my life in the trenches during the Great War. I owe him, so I vowed I would watch over little Charles. Now the lad has gone off to war, and, well, you and Theodore are my mission now, my lady. If I keep you both safe, Charles will come back home, won't he?"

She placed her hand over the butler's. "Lonsdales never die," she said. This time she believed it.

The vision she'd had of Charles and his men fighting hadn't left her mind. She had *seen* him—not that she knew how, only that she had. *Alive.* Fighting for her, for England, for the son he didn't know he had. God help anyone who stood between Charles Humphrey and those he loved.

CHAPTER 36

D*ecember 7, 1941*

ELIZABETH, HETTY, AND ISABELLE AGREED TO SPEND THE holidays in the country at Cunningham House with Eva and Marcus. Elizabeth, with Hetty's assistance, pooled everyone's ration books and purchased as much food as they could from the shops where they were registered and then packed Hetty's Morris Eight with their luggage.

Jarvis remained in London to keep an eye on the townhouse while they were away. Hetty, little Theodore, Elizabeth, and Isabelle all bundled up in their warmest clothes and headed out of London.

Elizabeth had told Philip the previous night when he'd telephoned her that they would be in the country through the new year. If he was able to get leave for the holidays, he and Nathan were to come stay with them.

She longed to see him. Ever since he'd returned to his base, she'd had so little time with him. Granted, she and the others had been busy with the bureau's business and the Auxiliary Fire Service, so much so that she collapsed into bed each night. Yet whenever Philip called, it rallied her spirits to hear his voice.

Snow was falling as they arrived at Cunningham House that evening. Elizabeth parked the car and took Teddy in her arms while Hetty and Isabelle climbed out. The little baby was nearly seven months now and was growing up to be the most adorable little fellow. His eyes were a light gray like his father's, his hair a light gold like both his parents. Yet his behavior was so much like Hetty's that it always made Elizabeth tease her friend about carrying around a miniature version of herself.

The front door of the house opened, and Hetty's parents along with Charles's came down the steps to greet them. Both families had been invited, including Hetty's grandmother, Agnes, to stay with them for the holidays. With twenty-three rooms, Cunningham House had more than enough to spare.

"Where is our Teddy?" Mrs. Byron demanded in a possessive, grandmotherly tone.

"Here, Mrs. Byron." Elizabeth passed Teddy over, who cooed and gurgled in delight. Lady Lonsdale hovered at Mrs. Byron's shoulder and spoke softly to the baby, making him squirm and kick his chubby legs. Brigadier Byron ruffled the hair on Teddy's head before he hugged his daughter, then Elizabeth and Isabelle. In the years since the Marriage Bureau had been born, Brigadier Byron had decided he was a surrogate father to Elizabeth, much like Colonel Cunningham had become.

"How are my girls?" the brigadier asked her and Hetty.

"We are fine, Father." Hetty kissed his cheek, then greeted her in-laws while Hetty's father helped Elizabeth and Isabelle with their travel cases.

"Come in, you lot, before you freeze," Mrs. Harrow called out from the doorway.

Eva came down the stairs, beaming at everyone, her cheeks flushed with color and her eyes bright with joy. She'd been running the bureau's financial affairs from the country while Hetty and Elizabeth handled the meetings in town. Marcus wasn't far behind his sister. He too looked well. In the last seven months, he'd been taking lessons from the colonel and Nathan about everything to do with hunting, riding, tracking, and all manner of gentlemanly activities that took place outdoors, and it seemed to be making him quite happy.

"Everyone getting on all right?" Elizabeth asked the brigadier.

"Oh yes, splendid." Hetty's father smiled warmly. "I've been glad to reconnect with Colonel Cunningham of late. Good man. Glad to see he's back in his own house, even if he doesn't own it. I heard about that sorry affair when he came back from the Great War. Terrible business, that."

By the time Elizabeth joined the others inside and the door was closed against the cold, she was astounded at the gathering of friends and family. Marcus had turned sixteen this past spring, and his coltish limbs were vanishing beneath the tall, muscular form of a young man. He had grown another two inches and was now the same height as Colonel Cunningham.

"I am surprised Lord Sheridan's boy isn't here. Wasn't he living in the house?" Hetty's father asked Elizabeth.

"He was temporarily, but Nathan had to return to Biggin Hill. Even though he can't fly anymore, he's a flight instructor for the new recruits. He promised he'd be back for a few days with Philip soon if they can get leave. We should be expecting them any day." Elizabeth couldn't wait to see Philip. It felt like a lifetime since she'd last seen him.

Elizabeth stepped back and had a moment to watch everyone in the entryway. Hugs and smiles were shared, and for a moment the war seemed so very far away.

The colonel and Mrs. Harrow had settled even more deeply into their affectionate rivalry over the last half of the year. Elizabeth marveled at the pair as the colonel offered the housekeeper a reassuring smile when she asked if anyone was hungry or needed a drink.

Little Teddy was passed about the room and seemed utterly content, regardless whose arms he ended up in. The house had been decorated with garlands, and the colonel announced that he, Marcus, Hetty's father, and Lord Lonsdale would be in charge of selecting a tree to cut down and bring back to the house at some point over the next week.

"You'd better not chop off any fingers out there. I won't be stitching any of them back on before Christmas," Mrs. Harrow warned the men. "Now then, anyone wish to help me with dinner?"

Elizabeth, Isabelle, and Eva volunteered. Hetty and her mother, along with her mother-in-law, took up the job of making everyone drinks in the drawing room.

The large kitchen was cozy and warm. Hints of candied orange peels and freshly mixed vanilla and cinnamon filled the air. Elizabeth wondered who in town Mrs. Harrow had negotiated with to get such rare ingredients.

Eva pulled on an apron and tied it around her waist. "Turn on the radio, Lizzie. Let's have some music."

Elizabeth leaned over the wide counter space by the window in order to reach the radio. Snow frosted the panes and framed the glass, each snowflake tiny and perfect. Music came through the speakers as she brought the radio to life.

Mrs. Harrow set out several bowls on the counter. "The BBC Home Service should be on soon."

Eva hummed along to the music on the radio as she and Mrs. Harrow prepared a Christmas pudding. Elizabeth retrieved an apron for herself and joined in. This was something she loved about Cunningham House. Cooking in the kitchen with Mrs. Harrow and the other girls was always fun, even with the ever-tightening rations. Before the war, she'd tried to cook with her mother, but she had always made it such a chore.

"We want to save our eggs," Mrs. Harrow told her and Eva. "So I've devised a new recipe for Christmas pudding. Eva, fetch the flour. Lizzie, tear up some wholemeal bread into crumbs."

The housekeeper opened one of the cupboards and removed a tin of mixed sweet spice, which she mixed with the flour. She then grated one potato and one carrot over a bowl. Elizabeth passed her the breadcrumbs, and then Mrs. Harrow added a teaspoon of bicarbonate of soda dissolved into two tablespoons of hot milk. It formed a well-greased pudding basin, which was one of Mrs. Harrow's white pots made for baking pudding. After mixing the rest of the ingredients, she set it onto the stove. "Now we'll boil it for four hours."

"What's next?" Eva asked.

"We could make a bit of Christmas sparkle," Mrs. Harrow mused, her hands on her hips as she surveyed the kitchen. "It's hard to make a meal feel special these days. A bit of sparkle might help with that."

"Christmas sparkle?" Elizabeth asked.

"You two have never made Christmas sparkle?" When they shook their heads, Mrs. Harrow sighed dramatically. "Lord, what is the world coming to? Come here, both of you, and watch."

A tune sung by Vera Lynn started up on the radio as Mrs. Harrow retrieved a bowl of holly sprigs she had collected earlier.

"We'll meet again . . . Don't know where . . . Don't know when . . ." Mrs. Harrow sang along with the song. "But I know we'll meet again some sunny day . . . Keep smiling through, just like you always do . . . 'Til the blue skies drive the dark clouds far away . . ."

The song was strangely sad, despite the upbeat notes. A shiver rippled beneath Elizabeth's skin as she thought of all the people she'd met since the war began, and she couldn't help but wonder, would there be anyone she'd never meet again?

Mrs. Harrow interrupted her thoughts. "Come and watch, Lizzie." She showed them how to create a strong solution of Epsom salts, and she then dipped the holly into the solution, making sure to coat each piece fully before she set it down on a plate to dry.

"There. Once it's done, it will look beautifully frosted, like ice," Mrs. Harrow announced proudly and wiped her hands on her apron.

"How very clever!" Elizabeth praised.

The housekeeper preened at the compliment. "Isn't it? My mother taught me that. She always used to say—"

The song on the radio was abruptly cut off, and the broadcaster for BBC Home Service came on. All three women turned to face the radio, their bodies rigid with dread.

"This is the BBC Home Service. Here is the news, and this is Alvar Lidell reading it. Japan's long-threatened aggression in the

Far East began tonight with air attacks on United States naval bases in the Pacific."

Mrs. Harrow gasped. "Oh God . . ."

"Fresh reports are coming in every minute. The latest facts of the situation are these: messages from Tokyo say that Japan has announced a formal declaration of war against both the United States and Britain. Japan's attacks on American naval bases in the Pacific were announced by President Roosevelt in a statement from the White House tonight. The first statement said that the naval base of Pearl Harbor and other naval and military targets on the chief Hawaiian island of Oahu have been attacked from the air. Almost immediately after came the announcement that Manila in the Philippines had also been raided.

"A little while ago, Mr. Stephen Early, White House press secretary, said, 'As far as we know at the moment, the attacks are still going on.' In other words, he said we do not know if the Japanese have bombed and left. Acting on his executive authority, President Roosevelt has ordered the mobilization of the United States Army and given instruction for both the army and the navy to carry out undisclosed orders in preparation for the defense of the United States."

Alvar Lidell paused briefly to draw a breath.

"So much for the official news. Press messages and radio observers on Oahu stated that attacks on the island began early in the morning, and it seemed a hundred or more planes took part. Some reports say that an oil tank was set on fire and the airfield hit. As soon as the planes appeared overhead, antiaircraft guns opened fire and American fighter aircraft also went up. A number of planes are said to have been brought down. Citizens were soon cleared from the streets by naval and military units with the aid of volunteers. Many people went up to the hills to watch the raid. The radio observer said that some damage had been done to Pearl Harbor and that the United States battleship *Oklahoma*, built in 1914, has been hit and a fire started . . ."

Mrs. Harrow dropped the small bowl she'd been holding, and it shattered on the floor. "We're at war with Japan now too?"

"Why would the Japanese attack America?" Eva said in shock. Elizabeth put an arm around Eva's shoulders to comfort her, but her own ears were full of a strange ringing.

The colonel's voice bellowed from the other room, making all three women jump. "Bloody hell!"

Marcus sprinted into the kitchen, skidding to a stop when he saw them.

"Did you hear?" he demanded. "The Japs bombed the Americans."

"Yes, we heard," Eva whispered.

Eva, Elizabeth, and Mrs. Harrow all went into the drawing room, where everyone else was gathered around a second radio, which was still reporting news.

"What does this mean, Colonel Cunningham?" Elizabeth asked. "Is it a good thing?"

"It means the Americans have finally taken a side. *Ours.*"

"It's about bloody time," Hetty's father said. "They've done a decent job of helping us on supplies, what with the Lend-Lease Act, but now they'll be sending troops. What we've needed since '39 were boots on the ground."

The colonel faced the flames crackling in the hearth while the snow fell thick outside. His face was serious and focused as he watched the logs burn.

"We need a full-scale invasion if Europe is to be saved. We lost Africa, Greece . . . even Russia is falling. The Russians are giving it all they've got, but it's villagers against an endless army of Germans."

"I've never been overly fond of Russia," Hetty's mother said. "But the reports we're hearing . . . It says they're fighting in the streets. Every man, woman, and child."

"Yes," Hetty's father agreed. "They're fighting for their home, just as we are. If we can get the Yanks over here . . . we'll finally stand a chance."

Finally stand a chance . . . The words rang inside Elizabeth's head like an ancient bell. Had England been fighting a losing battle all this time? She didn't want to believe that. Men like her brother, Alan, were fighting upon the sea, Philip was fighting in the sky, and Charles was fighting on land. Had none of them risking their lives even mattered until now? She had to believe that good, brave men and women were going to win, that the pure of heart could triumph over the shadowy spread of evil. If they couldn't . . . then what was the point of anything? Evil had no right to even one inch of this beautiful earth.

"Dinner is just about ready," Mrs. Harrow announced. "Why don't we eat? I'm sure they'll update us with more news once they have it." The housekeeper seemed quite determined to distract everyone from the trend of grim thoughts.

CHRISTMAS CAME TWO AND A HALF WEEKS LATER, AND everyone was still in the countryside at Cunningham House. The fir tree that Marcus, the colonel, and Hetty's father had finally chosen stood tall and proud in the largest drawing room on the ground floor.

Mrs. Harrow found a box in the attic that held bits of old

tinsel and other small trinkets that were now being used to decorate the tree. Apparently, the box of decorations had once belonged to the colonel, and he blustered about a bit, directing Elizabeth and Marcus where to put the tinsel and decorations, while the others were busy setting the large dining room table for dinner. Once he seemed convinced they needed no more supervision, he wandered off to find a cigar.

"Do you think we'll still be at war in two years, Lizzie?" Marcus asked. He carefully placed a red painted glass orb on one of the branches.

"Two years? No, we'll have beaten them back by then," Elizabeth said confidently, but they both knew her words were more hope than certainty.

"Eva won't like it, but I want to be a Commando someday, like Charles. I've been training with the colonel four days a week after I finish my schoolwork. I'm a crack shot now, he says. He's taught me all sorts of things, like survival in the woods, camouflage, and hunting for food," Marcus declared with pride, but Elizabeth saw no boyish foolishness in him. Where other lads his age might think to play soldier, Marcus knew the reality of this war as a man.

His homeland had been overrun, his parents murdered and thrown into a mass grave. He'd left his world behind and bravely grown into another. He wasn't a boy, hadn't been for a long time, and Elizabeth had to remind herself of that.

"I know you want to fight, Marcus." She set down the bit of leftover tinsel in the box he held out as he stood next to her. She had to tilt her head up to look at him.

"You won't try to stop me, Lizzie?" he asked in a low voice, afraid of being overheard by his sister.

"No, I won't. But if you go, you make a promise that you'll

come back. You understand? You come back *alive*. None of us here would survive burying you."

Marcus held a sad smile. "People always think Hetty is the tougher of you two. She's hard on the outside, soft on the inside. But you . . . you're all smiles and sweetness on the outside—and unbreakable steel underneath." Marcus's brown eyes moved over her face as if truly seeing her for the first time. "And if I didn't come home, you'd hold everyone together, wouldn't you." It wasn't a question.

Trying to tease him and failing, she said, "You'd better not give me such a task."

A terrible sense of doom filled Elizabeth like black smoke until she felt sick with it. How many people had to perish before enough was enough?

Eva spoke up from the doorway. "Lizzie? We have some unexpected guests I thought you'd like to welcome." Her lips carried a soft smile, as though trying to hide her excitement.

Elizabeth gave Marcus a brief, tight hug and then rushed toward the front of the house, wondering who it was.

Five men stood in the entryway, dusting snow off their uniform coats. Nathan and Philip were the closest to her.

"Lizzie." Nathan captured her in a warm hug before he surrendered her to Philip.

"Hello," Philip said solemnly, but there was a twinkle in his eyes as he caught her by the waist and pulled her against him.

"Hello," she replied, blushing. "I didn't know you were coming." She'd only been watching the windows for the last week, hoping to see him and Nathan arrive. He hadn't been sure he'd be able to get leave, but she'd still been hopeful.

"We were at the train station, and we found a few stray pups.

We thought you wouldn't mind taking them in over Christmas," Philip said with that twinkle still in his eyes.

"Stray pups?" Elizabeth said as the men behind Philip and Nathan turned around. The one in the middle made her quake with joy.

"Alan!" She threw herself at her little brother.

Alan laughed and held her tight. "I hope you don't mind? We were just leaving Mum and Dad's, and I thought we'd spend a few days here before reporting back for duty." Without letting her go, he nodded to the two naval officers beside him. "This is Cecil Brown, and that is Robert Butler, but we call him Pete. We met during officer training. We're all assigned to the same ship."

The two young men were close to Alan's age. All of them were indeed pups, as Philip had called them. Young, bright-eyed, and full of life. Seeing her brother here was a wonderful surprise.

"We would love to stay through Christmas, if there's a few rooms left? We can bunk together if we need to." Alan chuckled, and his friends laughed too, as though at some private memory they had of sleeping cramped in bunk beds in the barracks.

"Nonsense," the colonel said as he stepped into the entryway. "There's plenty of room for lads like you. Welcome." He shook hands with the three newcomers. "So, you're Lizzie's clever brother? The one who handles the radar on ships?" the colonel asked as he sized Alan up.

"I am indeed," Alan answered respectfully.

"What ship do you lads sail with?"

"We were on the HMS *Penelope*, but we're transferring soon to the HMS *Charybdis*. It's a Dido-class light cruiser."

"Well, it sounds like you lads will be close to home. That ship tends to prowl the Channel frequently to keep U-boats from reaching the Atlantic, or so I hear."

Elizabeth shot a surprised glance at the colonel, wondering how he managed to know so much about the navy while living way out in the country. The man still had his connections, it seemed.

Mrs. Harrow interrupted. "You'll have enough time to talk about all that nonsense later." She beamed at the three young sailors. "You'll be needing a cup of tea, I expect, won't you, lads?"

Everyone followed the housekeeper into the kitchen, except for Philip and Alan.

Elizabeth hugged her brother again. "Oh, Alan . . . You've grown!" She chuckled as she realized he truly had grown, both up and out. He now had the strong, broad shoulders of a man. Gone was the boy of eighteen he'd been when she'd last seen him. The man before her was twenty..

"You're still *you*," her brother said with delight. "God, Lizzie. It's so good to see you."

"How long can you stay?" She wanted him to stay forever, but she'd be lucky to have but a blink of time with him.

His eyes shadowed a little with disappointment. "Only three days."

"Then we'll make the most of it."

She turned to Philip. "Thank you," she mouthed at him. He smiled and nodded at her, as though she were his queen and he was happy to obey her command. Elizabeth blushed as she and Alan walked toward the kitchen.

Her brother leaned in to whisper, "I like him, Lizzie. He seems like a good chap."

On that, Elizabeth agreed.

THE NEXT THREE DAYS WERE SOME OF THE HAPPIEST Elizabeth had had in a long time. Every room in the house was filled with smiling faces and laughter. Music echoed through the corridors late into the night. They danced after dinner in the library and played games like charades and bridge every evening before dinner. Little Teddy became enamored with the Christmas tree and kept trying to pull the tinsel from it. Lady Lonsdale and Mrs. Byron quickly developed a sixth sense of whenever their grandson seemed to make a crawl toward the tree, causing one or both of the adoring grandmas to be there to scoop him up and cover his face with kisses.

Presents were exchanged and songs were sung by the fire while Mrs. Harrow passed out glasses of sherry. Through it all, Elizabeth felt the invisible stirrings of her heart tying around each person in the room.

During the final night of their stay at Cunningham House, Alan and his friends fell asleep by the Christmas tree, stretched out, sleeping the deep sleep of children. She stood there a long moment and gazed fondly down at them all. It was one thing to receive frequent letters from Alan, but it was such another thing entirely to have him here with all of the other people she loved. She couldn't have wished for a better Christmas.

Elizabeth draped blankets over the three young men before adding a few more logs to the fire and sneaking back up to her bed. Philip waited for her in the corridor in his pajamas and housecoat. He always seemed to be there whenever she needed him.

He gently caught her in his arms as she started to tremble. "Everything all right?"

"Oh, Philip, they're so young. Still so very young. I wish . . ."

He tilted her chin up to see her eyes.

"I wish we had more time . . ." It felt like she held the remnants of a shattered hourglass, and all the grains were slipping through her fingers. It was like trying to catch fallen leaves as winter winds began to blow them away, erasing all memories of the warm and happy summer that had come before. She buried her face against his chest to hide her tears. "I'm so tired of winter."

Philip kissed the crown of her hair. "I know, darling, I know."

After a long moment, she lifted her hand up to take one of his and pulled him toward her bedchamber.

They paused in the doorway, and she reached up to loosen the belt of his housecoat just as he threaded his fingers through the hair at the nape of her neck and held her for a long kiss. He was leaving in the morning with Nathan and the others, and she couldn't waste any more precious time.

"Stay with me?" she asked when their mouths finally broke apart.

"I'll take every night with you in my arms that I can have," he whispered before leaning in and kissing her. The feel of his warm lips made her heart swell.

The moment the door closed, Elizabeth sought his lips with hers again, and his strong arms surrounded her body. She was *home*, and for now home was safe and whole. It would have to do. She would meet whatever came in the morning with undaunted courage and unbreakable steel.

CHAPTER 37

F *ebruary 1943*

"No, no, Teddy darling. Put that down." Hetty gently removed the telephone cord from Teddy's chubby little fingers. He had been ringing the phone by yanking the cord over and over. Then he turned to his mother and grinned cheekily. Even after all these years, they still hadn't been able to fix that.

Elizabeth laughed. "Clever little thing, isn't he? He knows exactly what he's doing."

Hetty sat on the floor by her desk and pulled her almost-two-year-old son into her arms.

"Mama!" Teddy proclaimed proudly.

Elizabeth could scarcely believe that it had been almost two years since Teddy had been born at the Ritz hotel in the middle of a bombing. Charles still had no idea that he was a father, and Elizabeth knew that weighed heavily on Hetty. They'd been trying to send letters to him, but they never seemed to make it to him. The commandos traveled too fast and their missions were too secretive for them to be found and reached easily. Elizabeth knew Hetty was silently cataloging all of the moments in Teddy's life that his father was missing. The boy's first steps, his first words, his first laugh and smile had all been missed by a man who would have given *anything* to be here to see it.

"You are as incorrigible as your father, aren't you?" Hetty asked the little boy, then kissed his cheek. He bounced up and down on his legs. Now that Teddy could walk, the little chap mucked about everywhere. Elizabeth couldn't stop laughing at his antics whenever he got into places he shouldn't.

"I know I should let Lady Lonsdale take him to the country house, but the thought of being separated from him leaves me restless. When the air-raid sirens start, I'm frantic to have him with me."

"It's all right, Hetty. You're his mother. It's natural." Elizabeth brushed a hand over Teddy's blond curls, and he grinned up at her, knowing full well that he could do anything and she and Hetty would let him.

Miss Plumley came into the office, her face radiant. "We have two clients outside ready to pay their after-marriage fee."

Elizabeth brightened. "Oh? Send them in."

The secretary stepped into the hallway and then opened the door again to let John Kirby inside. Hazel Cochran, the young woman who'd found herself with child nearly two years ago after being attacked during a bombing, was with him, her arm linked with his. The young woman smiled at them shyly, but Elizabeth saw joy in the woman's eyes.

"We really should have come in sooner," John began apologetically. "We've been married a year and a half, but, well, I enlisted in the army and was away on deployment. But I'm home now, if only briefly, and we wanted to come in and pay our fee together."

"Heavens, has it really been that long?" Elizabeth asked. Hetty lifted Teddy up on one hip as she joined them. Most of the time they kept careful track of the after-marriage fees, but now that men were deploying, they were learning that many marriages had occurred quickly and the couples were finally writing to them and enclosing money, or their wives were dropping by the office to pay the fees.

"Tell us how it happened. Don't leave anything out." Elizabeth pulled them both into chairs by the desk.

"Well . . . where to start?" John's face reddened as he looked at Hazel. She took over the story.

"We went out for a dinner that night we first met in person after writing to each other. I couldn't do a lunch meeting because of my employment. But then we heard the sirens go off, and it was simply chaos. We were running, and . . . oh, it was all terribly embarrassing."

"We happen to be passing the Windmill," John said with a chuckle. "That's a place where the Yanks go to see scantily clad women pose for an audience in artistic ways. We took shelter in a café across the street and met a few of the Windmill girls there who were also hiding from the bombs." John cleared his throat. "They were clothed, of course."

Hetty and Elizabeth shared an amused look. They both knew about the Windmill. It was quite popular, especially with all the American soldiers who had flooded London since early last year after the Pearl Harbor attacks.

"Anyway," Hazel continued. "There was a stable nearby, and it caught fire. The horses were screaming, and the sound was simply awful." Hazel shuddered, and John put a hand over hers.

"We got in and started covering the horses' eyes with anything we could find," he added. "Then we led them out of the stables one by one until we freed them all. We were wandering around London for three hours during the bombing with eight horses in tow. Two of the girls from the Windmill helped us. We finally found a police station with enough room in their stables to take all of the horses." John smiled at his wife. "After that, I got down on one knee right in front of a startled constable and asked Hazel to marry me in the middle of a bombed-out street at four o'clock in the morning."

"And I said yes." Hazel beamed at him before she opened her handbag and held out a photo that showed a child. A boy of a year or so old.

"This is Andrew." She gave the photo to Hetty, who then showed it to Teddy.

The boy pointed a little finger at Andrew. "Baby!"

"Yes, that's a baby named Andrew," Hetty told him. He clapped his hands in delight.

"Oh, this is wonderful." Elizabeth took the photo from Hetty and admired the child.

"Andrew is a fine lad, and a fine son," John said, his face full of pride.

Elizabeth's throat tightened as a flood of strong emotions rolled through her. The child that had been conceived in a nightmare had become a blessing for John and Hazel.

"It's like you said." Hazel looked at Hetty and Elizabeth. "He's a part of me. Once I accepted that, nothing else mattered."

"He's every inch my son, no matter how he came into this world." John said this with such open honesty that even Hetty sniffled. He looked at his wife, his gaze softening. "I knew the moment I heard her story that day in the office, she was the one for me."

"He's right, Hazel—he told us that day he believed you were his destiny," Elizabeth said.

Hazel's lashes lowered, and a fresh blush stained her cheeks. "It's strange to think of how happy one can be in such times, isn't it? That there is still light illuminating the darkness."

"Indeed," Hetty agreed. Elizabeth knew she was thinking of Charles and worrying about him.

"Anyway, we finally had time to come see you at the same time, pay our fee, and offer you our heartfelt thanks in person." John reached into his coat for his pocketbook. "How much do we owe?"

"Let me go check the amount." Hetty handed her son to Elizabeth and went to retrieve the paperwork.

John stood and chucked Teddy under the chin. Teddy giggled. "He's Hetty's boy isn't he?"

"Oh, yes, and he's just as delightful stubborn as she is."

"Has she heard from her husband lately?"

"Charles?"

John nodded.

"We haven't had any letters in almost a month, why do you know him?"

"I had the fortune of meeting recently. The man saved the lives of more than thirty men three months ago, including my own."

Hetty gasped as she stood in the inner office doorway clutching their bureau file. "He what? You saw my Charles?"

"I did. We were in France . . ." John's eyes softened. "Christ, I imagine you couldn't hear from him often, not with the way the Commandos work."

"No, I get a letter every month or so, but I can't seem to get any letters to him in return. He is on the move all the time." Hetty passed Elizabeth the paperwork, and Elizabeth returned her son to her.

"What happened, Mr. Kirby? How did your paths cross?" Elizabeth pressed. She knew how desperate Hetty was for even the smallest bit of news about her husband.

"I'm afraid I can't give too much detail. My unit was pinned down while a pair of Panzer tanks rolled toward the only place we could hide. One of the Commandos threw an incendiary on top of the tank, and as the Germans tried to escape, the Commandos took them out. God knows where they were hiding, but they showed up just in time. I saw Charles—I didn't know his name at the time, of course. He and three men stormed the tank and took out the driver. Then they started to drive the tank and fired on the second one that had been coming toward us. They blew the damn thing sky-high."

John cleared his throat. "After that, we were able to take the remaining Germans as prisoners. It's why I'm here. I was part of a prisoner escort to England. That night after he saved us, I met your husband as we ate around the campfire. The Commandos stayed with us until just past dawn, then vanished into the mist like ghosts."

"Charles was unhurt?" Hetty asked in a small, frightened voice.

"He had a scratch or two, but not more than that. He's a good man, your husband. Bloody brave." John was quiet a moment, his next words solemn. "The shadow of war hasn't touched him the way it has the others. When he spoke of his wife, he looked like he was lounging on Brighton Beach on holiday, not huddled around a small fire in a bombed-out French village."

Elizabeth put an arm around Hetty's shoulders before she started to cry.

"I hope that my news of him is welcome?" John asked, seeing the pain in Hetty's eyes.

"Yes, it is. We worry about him. That's all," Elizabeth assured him.

"John dear, let's pay our fee and give Mrs. Humphrey some time alone," Hazel said gently.

"Yes, of course." John's face reddened a little, but he paid the fee and hugged Elizabeth once more, and Hetty too. Then he and Hazel bid them farewell.

"Be safe, John," Hetty managed to say as the veterinarian reached the doorway. "*Please* be safe."

"I will. I have everything to fight for, don't I?" he said and kissed his wife's forehead. "*Everything in the world*," he said more softly. Then he and Hazel left.

Hetty's legs gave out once she and Teddy and Elizabeth were alone. She collapsed into her desk chair, holding her son close. Teddy played with the strand of pearls about Hetty's neck, clinking them softly together.

"Oh, Lizzie." Hetty's eyes filled with tears. "He's storming tanks . . ."

"And saving lives," Elizabeth reminded her.

"He doesn't even know about Teddy. It's been two years. He's missed so much—he's missed everything. What if he . . . ?"

Elizabeth knelt beside her. "What if he comes home and sees

Teddy and you waiting for him at the train station? Can you imagine how his face will look?"

Hetty closed her eyes and drew in a deep breath before slowly letting it back out.

"Yes, I can see his face," Hetty murmured as she started to smile.

"Then all will be well, won't it?" Elizabeth asked.

"All will be well." Hetty smiled.

*J*UNE *1943*

Elizabeth was at her desk in the bureau when a young man in uniform stepped into the room. Elizabeth stood automatically, ready to offer him a registration form. They'd had so many soldiers coming through in the last few months they'd almost wondered if they'd ever have any nonmilitary clients again.

"Can I help you, Mr.—" Her words died abruptly as she recognized the man's face when he removed his cap.

"Hello, Lizzie." The young soldier smiled at her bashfully. "How do I look?" He waved a hand down the front of his new uniform.

"Marcus . . . ," she whispered. "Oh Lord, does Eva know?"

His smile faded. "I just came from Cunningham House. She knows, and she's not very happy with me at the moment. I leave tomorrow. I only just found out."

"You're leaving already? For where?"

"Africa."

"Africa?" Elizabeth said faintly. "That's so far away . . . Eva needs you."

"She'll be fine," Marcus said solemnly. "Nathan is planning to propose to her—not that I'm supposed to tell anyone, mind you." He smiled again. "But he wanted me to know his intentions before I left and have my blessing. I gave it. He is good for her, isn't he?"

Elizabeth was too stunned to speak for a moment. Marcus wasn't even eighteen. His birthday wasn't until later that year. They'd had plans for a big celebration. She couldn't even think about Nathan and Eva for the moment.

Marcus took her hands in his. She stared up at him in wonder. He was a man now, and she saw that. But there would always be a part of her that would cling to the memory of the fourteen-year-old boy she'd first met.

"Can you wait a few more months?"

He tucked his cap under one arm in a way she'd seen so many handsome young men in uniform do. The look on his face was one that broke her heart. It spoke of all the pain he'd carried over the last few years.

"Even one day more is too much. You were there when the *Times* reported that Jews were being massacred. More than a million have been killed since the war began. The news of the extermination camps, Lizzie . . . I have nightmares about those gas chambers. The Germans are exterminating people as if they were nothing. Every day I'm not out there fighting, that's one more day those camps stay open."

Marcus paused, his eyes full of agony as he looked at her.

"I can't help but think of what the world has already lost. Artists, scientists, dreamers. Men and women who could have made this world a better place . . . And the children. Children like Eva and I who couldn't escape in time. I think about them the most . . . those little innocent lives ended so violently, so cruelly." He suddenly halted in his speech, his voice rough with emotion as he continued. "I remember the colonel asking me what I would do if I faced the men who wanted the world to burn. Well, now I can do something. If I fight for no other reason, I fight to save those children. Tell me you understand, Lizzie." He squeezed her hands in his, the desperation in his voice making her tremble.

Elizabeth nodded, biting her lip. She did understand, even though she didn't want to. She thought of that little girl across the street from Isabelle's old home who'd died in her arms. Even one death was too many.

"You can't leave without saying goodbye to the others," Elizabeth whispered. It felt like she was swallowing glass.

"I said goodbye to Nathan and my sister, Mrs. Harrow, and the colonel too. He's done everything he could to prepare me. I feel as if I can handle whatever I need to."

Colonel Cunningham knew better than most what Marcus would be facing in the war. It might not be a war fought in trenches, but it was a war full of blood and death all the same. Elizabeth had to trust that he'd given Marcus every lesson he could to help him survive.

"Oh, but Hetty isn't here."

"Not here for what?" Hetty asked from the doorway, a bag of groceries in her arms. She gasped when she recognized the soldier. "Marcus? Is that you?"

"Hello, Hetty," he greeted and hugged her after she set her groceries down.

"So you're off?" Hetty asked, her voice a little shaky.

"To Africa."

Hetty nodded and cleared her throat. "Well . . . Do your duty, soldier. And you'd better come back, understand?"

"Of course. I wouldn't dare disobey you, would I?" he teased.

He was like all the other young men who'd come in through the bureau's doors in the last few months. All smiles and playful words, yet she could see they knew what was to come and wanted to cling to sunny days and happy memories for as long as they could. She remembered thinking once that it was better to see the boys off with smiles rather than tears, better that they carry laughter and gaiety in their hearts as long as they could. Because some would never return, and those who did would carry things far heavier than shadows within them. It was like the Great War all over again, only this time it was far, far worse.

"You'll come back. We'll see you for Christmas," Hetty said, as if it was a guaranteed thing. She wouldn't say goodbye, neither would Elizabeth, and Marcus seemed to understand.

"Until Christmas, then," he agreed. "Though I might need a second bicycle if I meet a nice girl." He winked at Hetty, and her lower lip quivered. Children grew up too fast. In the blink of an eye, Marcus had gone from a boy to a man. The fate of so many rested on the shoulders of those who were so young.

I wish I could fight in his place, Elizabeth thought with a breaking heart.

They embraced again, neither of them wanting to let him go. Elizabeth saw Hetty tremble as she tried to smile one last time as Marcus walked out the bureau doors.

"How many more?" Hetty asked after Marcus had departed. "How many?"

"I don't know . . . ," Elizabeth said.

"What if we're still at war when Teddy is . . ." Hetty choked on the rest of her words and buried her face in her hands until Elizabeth came over and wrapped her in a fierce hug.

"That won't happen. Teddy won't have to fight, because men

like Marcus, Charles, Alan, and Philip are out there right now fighting for him. For all of us."

Hetty sighed and steadied her breath. "I know. It's not like me to be such a watering pot, but ever since I had Teddy, I just worry so."

Elizabeth stared at the stacks of letters from new clients on their desks. For the first time since they'd opened the bureau, she hadn't really thought about what this job meant aside from people finding love. But it meant so much more. Not just to her, but to everyone they worked with.

Dozens of cards and letters, even photographs of smiling couples, were propped open on windowsills or pinned to a large corkboard on the wall. Dozens of reminders of why their work mattered. For every man who left to fight, they did their best to give him a reason to come home alive. They'd given the women a reason to stay strong and hold England together. Love was the essence of that strength for those who fought far away, and for those who defended the innocent here at home.

Elizabeth pulled the stack of letters toward her and handed Hetty half of them.

"We have work to do," she said.

Hetty took a deep breath. "Yes, we do."

The bureau would stay open and keep hope alive for everyone as long as they could.

OCTOBER 30, 1943

England seemed to try to fight to hold winter at bay as warm weather clung to the isle long after it normally would have turned cold. Elizabeth and Hetty joined Eva at Cunningham

House for a week to celebrate Halloween. It was Elizabeth's favorite holiday, and she never missed a chance to play snap-dragon or duck for apples.

Eva had managed Marcus's departure well, but Elizabeth suspected that Nathan's frequent visits to Cunningham House helped her. Nathan's warm smiles, affectionate manner, and positive mood always seemed to pull Eva up whenever sorrows began to weigh her down. Today she was smiling and telling Hetty and Elizabeth all about her work on the latest bookkeeping for the bureau and how Mrs. Harrow and the colonel had been arguing about the funniest things. Elizabeth had missed such moments and was glad to hear her friend recount them with such amusement.

It was rather strange to think that Cunningham House had begun as a refuge for the bureau offices in case London was destroyed by the bombings, yet it had transformed into a second home, a place of escape for whenever escape was most needed. Elizabeth smiled a little at the thought of the big country manor house standing for centuries to come, unchanging, reliable.

The three of them had gone to pick blackberries in the woods, but the bushes they'd found yielded few decent berries since it was so late in the fall, so they decided to walk and talk instead. It had been months since the three of them had been in the country together. Elizabeth missed the comfort of the old rambling manor more than she'd ever realized.

The gold grasses of the meadows felt warm, though the trees were starting to yield to winter's harsh approach. Polished chest-nuts and green-buff acorns littered the forest floor beneath the trees, causing the girls to slip when they walked, which made them all giggle and shriek as they caught each other to steady themselves, and for a brief moment they felt like young girls again. Girls who'd never seen German bombers, dead bodies, or felt the heat of burning houses. They were, for a brief time, innocent again.

The mix of woods and fields near Cunningham House remained unchanged despite the war. Nature still held its dominance over the land, unmarred by bomb craters. Elizabeth wondered what all the craters would look like in a decade. Other places in England had suffered bombings. Once-fertile fields had been wrecked by massive holes, and pieces of shrapnel had been embedded into the trunks of trees, leaving them scarred. She couldn't help but wonder how nature would fight against the destruction in the fullness of time.

"Lizzie, Hetty, I must speak to you about something." Eva's face was suddenly red as they reached the road that would lead back to Cunningham House. "I have something to confess."

"Oh?" Elizabeth and Hetty shared a glance of surprise.

"I have been seeing Mr. Sheridan. *Nathan.* He's been courting me for a long time. We . . . we wanted your blessing to marry."

"Our blessing?" Hetty's brows rose. "Eva, you have it, of course."

"Oh, thank heavens. I know you both worked so hard to match Nathan to other clients, but, well, he told me he's loved me ever since that night he saved Marcus and me, when we first met Hetty. He said there's never been anyone else for him for a long time. Are you upset?" Eva's hands shook around the nearly empty basket of blackberries.

Hetty chuckled. "Upset? No, of course not."

"We knew Nathan was in love with you," Elizabeth said, feeling a little glow of joy light up within her. "He stopped letting us introduce him to clients a long time ago."

"Did he?" Eva asked.

"Oh yes, we suspected he had feelings for you then," Hetty added. "When did you know you felt the same about him?"

Eva's face reddened further. "I was so worried about Marcus and the war and just remembering to breathe that I'm not sure I was really paying attention. Then one day I realized I was holding Nathan's hand as we were walking and talking together. I hadn't even realized I'd reached for him. We just . . ." She smiled. "I didn't think love was supposed to be easy. But with him, it is."

"I know what you mean." Hetty's expression was soft and wistful. "The right person doesn't make love a struggle. Life has struggles enough—love should be easy so it can help us endure."

"After Marcus enlisted I was so lost, but Nathan was there. He's *always* been there. I just ran to him and he held me, and I knew that as long as I had him, everything would be all right."

The three of them continued up the road toward the house, feeling like the last bit of fall would linger perhaps, just a little bit longer before winter finally triumphed.

"We should celebrate. How about a toast?" Hetty proposed as they stepped inside the house.

"Yes, a toast!" Elizabeth agreed. "Mrs. Harrow? Some glasses of sherry with our luncheon, please."

"Sherry?" the housekeeper called from the corridor. "What are we celebrating, dear?"

"Eva is getting married."

"What's that? Someone's getting married?" The colonel popped out of his study and met them in the corridor, clearly curious. He tucked an unlit cigar into his waistcoat pocket and peered at the three ladies facing him.

"I am, sir. To Nathan," Eva replied bashfully.

The colonel smiled, his mustache twitching. "Well, that *is* good news, isn't it?"

Hetty nudged Eva with an elbow and flashed her a teasing grin. "It certainly is."

The five of them celebrated after lunch with glasses of sherry.

"To Eva and Nathan." Mrs. Harrow sniffed and wiped tears from her eyes.

"Indeed. Here's to our darling girl," Colonel Cunningham said to Eva. He sipped his glass along with the ladies. Suddenly, the colonel straightened in his chair, his body stilling as he looked at something out the window behind Elizabeth.

Elizabeth turned around in her seat at the table and saw a car had come down the long drive and parked in front of the house. Two men in naval uniforms had gotten out of the car and were headed toward the front door. A moment later the bell rang.

"I'll get it," Mrs. Harrow said and started to rise.

The colonel placed a hand on the housekeeper's shoulder as he stood. "No, let me. Finish your drink, Maggie."

The colonel left the dining room. Elizabeth got to her feet, compelled to join him. She hoped it might be Alan. He had said he would have more time ashore now that his latest assignment had brought him closer to home. She reached the door and smiled as she saw Alan's friends Cecil Brown and Pete Butler speaking softly to the colonel.

"Cecil, Pete, is Alan with you?" Elizabeth asked.

The colonel turned to face her, his eyes dark with pain. Cecil and Pete slowly removed their hats and straightened their shoulders. No one was smiling. No one was . . .

Elizabeth's ears began to ring.

"Elizabeth." The weight of that one word crushed every castle of hope she'd ever built.

"Alan's been killed," the colonel said.

Elizabeth's eyes flew between the three men as the words pierced her in place. Everything said after that seemed to slow down.

"Our ship sank in the Channel. Four hundred men were lost, including the captain." Pete cleared his throat and took a step forward. "Alan . . ." He struggled for words. "He saved our lives, Lizzie, mine and Cecil's. He went down fighting for all of us."

Elizabeth's chest burned, and when she finally was able to draw breath again, it felt like she was dying, as though her body no longer wanted to go on.

"When did . . . ?" She could barely get the words out. A cold feeling crept through her body, freezing her soul.

"About a week ago. We've only just been able to get back to shore to make notifications to the families. We went to Cambridge first to see Mr. and Mrs. Mowbray this morning."

Strangely, she remembered that day. The wind had howled like a wolf and rattled the shutters of Cunningham House as she had lain awake most of the night with a strange, unsettling stillness inside her. It was as if her heart had already known what her mind could not.

"Thank you for coming to tell us," the colonel said. "Do you want to stay for a bit?"

"I wish we could, but . . . we have more notifications to give. Too many," Cecil said. "We came here first after visiting Cambridge. We knew that was important to Alan. He . . ." Cecil didn't finish. He cleared his throat and glanced away. "Now we have other calls to pay, other families to notify . . ."

"Yes, right . . . of course." The colonel seemed to understand what Cecil couldn't bring himself to say.

There was one thing above all others that Elizabeth hated about war besides losing the people she loved. It was the way war robbed people of speech. So many things were left *unsaid*, so many words became too hard to say. Too many bright and beautiful things were broken by war. It was as though someone had taken a knife and sliced a piece of her heart from her chest.

She remembered how their neighbor Mrs. Wesley had screamed as she held her dead daughter in her arms that night of the bombing. That animalistic sound of rage and grief so violent it went beyond one's humanity. That cry echoed in Elizabeth's head, and she dared not open her mouth lest it escape.

Cecil and Pete placed their hats back on their heads with polite and sober nods. They cast one more look at her before walking out the door.

The colonel closed the door behind them and wrapped Elizabeth in his arms. She did not break, even as he held her. She shuddered violently; it was as though an entire world of war was contained within her, trying to get out. She wanted to scream, to rage, to fight and claw at she knew not what . . . But none of that would bring Alan home. Nothing ever would.

Her teeth chattered now as though some chill had lodged itself in her very soul. The colonel said nothing as he continued to hold her. Words had no meaning in this place of grief, and so he gave what small comfort he could to her now.

She wasn't sure how long they stayed there in the entryway. Her mind drifted through the past, beating against the currents of time. A thousand brief memories of Alan and their childhood drifted past her as though she were sailing in a shallow boat on a river that reflected her life. She reached out in her mind for each memory, watching them ripple into eternity. Elizabeth wanted to disappear into those memories forever and never come back. She didn't want to live in a world where Alan wasn't alive.

"It's all right to cry," the colonel said. "Your tears honor him.

The pain you're feeling, that is a testament to *how much* he is loved. That boy is *loved*, Lizzie, and he knows it. Wherever he is now, he feels it," the older man whispered as he stroked her hair.

His words undid the last bit of control she had, and she cried. Her great, heaving sobs went deep, and the halls of Cunningham House echoed with them.

"I'd hoped never to feel this again . . ." Mrs. Harrow's voice came from behind Elizabeth. "All those beautiful boys with such bright futures and sunny dreams. They fight a war that never should have been, and so many never come home. I lost my husband, Jim, in the Great War . . ."

"I never knew, Maggie," the colonel said. "You never said . . ."

Elizabeth didn't open her eyes. Her breathing slowed as she listened to Mrs. Harrow.

"I never talk about him. His memory is so precious that it pains me to do so. But now I wish I had. Isn't that what we do to keep those we love alive? So long as we speak of them, they're still here with us, aren't they?"

The colonel nodded. "We owe them nothing less."

Elizabeth finally lifted her face and opened her eyes as a heavy, hollow void opened up and grew in her heart, creating a cavern filled only with pain. She looked to the housekeeper, tears clinging to her lashes.

"How did you go on?" she asked.

Mrs. Harrow came over and placed a hand on her shoulder, giving it a gentle squeeze.

"My Jim loved me, and I knew he'd be cross with me if I didn't manage without him. Do you think Alan would be pleased if you sat down and gave up?"

"No . . ." Elizabeth caught a flash of memory of Alan racing her down the road past the colleges of Cambridge one summer.

He'd been preparing for a footrace, and she'd been helping him practice. She'd been tired and called for him to stop and wait for her. Even though he was years younger than her, he'd always had much longer legs. He'd stopped and laughed and called out, "Come on, Lizzie! You can do this all day!"

She could see his face so clearly. Those bright blue eyes so like hers and that irresistible smile. She could hear his voice as though he was right beside her. The war had claimed his body, but she held his heart and soul.

Mrs. Harrow was right. Whatever bright future that might have been his was lost beneath the waves, but his memory could never die, not as long as she held fast to it.

She swallowed thickly, wiping tears from her eyes as she saw Eva and Hetty standing behind the housekeeper, their faces shining with tears. Little Teddy clung to Hetty's skirts and stared up at Elizabeth with worried gray eyes.

"Lizzie no cry," he said, his lower lip quivering as though he was on the verge of tears because she was.

"Oh, Teddy darling." Elizabeth knelt, and the little boy ambled toward her. She folded him into her arms, holding him tight. Teddy's tiny fingers twined in her hair, and he whispered softly in her ear, "No cry . . . no cry . . ."

When Elizabeth looked up, she saw Hetty had covered her mouth to keep from making a sound.

"I won't cry anymore," she promised the boy. "Except perhaps happy tears." She kissed the golden crown of his hair and promised herself that she would only cry from joy for now on. For Alan, for all the boys who would never come home, she would remain strong.

Elizabeth wiped her eyes again. "I should ring my parents."

"Here, let me take him. I'll feed him a few biscuits in the

kitchen." Mrs. Harrow picked up Teddy, and Elizabeth walked back toward the study where she could call her parents and help make plans for a service.

❦

AN EMPTY GRAVE MARKED THE MEMORY OF ALAN MOWBRAY. The service was small and private, but Elizabeth was glad that Philip and Nathan were able to attend. Colonel Cunningham had called the base at Biggin Hill to tell them the news, and Philip had been given two days leave to come and stay with Elizabeth at Cunningham House while she and her parents made preparations. Even without a body, they'd still wanted to plan a service.

As the empty casket was lowered into the cold November ground, Elizabeth removed her gloves and bent, digging her fingers into the English soil Alan had died defending. She sprinkled the dirt upon the engraved plate that bore Alan's name. Beneath his name was a quote she'd heard Alan say last Christmas when he'd been visiting her.

"Warriors are those who choose to stand between an enemy and all they hold sacred."

The vicar now ended the service. "We honor Alan James Mowbray, son and brother. Your day of duty is done, Alan. Now your day of rest has begun."

Elizabeth turned to face her parents. In all the years since she'd returned home from India, she'd felt like a stranger in her own family. Yet now, in grief, she felt part of herself connected to her mother and father again. It would never be a relationship of love and laughter like what the colonel and Mrs. Harrow gave her, but she'd reconciled her feelings since losing Alan.

"Thank you for helping us plan this, Lizzie," her father said. He kept his chin high with pride for his son's sacrifice, but Elizabeth knew he was hurting so deeply it would carve rivers into his soul.

She and her mother looked at each other, and her mother's mouth trembled before she embraced Elizabeth.

"It's all right," Elizabeth whispered in her mother's ear as her mother softly wept. "It's all right."

"We only have you now, don't we?" her mother said in a broken voice.

"And I'll always be here if you want me," Elizabeth promised her.

Philip kept his arm around Elizabeth's shoulders as they began to walk toward the gates of the cemetery. When Elizabeth reached Hetty's car, she turned back once more, staring at that lonely hill.

"We'll meet again someday, in a place where there is no more darkness," she promised.

For a moment, she thought she could hear her brother's voice. *"Come on, Lizzie . . . You can do this all day . . ."* And she would. She would keep going because her love for her brother was stronger than the pain of his loss.

CHAPTER 38

A *pril 1944*

It had been nearly six months since Alan died. Elizabeth found herself settling into a steady rhythm of work and life. With intermittent bombings and less frequent air raids, life had seemed strangely more bearable in many ways. She'd focused on her friends and the unofficial family she'd formed in the last five years. As an aunt of sorts to little Teddy, she found joy in the small moments, the quiet moments when sunlight poured in through the windows and the way the flowers bloomed in the pots on the roof of the Marriage Bureau's office.

Every day the mailman delivered letters, she felt renewed with hope, knowing she had a chance to help other people find love. It was the only purpose in life that could have kept her afloat on a sea of grief after her brother's death. She'd learned only the previous day that their clients Damien Russell and Penelope had formally adopted Cliff and Nella after learning their parents had died. It was bittersweet news. Elizabeth mourned the loss for the children, but they'd grow up the rest of their lives loved and cared for by two wonderful new parents.

One spring morning, Elizabeth carried a stack of files into the main interview room on Bond Street where Miss Plumley and Hetty were sorting completed marriage files. They had been receiving letters for the last two months with after-marriage payments, and it was finally quiet enough to set the account books straight on couples who had paid their final fees.

"Well, look at that! Mary Midland tied the knot!" Hetty exclaimed with a shocked little laugh.

Miss Plumley took the letter from Hetty and peered at it. "Which one was she again?"

"The one who wore all those black clothes," said Elizabeth.

"The *vamp*," added Hetty. "I remember thinking she must be terribly hot wearing all that. Not to mention it did nothing for her looks. Apparently, she's married Mr. Garfield, the retired diplomat. I'd forgotten we had introduced them. Here's a photo." Hetty passed Elizabeth a picture.

Elizabeth's eyes widened. This was certainly not the Mary Midland she remembered. This woman wore a light floral-patterned frock and held a bouquet of flowers. She looked years younger than she had when she'd first stepped into the Marriage Bureau. Mary stood next to Mr. Garfield for their wedding photo. She looked wonderfully happy, as did her husband, who beamed proudly at her side.

"And who is this?" Hetty handed Elizabeth another photo of

a young soldier and his fresh-faced bride, which she retrieved from another opened letter. "I don't remember this one."

"Oh . . ." Elizabeth put a hand to her mouth as a smile crept across her lips. "That's Wyatt Harding. He was a soldier I met years ago at the train station. He was all alone when he shipped off, and I couldn't bear to think he had no one to tell him to come back, so I did. I also told him to write to us and register. I was worried it would be hard for him to get any letters where he was going, but he managed to write back quite a few times. It says here that thanks to one of our introductions he married a young woman from his little village who'd been in love with him since she was a little girl."

"One of our introductions?" asked Hetty.

"Apparently we matched him with the girl who'd registered with us. We didn't know their connection when we matched them and they were delighted to get reacquainted. He married her last month. And he's enclosed their fee."

Elizabeth held the photo a long moment, her heart fuller than it had been in a long time. Ever since Alan died, she'd felt like she had been drifting. To see a young man so close to her brother's age, happy, married, and alive boosted her spirits considerably.

"Why don't I sort the rest of these out," Miss Plumley suggested as she collected the stack. "You both deserve a break."

Hetty blew out a breath, and a lock of hair fell into her eyes. "Do we?" She swatted the hair away and sighed.

The secretary tutted at them. "Yes, you do. The pair of you have been working like mad these last few months. I'm beginning to think neither of you sleep."

"Well, it feels good to be busy," Elizabeth said. She couldn't admit to either of them that being *busy* was the only way she could forget about what she had lost.

The secretary arched a brow. "Sometimes it's all right to pause and let oneself grieve."

Grieve. Elizabeth hated that word. *Grief* wasn't powerful enough of a word for what she felt.

"Yes, *grieve*, Miss Mowbray." The secretary marched off with the files, and Elizabeth sank into her chair at her desk. She toyed with the phone line with the tip of her shoe, and like always, it rang. She and Hetty both burst out laughing.

"We ought to fix that," Hetty said.

"Oh, let's not. It's come in handy before—one never knows when we might need it again." The faulty wiring was one of Elizabeth's fondest memories of the bureau's early days.

"You are such a sentimental darling, Lizzie," Hetty said with affection.

Elizabeth lifted her chin. "I am, and I make no apologies."

"Good. You shouldn't." Hetty stood and smoothed her skirts. "Fancy a cup of tea?"

"Oh yes, please."

The phone suddenly rang, and Elizabeth answered it. It was Miss Plumley downstairs.

"There are three army officers here to see Miss Mowbray. Americans. Shall I send them up or schedule them for later?" There was a slight hesitation in the secretary's voice that made Elizabeth curious.

"Send them up. We might as well. We have no other appointments for the day."

"Yes, Miss Mowbray."

Hetty emerged from the inner office with the tea tray just as the door to the outer office opened. Three men in United States

Army uniforms came in. She understood now why Miss Plumley had been hesitant. The three gentlemen were black. They hadn't had any black clients register before, but Elizabeth and Hetty didn't mind. Love had no boundaries to them.

"Excuse me, are you Miss Mowbray and Mrs. Humphrey?" the first man asked with a gentle politeness that immediately put Elizabeth at ease with the three men.

"Yes, I'm Elizabeth Mowbray, and this is Hetty Humphrey. Are you here to register with the Marriage Bureau?"

"Yes ma'am, if we're allowed to."

Hetty smiled warmly at them. "Of course you are."

"Would you care to sit?" Elizabeth stood and collected three clipboards with new registration forms for them and pens to fill them out. The men were all in their midtwenties and quite attractive. Elizabeth suspected they'd have an easy time of matching the gentlemen.

"Thank you, ma'am," the first man said as he passed the other clipboards to his two companions.

"Please fill these out. When you're done, we'll interview you right away, if that's all right? It should only take fifteen to twenty minutes per person."

"That's fine with us, ma'am. We're off duty today."

Hetty set the tea tray down and hastily retrieved more cups. "Would anyone like some tea?" she asked.

The men all politely accepted, and Hetty prepared cups for them as they filled out the paperwork.

Once they were done, Elizabeth collected the clipboards and examined the names. "Hetty, you take Mr. Anderson. I'll take Mr. Jackson. Mr. Nolan, you can wait in the hall, and whichever of us finishes first will take you next."

Mr. Anderson followed Hetty into the inner office, while Mr.

Nolan waited in one of the chairs in the hall. Mr. Jackson sat opposite Elizabeth's desk. She scanned over his completed form.

"You are a United States citizen?" she clarified. With soldiers, it was important to be certain of citizenship. Several Polish and Czech soldiers had recently registered, and while they were enlisted in the British Army, they were citizens of Poland and Czechoslovakia.

"Yes, ma'am, I am."

"And will you be returning to America after the war?"

At this, Mr. Jackson hesitated a little. "Well, that's the thing, ma'am. I am planning to remain in England once the war is over." He was silent a long moment. "Do you mind if I'm frank with you, Miss Mowbray?"

"Not at all. Everything spoken here is entirely confidential."

"Right, well, the truth is it's easier here, as a colored man. The English aren't so bothered. I couldn't marry a white woman back home. It's actually against the law. Not to mention danger-ous. My family is all gone, and I'm all that's left now. I thought I could have a fresh start here. I'm not saying I have to marry a white woman, I'd just like to find someone who would be a good match for me."

Elizabeth's heart hurt for Mr. Jackson. She had seen how some US soldiers—not all of them, but enough—treated the black soldiers with derision and cruelty. When black soldiers had first arrived in England after Pearl Harbor, many English people had been hesitant, but once they had seen how some of the Americans treated their fellow countrymen, it distressed many Londoners. Shops began placing signs out front, encouraging black soldiers to visit. Restaurants also welcomed them. English girls were especially drawn to the polite, hard-working, and intel-ligent black soldiers. They were kind and honest men, and women loved that. Elizabeth knew that matching these three soldiers would be easy if they planned to stay in England.

"I brought a dozen photos of myself." Mr. Jackson held up a stack of printed military photos. "I thought it would be helpful for any woman I write to see one so that she'll know exactly what I look like. I don't want to confuse anyone."

Elizabeth took one of the photos and studied it, noticing how dashing Mr. Jackson looked in his uniform. They hadn't had any black clients register yet, but Elizabeth knew she had plenty of British women and even women from other countries who were war refugees who had specifically mentioned they had no prejudice when it came to race as far as their potential matches were concerned.

"That's an excellent idea, Mr. Jackson. I do have a fairly extensive list of young women who indicated they had no preference of race when it came to introductions. We'll start with these ladies. Now, let me ask you, what is the most important quality in a partner for you?"

Mr. Jackson's gaze softened, and he smiled. "I want a woman who likes to laugh and cook. She doesn't have to be good at cooking, I'm a good cook myself, but I'd want to spend time with her in the kitchen, even teach her to cook if she liked."

"That sounds wonderful," Elizabeth admitted with a smile. She ran him through the other standard questions and was quite satisfied, with at least a dozen possible matches in mind for him. He then paid a small fee to register, and she interviewed Mr. Nolan next. When the three soldiers left, Hetty sat down beside Elizabeth.

"Well, that was unexpected," Hetty admitted.

"But certainly welcome. I was quite happy to know they wanted to see us, that they felt they could come here and be

treated fairly. They all want to stay in England after the war."
Elizabeth created a trio of folders for their new clients.

"Can you blame them? I saw a fight last week on the street
between several soldiers. It was terrible. Did you know that
every American soldier both white and black needs his
commanding officer's permission to marry?"

"What?" Elizabeth nearly spilled her tea.

"Yes, and the three gentlemen we just met with have been
given permission to marry *if* they promise to stay in England.
Apparently, their commanding officer doesn't want them to
return. What a prig," Hetty scoffed.

"That's such nonsense," Elizabeth muttered. "If there's one
thing I've learned, it's that love isn't restrained by boundaries.
Love can exist anywhere between anyone." Uncle George and
Aabha were a perfect example of that.

Hetty nodded, her gaze suddenly distant. "Mr. Anderson said
something to me that worried me, though," she replied.

"Oh?"

"He said that in June we ought to be careful. We should stay
in the country for a while."

Elizabeth tucked the files into the filing cabinet. "Why
would he say that?"

"He couldn't tell me, but he said that if I noticed troops
moving south, it was time to leave London for at least a few
weeks. It sounded terribly ominous."

"Perhaps it's some kind of military signal? We can ask the
colonel about it."

"I think that's a good idea."

That evening, Elizabeth phoned the colonel, who confirmed
that something was definitely in motion. Thousands of soldiers
were arriving in England each day, and hundreds of planes had

flown over Cunningham House in the last few days. All of them were headed toward Biggin Hill.

"If those soldiers told you to leave London, I would listen to them," the colonel advised.

***

OVER THE NEXT TWO MONTHS, THE STEADY FLOW OF TROOPS trickled to a stop and the streets of London were suddenly eerily empty after everyone had become used to the lively activity of the American GIs roaming the streets with their boyish smiles and money to spend. By early June, it was as if the American soldiers had never been in London at all.

"I miss them, the Yanks," Hetty said as she and Elizabeth closed up the bureau offices for the day. "They were so merry, and now everything is so quiet. All the shops and restaurants are practically empty."

Elizabeth sighed. "I miss the stockings."

More than half a dozen soldiers had paid for their registration fees at the bureau using fresh stockings. Elizabeth, Hetty, and even Miss Plumley had benefited from them. It had been bad enough that a few days a week Elizabeth had to draw a seam line on her bare legs with ink to make it look like she wore stockings. Now, thanks to the GIs, she had several new pairs.

"Do you think London will ever feel the way it used to?" Elizabeth asked as they passed through the darkened reception toward the front door.

"I think it will, though it may take a very long time."

When they stepped outside, Elizabeth was met with the welcome sight of a dashing RAF pilot leaning against the brick wall by the steps of the bureau's front door. His arms were crossed over his chest, and his hat was tipped at a rakish angle.

"Philip!" She flew down the steps, and he caught her in his arms. "What are you doing here?"

"I'm off for a few hours tonight," he said. "I was in London for a meeting with the Americans, specifically the US Army Air Forces."

"The colonel mentioned he'd seen several planes overhead recently." She pressed a kiss to his cheek, and he tapped the tip of her nose with his finger.

"I'm sure he did. We've been slowly building a joint task force." Philip met Hetty's gaze as she came down the stairs to join them. "I'm afraid I need to speak to you both, though. Somewhere private."

"Let's go home," Hetty suggested.

The three of them walked back to Hetty's townhouse, where Isabelle had dinner waiting for them. She'd made some mince pies, shortbread, and she'd even found honey to spread on wholemeal bread for tea. She had also crafted a gooseberry tart that she'd baked in a deep dish.

"Thank goodness Isabelle can cook," Hetty said with a chuckle.

Jarvis collected the plates from the table, then went to check on Teddy, who had been put to bed half an hour before. The butler had grown fiercely protective of the little boy. Philip finished his glass of scotch and then cleared his throat.

"What I'm about to say must not leave this room. You understand?"

The women all answered in agreement.

"There are plans to move on Europe soon. Very soon. I want all three of you to go to Cunningham House tomorrow, or at least leave London. Pack everything of value and stay there for a few weeks."

Elizabeth reached for his hand on the table and covered it with hers. "Philip—"

"Please, Lizzie, I can't say more. All I can tell you is that we've heard rumors of a revenge weapon, as the Germans call it. We do not want any of you caught up in whatever happens with it."

"We'll make plans to leave in the morning," Hetty promised. "We can work from the country, after all," Hetty said. "We'll tell Miss Plumley to come with us. Isabelle, what about you? Will you join us at Cunningham House?"

"I think I'll go to Scotland again. Mr. Hartnell is looking for more designs for countrywear, and the Highlands always inspire me the most."

Elizabeth watched Philip. That creeping stillness she had felt the night of Alan's death was back. She had a terrible feeling that whatever Philip wasn't saying was something he didn't want to worry her with, but that only made her worry all the more.

After dinner, the others went upstairs, leaving Philip and Elizabeth alone in the drawing room. He sat on the sofa, and Elizabeth curled up beside him, wrapping an arm around his chest as they listened to music playing on the wireless. She tucked her head against his neck and closed her eyes.

"You would tell me if you're planning to do something dangerous and reckless, wouldn't you?"

He chuckled, but the sound didn't carry the same mirth it usually did.

"You know me, Lizzie. Dangerous is all this war is. I have to do whatever I'm called upon to do."

"I mean it, Philip. Don't you dare play the hero and get yourself killed."

He curled his arm around her waist as he slid her onto his lap to hold her closer. "You deserve a hero," he whispered. "You deserve everything a man can give of himself."

She placed her fingertips against his lips, silencing him. "No. No more of that talk. That's the sort of thing a man says before he goes and does something bloody noble and dies. I won't let you, do you understand? You aren't free to let go like that."

There was silence between them as she composed herself. "I've already let this war take a part of my heart. I won't let it have the rest. I won't let it have you." She dropped her fingers from his lips and leaned in, softly kissing him. Her heart ached, and that cavernous space left by Alan's death rumbled ominously within her, reminding her what it felt like to lose someone. Her mouth trembled against his, and tears coated her cheeks as she clung to him.

"If I had my life to do all over again," he said softly, blue eyes glowing bright, "I would do everything to find you sooner, so I might love you longer."

She buried her face in his neck, crying softly for everything they might never have if he never came home. What she felt in Philip's arms was *unending*, like an ever-expanding universe with new stars born every minute from swirling cosmic dust. New worlds, new horizons lay before her so long as he was alive. To lose him now would leave her universe dark and cold, without a hint of starlight.

"Love me tonight?" She spoke the word without fear now. *Love.* It was the only word that held any power for her now, and she would wield it as a shield against the darkness.

"Now and always, for as long as you'll let me." He lowered his head to hers, and Elizabeth surrendered to his kiss, even as her heart feared what the future held.

JUNE 6, 1944

The D-Day landings marked the beginning of the liberation of France and Western Europe, the largest amphibious operation in history. Relying on the knowledge of meteorologists, scientists, inventors, and the combined might of the militaries of thirteen nations, along with tens of thousands of members of the French resistance, it would become one of the most significant battles in the history of humanity.

Just after midnight, 23,400 allied paratroopers were dropped into Normandy, providing tactical support to the troops landing on the beaches. The Allied fleet opened up their guns along the beaches of Normandy, encompassing fifty miles of coastline to keep the German bunkers distracted as the Allied troops landed. Their actions secured a foothold in mainland Europe for the first time in three years.

At ten o'clock in the morning, Elizabeth, Hetty, Mrs. Harrow, Eva, Miss Plumley and Colonel Cunningham sat in the drawing room, listening to the BBC Home Service as John Snagge announced the words that would change their world forever.

"D-Day has come. Early this morning, the Allies began the assault on the northwestern face of Hitler's European fortress. The first official news came just after nine thirty, when the supreme headquarters of the Allied Expeditionary Force issued communiqué number one. This said: Under the command of General Eisenhower, Allied naval forces, supported by strong air forces, began landing Allied armies this morning on the northern coast of France."

Elizabeth held her breath as the announcer's words had her complete focus.

"Supported by strong air forces . . ." Philip was flying at that moment along the coast of France. He was a part of this. That was what he hadn't been able to tell her.

"Dear God. They just might do it." The colonel collapsed into the nearest chair as tears rolled down his cheeks. "Our boys will win now . . . My God, they'll win."

"How can you be certain?" Hetty asked, her eyes full of tears. No doubt she was thinking of Charles.

"Because of the number of men, the concerted effort of all three branches of the armies, navies, and air forces of thirteen nations at last unified on the side of right. If they successfully manage this landing and keep gaining ground, the Jerries won't be able to drive them back. They no longer have the resources, not against this many Allied troops working together." The colonel wiped the tears from his face, still smiling.

Elizabeth wished she felt as certain about winning the war as the colonel did. All she could think about was Alan and how he hadn't lived to see this day. So many other lads like him were gone, and men like Charles, Marcus, Philip, and Nathan were still out there fighting ever onward toward that final victory, no matter what it might cost.

The week that followed D-day, all of England—all of the world, in fact—was abuzz with the news. For the first time, hope bloomed like the golden crocuses in the little flower beds near the Marriage Bureau's doors.

But the warnings they'd been given had not been forgotten. Within a week, word reached Cunningham House that a new danger far more terrifying than the bombs England had faced during the Blitz had arrived. Elizabeth was never more glad they had taken the advice of the American soldiers who'd visited their office.

V-1 flying bombs were suddenly launching off the coast of France and reaching London. These were indeed weapons of vengeance, a repayment to innocent civilians for the brave actions of the forces who had landed on Normandy's beaches.

It felt like the world was ending all over again as the city became a ghost town for a second time. The V-1s, sometimes called buzz bombs or doodlebugs, filled everyone with fear. They were much harder to see coming than fleets of German bombers, and the destruction from a single V-1 was much bigger than what previous Blitz bombs had managed. Hetty sent Teddy to stay at Lord and Lady Lonsdale's country estate until the war was over. It broke her heart to be separated from her son, but it was the only way she could keep him safe. Even Cunningham House was too close to London and the V-1s for it to be entirely free of risk. The unpredictability of the V-1s meant that they often didn't reach London itself and instead would explode in smaller towns and the countryside.

More than once, Elizabeth heard the V-1s flying past overhead, and at any moment, she knew the pilotless devices could simply drop and obliterate everything around them. Everyone was glad not to be in London, yet at the same time, their hearts were breaking at the further destruction of their beloved, defiant city.

Elizabeth buried herself in work each day, sharing the desk with Eva in the study, as she silently prayed for the rare call or hastily written note from Philip between missions.

But finally, she knew she had to return to London along with

Hetty. They couldn't stay in the country forever. So once more she was back at her office in Bond Street to see to the Bureau's affairs. The only bright spot in Elizabeth's life was the steady stream of letters still delivered by their beloved postman, whom they had married off two years before.

"Another full bag today, Miss Mowbray," Harry said as he poured the letters on her desk. At least a hundred covered the surface. Postmarks from Ireland and Scotland and places all over England, even a few from America, showed how word of the bureau had spread since their doors opened five years ago.

"Thank you, Harry."

Elizabeth began sorting the letters. A strange sort of melancholy crept into her heart as she sat alone in the office. Hetty was out running errands, and Miss Plumley had the day off. It was just her now, and she didn't like being alone. It was too quiet.

She opened several letters on the top of the pile, but no matter how hard she might try, she couldn't bring herself to focus on the words contained within. She knew what Hetty would say: "Call it a day and go home."

Finally, she packed her things and locked the doors before heading downstairs. She stepped out onto the landing and saw Nathan coming toward her on the street. He was wearing his uniform, which was smartly pressed. As they met at the bottom of the stairs, she saw the look on his face.

"No . . . ," she begged him, praying he wouldn't speak.

He held out a letter in a trembling hand and leaned on his cane as though it was the only thing holding him up.

"Lizzie, I'm so sorry . . . It's Philip."

With those words, the last starlight in her once bright and glorious universe died.

CHAPTER 39

Elizabeth took the letter from Nathan. Her fingers shook so hard that she nearly dropped it.

"He was flying back from France with a few younger pilots. Most Spitfire pilots only have a life expectancy of four weeks . . . Philip was trying to keep the newer lads alive." He swallowed hard before continuing. "He radioed in that one of the lads went down into the water. He circled back to see if the boy made it out of his plane, but a German plane shot him down as well. His last radio communication said he was headed into the Channel."

Elizabeth clenched the letter tight as she clung to those last few words.

"You haven't confirmed that he's . . . ?"

"No. Not yet. But he'd be lucky to survive a crash, even on the water. I should know. It's how I wound up with a limp. I went down just off the coast while in a dog fight with a German plane. Barely made it to shore. He went down too far from land..."

She still clung to the hope, however small. "He's not gone," she said firmly and tried to give him back the letter.

"Lizzie, please." Nathan's voice was rough as he struggled to speak. "I know you've lost so much, and it seems like this is the last thing that you can bear, but you must accept it. Philip is gone." Nathan curled his hands around hers and closed the letter within her fingers more firmly.

Elizabeth sank to the ground, the letter now pressed to her chest. Nathan removed his hat and eased down beside her. The silver lion's head of his cane glinted in the sunlight as he rested it on his lap.

Long moments later, she opened the letter. The fact that Philip had written it made the words all that much more precious and yet unbearably hard to read. Her grief was so strong that it almost blinded her, but she forced herself to focus on Philip's last words.

My darling,

How much I shall miss calling you that. It's going to be the small things, the little words, the moments our hands touched and the feel of your lips on mine that I'll miss so desperately. I'll miss the way you smile early in the morning light as you lie beside me and the frown you make whenever I tease you. I'll miss the way you always seem to see into my soul. You have the biggest heart of anyone I've ever met. If more people loved the way you do, there would be no more war in the world.

I know you warned me not to be reckless, and please know that whatever happened, I wasn't. I wanted more than anything to come back to you. To walk through the bureau's doors and tell you that I'm yours now and always. I wanted to tell you that we would see the world together. We'd go visit your beloved uncle George in India and live the sort of lives only dreamers could ever have.

But if you're reading this, it means poor Nathan has come to tell you the news. I wish with all that I am that you never faced this pain. Knowing that I've been the one to do this to you pains me. Wherever I am, I will do what I can to wish your pain away.

I meant what I said. If I could go back to the beginning of my life and start anew, I'd spend every moment searching for you so that I could find you and love you all over again and for far longer.

Yours always,
The scoundrel who loves you

SHE STARED AT THE HORIZON WITH ITS CLEAR SKIES. THE SUN was setting, painting the world in shades of gold and fuchsia.

"I have no more tears left," she whispered. The cavern in her chest had widened to fit the entire universe.

"You know he would never want them. He would much rather you were smiling. You know how the old boy was, the way he teased you so often. He loved you to distraction."

"He certainly did love to tease me."

"Did he ever tell you what he told me the night after we first met you? When we left you after that first bombing?"

Her heart clenched at the memory of that hour in the basement, and she shook her head. He had kissed her in the doorway of a shop, even as the world burned around them. She'd felt that so long as he was there, life would go on. The world wouldn't end.

"As we hopped on that fire truck and rode toward the flames, he leaned over and told me, 'I'm going to marry that girl,

Nathan.' I remember I mocked him mercilessly about it. He simply smiled and said, 'We're the same, her soul and mine. Wherever the universe made us, we came from the same place, the same cosmic dust. She and I . . . we belong together, as natural as the sea and the shore.'"

They were quiet for a time after that. Lizzie didn't want to move from the bureau's front steps, even though darkness would soon be upon them. As soon as she stood and took that first step, she would be moving forward in a life without Philip in it. She wasn't ready. She just needed to take a little longer to hold on to the past . . . to him.

"Do his parents know?" she asked.

"Yes. I drove to their estate this morning. Baron Lennox is not convinced he's gone either. Lady Lennox . . . she's harder to read. Such a lovely woman, but so very quiet in her grief."

She finally stood. "I was supposed to meet them." Elizabeth and Nathan began to walk back toward Hetty and Charles's townhouse.

"You hadn't yet?"

She shook her head. "It's been four years, and yet we never found the time. He didn't want his parents coming to London, not with the bombings, and he couldn't take enough time from the base to visit them with me."

"You should see them. They would want to meet you."

"I don't know if I could face them now. It would hurt too much."

"Some things in life are worth the pain," Nathan said. "I cursed myself when I bashed my leg. I thought it ruined my life. But if I hadn't been injured, I would still be flying on missions, and I wouldn't be here to watch over Eva and Marcus." He smiled. "When I came into your office and saw Eva again the day that I registered, I knew she was the one for me. But I thought I would frighten her too much, so I let you match me with other ladies so that I would have an excuse to come see her all the time."

Elizabeth stopped as they reached Hetty's house. "Why didn't you say something?"

"Because real love, even when it strikes as fast as lightning, still requires faith and trust."

Faith and trust.

Elizabeth's hand slid into the pocket of her dress where Philip's letter was tucked away. She still didn't fully believe he was gone. Philip was too alive, too *real* to simply be there one day and gone the next. She refused to believe it, because he had been right—they were the same. Two pieces of a whole. She would know in her very soul if he was gone, wouldn't she?

"Will you be all right tonight?" Nathan asked. "I could stay here if you need me." He was so earnest and full of compassion, his warm brown eyes a reflection of her pain.

"I'll be all right," she promised. "Will you?" He had to be hurting as much as she was. For the first time since she had met Nathan Sheridan, he couldn't manage his usual smile. He shook his head and swallowed hard.

"It was a group of us lads—Charles, Philip, Will St. Laurent, and myself. We did everything together. I don't know what it will mean to wake up tomorrow and not have him here. I have such a strange feeling, like I've left all my lights on and the blackout curtains open. It's a terrible sense of something left undone, you see. I can't shake the feeling. There's a part of me that keeps thinking he'll just fly back to the base any minute and ask if I missed him."

Elizabeth understood all too well what Nathan meant. The

war took goodbyes from the ones they loved most and left only empty graves and futile expectations of men walking back in through doors that they never would again.

"Maybe he isn't . . . ?" she began again.

Nathan shook his head. "We can't think like that. The moment we do, it will make the reality that much harder to accept."

Elizabeth wrapped Nathan in a tight hug for a long moment.

"I'll be in London tonight, but I return to Biggin Hill tomorrow. Once the funeral arrangements are made, I'll let you know." He leaned in and kissed her forehead like a beloved brother. Longing for Alan dug into her heart all over again.

"Thank you, Nathan."

She watched Nathan walk away as darkness crept across the city. The sound of his cane tapping on the pavement echoed in the silence until he turned the corner. Then she went inside.

"Is everything all right, Miss Mowbray?" Jarvis asked as he took her handbag.

"No . . ." She could feel the pain deep inside her clawing its way to the surface. "Is Hetty here? I need to—"

"She's in the drawing room." Jarvis touched her arm, his face lined with worry. "Is there anything I can do for you, miss?"

"No, thank you, Jarvis. You're such a darling." She hugged the butler, much to his surprise, but then he gently patted her back.

"Do you wish to tell me about what's bothering you?"

"It's Philip. His plane was shot down this morning. He's gone."

The butler stiffened. "Not the Lennox boy . . ."

It was then she realized that the butler must have known Philip almost as long as he had known Charles. How he would miss Philip almost as much as he would Charles if something happened to him . . .

"What's the matter, Lizzie?" Hetty's voice echoed in the entryway.

Elizabeth released poor Jarvis, who hastily excused himself to grieve in private.

"Oh, Hetty . . ." She walked into her friend's arms. "Tell me this is all a bad dream. Tell me that I'll wake up tomorrow and it will be over."

"Philip?" Hetty asked, on the verge of tears now too. Elizabeth simply nodded.

"Oh no," Hetty gasped. "*Oh no*, Lizzie."

"I have nothing left," Elizabeth said in a whisper. "Nothing."

"You have *you*," Hetty said. "You are still here. You have me. You aren't alone."

A long while later, Elizabeth crept to the window in her bedchamber and parted the blackout curtains. With no light to escape into the night, she was able to steal a look at the sky. Distant stars burned millions of miles away. Endless stars. She began to count them.

It made her think of something Marcus had said before he left. He had mentioned a rumor that Jews were being identified with bright-yellow patches of cloth cut into the shape of stars and sewn onto their clothes. Hitler had sought to mark those he wished to destroy, but he had done so with the most powerful symbol of hope that ever existed. Even if one destroyed a star, new life was always born from it.

No one could ever count all the stars—their numbers might as well be infinite. Elizabeth continued to stare up at the sky. Was Philip among these glittering stars now? When this war was over, Elizabeth would see a vast sky of stars and she would never forget what each one meant.

⊛

SOMEHOW, LIFE DID GO ON IN THE WEEK FOLLOWING PHILIP'S death. Each day Elizabeth woke, dressed, ate a light breakfast, and headed to the bureau's office on Bond Street. The V-1 flying bombs still flew across the Channel into England, their buzzing engines cutting short just a second before they fell to the earth and exploded. Elizabeth had witnessed several over the last few days, and despite the fresh fear they inspired in the already devastated city, Elizabeth was unafraid. Her greatest fear had already happened. What more could they take from her? It seemed so silly to cower and hide now, so she didn't. She stopped retreating to the Anderson shelter and stayed in her bed whenever the sirens went off. If she was fated to go, it would be on her terms.

Both Hetty and Miss Plumley grew concerned about her new bravado, but Elizabeth didn't care. She poured herself all the more into the work of matching couples with a level of intensity that exhausted even Hetty.

But her strength was soon tested. On the sixth day after Philip's plane was lost, Lord and Lady Lennox came to the bureau.

When Miss Plumley informed her of their arrival, she had them sent up immediately. Hetty was out having lunch with her father, and with no appointments that afternoon, Elizabeth could take her time talking to them in private. Her heart beat so hard in her chest that her ribs began to ache. She drew a steadying breath and opened the door.

Lord Lennox was tall and in fine shape, with silvery blond hair and bright-blue eyes, every inch the dashing flying ace he'd been during the Great War. It was easy to see where Philip got his looks. Nothing in his face suggested weakness, except perhaps his eyes, which held a vast pain she recognized all too well.

Lady Lennox was a stunning brunette with soft gray eyes, and she was dressed as elegantly as her husband. Something about her face reminded Elizabeth of Philip—a softness, a compassionate playfulness that was now marred with heartbreak. They were exactly how Elizabeth had always envisioned Philip's parents to be.

"Are you Miss Mowbray?" Philip's father asked.

Elizabeth shut the door, giving them all some privacy. "Yes."

"I am Andrew Lennox, Philip's father. This is Louise, his mother." He cleared his throat. "We were supposed to meet you soon, before . . ." Andrew didn't continue.

Elizabeth found it almost impossible to speak but managed to say, "Yes." The love she bore for their son was so strong that it burned bright within the wintry world where her heart was covered in snow and encased in ice.

Andrew cleared his throat. "I apologize for showing up without scheduling an appointment. It's just that . . . we wanted to meet you, to see his Lizzie for ourselves. Our boy has talked of nothing else over the past few years." Lord Lennox's strained smile was heartbreaking. "We want you to know that we consider you the daughter we never had, even with Philip gone. You were his, and now you are ours. If you'll have us as a family, that is."

Louise's hands shook as she set her handbag down on Elizabeth's desk. Then she placed her hands on Elizabeth's shoulders as she appraised her with motherly affection.

"You are so lovely, my dear, so very lovely. I can see what drew him to you." She smiled. "He told us so much about you, we feel as though we've known you forever. Don't we, Andrew?" Her husband nodded.

Elizabeth was surprised by that. "You do?"

"Oh yes, we know all about your adventures in India, about the bureau and everything," Louise said. "It was then we understood how he fell in love with you. You see, no one before you has ever turned his head. My son is a notorious flirt, but the moment he met you . . . you were all he could talk about. You were his world." Louise was smiling as she said it, but the smile was full of the pain only a mother could feel.

"I . . ." It took Elizabeth a moment to collect herself before she could continue. "Philip was my second chance. I made a mess of things when I first thought I fell in love—what I *thought* was love. It was only after I met Philip that I learned what real love is, how it makes you feel. Loving him made me fearless. Even now, I'm still fearless, perhaps even more so." She shook her head. "I'm sure that must sound like nonsense."

"Not at all," Louise assured her.

"I . . . I miss him so much," Elizabeth confessed. Louise's eyes filled with tears.

"As much as I never wanted my son to fight in this war," Andrew began, his voice quiet, "as a parent, you learn that you can't hold your child back. You can't let them shun life and be afraid of things, or else your child will someday become an old man who never tasted the sweet fire of life. And death is a part of that . . . but no parent should ever have to bury their child. My boy was supposed to live to a ripe old age, surrounded by grandchildren and great-grandchildren. Now we have only ourselves, but thankfully, we still have you."

The honesty and love in Andrew's eyes and voice struck a chord so deep that Elizabeth would feel the vibrations for years to come.

"You don't know what it means for us to meet you," Louise went on, tears dripping down her face. "To look at you, to see your courage and know what you do each day for others—it eases the ache in my heart to know that my son loved you and that you loved him. When I think of all these lads who don't come home, how our boys trained, were forced to endure things and to go on and kill other mothers' sons, how the light from all these mothers' faces must die when they learn their lads are gone . . . I have to hold on and think that as long as women like you are here, you will hold the world together for the men who do come home."

"No one is a lost cause," Elizabeth said. A sudden memory of Philip came to her. "When Philip smiled at me or teased me, which he did so often, it always gave me the most wonderful feeling, like I had left a dark bit of woods and found myself on a hillside full of yellow gorse and poppies in bloom, with the warm summer sun surrounding me in all its splendor. When he made me feel like that, nothing was impossible, nothing. His love gave me an undying flame. I only wish I could have given him half my life so that we would have had more time together . . ."

Louise covered her mouth with a trembling hand as she shared a look with her husband.

"Even a thousand years isn't enough when you love someone that deeply," Lord Lennox said.

"No, it isn't," Elizabeth agreed. "Would you . . . would you tell me about him, what he was like as a boy?" She hoped desperately they would be able to give her new memories to cling to.

"We would love to tell you everything," his mother said.

Elizabeth gestured for them to sit with her. "Start at the beginning." The three of them lost themselves in recounting Philip's life and stories of his mischief and cleverness. By the time Louise and Andrew had to leave, Elizabeth was wiping away fresh tears and smiling.

"Come and stay at our estate next week," Louise offered. "Please. We've arranged for Philip's service, and we would like you to stay a few days afterward, if you'd like."

"I would like that, Lady Lennox. Thank you."

"It's Louise and Andrew to you, my dear," Philip's mother said, and she stroked a lock of hair from Elizabeth's face like a mother would her daughter.

"Thank you so much." Elizabeth suddenly remembered that she still wore the RAF sweetheart pin on her dress, and she reached up to unbutton it. "Philip gave this to me. You should have—"

"It's yours, my dear. Keep it safe for him," Andrew said with loving but sorrow-filled eyes.

"I will. Always." It was a promise. The pin would never be left anywhere. It was part of her now, just as Philip's love and memories were a part of her.

"We will ring you once we know when you should come down for the service. We'll send our car."

"Oh, but the petrol . . ."

"Don't worry about the petrol, dear," Louise said. "We stayed in the country so much that we saved up our rations quite cleverly."

Elizabeth hugged them both goodbye and sat at her desk

again once they were gone. It was a strange thing to see what her life might have been like if Philip hadn't died. Andrew and Louise would have been her mother- and father-in-law.

Hetty returned from her lunch with her father and saw the odd look on Elizabeth's face. "Are you all right, Lizzie?"

"Yes, I feel strangely at peace," Elizabeth said. "Not that I deserve any, but somehow I do feel steady inside, like a flowing river. The pain is still there, but there's a peace to that too."

"I'm glad you're feeling better. I hope you are up for a bit of good news," Hetty said, and with a small smile, she removed a letter from her handbag.

"Of course! What is it?" Elizabeth asked.

"Charles finally knows. My father was finally able to get a private message to him about Teddy when his unit checked in from Europe. My father couldn't find out where Charles was, of course, but he finally knows he has a son. He was able to send a quick message back." She held up a handwritten note. "One of my father's friends was able to get it back to my father, who just gave it to me."

"That's wonderful! What did Charles say about Teddy?"

"Here, you read it." She passed the letter to Elizabeth.

My darling Hetty,

You've given me sunlight to pierce this dreaded fog of war. You know, every day I fight to return to you and now to our son. I hope he'll know me. Please tell him about me. I don't want to be a stranger to him when I come home. Hold on a little longer, and I'll be back to you both.

Yours forever and a day,

Charles

. . .

"Is the war ending soon? Perhaps Charles knows something we don't?" Elizabeth asked her friend.

"I hope so, or I'll have to join the paratroopers and settle things in Berlin myself," Hetty said. They both laughed, but it didn't ease the nagging worry that hovered about Elizabeth.

Hetty pushed aside the stack of client questionnaires sitting in front of Elizabeth on the desk. "Let's go home. A storm is rolling in, and the bombers won't be out tonight. I want to curl up and read by the fire."

"Good idea." Elizabeth packed up her things and joined Hetty on the walk home. Isabelle was spending the night at a friend's townhouse in Grosvenor Square while they worked on some sketches for work which meant Jarvis would be in charge of dinner for the three of them since Elizabeth and Hetty were not the best cooks.

The skies opened up an hour after they arrived home. Thunder rattled the windows, the doors, and their hinges. Lightning flashed through the edges of the blackout curtains, and the power flickered.

"Oh heavens. We'd better not lose our electricity again," Hetty grumbled.

Jarvis fetched a few torches from the hall, and they gathered the remaining candles once again, just in case. They ate a meal of steak, baked mushrooms, peas, and chips that Jarvis had prepared in the cozy kitchen rather than the dining room. Jarvis had managed to find some beer in the wine cellar, and the three of them ate and talked long into the night while the storm raged.

At last, Hetty yawned and excused herself to bed. Jarvis inquired if Elizabeth was in need of anything else. She wasn't, so he also went up to bed.

Elizabeth headed to the drawing room, clutching her sweetheart pin between her fingers as she sat on the couch by the fire. It glowed in the light as she examined it.

Brushing her thumbs over the shiny surface of the RAF letters and silver wings, she whispered, "I'll never love anyone but you."

The fire popped and crackled, followed by a crash of thunder that rumbled through the house. She knew she wouldn't be able to sleep with the storm raging so. She plucked a book off the shelves, hoping Hetty had something that would distract her. She found an old Gothic novel, rather fitting her mood, given the weather. She'd started back toward the sofa when the front door chime sounded.

She glanced at the clock. It was already half past one in the morning. She almost went to wake Jarvis, but he needed his sleep. He had been working so hard since they had sent Charles's other servants to the country to keep them safe from the buzz bombs.

She slipped out of her heels and padded on stocking-clad feet to the front door so she wouldn't wake anyone with the click of her heels. Then she unlocked the old oak door and pulled it open.

A figure stood wreathed in darkness. Lightning flashed from behind him just as the gold light from the house washed over his front.

Lizzie sucked in a breath as she saw the figure's face, and everything went black.

ELIZABETH WOKE SLOWLY, HER BRAIN FUZZY. SHE SHIFTED IN discomfort as she realized she was in the drawing room, and she was dripping wet. She blinked down at herself and the strange way her clothes were soaked all over when she hadn't even gone out in the rain. Still confused, she lifted her head to stare at the face of the man who held her cradled in his arms on Hetty's sofa.

Phillip smiled back at her.

"My God . . . you are the most beautiful thing I've ever seen." His boyish grin held a hint of mischief about it.

"No . . . You . . . you died . . ." Elizabeth covered her face with her hands, trying to stop the dream before it went any further. Whenever she dreamed of him, she always wept so bitterly the next morning that she ached for hours.

Philip chuckled as he gently pried her hands away from her face. "I'm here. I'm really here, darling."

She stared at him again, feeling the warmth of his body. She breathed in the scent of his clothes. She touched the very shabby, strange coat he wore that didn't fit him quite right. He smelled of tobacco, shaving soap, and something of the storm, mixed with the scent that was uniquely his. Even her dreams couldn't resurrect a scent like this.

"What are you wearing?" she asked, unable to think of anything else to say. She played with the collar of his shirt. It wasn't part of any uniform she'd ever seen him wear.

"It's a long story, and you seem ready for bed. I shall tell you tomorrow."

"If you don't tell me now, Philip Lennox, I swear I'll throttle you."

He grinned and pulled her tighter to him. A lock of wet hair fell into his eyes, and she brushed it away before cupping his cheek in her hand. There was a cut across his brow that seemed to be healing, and bruises shadowed both his eyes. He turned his head to kiss her palm. She couldn't help but wonder what he'd been through when his plane went down.

"I'll tell you everything in more detail tomorrow. Right now I'm damned tired and just want to hold you, darling."

"What happened?" she pressed.

"I was flying back with a few younger pilots when we were attacked. One of the boys went down, and I thought I saw him get free of his plane, so I circled back to check on him. I got hit by the Germans and had to bail out.

"As luck would have it, I managed to find the other pilot once I landed in the water. We inflated one of the rafts we had in our crash kits and paddled back toward England. It took us nearly five days. We had a bit of food and water, enough to last us if we shared. It was a bloody miracle we made it to shore with the currents against us and the Jerries circling the Channel like vultures.

"We washed up on a beach, and I managed to get the young lad a cab back to base. I borrowed some money and clothes from an old couple in the village we washed up by. I took several buses for the last day and a half just to get back here . . . to you. I'm sure my commander will be furious, but sod him—I had to see you first."

She stared at him, unmoving, and his grin slipped a little.

"Lizzie?" He wrapped his arms tighter around her.

"We . . . we planned your funeral service. It's this coming weekend . . . and . . . and I met your parents and . . . Oh my God, we must call everyone!" She struggled to get off his lap, but he held her still.

"Easy, Lizzie, my girl. You can resurrect me from the dead tomorrow. Tonight, I just need to be here with you."

She finally pulled herself free of his arms. "We need to get you out of those wet clothes. Come along. Let's go upstairs. I think there's a few pieces of Charles's clothes in an old wardrobe in my room." She grasped his hand, and they crept upstairs to Elizabeth's bedchamber. When he closed the door behind them, she pulled off his coat and shirt, desperate to bare his skin so she could feel his heart beating.

"You're wet too," Philip said as he began to undo the buttons on the front of her dress.

"Charles's clothes are . . ."

"Let's forget the clothes for now, hmm?"

She couldn't disagree with him on that.

They were skin to skin a few minutes later beneath the warm covers of her bed, and he stroked her hair back from her face as he looked into her eyes.

"All I could think about was you, Lizzie. Every single moment, just getting back to you," Philip whispered. "You guided me home."

She buried her face against his neck, the beat of her heart matching his. "I didn't really believe you were gone. I grieved, I had to accept it, but deep down I knew I would feel it if you were really . . ." She couldn't finish.

"I would never break my promise to you," he said.

She lifted her face to his as she tried not to cry all over again.

"Never, my heart, never."

And there it was, that feeling he always gave her. The one where she stepped out onto that sunny hillside, full of yellow gorse flowers and red poppies and all the splendor of life around her.

"I got the chance to find you and love you all over again, and this time for far longer . . . ," she murmured, almost to herself.

Then she kissed him and felt his lips beneath hers curve into a smile. "Scoundrel," she laughed.

"*Your* scoundrel," he said most earnestly.

The war was not over, but whatever came next, Elizabeth knew she and Philip would be all right. She knew it with that same certainty she felt when it came to other people, like the night she had met Hetty at her father's party.

Grief was love enduring, but joy . . . joy was love embraced.

CHAPTER 40

M*ay 8, 1945*

NEARLY A YEAR HAD PASSED SINCE THE D-DAY INVASION, turning the tide in the war. Allied forces had pressed the advantage after Normandy, pushing deeper into Europe, and were now making progress toward Berlin. Even though the world was still at war, there was a sense that it was all close to coming to an end. The men would come home, and after a time life would return to some sense of normalcy that had almost been forgotten after six years. For the first time, the world *had* hope.

Elizabeth and Hetty were ensconced in the study at Cunningham House, poring over another set of letters from clients who had married and were settling their after-marriage fees. Dozens of their clients were returning each week as troops began to come home at last. Everyone could feel it, that sense that the end of this dreadful war was near. They had already heard in the last twenty-four hours that Germany was going to surrender.

"So many of the men are coming home. It's wonderful." Hetty sighed, and her gaze drifted to Teddy, who sat on the floor playing with a train set the colonel had given him for Christmas. It was an old toy, one left collecting dust in the attic, but it had found a new life with the four-year-old who now moved the train carriages and engines around the little metal tracks.

He'd lost that baby look and was now a little boy, his cheeks thinner, his limbs longer and leaner. Elizabeth knew Hetty was worried that he'd grow up before his father came home.

"Any word of Charles?"

"Not yet. But my father is trying to find him. There are so many men in Europe, it's hard knowing where one man is among thousands. What about Philip?"

"He'll be home in a few days, I think. They have no more missions being assigned. There's still fighting in the Pacific, but he is certain he won't be sent there. He's paid his time more than enough and brought so many of our boys home safe."

"Thank God. I don't think either of us could handle that man flying off to unknown horizons again," Hetty grumbled. "I shall never forget coming down to breakfast and finding him sitting at my dining room table, buttering a bit of toasted bread as if he hadn't just been declared *dead* for six days."

The memory made Elizabeth laugh. "He insisted. If you could have seen your face . . . You went as white as a sheet, and then you started throwing napkins at him and lecturing him

602

about scaring us all to death. I rather think he was glad to know you missed him."

"Of course I did, the damned fool," Hetty said, smiling.

After Philip had seemingly come back from the dead, everything had changed for Elizabeth. Every moment they had together now had become precious, and she vowed never to hesitate about anything in her life again.

"Speaking of that ace of yours, when is he going to propose? It's only been five bloody years. Or shall I have Charles talk some sense into him when he gets home?"

"He'll ask when the time is right. We want the war to be over, so it leaves no shadow on our future."

"Well, you oughtn't dally, not if you want any children. Besides, Teddy needs someone to keep him out of trouble. You and Philip need to produce a child or two at once, so he has friends."

Elizabeth blushed. She did want children, but after seeing Hetty endure such fear for her child during the war, Elizabeth needed to hear the church bells ring and victory announced before she could bring a baby into this world.

"I hope we never see days like these again," Hetty said as she set her pen down and sat back in her chair.

"You mean the war?" Elizabeth asked. She sorted a stack of wedding photographs from their clients, marveling at all the happy faces and knowing that their lives too had been forever changed.

"Yes. I hope for Teddy's sake that the young men and women being born into the world can see the beauty in what we have and why it must be protected. I just hope for peace in our time."

"I don't know if we will ever have peace in our time, but if we can find peace within ourselves, that will be enough."

Hetty studied her. "War has changed you, Lizzie. I don't think I noticed until now."

"Has it?" War had changed everyone, but she hadn't given much thought to the changes within herself. The world was different, just as it had been transformed after the Great War. The landscape of human interaction and understanding would never be what it once was. In some ways, an innocence had been lost and was forever out of reach. For them, at any rate. There was still hope for those yet to come.

"When we first met, you were so delicate I feared a harsh wind might break your beautiful wings, but now I see you've emerged from the war as something far stronger than a butterfly."

Elizabeth leaned in her chair and stared back at Hetty. "What am I now?"

"A stormy petrel. You ride the winds of change, never having to land. You have wings that can carry you anywhere for as long as you need them to."

The compliment made Elizabeth flush with pleasure. "You've changed too," she admitted. "You used to be so hard and inflexible before, but now you're a willow that bends in the storm but never breaks. You've grown your roots and flowered in your life, and it's utterly stunning to see who you've become."

Hetty's cheeks pinkened. "Look at us, acting so maudlin and philosophical. I think we ought to see what Mrs. Harrow has made for dinner and leave all this nonsense for another day."

Eva burst into the study. "Come quick! Churchill's on the wireless!"

Elizabeth and Hetty collected little Teddy and hastened to the drawing room, where Mrs. Harrow and the colonel stood close to the wireless. Winston Churchill's voice echoed through the room as if the old bulldog were there with them in this moment.

"God bless you all. This is your victory! It is the victory of the cause of freedom in every land. In all our long history, we have never seen a greater day than this. Everyone, man or woman, has done their best. Everyone has tried. Neither the long years, nor the dangers, nor the fierce attacks of the enemy, have in any way weakened the independent resolve of the British nation. God bless you all. My dear friends, this is your hour. This is not victory of a party or of any class. It's a victory of the great British nation as a whole.

"We were the first, in this ancient island, to draw the sword against tyranny. After a while, we were left all alone against the most tremendous military power that has been seen. We were all alone for a whole year. There we stood, alone. Did anyone want to give in? Were we downhearted? The lights went out and the bombs came down. But every man, woman, and child in the country had no thought of quitting the struggle. London can take it. So we came back after long months from the jaws of death, out of the mouth of hell, while all the world wondered: When shall the reputation and faith of this generation of English men and women fail?

"I say that in the long years to come, not only will the people of this island but of the world, wherever the bird of freedom chirps in human hearts, look back to what we've done and they will say, 'Do not despair, do not yield to violence and tyranny, march straightforward and die if need be—unconquered.'"

Elizabeth felt a chill at Churchill's last word. *Unconquered.* That was the word that she had been feeling these last few months. She had fought and fought time and again against fires, incendiaries, bombs, against German airmen falling from the sky, and against the despair of facing the end every day—and yet she was still here, still unconquered.

She saw Hetty and Eva's eyes glimmer with tears as they smiled in sweet relief. The colonel removed a handkerchief from his pocket and wiped his eyes.

"We beat them back. It's over. Thank God, it's over," the colonel whispered. He swallowed hard before he faced the ladies in the room. "You all should remember this moment for the rest of your lives. You were a part of this nation's victory. Never forget it."

There was something in the way he said this that made Elizabeth wonder if perhaps the pain of the Great War had been so vast that no one wanted to remember that they had won that war, however great the sacrifice it had taken. But not this time—this time they would remember this victory for centuries to come.

She thought of the words Churchill had spoken as the Battle of Britain raged over their heads, when men like Philip were risking their lives to protect the skies over England. "If the British Empire and its Commonwealth last for a thousand years, men will still say, 'This was their finest hour.'"

"We will never forget, William," Mrs. Harrow said. Her chin wobbled as she tried to smile, fighting back a sob of relief. "And if you hadn't been here to keep us all calm, I don't know what we would have done. And Marcus . . . he'd be . . . oh . . ." Now she started to cry, but they all knew what she'd been trying to say. Marcus would never have learned how to survive if he hadn't been taught by a hero of the Great War like the colonel.

The colonel pulled Mrs. Harrow into his arms and kissed her forehead. The housekeeper burst into tears, and yet when they broke apart, she was smiling again. She brushed her hair back with another sniffle before she lifted her apron up and dabbed at her eyes.

Teddy tugged on his mother's dress. "Why is Miz Arrow crying?" he asked, trying to say Mrs. Harrow's name in that silly way of his.

Hetty pulled her son into her arms, and the little boy whispered softly to her, asking again why the housekeeper was crying.

"Because your papa will be coming home soon, darling." Hetty kissed the crown of his hair. "We're all just so happy."

"My papa?" Teddy's mouth opened in a little childlike gasp of wonder, which made Elizabeth laugh.

"Yes, your papa. And he is so excited to finally meet you," Hetty promised the little boy.

"Marcus will come home too," Eva said with hope in her eyes. She and Nathan had married after Marcus had left for Europe, and she was anxious to see her little brother again. It had been two months since they'd had a letter from him, but Elizabeth had faith that he was all right. He'd been among the troops liberating concentration camps in Germany, but he would soon be home.

"They'll all come home," Mrs. Harrow said. "Oh heavens, I'd better start cooking. We'll need enough food to feed an army when those lads return." She rushed off to the kitchen.

"You'll have to have all your men over and let her fuss over them," the colonel said with a chuckle. "They're all her boys now, whether they wanted a second mother or not."

"Everyone is going to be celebrating in London." Eva smiled as she looked out the window. "Can you imagine how packed Trafalgar Square will be?"

Elizabeth joined her and put her arm around her friend. "I bet the streets will be filled for miles."

The entire world would be celebrating, Elizabeth thought. Even the Germans would have to be glad it was all over.

Elizabeth left the rest of her family inside the house. She went into the back gardens and sat down on the marble bench that had been a place of escape in the early weeks of the Blitz. She eased down onto the stone, which had warmed in the sunlight, and tilted her face up to the sky, closing her eyes. She thought of all the young soldiers who'd gone to war, those coming home soon and those not coming home. She thought of Alan most and the life that had been taken from him. His loss still left a deep ache inside her, but the sting of it was somehow less, and her memories of him when he'd been alive were stronger than those of losing him. That was what mattered most. The good memories, the ones of his life, not his death, were strongest.

Birds chirped excitedly as a gentle wind rippled through the trees, creating a pleasant rustling sound. A distant purr of airplane engines drew her focus. She opened her eyes to see a squadron of Spitfires flying low overhead, and a smile curved her lips.

Church bells that hadn't rung in six years sounded in the distance, and their musical notes echoed between the rolling hills until the earth itself vibrated with the sounds of victory.

"Come home to me, Philip," she whispered to the passing planes. "We have so many dreams to live for now."

THREE DAYS LATER

Elizabeth sat in a chair at the bureau's London office. She puzzled over a few prospective clients, the wheels turning in her head at the possible matches she could make. Most were soldiers returning from the war who wanted to have someone to hold and love so that they might banish memories of the war. She would do everything in her power to help them.

And yet the war hadn't just changed the men—it had changed the women as well. As for all the women who'd worked in the factories, for the Auxiliary Fire Service, and in the military branches, they'd kept the planes in the skies, the fires at bay, and the world running when the men left. They deserved to have a life of joy with someone who valued the work they'd done these last six years.

She wasn't sure how much time passed before she became aware of a man standing in the doorway, leaning in an arrogantly attractive way against the doorjamb. She lifted her focus from her files, and a smile broke out on her face.

"Philip!" She abandoned her work and ran to him. He removed his hat, tossing it to the nearest table, and caught her in his arms. "What are you doing here?" she asked between peppering his face with soft kisses.

"Isn't it obvious? I've come to register." He nodded at her desk. "I suppose I need to fill out a form or some such thing?"

"Register?" She blinked at him. He was teasing. He had to be. "But you don't believe in matchmaking."

"I believe in you, darling, so there must be something to this whole matching business. Let's see . . ." He went to her desk and picked up a clipboard, then with a flirtatious smile he made a grand show of settling into a chair opposite her desk as he started to fill out a registration form.

"Hair color . . . hmm . . . What do you think? Should I put blond?"

Elizabeth, still dumbfounded at him, sat down in her own chair and watched him complete the registration form quite diligently. After he was done, he stood and slid the clipboard across the desk toward her so she could look it over.

In the comment section he'd written, "Any prospective ladies must not mind marrying a scoundrel."

"Oh dear, I'm not sure we have *anyone* who would consider those requirements," she said quite seriously, fighting very hard not to laugh.

"Can't you think of at least one?" He got up from his chair and came around to her side of the desk, then slowly got down on one knee. "Not even you?" All teasing had gone from his eyes as he held up a velvet box and opened it. A diamond surrounded by tiny sapphires adorned a ring that sat on a cushion of velvet.

"Well, yes, I suppose I could find someone," she said with a chuckle, but inside her heart was pounding as a maddening joy raced through her.

"Is that a yes?" he asked.

"I suppose I ought to think on—" She was cut off as he stood and pulled her into his arms, kissing her soundly. The strings of her heart plucked like a harpist, striking notes throughout her soul.

"Think on that for a moment . . ." Philip's husky voice sent a delicious shiver through her.

"Well, when you put it like that, yes, I'll marry a scoundrel. But only if it's you."

He slipped the ring onto her finger and swept her into his arms. Their lips met in a fire of desire, longing, and answering joy. Fireworks exploded against the back of her eyelids as Elizabeth finally let her own shadows of the war recede. She could feel Alan there beside her, sense his smile and invisible touch upon her shoulder. She'd stood alone for so long—but no longer.

ONE MONTH LATER

Eva stood by the doorway to Cunningham House, quaking with excitement as she and Nathan waited for the car driving toward them. The colonel and Mrs. Harrow stood by her as the car finally stopped in front of the house, and they all went down to greet the new arrivals.

The cab stopped, and a man stepped out. He wore a British Army uniform and carried a military pack. He turned to face them, and for the first time in two years, Eva saw Marcus's face.

"Marcus!" she gasped.

"Eva!" He laughed as he embraced her.

His voice was deeper than she remembered. His shoulders were broader, and there was far more of him than there had been when he'd left. He'd transformed from a slender youth to a strong man. He stepped back and turned to the car, holding out a hand. A young woman with dark hair and lovely brown eyes stepped out. She was dressed in a cream-colored frock and held a battered traveling case.

"Everyone, I'd like you to meet my wife, Leonie."

"Wife?" Eva breathed as she took in the sight of the young woman, who couldn't be more than nineteen. Nathan tucked Eva's arm in his and gave her hand a reassuring squeeze.

Marcus smiled bashfully and put an arm around Leonie's shoulders.

"Hello," Leonie said in a French accent. "It is so lovely to meet you all."

"Well, don't just stand there. Bring her in for tea, silly boy," Mrs. Harrow admonished with motherly affection as she opened the door for everyone. The colonel and Eva lingered at the back of the crowd to speak to Marcus while Nathan escorted Leonie inside.

"How did you manage to get married in the middle of a war?" Eva asked.

His cheeks turned ruddy, and he rubbed the back of his neck. "I met her while my unit worked with the French Resistance. Her family was killed in the invasion, and . . . and she was all alone. When I met her, it was like something missing inside me had been found. We married two weeks ago so I would be able to bring her home as my wife. But now that we're here, we would love a real wedding with everyone present."

"Of course you would," the colonel grunted. "We'll have a big party thrown here, of course. I suppose I'd better find a rabbi?"

"Yes, Leonie is Jewish too, so that would be appreciated." Marcus chuckled, and the colonel smiled back at him.

"Consider it done, my boy. Glad to have you home." The colonel's eyes conveyed what his words could not, and Marcus clasped him in a tight but brief embrace.

"I wouldn't be here now if it hadn't been for you, sir," Marcus said with quiet honesty. "Most of the lads I fought with barely knew how to use a gun."

"It was the same when I fought," the colonel said. "All the lads who left quiet, gentle lives behind suddenly faced hell. It's a bloody miracle anyone survives war." He cleared his throat. "But you did, my boy. You did."

"I did," Marcus echoed.

Some terrible tightness inside Eva's chest finally eased. Her brother was home. He was alive and safe, and he would never have to fight like that again.

"Somehow he grew up when I wasn't looking," Eva whispered to the colonel after Marcus went inside the house.

"Children do that, and war has a funny way of making men out of young lads. You did a fine job with him, Eva. He's a good man. A hero. It does my old heart good to see all of you move forward with your lives. This is what we fought the war for, the beauty of life and the freedom and dignity to live it as we wish."

Eva wiped away fresh tears. The colonel was right. This was what the world had fought for, the right to live and love as they wished.

HETTY STOOD ON THE TRAIN STATION PLATFORM, HOLDING Teddy's small hand in her own. She'd dressed her son smartly in his best Sunday clothes, and she wore her own favorite dark-blue dress that Charles always said made her eyes glow like sapphires. It was silly, but she wanted everything to be perfect.

The train rolled into the station, steam hissing from it like a great black dragon coming back to its cave to rest. Sunlight cut through the glass ceiling and penetrated the steam with shafts of light, which formed flickering rainbows every now and then.

People anxiously gathered on the platform as the train finally stopped and the compartment doors started opening. Soldiers by the hundreds began piling out, brown canvas bags slung over their shoulders. Women and children started to cry and rush toward the returning men. There were fathers, brothers, sons, all being welcomed back with happy tears.

Teddy gave a slight tug on Hetty's hand. "Where's Papa?" She looked down at her son and saw worry in his eyes.

"He'll be here." He had to be. Her father had said he would be on this train. Surely he hadn't stayed behind or been delayed? She couldn't bear one more day without him.

She and Teddy stood on the platform long after the crowds had gone and only a few soldiers were still exiting the train. The hope inside her chest began to wither . . . until a shape emerged from the steam at the end of the farthest train carriage. A tall man with a golden mustache and a short, trimmed beard walked toward them, a bag slung over his shoulder. He had a dark hunter-green beret on his head, belonging to a British Commando's uniform. But this man couldn't be Charles. He was too gaunt. His face was hollow and his eyes shadowed.

The man stopped ten feet away. Clear gray eyes met hers. She took a step toward him, her heart pounding as she saw a hint of the man she loved beneath that short beard and mustache. She took another step, and another, until they were but two feet apart. The shadows in the man's eyes began to vanish the longer they looked at each other.

"Lonsdales never die," she whispered.

The man slowly smiled. She knew that smile. It was the smile he reserved only for her.

"My darling." Charles's voice was slightly rough as he opened his arms, and she threw herself at him. He caught her, hugging her tight. He lifted her up and spun her around, her feet clear off the ground. When he finally set her down, he turned to face the little boy who stared up at him. He knelt down in front of his son for the first time.

"Hello there," Charles said, his voice still slightly hoarse with emotion. His gaze seemed to search the child's, looking for features of his and Hetty's, anything that could tie this little stranger to him.

How many times had she done that as Teddy had grown up in the last four years? She'd watched all of his darling features as they became more like hers and Charles's and yet . . . Charles had missed those years. Four years. First steps, first words, first Christmases and birthdays . . . Hetty covered her mouth with her hand, holding in a sob.

Teddy glanced at Hetty uncertainly, then raised his tiny hand in a military salute in the way his grandfather had taught him. Charles saluted him back.

"At ease, soldier." Charles chuckled. The warm sound melted Hetty's heart as she crouched down to join them.

"Are you really my papa?" Teddy asked in a wavering voice, his lower lip trembling.

"I am," Charles said. He slowly reached out to Teddy, opening his arms again. "I would very much like to hug you, my boy, if that's all right?"

Teddy nodded, and with tears on his cheeks, he buried his face against his father's chest as Charles brought him in for a tight embrace.

Charles closed his eyes, but Hetty saw he was crying. Shiny tracks of tears reflected in the sunlight. At last he opened his eyes and looked up at her as he held their child.

Words weren't needed, but Hetty knew now, words of love should never be held back for any reason.

"I love you," she said.

"I love you too, my darling warrior." He stood, still cradling their son in his arms as though he would never let go of him. Teddy wrapped his arms around Charles's neck, apparently content to stay there.

"Your parents and mine will be driving Jarvis crazy with their worry," Hetty said. "I didn't want them all to come in case . . . in case you were delayed."

Charles chuckled. "Then I suppose we had better go rescue the old boy."

With a smile, Hetty curled an arm around Charles's waist while he carried their son as they left the station

Charles looked down at her with endless love. "Let's go home."

EPILOGUE

E ngland
June 1946

MARGARET HARROW HELD THE TIN OF SUGAR AGAINST HER chest, watching Marcus and Leonie from the kitchen window overlooking the back gardens of Cunningham House. As they walked past, their hands were linked, faces bright with laughter in a way that made the housekeeper miss her youth with a surprising ache. Just because she was no longer in the bloom of her youth didn't mean she didn't remember how it felt to be young.

Marcus and his bride had their whole lives ahead of them now, with no more shadows of war. Margaret had been so afraid that the little boy she had taken under her wing would have been damaged the way so many young lads had been from the last war.

But not Marcus. He seemed at peace. As though having gone to war and returned home, he had done what his heart had demanded of him, and now he was free to live.

And Leonie . . . such a sweet lamb, with doe-brown eyes and a gentle soul. Margaret simply adored her. Now she had one more unofficial daughter to spoil and share recipes with. Marcus often bragged about how brave Leonie was, given the things she had done in the French Resistance. Margaret could only think that it was because of girls like Leonie and boys like Marcus that they had won the war at all.

The colonel always said one could never know what the human spirit was capable of until it was tested, and then it would amaze you with all it could achieve against seemingly impossible odds.

Marcus and Leonie sat down on the marble bench, their heads bent as they shared a lingering kiss. Margaret turned away to give them privacy and found the colonel staring at her from across the kitchen. He held a letter in his hand.

"Oh Lord, tell me it isn't bad news," she begged him.

The colonel dragged a hand through his hair and shook his head, his eyes wide. "It's the house," he said.

"What about the house?"

"It's mine again."

"What? *This* house?" Margaret set the tin of sugar down on the counter and came toward him.

"That bloody Italian count has decided to stay permanently in America. He is delivering a set of documents to my solicitor this afternoon to review about transferring the house and estate back to its rightful owner, which is me."

"You're joking," Margaret gasped, but William shook his head.

"Our dear Lizzie arranged a match for the count, some English beauty who's headed to New York to meet him as we speak. To show his thanks, he said he would do anything for Lizzie. She had only one request, that he return the house to its rightful owner."

Margaret's heart swelled, and she clapped her hands together, sending a dusting of sugar from her fingers onto her apron.

"Oh William, that's wonderful. That's—" She halted abruptly as she realized that she would lose her position here. Cunningham House had been her home for so many years, and now she'd have to leave.

"What's the matter, Maggie?" William asked. "You've gone pale."

"I'll need at least a week to pack my things and find employment at another house."

"Employment at another house?" William's brows arched and his mustache firmed into a hard line over his lips.

"Yes, that *bloody count*, as you call him, was my employer. If he has no home, then I have no one to keep house for."

At this, William huffed. "No house? Woman, you have a house—*this* one." He waved an arm about the kitchen.

"Are you asking me to stay on, then, as your housekeeper?" Margaret asked slowly, not quite sure she understood. The colonel frequently blustered about her cooking and her always disturbing his afternoon cigar when she came in to dust.

William stared at her for a long moment. The man was still quite handsome, perhaps more so at his age. She'd always adored looking at him, except when he was scowling . . . even when he was scowling, if she was being honest with herself. That's why she so loved to dust whenever he smoked a cigar. The scent clung to his clothes, a sweet scent that made her think of long winter nights by a warm fire where she was cozy and safe.

He reached up and cupped her face in his hands, and a warm flush moved through her.

"Silly woman, I'm asking you to marry me," William said. His mustache curved with his lips into a smile. Then he leaned down and kissed her.

His warm and gentle lips made no demands, yet a fire slowly started to grow within her. She had never forgotten what it meant to feel like this, but she never imagined she would feel this way again.

She stood on her tiptoes and curled her arms around his neck. He moved his arms to band about her back as he held her close. She could feel his strength and steadiness, but also his passion, and Margaret wanted all of it. Her eyes were full of tears as she and William finally parted enough to draw breath.

"Say yes, Maggie, my girl. Make an honest man of this old warhorse." He waggled his brows, and she giggled, feeling every inch a girl of eighteen again. He reached one hand into his trouser pocket and produced a ring, holding it up for her inspection. Not that Margaret would have cared if it was made of tin. She'd take William with or without a ring.

"Oh all right, you sweet-talked me into it," she said with a laugh as she let him put the ring on her finger.

"Speaking of sweet, why do you taste like sugar?" William asked.

"I was baking a blackberry tart and had to sample the sugar."

"Hmm . . ." He nuzzled her nose with his. "I'd better have another taste."

LEONIE STIFLED A DELIGHTED GIGGLE AND POINTED OVER HIS shoulder. "Marcus, look."

He turned in the direction his wife gestured. Through the back kitchen windows of the house, he spied the colonel and Mrs. Harrow locked in a passionate embrace.

Leonie rested her head against his shoulder and sighed. "I was wondering when he would ask her. He's been carrying a ring box around in his pocket for weeks."

Marcus watched the couple, who had in some ways been his surrogate parents, and his heart swelled with quiet joy. Perhaps now was the time to ask his wife what he'd been putting off for several weeks.

"Leonie, the colonel asked if we want to stay here at Cunningham House. I would love to stay here, but what do you want? We could return to France, or go somewhere else."

His fierce little lioness smiled up at him. "I would like to stay here too. It reminds me of home. I do not think I could ever go back to France. The memories are too painful. But here . . . here there is peace . . . no ghosts."

He kissed her forehead and pulled her close to his side. "I agree." They sat on the bench facing the golden rolling hills and the dark woods beyond.

Both he and Leonie had lost their homes and families, but somehow in the middle of the darkest parts of their lives, they'd found each other and made a new family. He thought back to the boy he had been in 1939, too small to protect his older sister. Fate had intervened. Nathan and Hetty had stepped in to help him, and ever since then he had never felt alone.

Then he thought of all the men, women, and children he'd helped free in the concentration camps. He'd never forget the tattered, dirty yellow stars and colored triangles stitched onto their clothes. So many stars . . . And now those who had survived were free.

It was a sweet and beautiful revenge on all those who had wanted to kill people like him and Leonie. The Nazis had sought to eradicate them. But they'd failed. Now, he and so many others would live in love and go on. He could give a life to his children, and it would be a wonderful life. Marcus tipped Leonie's chin up so he could see her eyes, and then he kissed her. The sound of songbirds, singing clear and free, filled the gardens of their new home.

❧

"They're so tiny," Eva said in wonder as she held up the little hand of her son. The baby lay resting in a bassinet right beside his twin sister. They'd been born only two days before, but Eva never tired of looking at them.

Nathan stood next to the bassinet and gently traced the tiny fingers of his daughter's hand, which peeked out from her blankets.

"It's rather amazing, isn't it? To see something so perfect and so small." He smiled down at his children, and Eva turned to kiss his cheek. He flashed a dazzling smile at her. Even after six years, Nathan had a way of making her tremble with excitement.

"As soon as they are old enough to ride, I'll buy them the finest ponies—"

Eva started to laugh. Her husband loved horses. It was something that ran in his blood. Nathan, despite his limp, still managed to do quite a bit of country living, including horseback riding. He'd taken her on rides around their estate daily until she was almost ready for the twins. She had never been on a horse before she had met him. Now, she loved them as much as he did. There was an innocence about them that no amount of war had been able to tarnish.

She leaned into him and placed her hands on his shoulders. "Nathan."

"Yes?" He brushed his knuckles over her cheek, his warm brown eyes so full of love that Eva felt truly blessed.

"Tell me we'll always be this happy."

He gave her a gentle kiss and then drew back. "I promise that no matter what happens, we'll be together. And as our love grows, we'll never lose our joy." He said this with such certainty that she believed him. Whatever came next in their lives, they would face it together and joy would follow.

❦

CHARLES SPOTTED HETTY LOUNGING IN A CHAIR, A BOOK IN her hands. "Where's Teddy?"

"In the Rogues Gallery." She closed her book and shot him a bemused look. "He's playing Commandos again."

At this, Charles could only laugh. "Is he, now?"

Hetty set her book aside and stood, coming toward him. "Oh yes, he is determined to be just like you. I swear he's a miniature version of you."

Charles waited until his wife was close enough to touch. "How about we work on creating a miniature of you?" he asked in a husky voice.

Hetty turned those bewitching eyes upon him, and he fell in love all over again.

"That sounds like a marvelous idea." She tiptoed her fingers up his chest to his chin. He caught her hand and pressed a kiss to the backs of her fingers, loving the way his gentlemanly manner lit up his wife's eyes. He had waited years for Hetty to really see him, to love him, and it had been worth every moment.

"You truly are the most extraordinary woman I've ever known," he said.

She winked at him. "Well, you know how I feel about you. I wouldn't have just anyone's baby in the middle of the Blitz."

Once again, he was laughing. He held her hand as he led her from the sitting room through their house. They had been living in the countryside for the last six weeks to spend some time with his parents.

Teddy had become obsessed with all the rooms of the rambling old country home, and he especially loved the large portrait gallery. It was full of massive seven-foot-tall portraits of various Lonsdale lords and ladies throughout history. It also contained paintings of friends who had been as dear as family to the Lonsdales. Charming rogues and rebellious ladies in their day, according to family legend, which is why the hall had been affectionately dubbed the Rogues Gallery by some recent ancestor.

Charles and Hetty paused at the doorway to see Teddy and a trio of local boys playing together in the vast open space of the carpeted room. Teddy's blond hair was covered by Charles's hunter-green beret. As he played soldier with his friends, the sunlight from the windows caught silver and gold gleaming on Teddy's chest. Something in Charles's heart clenched tight as he realized his son wore his military service medals.

Joy and sorrow shared an equal place in his heart then, for those medals had come at a price. The lives of men, good men, lost in those hard years of war. He and Will St. Laurent had been among the lucky few to return from their unit.

He swallowed hard and looked to Hetty. "I'll never know how you raised him alone all those years."

She squeezed his hand. "I was never alone. Even when you were gone, I felt you were looking after me, after both of us." She looked back to where their son and his friends were playing.

He turned to her. "The night he was born, I was in Norway, fighting with my unit. We were badly outnumbered, but my God, the men with me followed me into the jaws of death, and we emerged victorious. I thought of you the entire time, as though I could feel you calling my name, driving me on."

Hetty's eyes grew wide in shock, then glistened with tears.

"I was calling for you that night," she whispered. "I saw you. As I was fighting to bring Teddy into this world, I blacked out and had a fantastical dream where I saw you fighting with your men. I always thought it was simply a fevered dream, but I remember I called your name."

Charles pulled her into his arms. "I heard you—I'll always hear you."

"I love you so much, Charles. I hate that I wasted so many years not knowing it." She pulled his head down to hers, and their foreheads touched.

"I know, but it's all right now. We have time enough now, darling." There would never be enough time with Hetty; life was simply too short. But he'd never dare tell her that. He always wanted her smiles, never her tears.

From somewhere in the Rogues Gallery, a little boy shouted, "Lonsdales never die!" The other boys echoed the battle cry as their games went on, games that were simply that, for they lived in a world where they could play without fear. And that had been worth fighting for.

Charles smiled against Hetty's mouth as he tasted heaven once more.

ASSAM, INDIA
September 1946

George Astley sat at his desk in his study, reading the latest London newspapers. He reached absently into his pocket for a cigar, but his hand came up empty. With a grumble, he stood and walked over to the brightly colored cabinet against one wall and dug around on the top shelf until he found his extra box.

He retrieved one from the box and lit it, then puffed a ring of smoke and started to close the cabinet door, but a framed photo tucked beneath some papers caught his eye. He picked it up and walked over to the tall windows overlooking the court-yard to get a better look. His nephew stared proudly out of the frame at him. Alan wore his naval uniform, and his hat was tucked under one arm. George's eyes misted, and he set his cigar aside on a nearby ashtray.

"Sometimes we lose the best too soon," he said to the boy in the photo. "The trumpets called you home, my boy. But we'll see you again."

George set the photo down on his desk, determined to look at Alan every day. He had been too afraid after the last war to see the faces of the friends he'd lost. He couldn't do that this time. There would always be pain, but at least now he could remember them with love, no matter how fierce the ache.

Movement in the courtyard below caught his eye. A young

woman dressed in a burnished gold frock and wearing a rakishly tilted red hat walked across the courtyard, arm in arm with a tall man in a smart suit. He couldn't see their faces, but the way the woman moved brought a smile to his lips. He sat down at his desk, knowing she had finally come home.

Soon after, Aabha opened the study door, mischief in her eyes. "I have a surprise for you," she said in a playful tone.

George leaned back in his chair and smiled. "Show them in."

Aabha stepped back as the couple walked into his study.

"Lizzie!" He greeted his beloved niece by getting up and hugging her for a long moment. Lord, he had missed his darling girl.

"Hello, Uncle George." Elizabeth blushed as she introduced the man beside her. "This is my husband, Philip Lennox."

George shook Philip's hand. "It's good to meet you, Lennox."

"It's an honor, sir. I've heard all about you." The man had an honest gaze, and his grip was firm, two things George valued in a man. But what really mattered was the way he looked at Elizabeth. George saw love, adoration, and devotion in the man's eyes. And she looked at him the same way.

Bravo, Lizzie. You finally found your match.

"Come and sit," George offered. "I hope you'll be staying for a while."

"A while," Elizabeth said. "But then we have more places to see. Oh, there's so much that's happened since I was last here, Uncle. I know most of my letters likely didn't make it to you."

"Eight years is a long time," George agreed with a smile. He had received the occasional letter, but with the war, he knew most of her letters would have been lost in transit.

Lennox nudged his wife with a chuckle. "You'd better tell him the whole tale, darling."

"Oh, but . . ." Elizabeth blushed again as she looked at George. "Do you really want to hear it? It's such a long story."

"A *good* story," Lennox corrected affectionately.

George reached across the desk and held out his hand to her. When she placed her palm in his, he squeezed it with a smile that came from deep in his heart and soul. "Lizzie, my darling girl, tell me everything."

HISTORICAL NOTE

The Real Matchmakers

Heather Jenner was the daughter of a brigadier-general and spent several years in Ceylon before she returned home to England along with her parents. Mary Oliver grew up in a simple farmhouse in Cambridgeshire. The two girls met in Ceylon on a boat coming home to England, and after some convincing by Mary, Heather agreed to create the Marriage Bureau. (Heather is the one who insisted on the name change from *Agency* to *Bureau*.)

Uncle George really existed and is one of the few real names that I have kept in honor of his memory. He did give Mary the idea to form a bureau, since she had the talent of matchmaking. Mary really did sever an engagement with a man who was controlling and had made it clear to her that their married life would not be one of a true partnership. After Mary broke off her second engagement while in India, she sold her wedding gifts for a boat ticket back to England, where she met Heather. Mary's parents were less than supportive of her returning home after two broken engagements, and she moved to London, where she could start a new life. The romances my characters have with Philip and Charles are entirely a work of fiction.

For a more detailed account of Mary and Heather's adventures, please read the books titled *Marriage Bureau* by Mary Oliver and Mary Benedetta and *The Marriage Bureau* by Penrose Halson listed in my bibliography. Mary Oliver's book was written about the origins of the bureau and includes the full story of how they got started and contains real letters and questions they received from clients. The book was written in 1942 during the war, and Mary penned the last words of the story while staring at a Blitz-bombed London. Nothing is more amazing than reading her firsthand account. Penrose Halson's book, published in 2017, does a wonderful job of picking up where Mary's book leaves off and giving an overview of the Marriage Bureau's legacy. The bureau itself lasted into the 1970s, still matching couples.

Creation of the Marriage Bureau

When Heather and Mary began to consult people about forming the bureau, they were accused of starting a brothel by an elderly attorney, and they did indeed baffle Scotland Yard policemen, who had no idea whether a matchmaking agency was legal. (It was not illegal, as it turned out). A young lawyer who was a friend of Hetty's assisted them in creating the bureau from a legal perspective, and according to the accounts I found, he actually had the surname of Humphrey. I couldn't resist keeping this name, as it was the surname of my Regency-era hero Charles Humphrey, the Earl of Lonsdale (from my League of Rogues series), which is how the legend of *Lonsdales never die* was born in this story.

While hunting for locations for the bureau's office, Mary and Heather did visit a location at Piccadilly Circus that was full of rude businessmen who smoked and teased them when they tried to reach the tiny desk in the corner. It was after this failed attempt that the girls found themselves looking for offices on Bond Street, where they rented space above a hairdresser's shop.

The bureau's office on Bond Street did have a faulty telephone cord that when tugged or kicked would make the phone ring. The incident of using the fake phone calls to persuade an early client that they had women to match him with did occur. While he sat for his interview with one girl, the other made the phone ring and pretended to talk to heiresses and other rich, influential young women.

Hetty's Grandmother

In real life, Heather's grandmother, who she feared would not approve of the bureau, did approve, and the words she told Hetty in my story were closely based on what she said about helping girls find husbands in a far less costly manner and with less effort.

Major Taylor

One of the bureau's first clients was a middle-aged army major. Mary and Heather recounted how wonderful he was while he interviewed himself because they were both so new at it and nervous. He insisted on paying his fee and then left. He won Mary and Heather's hearts. As I read the real accounts, I knew that he needed to have a happy ending to his story. And so I wrote into my fiction the darling character of Major Taylor. I sent him to Dunkirk, and it was to my shock during my research that I learned there really was an army major on the mole counting soldiers and rallying spirits as the men boarded naval and civilian vessels to evacuate the beaches. Once I read this, I knew I had to write this major into my story as Major Taylor's character—and most importantly, I had to bring him home safe.

Dunkirk

All of the scenes that you read in the Dunkirk chapters were based on true stories from soldiers and civilians. The British people worked together to gather lifeboats from the Lifeboat Institute, pleasure yachts, steamers, tugboats—anything that was seaworthy and could handle the Channel was collected and sent over. Average men and even some women assisted the Royal Navy with the rescue of British and French troops during one of the most remarkable rescues in modern history. Despite it being a massive military retreat, the civilian "little ships" rescue captured the public's heart and rallied England's spirits for the long war that lay ahead.

The stories of brothers meeting up on the beach, of sinking trucks into the water to create jetties to send men out to reach ships, men drowning from the heavy uniforms and gear they carried, and the desperation and desolation of the troops as they tried to escape the German aircraft bombing them from the sky was true. The story of the star above Dunkirk guiding troops through the only safe narrow passage through the countryside was recounted many times by soldiers. Many French troops remained behind as the rear guard to protect the beaches. They knew that final night they would never make the retreating ships, and they knew their job was to hold the Germans back as long as they could and likely die in the effort.

The Blitz, Bombs, Orphans, and Anderson Shelters

Where possible, the stories about the Blitz, from the bombs to the Anderson shelters, were all heavily researched. The scene where a little girl dies in Elizabeth's arms as she rescues her from the rubble was an account I read from an Auxiliary Fire Service fireman's firsthand story.

During the war, thousands of children were sent to the countryside to live with complete strangers while their parents stayed in London. Children from toddler age to middle school were packed up, name tags attached to their coats, and sent on trains, buses, and cars to places far from the danger of the bombings. Many children whose parents were killed in London were adopted, often by the families who took them in during the children's evacuation.

Dining and dancing at the Ritz in London was a way of decadent rebellion. People there seemed untouched by the war. The band was indeed knocked to the ground one night, and the piano player got back up to start singing "A Nightingale Sang in Berkeley Square." Dinner guests and hotel guests were allowed to stay the night in the hall on chaise longues. When Hetty gives birth to Teddy at the Ritz, this was based on a true account of a future duke (rather than an earl) being born at the hotel during the Blitz.

The Matches

Nearly all of the tales that my characters Hetty and Elizabeth share about their clients are based on true accounts from the real matchmakers, Heather and Mary. Even the story of the male client being hit by a car, or the woman who hired the bureau to find a way to introduce her to her neighbor, with Mary Oliver calling and pretending the unsuspecting man had an appointment for an interview with the bureau, were all true. The catching of a German spy was also a true. A man came into their office seeking a well-born and well connected English wife in hopes of getting information that could help him in Germany. It turned out the man was an exiled German who was wanting to get back in the good graces of the German government with any spy information he could provide. Scotland Yard was able to investigate him and arrest him thanks to Heather and Mary.

For a full, detailed, and fascinating account of the lives of Heather and Mary and real stories about their matchmaking, please read *Marriage Bureau* by Mary Oliver and Mary Benedetta and *The Marriage Bureau* by Penrose Halson. See the bibliography for more information on these titles. They provide a wealth of information that will have you laughing, smiling, and even tearing up.

The Windmill Horse Rescue and the Silent Massacre

Two young dancers from the Windmill did wake up during a Blitz bombing and hear that a nearby stable had been bombed. Instead of rushing for shelter, they went to rescue the horses and saved about eight of them. They walked the streets with all of these frightened horses in tow for several hours, until they located a police station that had a stable nearby that could house the horses.

When my character John Kirby, the veterinarian, tells the story of all of London putting their animals down, this was true. A well-meaning pamphlet issued to the public early in the war insisted that animals be "taken care of" so that they wouldn't be abandoned, starved, or suffer the bombings. Public bomb shelters did not allow pets, especially dogs, because they were afraid the barking would drive the humans in the shelters mad. So people all over the country euthanized thousands of pets. The story John Kirby tells of a duchess helping to rescue animals and create a sanctuary was true.

The Bureau Secretaries

The real Marriage Bureau had a few different secretaries over the course of the war. Miss Plumley was modeled off a real secretary who did in fact try to steal a client. She posed as someone he'd been writing to and met him on a date and was a little forward in her actions, which startled the man and caused a complaint. She did not stay employed at the bureau.

Eva acted as a lovely stand-in for another real secretary the bureau had who was rather sweet and innocent. This real secretary did receive a call where a gentleman asked if he could have a woman who enjoyed *fellatio*. Of course, the woman, being rather innocent, assumed it was a nonsexual hobby and thought he meant *philately*, the term for stamp collecting. Naturally, I had to include such a funny moment in the story.

Eva and Marcus

Eva and Marcus were inventions of my heart and mind. The names were specially chosen and borrowed with deep love from

Eva Unterman (her grandfather was Eli Wolman), a Holocaust survivor I have known for nearly twenty years. Her father was named Markus, which later became Marcus. For Eva Unterman's amazing story, visit this link: https://voicesofoklahoma.com/inter views/unterman-eva/

Cunningham House and the Colonel

The real matchmakers did rent a house in the country with dozens of rooms, which was on lease from an Italian diplomat who'd left London due to the coming war. One of the early renters was a grumpy naval admiral who spent the night and broke the bed in a terrible crash. He also complained about the food. It was this story of the admiral that I wove into Colonel Cunningham's story in my fictional narrative. The country office for the bureau didn't last long in real life, but for my story, I saw this home as a place of refuge. Colonel Cunningham and Mrs. Harrow, the housekeeper, became surrogate parents to Hetty, Elizabeth, and all the others.

For more information on the historical research used during the writing of this book, please turn the page to see the complete bibliography.

ACKNOWLEDGMENTS

This is the longest book I've ever written. It has taken more than a year and a half to complete, but I believe it was worth the work and, for readers, worth the wait. I had help from so many people I wish to mention:

Madeline Martin, a wonderful author and friend, inspired me to write a WWII-set story of my own and provided me with a list of research sources.

Evie's Café at the Market in Tulsa, Oklahoma, where I live, provided a lunchtime retreat where I could write for hours and people-watch (my favorite activity while I am writing).

The owner of The Hussar shop, a military history store in my hometown of Tulsa, Oklahoma, was incredible helpful in getting me books on uniforms for RAF pilots and other information pertaining to the Battle of Britain. I have been going to this shop since I was a child, when after breakfast I would admire the model ships and planes and the war memorabilia for sale.

My mother offered constant support during the writing of this story because she knew how emotionally draining it was to write something so real that had so much suffering in it. She reminded me every day that this story was worth the heartache and tears, that the story within these pages deserved to be told. She taught me from a young age that words matter and that stories change lives.

My father reads the *Wall Street Journal* every day and scoured its historical nonfiction book reviews to find excellent research material for me. He was the inspiration for Charles Humphrey. He fought in Vietnam and had to leave his young baby, my elder half-brother, behind with his wife, never knowing if he'd see them again. He also lost his dearest friend since childhood in the war. He showed me what it means to lose someone you love and to go on living a life of joy and meaning.

My high school Holocaust Studies teacher, Nancy Pettus, set me on a path that would define the rest of my life when she introduced me to real Holocaust survivors like Eva Unterman and Harriet Sherber. My understanding of people—and the idea that living a wonderful life is the best revenge against those who've wronged you—comes from these women. Their strength, undaunted courage, compassion, and fierce love will exist long after their stars have returned to the night sky.

Lastly, I must thank a person I had so little time to know in life—my grandmother. My grandmother, Mary Louise Shofner, had two brothers who served in the US Navy during World War II. Great-Uncle Girard came home, and Great-Uncle Walter died in one of the forgotten but hardest fought battles in the Pacific. Great-Uncle Walter served on the USS *Peary*, which was sunk along with many other ships in Darwin Bay, Australia, which suffered more damage and loss than Pearl Harbor. Ever since I was a child, I've felt a connection to my great-uncle that I couldn't explain. I have possession of his Purple Heart and his other campaign medals, and I cherish them dearly. My grandmother was pregnant during the war and gave birth to my father in 1942. As I wrote Hetty's story I couldn't help but think what my grandmother must have felt as she held her son in her arms, not knowing that in twenty-some years he would be fighting in Vietnam.

When I began to write this book, I had a dream one night where I saw my grandmother. I could feel in my very bones that she was visiting me in the way those we have loved and lost can do from time to time. I told her about this book in my dream, and she reached out and clasped my hand in hers, her eyes bright and full of wonder and curiosity. She said, *"Tell me everything . . ."* And so with this book, I did.

BIBLIOGRAPHY

Cockett, Olivia, and Robert W. Malcolmson. *Love & War in London: A Woman's Diary, 1939-1942*. Stroud: History Press, 2008.

Gardiner, Juliet. *Blitz - the British Under Attack*. London: HarperCollins Publishers, 2011.

Gardiner, Juliet. *The 1940s House*. London: Channel 4, 2002.

Grehan, John. *Dunkirk: Nine Days That Saved an Army: A Day by Day Account of the Greatest Evacuation*. Barnsley (South Yorkshire): Frontline Books, 2018.

Halson, Penrose. *The Marriage Bureau: The True Story of How Two Matchmakers Arranged Love in Wartime London*. New York: HarperCollins, 2017.

Hutton, Mike. *Life in 1940s London*. Stroud: Amberley, 2014.

Kay, Fiona, and Neil R. Storey. *1940s Fashion*. Stroud: Amberley, 2018.

Larson, Erik. *The Splendid and the Vile: A Saga of Churchill, Family, and Defiance during the Blitz*. New York: Crown, 2020.

Last, Nella, Richard Broad, and Suzie Fleming. *Nella Last's War: The Second World War Diaries of Housewife, 49*. London: Profile, 2006.

Lord, Walter. *The Miracle of Dunkirk: The True Story of Operation Dynamo*. New York: Open Road Integrated Media, 2017.

Oliver, Mary, Richard Kurti, and Mary Benedetta. *Marriage Bureau*. S.l.: Andrews UK, 2020.

Stavropoulos, D., J. Terniotis, S. Valmus, J. Varsamis, and S. Vourliotis. *Britain 1940: The RAF Fights a Desperate Battle against the Luftwaffe*. Periscopio Publications, 2009.

ABOUT THE AUTHOR

Lauren Smith is an Oklahoma attorney by day, author by night who pens adventurous and edgy romance stories by the light of her smart phone flashlight app. She knew she was destined to be a romance writer when she attempted to re-write the entire *Titanic* movie just to save Jack from drowning. Connecting with readers by writing emotionally moving, realistic and sexy romances no matter what time period is her passion. She's won multiple awards in several romance subgenres including: New England Reader's Choice Awards, Greater Detroit BookSeller's Best Awards, and a Semi-Finalist award for the Mary Wollstonecraft Shelley Award.

To connect with Lauren, visit her at:
www.laurensmithbooks.com
Lauren@laurensmithbooks.com

facebook.com/LaurenDianaSmith
twitter.com/LSmithAuthor
instagram.com/laurensmithbooks

Made in the USA
Middletown, DE
20 March 2024

51354876R00385